The Wilders

MARIE FERRARELLA

MARY J. FORBES

TERESA SOUTHWICK

MILLS & BOON

First published in Great Britain 2013
by Mills & Boon, an imprint of Harlequin (UK) Limited,
Eton House, 18-24 Paradise Road, Richmond, Surrey TW9 1SR

THE WILDERS © by Harlequin Enterprises II B.V./S.à.r.l 2013

Falling for the M.D., *First-Time Valentine* and *Paging Dr. Daddy* were published in Great Britain by Harlequin (UK) Limited.

Falling for the M.D. © Harlequin Books S.A. 2008
First-Time Valentine © Harlequin Books S.A. 2008
Paging Dr. Daddy ©Harlequin Books S.A. 2008

Special thanks and acknowledgment are given to Marie Ferrarella, Mary J. Forbes and Teresa Southwick for their contribution to THE WILDER FAMILY miniseries.

ISBN: 978 0 263 90548 9
ebook ISBN: 978 1 472 00121 4

05-0313

Printed and bound in Spain
by Blackprint CPI, Barcelona

FALLING
FOR THE M.D.

BY
MARIE FERRARELLA

Marie Ferrarella, a *USA TODAY* bestselling and RITA® Award-winning author, has written more than one hundred and fifty novels for Mills & Boon®, some under the name Marie Nicole. Her romances are beloved by fans worldwide.

To
Gail Chasan
And the Joy of
Family Sagas

Chapter One

He'd known this day was coming for a long time.

Death was not a surprise to him. As a doctor, it was all part of the circle of life. But while he always concentrated on the positive, Dr. Peter Wilder could never fully ignore the fact that death was seated at the very same table as life.

His mother, Alice, had died five years ago, a victim of cancer. Now that death had come to rob him for a second time, though, he felt alone, despite the fact that the cemetery was crowded. His three siblings were there, along with all the friends and admirers that his father, Dr. James

Wilder, had garnered over the years as a physician and Chief of Staff at Walnut River General Hospital and, toward the end, as the chairman of the board of directors. Despite the cold, gloomy January morning and the persistent snow flurries, there had been an enormous turnout to pay last respects to a man who had touched so very many lives.

Despite all of his professional obligations, James had never failed to make time for his family, was always there for all the important occasions that meant something to his sons and daughters.

Now both his mother and his father were gone, the latter leaving behind incredibly large shoes to fill.

Peter had become the patriarch. As the oldest, he would be the one to whom David and Ella and Anna would turn.

Well, maybe not Anna, he reconsidered, glancing over toward her.

They were gathered around the grave. Typically, while he, David and Ella were on one side of his father's final resting place, Anna had positioned herself opposite them. Ten years his junior, Anna was the family's official black sheep.

While he, David and Ella had followed their father's footsteps, Anna's feet had not quite fit the mold. He knew that she had tried, managing to go so far as being accepted into a medical school. But then she'd dropped out in her freshman year.

Anna didn't have the head for medicine, or the heart. So she had gone a different route, earning an MBA and finally finding herself when she entered the world of finance.

But there was an even greater reason why the rest of them considered Anna to be the black sheep. His father had been fond of referring to her as "the chosen one," but the simple truth of it was, Anna had been a foundling, abandoned as an infant on the steps of the hospital to which the senior Wilder had dedicated his entire adult life.

Since James Wilder lived and breathed all things that concerned Walnut River General, it somehow seemed natural that he should adopt the only baby who had ever been left there.

Or so he'd heard his father say to his mother when he was trying to win her over to his decision. His mother tried, but he knew that she could never quite make herself open her heart to this child whose own parents hadn't wanted her. Maybe because of this, because of the way his mother felt, his father had done his best to make it up to Anna. He had overcompensated.

For years, James went out of his way to make Anna feel accepted and a wanted member of the family. In his efforts to keep Anna from feeling unloved, James Wilder often placed his adopted daughter first.

Despite all his good intentions, his father's actions were not without consequences. While they were growing up, Peter and his siblings were resentful of the special treatment Anna received. Especially David, who began to act out in order to win his own brand of attention from their father.

Slowly, so slowly that Peter wasn't even certain when it actually happened, it became a matter of their breaking into two separate camps—he, David and Ella on the one hand, and Anna, by herself, on the other. The schism continued to grow despite all of their father's efforts to the contrary. Time and again, James would try to rectify the situation, asking them each what was wrong and what he could do to fix it, only to be told by a tight-lipped child that everything was fine.

But it wasn't.

He, David and Ella felt that Anna had their father's ear and the bulk of his love and attention. At the same time Anna, he surmised as he looked back on things now, probably felt like the odd woman out, doomed to remain on the outside of the family circle, forever looking in.

Maybe now would be a good time to put a stop to it, Peter thought. To change direction and start fresh. As a tribute to his father, who simply wanted his family to all get along. They weren't all that different, really, the four of them. And Anna had loved James Wilder as much as any of them.

Snow was dusting Peter's dark brown hair, making it appear almost white. He brushed some of it aside. The sudden movement had Ella looking up at him. Ella, with her doelike eyes and small mouth that was usually so quick to smile shyly. Ella, whose dark eyes right now looked almost haunted with sadness.

Leaning her head toward him, she whispered, "I can't believe he's really gone. I thought he'd be with us forever, like some force of nature."

Standing on her other side, David couldn't help overhearing. "Well, he really is gone. They're about to lower the coffin," he murmured bitterly.

Ella's head jerked up and she looked at David, stunned at the raw pain in his tone, not just over the loss of their father, but the opportunity to ever again make things right between them. James and David had not been on the warmest terms at the time of the senior Wilder's death and Peter was certain that David chafed over words he had left unsaid simply because "there was always tomorrow."

Now tomorrow would never come.

Peter turned away, his attention on the highly polished casket slowly being lowered into the ground. With each inch that came between them, he felt fresh waves of loss wash over him.

Goodbye, Dad. I wish we'd had more time together. There's so much I still need to know, so much I still want to ask you.

Peter waited until the coffin was finally placed at the bottom of the grave, then he stepped forward and dropped the single red rose he'd been holding. It fell against the coffin and then, like the tears of a weeping mourner, slid off to the side.

"Rest well, Dad," Peter said, struggling to keep his voice from cracking. "You've earned it." And then he moved aside, letting Ella have her moment as she added her rose to his, her wishes to his.

One by one, the mourners all filed by, people who were close to the man, people who worshipped the doctor, dropping roses and offering warm words for one of the finest men any of them had ever known.

Peter had expected Anna to follow either David or, more likely since she'd once been close to her, Ella. But she stood off to the side, patiently waiting for everyone else to go by before she finally moved forward herself.

He should have realized that she wanted to be alone with their father one last time.

Last but not least, right, Anna?

She was saying something, but her voice was so low when she spoke that he couldn't hear her. He caught a glimpse of the tears glistening in her eyes even though she tried to avert her head so her grief would remain as private as her parting words.

Peter felt a hint of guilt pricking his conscience. This was his sister. Adopted, yes, but raised with him from infancy. She'd been only a few days old at most when his father had brought her into their house.

"I brought you an early birthday present, Alice," the senior Wilder had announced as he came through the front door.

Until the day he died, Peter would remember the look of surprise, disbelief and then something more that he couldn't begin to fathom wash across his mother's face when she came into the living room to see what it was that his father had brought home for her. He was ten at the time and David was six. His mother had just crawled out of a depression that had her, for a time, all but confined to her bed. He remembered how afraid he'd been back then, afraid that there was something wrong with his mother. He'd fully expected her to fall head over heels in love with the baby—that's what women did, he'd thought at the time. They loved babies.

But there had been a tightness around her mouth as she took the bundle from his father.

"She's very pretty, isn't she, boys?" his father had said, trying to encourage them to become part of the acceptance process.

"She's noisy," David had declared, scowling. "And she smells."

His father had laughed. "She just needs changing."

"Can we change her for a pony?" David wanted to know, picking up on the word.

"'Fraid not, David. What do you think of her, Peter?" his father had asked, turning toward him.

"She's very little" had been his only comment about this new addition. He remembered watching his mother instead of the baby. Watching and worrying. His father had once said that he was born old, and there was some truth to that. He couldn't remember ever being carefree.

"That's right," his father had agreed warmly. "And we need to look out for her." His father had placed his large, capable hand on his shoulder, silently conveying that he was counting on him. "You need to look after her. You're her big brother."

He remembered nodding solemnly, not happy

about the assignment but not wanting to disappoint his father, either. He also recalled seeing his mother frown as she took the baby from his father and walked into the other room.

And so began a rather unsteady, continuing family dynamic. David saw Anna as competition, while Peter regarded Anna as a burden he was going to have to carry. And things never really changed.

For one reason or another, things were never quite harmonious among them. Whenever he would extend the olive branch, Anna would hold him suspect. And whenever she would seek common ground with him, he'd be too busy to meet her halfway. Things between her and David were in an even worse state. Only she and Ella got along.

And so the years melted away, wrapped in misunderstanding and hurt feelings, and the gap continued to widen.

It was time to put a stop to it.

"Anna," he called to her.

David and Ella, standing nearby, both turned to look at their older brother. About to melt back into the crowd, Anna looked up and in Peter's direction. The wind whipped her light blond hair into her eyes. She blinked, pushing the strand back behind her ear, a silent question in her pale blue eyes.

Peter cut the distance between them. He

couldn't shake the feeling that he was on borrowed time, that there was a finite amount of it during which he could bring peace to the family. He had no idea where the feeling had come from.

However, once he was beside her, words seemed to desert him. Ordinarily, he always knew how to sympathize, how to comfort. His bedside manner was one of his strongest points. He had absolutely no trouble placing himself in his patient's drafty hospital gown, understanding exactly what he or she was going through. Like his father before him, Peter's capacity for empathy was enormous, and his patients loved him for it.

But this was different. This was almost too personal. This came with baggage and history. His and Anna's.

Peter did his best to sound warm when he spoke to her, knowing that she had to be feeling the same sort of pain he was.

"There's going to be a reception at my house." David and Ella were standing directly behind him. He wished one of them would say something. "I didn't know if you knew." Once the words were out, he realized it sounded like a backhanded invitation.

"I didn't," she replied quietly. Her eyes moved from David's face to Ella's to his again.

She looked as if she wanted to leave, Peter

thought. He couldn't really blame her. He knew there'd be less tension if she did. But then again, it wasn't right to drive her away.

Peter tried again. "I thought it might help everyone to get together, swap a few stories about Dad. Everyone seems to have a hundred of them," he added, forcing a smile to his lips.

He waited for her response, but it was David who spoke next. "Sounds great, Peter, but I'm booked on a flight that leaves in a couple of hours." He glanced at his watch. "I've just got enough time to get to the airport and go through security."

"Take a later flight," Peter urged.

He knew that David could well afford to pay the difference for changing his plans. The younger man was, after all, a highly sought after plastic surgeon. *People* magazine had referred to David as the surgeon to the stars in a recent article. He was certainly the family's success story—at least, financially. In contrast, Ella had just recently completed her residency. And God knew that he wasn't making a pile of money, Peter thought. About forty percent of his patients had no health insurance and could barely make token payments for their treatment, not that that would stop him from being available to them if the need arose.

However, Anna probably did quite well for herself in the business world. Her clothes certainly looked expensive, as did the car she drove. She never elaborated about her job, though, so it was left to Peter's imagination to fill in the blanks.

David shook his head. "You know I would, but I've got a surgery scheduled first thing in the morning. It was a last-minute booking," he explained. "Flying always tires me out and I need a good eight hours to be at my best." He paused for a moment, looking at his older brother. It was obvious that he did feel somewhat guilty about grieving and running. "Are you okay with that?"

No, Peter thought, he wasn't okay with that. But that was life. There was no point in creating a fuss, so he nodded and said, "I understand. Duty calls."

Squeezing through the opening that David had inadvertently left for her, Anna was quick to say, "I have to be going, too."

She deliberately avoided Peter's eyes, knowing that they would bore right through her, not that it really mattered. She'd come here for her father, not for any of them. She knew what they thought of her. She'd hoped that their father's passing might finally bring them together, but that obviously wasn't happening. In their eyes, she knew she would always be an outsider. There was no getting away from it.

"There's a meeting I need to prepare for," she told him.

She was lying, Peter thought. Anna always looked extremely uncomfortable when she lied.

But he wasn't about to press. "You'll be missed," he told her.

Now who was lying? he asked himself.

She debated leaving the comment alone and retreating while the going was good. But she couldn't resist saying, "I sincerely doubt that." She saw both her brothers and Ella look at her in surprise. Was the truth that surprising? Or was it because she'd said something? "No one will even miss me."

"I will," Ella told her.

It was Anna's turn to be surprised. She looked at her sister. Only a year separated them and if she was close to anyone within the family, with the exception of her father, it was Ella. So much so that she'd taken time off from her impossibly hectic schedule to attend Ella's graduation. Aside from that, she'd only been home for the holidays and her father's birthday.

Now that he was gone, she doubted she'd be back at all. What was the point? There was no reason to return to this den of strangers. She had a feeling they would be relieved as well not to have to pretend that they cared whether or not she visited.

But for now, she smiled at Ella, grateful for the sentiment the youngest Wilder had expressed. Anna squeezed her sister's hand. "Thanks, El. But I still have to go."

"An hour?" Peter was surprised to hear himself say. Maybe it was the look on Ella's face that had prompted him to try to get Anna to remain. "Just stay an hour." He saw her reluctance to even entertain the suggestion. "For Dad, not for me."

"You can stay for both of us," David told her flippantly. Embracing Ella, he kissed his younger sister on the cheek affectionately, then gripped Peter's hand. "I'll be in touch," he promised his brother. And then he nodded at Anna, his demeanor polite but definitely cooler. "Anna, it was good to see you again."

Peter saw Anna's shoulders stiffen.

So much for a truce. Maybe some other time, he told himself.

He began to guide Ella to the parking lot and the limousine that had brought them here.

He didn't see Bethany Holloway approaching until she was almost at his elbow. Beautiful women occasionally captured his attention, and this woman was a classic beauty, with porcelain skin, luminous blue eyes and breathtaking red hair.

Wanting to get Peter's attention, Bethany lightly

placed a gloved hand on his arm. Surprised, he turned to look in her direction.

"Oh Peter, I just wanted to say again how sorry I am about your father. Everyone loved him."

That much he knew was true. To know James Wilder was to admire him. His father had had a way of making people feel that they mattered, that he was actively interested in their welfare. In exchange for that, people would regard him with affection. It was a gift.

"Thank you."

He was trying to be gracious, but his words rang a little hollow. Maybe it was selfish, but for a moment, he wanted to be alone with his grief. And yet, he knew he couldn't. He didn't have that luxury afforded to him. No matter his emotions, he needed to hold it together so that everyone else could mourn as they needed to.

It certainly wouldn't help Ella cope with her grief if she saw him break down, he thought.

"But maybe," Bethany went on, falling into step beside him, "in a way this might have been easier for your father."

"'This'?" Peter echoed.

Bethany nodded. "His passing."

Peter stopped walking and looked at her sharply. He wasn't following her logic. "What?"

Bethany looked as if his reaction wasn't what she'd expected. "Think how Dr. Wilder would have felt, having Northeastern Healthcare take over."

Peter felt as if his brain had just been submerged in a tank of water. None of this was making any sense to him. "Take over what?"

Bethany looked at Peter in surprise. "Why, Walnut River General, of course."

Chapter Two

For a moment, it was so quiet Peter could hear the snow falling, the snowflakes touching down. He was only slightly aware that both Anna and David were still standing nearby.

"What are you saying?" Before Bethany could answer, he looked at Ella. His sister looked completely encased in her grief. He didn't want her subjected to anything more right now. "You look cold, Ella. Why don't you go on to the limousine and wait for us inside?" he suggested.

In a haze, Ella nodded and left the group.

Wilder hadn't heard, Bethany realized. What's

more, he looked obviously upset by the news. She hadn't thought he would be. As far as she saw it, the proposed takeover was good news. Only people who resisted progress would view it as anything else.

Still, a qualm of guilt slid over her.

"I'm saying that it's official," Bethany explained. "NHC came out and announced that they were interested in acquiring Walnut River General." Her smile widened. "They're saying that it would be an excellent addition to its family of hospitals. Your father helped turn the hospital into a highly regarded institution, and he did a wonderful job," she added.

Maybe too wonderful, Peter thought. Otherwise, they would have continued operating under the radar.

"He didn't do it to have the hospital pillaged by an impersonal corporation," Peter declared, feeling his temper suddenly rise. If he needed proof of the organization's insensitivity to the human condition, he had it now. The conglomerate was putting in a bid before his father's body was barely cold. "Those sharks wouldn't know what a family was if they were hit over the head with one."

"Don't hold back, Peter," David urged wryly. "Tell us what you really think."

Bethany glanced at the younger Dr. Wilder.

She knew he wasn't part of the hospital staff, but she'd expected to hear something more in favor of what seemed inevitable than a joke. After all, a plastic surgeon, especially one of David Wilder's caliber, could appreciate a highly efficient organization.

Feeling slightly uncomfortable, like the bearer of bad news instead of good, Bethany cleared her throat. "Well, anyway, the board is going to be meeting tomorrow morning about this," she told Peter. "I thought I'd give you a heads-up, seeing as how this will be your first time and all."

She was referring to the position on the board he'd assumed. Not his father's position—that had gone to Wallace Ford. With Wallace assuming the chairmanship, that had left a seat open and, out of respect for James Wilder, the board had offered it to Peter. He'd accepted it out of a sense of responsibility and not without more than a little dread. He simply wanted to be a doctor. The seat on the board would get in the way, but for now he had no choice.

Peter nodded in response to her words, trying not to look as disturbed by the news as he felt. Right now, he was here for his father and that was all that mattered. There was time enough to worry about this newest development later.

"Thank you." Realizing how stiff he sounded, Peter made an effort to be more congenial. "Will I see you at the reception?"

A trace of Bethany's smile entered her eyes as she answered, "Of course. Again—" she took hold of Peter's hand and looked up into his eyes "—I am very sorry for your loss." She glanced over toward the limousine where Ella sat waiting. "And your sister's," she added.

At least it was death that had taken the man from Peter and his siblings, she couldn't help thinking. Her parents had simply left her years ago—if they had ever been there to begin with.

A quick smile flashed across her generous mouth. "I'll see you later," she promised, and then she slipped back into the dispersing crowd as they all made their way to their separate vehicles.

David stood beside Peter for a moment, watching Bethany's back as she walked away. His thoughtful expression hinted that he was envisioning what she might look like beneath the white winter coat she had on.

"Well, that's a new face." He turned back to his brother, for the moment ignoring Anna's presence. "Nice structure. Good cheekbones."

Anna made a small, annoyed noise. "Do you have to look at everyone like a work in progress?"

Her disapproval was evident despite the fact that she kept her voice low.

David's shoulders moved in a half shrug beneath his camel hair overcoat. "Sorry, occupational hazard. It's the artist in me. Although—" he addressed the rest of his remark to Peter "—there doesn't seem to be anything to improve on with that one. Who *is* she?"

"Bethany Holloway," Peter answered. His and Bethany's paths had crossed perhaps half-a-dozen times, perhaps less, since she had come to Walnut River. "She's on the board."

Mild interest traced itself over David's handsome features. "New member, I imagine. As I remember it, the board was a collection of old fossils."

Peter laughed shortly. "Not anymore. Things have changed since you left for the West coast. Dad's been the oldest one on the board for a while now. Or he was," he corrected himself. God, but it was hard thinking of his father in the past tense. "Some of the others retired.

"Bethany's an efficiency expert. She's been on the board for as long as she's been in town. About six months or so, I think." Peter thought of what he was going to be facing tomorrow. "I guess I'd better start becoming more involved with the business end of things now that I'm part of it."

David looked impressed. "You're taking over Dad's old seat?"

Peter shook his head. "No, not exactly. Dad was the chairman. I've got a long way to go before I'm experienced enough for that position—not that I want it," he added quickly. As far as he was concerned, being on the board was a necessary evil. "Dad always regretted how much time being chairman took away from doing what he really loved."

A comfortable silence hung between the two brothers for a moment. "They don't make 'em like Dad anymore, do they?" And then David looked apologetically at his older brother. "No disrespect intended."

"None taken," Peter replied easily. "James Wellington Wilder was one of a kind. We shall not see his like again."

David rolled his eyes, his natural humor returning. "You're starting to quote Shakespeare, time for me to leave."

Peter hated to see his brother go. David was around so infrequently and there never seemed to be enough time to catch up. "Can I give you a ride to the airport at least?"

David shook his head. "I've got a taxi waiting." As if to prove it, he nodded toward the lot. Peter made out the yellow body and black lettering of a local cab service. "You know I hate long goodbyes."

Peter nodded. "I know it. Ella knows it."

"Don't worry about NHC," David advised.

Peter laughed shortly. "Hard not to," he said honestly. "What is their motto again? Whatever NHC wants, NHC gets?"

David grinned. His money was on Peter. His brother might be a man of few words, but in Peter's case, still waters ran deep. Very deep.

"No, I think it's: 'We've never met a dollar bill we didn't like'." He felt compelled to give his older brother a few words of encouragement. "Which is exactly why Walnut River General won't be joining their so-called family. People feel cared for when they come to Dad's hospital—excuse me, your hospital—"

"It's not mine," Peter corrected. "You were right the first time. Dad's hospital."

David ignored him because they both knew that wasn't true. Walnut River General was the mistress in Peter's life, the lover he lavished his attention on and from whom he'd never strayed. Peter's life was filled with relationships, but they were all with his patients and friends. Not a single one of them was a romantic entanglement.

From the moment he first took his Hippocratic

oath, Peter had been devoid of any sort of relationship that might eventually become permanent. There'd been one in college, but that was all behind him. Beyond caring about his own family, Peter had told David more than once that there wasn't time for anything else.

"You can't put a price on that," David concluded, as if Peter hadn't interjected anything. He paused to embrace his older brother before taking his leave. "It'll be all right." he promised. "Call me if you need me. I'm only a five-hour flight away— if you don't factor in inclement weather and mile-long security lines," David added with a grin.

Crouching for a moment, he peered into the limousine. Ella rolled down the rear window and leaned forward. "Make me proud, little sister."

Peter smiled, shaking his head. "Just what she needs, pressure."

David raised his shoulders and then lowered them in another careless half shrug. "We all need a little pressure." He glanced toward Anna as he made his pronouncement. "Keeps us on our toes and keeps life interesting."

Anna shifted uncomfortably as David told her goodbye again and then hurried off to the cab.

"I'd better be leaving, too." She looked at Peter, loathing to ask for a favor but she'd been so overwhelmed with grief, she hadn't been thinking straight when they set off to the church. "If you could drop me off at my hotel on the way back to your place, I would greatly appreciate it."

She sounded as if she was talking to a stranger, Peter thought. "No problem," he told her.

The limousine driver had popped to attention the moment they'd approached the vehicle, and he was now holding the rear passenger door open for them. Peter waited until Anna climbed in beside Ella, then got in himself.

"Are you sure you won't come to the reception?" Peter prodded. "Just for a few minutes."

But Anna remained firm. "I'm sorry, I really do have to leave. I have a flight to catch, too. I realize that I won't be reconstructing some Hollywood wannabe starlet's breasts in the morning, but what I do is important, too."

"No one said it wasn't, Anna," Peter pointed out.

Why did everything always devolve into an argument between them? Right now, he really wasn't in the mood to walk on eggshells.

Unable to take any more, Ella spoke up. "Please, we just buried Dad. Do you two have to do this now?"

Their father's death had brought everything too close to the surface. Like nerves and hurt feelings.

It was Peter who retreated first.

"Ella's right." It was on the tip of his tongue to say *We shouldn't be acting this way,* but he knew Anna would take the statement as accusatory and it would only add kindling to the fire. So instead, he changed the subject, hitting on what continued, thanks to Bethany's announcement, to be foremost in his mind. "Anna, I'm going to need your help."

It was obviously the last thing she had ever expected to hear from him. Anna looked at Peter, utterly surprised. "You need *my* help?"

He could feel Ella looking at him, mystified. But it was true. He did need Anna's help. "Yes."

This was definitely a first, Anna thought. An uneasiness immediately slipped over her. An uneasiness because she had a feeling she knew what her older brother was going to say. And if she was right, she was going to have to turn him down. Because she was facing a huge conflict of interest. So, she made a preemptive strike, nipping a potential problem in the bud before she was faced with it. "I'm sorry, Peter, but all my time is already accounted for over the next few months," she said firmly.

"I see." He let the matter drop, silently upbraiding himself. Given their distance recently, he should have known better than to ask.

Peter's small, two-story house was stuffed with people. Nearly everyone who'd attended the service and gone to the cemetery had followed the stretch limousine back to the reception.

Peter mentally tipped his hat to Ella. He had no knowledge of these kind of situations, no idea what was expected beyond the necessary funeral arrangements. Ella had handled all the subsequent preparations, securing a caterer and telling the man what to bring, where to set up and when.

Initially, when he'd seen how much food was going to be on hand, Peter had envisioned himself having to live on leftovers for the next six months. Watching his various guests help themselves, he smiled now, thinking that if there was enough left over for a sandwich for lunch tomorrow, he'd be doing well.

He supposed that sorrow brought out the hunger in some people. As for him, the exact opposite was true. He wasn't sure if he'd had more than a single meal since his father had suffered the fatal heart attack that had taken the man away from them.

Damn, but I am going to miss you, Dad. You left too soon, he thought not for the first time.

"You're not eating."

The words took him by surprise. Or rather, the

voice did. Bethany Holloway, the Jill-come-lately to the hospital's board of directors.

As he turned to look at her, he caught himself, thinking that David was dead-on in his evaluation of her appearance. But he had a sneaking suspicion that they might find themselves on the opposite sides of an opinion.

Pity, he thought.

"That's because I'm not hungry," he said, punctuating his statement with a half-hearted smile.

"You really should have something," Bethany advised. The next moment, she was putting into his hands a plate containing several slices of roast beef and ham that she had obviously taken for herself. "You're looking a little pale."

Trying to return the plate to her proved futile. "You have a degree?" he asked amiably.

Bethany knew he meant in medicine, but she deadpanned her answer.

"In observation." She quickly followed up with, "And it doesn't take much to see that you haven't been visiting your refrigerator with any amount of regularity." That actually stirred a few distant memories within her. She really had so few when it came to her own home life. "My father used to get too caught up in his work to remember to eat," she added, hoping that might persuade him to take a few bites. She could well imagine how he had to feel. It wasn't easy losing family, and from what she'd observed of father and son, they had been close.

"Used to?" Peter echoed. "Is he—" He couldn't bring himself to finish the question. The word *dead* stuck in his throat like an open wound, the kind sustained by swallowing something that was too hot.

"Gone?" she supplied. It was a nice, safe word for what he was implying, she thought. "No, actually, I'm the one who's gone. From the state," she added quickly when she saw his eyebrows draw together in minor confusion. "As far as I know, both of my parents are still working like crazy." Bethany lifted one shoulder in a quick, careless shrug and then took a sip from the glass of diet soda she was holding in her other hand. "It makes them happy so I suppose it's all right."

From her tone, Peter inferred that it was *not* all right with her. Questions about her began to form in his mind.

Bethany looked around the tightly packed family room and beyond. There was barely enough space for people to mill around without rubbing elbows and other body parts against one another.

"This a very large turnout." She smiled at him. "Your father had a lot of friends."

To know his father was to like him, Peter thought. "That he did."

"I didn't know him very well," Bethany began, picking her words carefully, "but the little I did know, I liked a great deal." Her smile widened and Peter caught himself thinking that she had an extremely infectious smile. "He reminded me a little of Jimmy Stewart in *It's A Wonderful Life*, always thinking about other people and what they needed." She raised her eyes to his and, just for an inkling, Peter thought he felt something inside himself stirring, reacting to the soft blue gaze. "You kind of look like him." He perceived a hint of pink along her cheeks. "I mean, like the portrait of him that's hanging in the hospital corridor outside the administration office. Same strong chin, same kind eyes."

And then she laughed. "I'm sorry," she apologized. "I always speak my mind. My mother told me it would get me in trouble someday." Lectured her, actually, but Peter didn't need to know that.

"And has it?" he asked. "Gotten you in trouble I mean."

She shook her head. "Not yet, but there's still time." Bethany looked past his shoulder. A curious expression slipped over her flawless features. "I think that man is trying to get your attention."

Peter turned to look over his shoulder and saw Fred Trinity, his father's lawyer. The latter looked relieved to make eye contact and waved him over.

What's this all about? Peter wondered. The formal reading of the will, not that it was really necessary, was set for tomorrow.

Well, he might as well find out, he thought. "If you'll excuse me," Peter murmured, handing her back the plate she'd given him.

"Of course." Bethany frowned at the untouched fare on the plate. "Don't forget to eat something," she called after him. And then, with a resigned sigh, she turned back to the crowd.

It took him a minute before he realized that he was just standing there, watching her walk away, thinking that the woman looked good going as well as coming.

Chapter Three

With his shaggy mustache and gleaming bald head, Fred Trinity looked like a walrus in an outdated suit that might have fit him well some twenty-five, thirty pounds ago. His carelessness, however, only extended to his appearance. His mind was as sharp as the point of a sword.

Placing a solicitous hand on Peter's arm, the lawyer lowered his voice, as if the weight of his words wouldn't allow him to speak any louder.

"Could I see you alone for a minute, Peter?"

The grave expression on the man's round, ordinarily amiable face was not reassuring. A chill passed over Peter's shoulder blades and he couldn't help wondering if this had anything to do with the threat he'd so recently been made aware of, the one posed by NHC. Fred had been his father's lawyer for as long as he could remember, but he wasn't the legal counsel that the hospital board turned to. Still, Fred might have been privy to some sort of inside information. Lawyers talked among themselves like everyone else, didn't they?

Bracing himself, Peter nodded. "Sure." He indicated the doorway leading to other parts of the house. "We can go to my study. It's just down the hall."

Crossing the living-room threshold, Peter led the way out.

"I've never been to your house before," Fred commented, looking around.

"It's not much of a treat," Peter confessed. "I'm afraid I've let things get away from me. You know how it is."

"Actually, no," Fred replied. "Selma handles all that. You need a wife, Peter."

"I'll put it on my list of things to do," Peter promised.

The house was older than Peter and in need of attention and a fair amount of updating. Other than hiring an occasional cleaning crew to do battle with the cobwebs and the dust, nothing had been changed since he'd moved in shortly after graduating from medical school. He honestly couldn't remember the last time he'd had the house painted, but then, he rarely spent much time here.

He was always at the hospital, either in the O.R., the emergency room or in his fourth-floor office. His house was just the place where he received his mail, did his laundry and slept. Beyond that, it really didn't serve much of a function.

Like the rest of the doors in the house, the door to his study was wide-open. He didn't like closed doors. Closed doors meant secrets. It was a holdover from his childhood. On the rare occasions when his parents would have words, the doors were always closed. When they were opened again, his parents would emerge, each with sadness in their eyes.

As he walked in, Peter flipped a switch on his desk lamp, which cast a dim light.

He switched the three-way bulb on high, then turned around to face the man he had ushered in.

"What's wrong, Fred?"

Fred looked somewhat uneasy. Peter couldn't remember ever seeing the lawyer look anything but comfortably confident. Fred reached inside the breast pocket of his jacket and took out a bulky-looking white envelope. Watching Peter's face, Fred held it out to him.

Across the front of the envelope, in his father's very distinct handwriting, was his name.

"Your father wanted me to give this to you. It was only to be opened in the event of his death," Fred explained and then sighed with genuine sorrow. It was no secret that he'd known James Wilder for over sixty years. They'd gone to school together. "Which is now. I am going to really miss that man. Did I ever tell you that he saved my life?"

Peter stared at the envelope before taking it. What could his father have written that he couldn't have said to him in person?

"Twice." A heaviness hovered over Peter as he took the envelope Fred was holding out. He had an uneasy feeling he didn't want to know what was inside. "When did he give this to you?"

"Five years ago. Shortly after your mother died." The man's small mouth curved beneath the shaggy mustache. "I think her death brought mortality into his life in big, bright letters. It hit him then that no one was going to go on forever, not even him, and he had some things he wanted to get off his chest, I suppose." Fred pressed his lips together. "Damn, I thought if anyone would have been able to cheat death, it would have been him."

"Yeah, me, too." His father was the most decent,

honorable man he had ever known, as well as the most dedicated. There were no skeletons in his closet, no real deep, dark secrets. His father's life had been an open book. "What makes you think my father had something he wanted to get off his chest?"

"Because, for one thing, there are no letters for David or Ella or Anna. I guess as the family's new patriarch, he was turning to you." Fred's bushy eyebrows rose in surprise as he watched Peter tuck the letter into his own breast pocket without opening it. "Aren't you going to read it?"

Peter shook his head. "Not right now. I need to get through this ordeal first before I'm up to tackling another problem."

Fred nodded, but it was obvious he was curious about the envelope's contents. However, it wasn't his place to prod.

"Makes sense," Fred allowed. His mission accomplished, he took a step toward the doorway, then stopped. "By the way, is tomorrow evening still convenient for the reading of the will?"

Convenient. What a strange word to use under the circumstances. Peter took a breath, doing his best to block the barrage of sadness that threatened to overwhelm him again.

"Tomorrow evening will be fine, Fred," he replied quietly.

Fred continued to pause as another thought

occurred to him. "What about Anna and David? I don't see either one of them at the reception."

"That's because they're not here," Peter replied simply. He could see the answer didn't please the man. Crossing back to the doorway, he turned off the light. "If there's anything out of the ordinary in the will—" which he was confident there wouldn't be "—I can always call and tell them."

Fred nodded as they walked out of the room together. "Rumor has it that NHC is about to come knocking on the hospital's door." He stopped short of the living room. "What are you planning to do about it?"

"Not answer," Peter replied with a finality that left no room for argument.

Fred grinned broadly and clapped him on the shoulder. He had to reach a little in order to do it. "Good man. You'd make your father proud." He lowered his voice again, assuming a conspiratorial tone. "He's watching over you now, you know that, don't you?"

Peter merely offered a perfunctory smile. He wasn't exactly sure how he stood on things like that. What he did know was he would have preferred to have his father at his side. Or better yet, leading this charge against the anticipated assault.

James Wilder was far better suited to staving off the barbarians at the gate than he was.

But he was going to have to learn. And fast.

The first person Peter noticed when he walked into the boardroom the next morning was Bethany Holloway. Out of respect for the late chief of staff, she was wearing a black sheath. It made her hair seem more vividly red, her complexion ever more porcelainlike.

Black became her, Peter thought absently. On her, the color didn't look quite as somber.

The eight other board members in the room were also wearing black or navy, undoubtedly prompted by the same desire to show respect, Peter mused. His father would have been surprised at how many people mourned his passing. But then, the man had always been so unassuming, never thinking of himself, only others.

His thoughts momentarily brought him back to the envelope Fred had given him last night. He'd left it, unopened, on the mantel in the living room, unable to deal with its contents. He knew that was making assumptions, giving it an importance it might not actually have, but he couldn't shake the uneasy feeling that whatever was inside the envelope was going to change life for him as he knew it.

So for the time being, it was going to remain unopened. At the moment, he had enough windmills to tilt at. Especially if this threat posed by NHC actually was genuine.

The January sun had decided to make an appearance, pushing its way into the rectangular room via the large bay window that looked down onto the hospital's emergency room entrance.

Despite the brightness, Peter felt a chill zip down along his spine as he walked into the room. Everyone was already there. He was on time; they were early. Was there some sort of a significance to that?

Wallace Ford, the newly appointed chairman of the board, walked up to him and shook his hand as if he hadn't been at the service and subsequent reception just yesterday.

"Good of you to attend, Peter," he said heartily. Dropping his hand, he sighed heavily. "Again, let me express my deepest sorrow regarding your father." He cast a glance about the room before looking at Peter again. "We all lost someone very special to us."

"Thank you, Wallace, I appreciate that." Peter looked around at the other board members, all sitting at the long rectangular table. It seated twelve. Only nine seats were filled. He'd never paid attention to the exact number of board members before. There'd been no need. Maybe he should have.

Hindsight wasn't helpful.

"Where do you want me?" he asked Wallace.

Wallace gestured toward the chair beside Bethany. "Why don't you take the empty seat next to Ms. Holloway?" And then the chairman smiled at Bethany as if they were both in on a secret joke. "I guess you're going to have to relinquish your title as the newest member of the board, Ms. Holloway."

"Gladly," Bethany replied.

Wallace waited until Peter took his seat and then, running his fingers along the gavel he refrained from striking, the newly appointed chairman called the meeting to order and addressed the group.

"Because this is an impromptu meeting and we all have other places we need to be, I'm going to dispense with the reading of the minutes today and get right down to the heart of the matter." His small, brown eyes rested on Peter for a long moment. "Or matters, as the case might be," he corrected himself.

"First of all, we, the board and I—" Wallace gestured grandly around the table before continuing, and it struck Peter that the man was a born showman who was given to dramatic pauses "—would like to offer the position of chief of staff to you, Dr. Wilder."

For a moment, Peter didn't know what to say. Chief of Staff had been his father's position. In his later years, James Wilder juggled that *and* being chairman of the board. Both were full-time jobs. It never ceased to amaze him how his father managed to do justice to both, but he had. In the end, it had probably taken a toll on his health.

That notwithstanding, Peter was flattered by the offer, but he knew his limitations. With a self-deprecating smile, he shook his head. "Thank you, all of you, but I don't believe I'm experienced enough to take that on."

Wallace laughed at the refusal. "Modest. You're your father's son all right. Actually, we're asking you to take the position on temporarily, just until we find a suitable candidate. Your father left very big shoes to fill. It's going to take us a while before we find someone who comes close to his caliber. Until then, we would consider it an honor, as well as a huge favor, to have a Wilder in that position for a little while longer." Wallace paused just long enough to allow the words sink in. "You'd really be bailing us out."

Very adroitly, the new chairman of the board had maneuvered him until his back was against the wall. Peter knew he had no choice but to agree. It helped somewhat knowing that it was only for a little while.

"Well, put that way, I don't think I can turn it down."

"Wonderful. Then it's settled. Peter Wilder is the new temporary chief of staff." Wallace grew somber, as if the next topic could only be spoken about with the utmost respect and gravity. "As for the second reason for this meeting, I think we're all aware of what that is, but I'll be the one to say it out loud. Northeastern Healthcare has expressed a great interest in acquiring our little hospital and I believe that their offer is worth discussing at length."

Peter could feel his stomach tightening. "As long as our final answer is no," he commented.

Wallace shot him a look as if he'd just violated some sort of sacred procedure.

He probably had, Peter thought. He wasn't up on the intricacies of parliamentary procedure and the kind of pomp and ceremony that went with conducting meetings properly. It had never aroused the slightest bit of interest in him.

What did interest him were people—patients—who needed his care, his skills. He couldn't help wondering how his father, a very simple man at bottom, had been able to put up with all of this.

Wallace narrowed his eyes as he continued to look at him. "Excuse me?"

Now that he was in the potential fray, he might as well speak his mind, Peter thought. "Well, you can't seriously be thinking about accepting their offer, Wallace."

Wallace frowned. "You haven't even heard the amount yet."

Peter laughed shortly. "I don't need to hear the amount. You can't put a price on what we do here."

"I'm sure that would come as a surprise to the insurance companies, Dr. Wilder," Bethany said. She saw the incredulous look on the doctor's face and quickly continued. She needed to make this man understand why he was wrong. "Patients pay for their care, that's the whole point. And if that care can come about more efficiently, more quickly, it's a win-win situation for us and for them." Her voice grew more impassioned as she continued. "Besides, we're just a simple hospital. One huge lawsuit could ruin us and force us to close our doors."

"There's never been a lawsuit against the hospital," Peter said, in case she was ignorant of the fact.

"That doesn't mean that there couldn't be," Bethany pointed out. "People are a great deal more litigation-crazy than they were when your father joined the staff here. With a conglomerate like NHC taking Walnut River General under its protective wing, we're all but invulnerable."

The other board members in the room faded into the background. One attempted to say something, but Peter ignored him. Because Walnut River General meant so much to his father, to him, this had suddenly become personal.

"And where does the patient fit in with all this?" Peter wanted to know. How could someone who looked like an angel be so cold?

"The patient is the one who benefits," Bethany insisted. She clearly thought he was oblivious to that. "NHC puts us on the map, makes us eligible to receive grants, updates our equipment, perhaps even gets us state-of-the-art equipment. You can't possibly ignore that."

"No," Peter agreed. "Updated equipment is extremely important, but that's what we have fund-raisers for. And so far, they've done pretty well by us."

The man just wasn't getting the big picture. He thought too small. "Personal donations," she said. "Think how much more we could do with allotments from a conglomerate with bottomless pockets."

He wondered if she was actually that naive, or

if it was a matter of her being heartless. He preferred thinking it was the former, but he had a feeling he was wrong. "Isn't that a little like selling our souls for thirty pieces of silver?"

Wallace cleared his throat, getting them to both look in his direction for a moment and breaking the growing tension.

"Aren't you being a little dramatic, Peter?" Wallace asked.

"No, I'm being pragmatic," he responded. "I didn't go to medical school to practice assembly-line medicine." His main focus wasn't Wallace, it was Bethany. He wanted to make her understand, to see the flaw in the way she thought. "The doctors here treat the whole patient, they don't deal with him or her piecemeal. I don't want some accounting analyst holding a stopwatch and looking over my shoulder, telling me that I need to move faster or I'll wind up pulling the hospital's batting average down."

"There's nothing wrong with seeing more patients," Bethany insisted.

"There is if you wind up shortchanging them because you have a quota to meet or a schedule to live up to. Can't you see that?"

Bethany's eyes flashed angrily. Was he accusing her of being obtuse? She'd never reacted well to criticism. She'd had to put up with a lot of it while she'd been growing up. She didn't have to anymore.

"You're ignoring all the benefits that being part of an organization like Northeastern Healthcare can provide for the hospital. They have access to far more facilities than we do."

"Looks like someone has done their homework," Wallace said. There was no missing the admiration in his voice or the approving look on the chairman's face as he looked at Bethany.

Was Wallace for the takeover, or was he just trying to score points with Bethany? Peter wondered in mounting frustration.

He didn't often lose his patience, but his father's death had changed the rules and shaken him down to his very foundation.

"Then give her a gold star, Wallace, but don't give NHC the hospital. Everyone will regret it if you do, most of all, the patients." Peter rose from his chair. The legs scraped along the floor as he pushed it back from the table. "Now, if you will all please excuse me, I have patients waiting to see me."

It was only by calling up the greatest restraint that he didn't slam the door behind him as he left.

Chapter Four

Bethany could feel the vibrations created by Peter's exit long after he'd left the room. Even after the meeting had abruptly broken up less than fifteen minutes later. Until she'd witnessed Wilder's reaction she'd figured the takeover to be a slam dunk.

So much for intuition.

She wouldn't have thought it to look at him, but Wilder was positively archaic. The man was standing in the way of progress, pure and simple. He was obviously so stuck in the past, he refused to open his eyes and see the future, or even acknowledge, much less read the handwriting on the wall.

Bethany's mouth curved as she walked down the fourth-floor corridor. It looked like it was up to her to make the temporary chief of staff see the error of his ways. She'd made up her mind about that the moment the meeting broke up. All the other board members already had some sort of relationship with Peter and seemed obviously wary of upsetting him, whether because they liked him, or were still treading on eggshells because of his father's recent death. Just as possibly, their hesitation arose out of respect for the late James Wilder.

Whatever the reason, she didn't know and she didn't care. No single person should be allowed to stand in the way of bettering a situation that ultimately affected so many just because clearly he viewed all change as bad and something to be avoided.

She knew people like Peter, had dealt with them before. People so set in their ways they felt there was no true path except the one they were standing on. They were stuck there, like the prehistoric creatures had been in the La Brea tar pits. The only difference was, the animals hadn't wanted to be stuck—they'd wandered in and had no choice. Wilder had a choice and he'd focused on the wrong one.

Knowing she couldn't confront the man while he was seeing patients, Bethany positioned herself outside his office a few minutes before noon. She assumed that, like every other physician she had ever known, he would break for lunch around that time. So she waited.

At one o'clock, she was still waiting.

Mystified, Bethany moved to the door and tried the knob, intending to check whether Wilder was still actually in his office or had somehow managed to leave by a back door without her knowing it. Her hand was on the knob when the door suddenly opened. Jerked forward, she stumbled and found herself bumping up against the doctor full force.

He was quick to grab her by the shoulders so the collision wouldn't send her falling backward. Caught off guard, she sucked in her breath, stifling a noise that sounded very much like a gasp.

She wasn't accustomed to being at an awkward, physical disadvantage. She liked being in control. Complete poise had been her credo since college. To her credit, she managed to collect herself almost immediately.

"Oh, Dr. Wilder—"

"That's what it says on the door," he acknowledged, unable to see why she should sound so surprised at seeing him walk out of his own office. Ever the doctor, his dark eyes swept over her, checking for any minor signs of damage or bruising. There were none visible. Still, he asked, "Are you all right?"

"Yes." Bethany brushed absently at her dress, smoothing it out. "I'm a lot more resilient than I look."

"Good." With a satisfied nod of his head, Peter began to walk toward the elevator.

Bethany had expected him to stand still so she could talk to him. Instead, she had to fall into step to gain his ear. Moreover, she found she had to fairly trot in order to keep up with the man. If she didn't know better, she'd speculate that he was trying to avoid her.

"I was hoping to run into you—"

He glanced at her with mild, amused interest. "And you decided to do that literally?"

She frowned. Was he teasing her, or did it go deeper than that? Her childhood was steeped in ridicule and the wounds from that had never quite healed. "That wasn't the plan."

Stopping by the elevator, Peter pressed the down button on the wall. A faint glimmer of a light went on, circling the button.

"What *was* the plan?" he asked, feeling that he was probably setting himself up. Braced, he sank his hands into the deep pockets of his lab coat and waited for her to answer.

Bethany psyched herself up for exactly half a second before saying, "I wanted to talk to you about NHC's offer."

He looked at her for a long moment. The woman didn't appear to be someone who had adult attention deficit disorder. But then, you just never knew, did you? From what he'd gathered, she was an overachiever. That could be a sign.

"I believe you already did," he reminded her.

"But you walked out," she countered. Walked out before she could even get warmed up, she added silently.

"Not very polite," Peter granted amicably. "But in all honesty, there was no point in wasting your time or mine. I'd heard enough."

"You hardly heard anything at all."

There they had a difference of opinion. "I heard the words 'Northeastern Healthcare' and 'takeover.' In my book, that's really enough."

The man really *was* closed-minded, Bethany thought, annoyed. Which meant that she had her job cut out for her. But she was up to it. She liked Walnut River, liked working at the hospital. And she wasn't going to allow this man to stand in the way of the takeover.

Bethany did her best not to let her emotions surface as she argued. "You could at least listen to what they have to offer, Dr. Wilder."

"I'm not some hermit living in a cave, Ms. Holloway. I know exactly what NHC has to offer." He enumerated. "A lot of gleaming, brandspanking new equipment they ultimately resist letting us use because of the prohibitive cost of operating the same gleaming, brandspanking new equipment." The look he gave her felt as if it was going right through her, straight to the bone. "I'm not some child who can be bribed by the promise of an expensive toy."

The elevator arrived, empty. Peter stepped in. Bethany was close behind him. As the steel doors closed, she suppressed a sigh. Losing her temper was not the way to go.

"I don't think of you as a child, Dr. Wilder."

His mouth curved and she felt something within her responding to the expression. The man did have charisma, she couldn't help thinking. "I'm sure the medical board will be happy to hear that."

This wasn't funny and she didn't like being the source of his amusement. "But I do think of you as a throwback."

The smile remained as he arched an eyebrow. "Speaking your mind again?"

Bethany squared her shoulders. Her chin went up. "Yes."

Peter faced forward and shook his head. "It's not charming."

"I'm not trying to be charming."

"Good." He continued looking at the steel door before him. "Because you're not succeeding."

Knowing the value of temporary retreat, Bethany backpedaled. A little. "Maybe *throwback* wasn't the right word."

He nodded, watching the floors go by. "Maybe."

She stopped backpedaling. "But you have to admit, you're stuck in the past."

That got to him. He turned his head to look at her. "No, I am in the present." He felt his temper flare, something that very rarely happened. What was it about this woman that got his jets flaming? "And I won't give up this hospital without a fight."

It was her turn to appear amused. "That's a little melodramatic, don't you think?"

"Whatever it takes, Ms. Holloway." Peter faced forward again, mentally counting to ten. "Whatever it takes."

The elevator arrived in the basement and he got off. All he wanted to do was to get a bite to eat before he went back to seeing his patients. Bethany was interfering with the smattering of peace and quiet he was hoping for. He *knew* he should have brought his lunch with him and remained in his office. But there hadn't been anything in his refrigerator to bring. He needed to get around to shopping, and soon.

He spared her a glance as he walked into the cafeteria. "Are you planning to follow me around all afternoon, Ms. Holloway?"

Bethany responded with a wide smile, paraphrasing his earlier words, "Whatever it takes, Dr. Wilder. Whatever it takes."

He inclined his head. "Touché."

She grabbed at what she felt was a temporary truce. "Won't you at least listen to me?" she pressed, following Peter into the main area where all the food was served. There were steam tables on two sides of the opposite wall and a bed of ice for cold beverages and desserts on the third. Just before the exit were the coffee dispensers.

Peter picked up a tray and handed it to her. She looked a little uncertain as she accepted it.

"I'm assuming you want to keep up the ruse that you actually want to be here," Peter said, moving to the left wall. "That means buying some food."

"Right," she murmured. Bethany looked around the cafeteria. This was actually her first time down here. She usually left the grounds at lunchtime, preferring to get her meals at one of several nearby restaurants. "*Then* will you listen to me?"

"I've been listening to you since you pounced on me outside my office," he told her innocently.

His comment earned him an interested look from the young nurse who walked by, her tray laden with what passed for a nutritious lunch. The woman's hazel eyes went from him to Bethany and then back again before a very wide smile sprouted on her lips.

Terrific. "I think you and I just became the latest rumor that's about to make the hospital's rounds," Bethany noted glibly.

He nodded his head, as if that was fine with him. "They have little else to talk about this week," he said drily. Nodding at the small row of dispensers, he asked, "Coffee?"

Her attention was already drawn to another dispenser beyond the quaint coffeemaker that contained the simple fare. "I'll take a latte."

"Of course you will." He supposed he would have been disappointed if she hadn't. It would have meant that he was off target about her. And he knew in his gut that he wasn't. "I should have known that."

She proceeded to fill her cup. "Lattes are something else you don't approve of?" she asked.

He heard the high-handed note in her voice

but went on as if he was talking to a friend. "What I don't approve of is pretentiousness, or change for the sake of change and not because it's a good thing."

Bethany grabbed her tray and quickly followed him. He stopped by a display of already wrapped sandwiches and grabbed one without even noting what it was.

"If you're talking about the takeover, it *would* be a good thing," she insisted emphatically.

Peter made a low, disparaging noise to show his contempt for the thought, not the woman.

"I've been to other HMOs, Ms. Holloway. I know the kind of medicine that's practiced there. I categorically refuse to see that happen here. At Walnut River General, we treat the whole patient. Not his arm, not his leg, not his liver, but the *entire* patient, no matter what his or her complaint might be."

That sounded good in theory, but it was a completely other thing in practice. "Don't you think that's rather time-consuming?" *Not to mention costly*, she added silently.

He knew she'd see it that way. This would be exactly the same argument he would be having over and over again with the administrators if they joined NHC. "Perhaps, but if you don't treat the

entire patient, you might miss something very
relevant and specific to his or her case."

"And how many times does that actually happen?
Finding something that doesn't apply to anyone
else with the patient's condition?" she challenged.

That would be the efficiency expert in her
coming out, Peter thought. "More times than you
would think." He paused to look directly at her.
"Once is enough if it's you," he told her, his voice
low as he placed a very personal point on the matter.

Okay, he was right, Bethany allowed as she
followed him to the checkout area, but she was still
willing to bet those kind of patients only surfaced
once in a blue moon. The rest of the time it was
business as usual.

"But in the long run—" she persisted.

Nodding a silent greeting at the cashier, Peter
took out his wallet and indicated to the man that
he was paying for both his and her selections. He
handed the man a twenty.

"In the long run, we will keep on doing as much
good as we have been," Peter told her firmly.

She saw the exchange of nods and money.
Bethany was quick to take out her wallet from her
purse. "I can pay for my own food."

Peter picked up his tray and walked away.
"Never doubted it for a moment, Ms. Holloway."

"Thank you," she replied primly, grabbing her own tray and quickly following him into the dining hall. "Do you realize that you just said my name as if it was some sort of evil incantation."

He didn't bother turning around to look at her. "Maybe that's your guilty conscience making you think that."

"I don't have a guilty conscience," she said with more than a note of indignation managing to break through.

"I would. If I voted for the takeover." Finding a small table in the back, he made his way toward it and then placed the tray in front of him on the table before sitting down. "Fortunately, that isn't going to happen."

She stood at his elbow for a moment, frustrated. "And your mind is made up?"

"Yes."

She shook her head, her voice fraught with disappointment. "You know, I never thought you would be the closed-minded type."

"Life is full of surprises." He watched her place her tray opposite his on the table and then slide in.

"Why have you singled me out?" he wanted to know. "I'm just the newest member of the board." And as such, he thought of himself as having the least amount of influence.

But that wasn't the way she saw it. "Because you do hold a lot of sway. You're Peter Wilder, resident saint. Moreover, you're James Wilder's son, an even bigger saint in his day. People look up to you, and they respect you. If you feel strongly about something, people think there has to be a reason." She tried not to notice that his smile made her stomach tighten again.

"There is."

"And," she continued, valiantly pretending that he hadn't spoken, "they'll vote the way you vote."

His smile was a thoughtful one. "But not you."

She slowly moved her head from side to side, her eyes never leaving his. "I don't vote with my heart, I vote with my head."

"Pity." He could see that she was about to take exception to his response so he elaborated. "You know, most of the time the heart is a far better judge than the head." He took a sip of his coffee, then set down the container and leaned forward. "I'm curious. Why are you so set on this takeover happening, Ms. Holloway? What do you get out of all this?"

She didn't even have to think, didn't hesitate with her answer. "Progress."

Peter shook his head. "I don't see it that way." He glanced at his watch. He could better spend what little time he had left before he opened his office again. Placing his sandwich in a napkin, he wrapped it up. He rose to his feet, sandwich in one hand, the remainder of his coffee in the other. "Now, if you'll excuse me, I have somewhere else to be."

Her eyes narrowed. He was lying, she was sure of it. Why come all the way here, then sit down just to leave? "Where?" she challenged.

"Appointments," he told her with a smile. And then, turning on his heel, he walked away.

Stunned, Bethany glanced around to see if anyone near her had overheard the exchange between them and, if they had, were they now looking at her with a measure of pity?

Even though she didn't see anyone looking in her direction, Bethany squared her shoulders and raised her chin defiantly.

She'd spent most of her life, both as an adult and as an adolescent, striving to be the highest achiever, the one who consistently was successful in grabbing the brass ring. Once acquired, she always went on to the next prize because, she had discovered, the getting was far more exhilarating than the having. Victory was exciting for only a few minutes—after that, it was hollow.

She felt that way about everything. It didn't stop her from hoping to someday be proved wrong.

But it hadn't happened yet.

Lifting the latte to her lips, she took a small sip, still watching Peter's broad shoulders as he made his way toward the exit, and ignoring the odd little flutter in the pit of her stomach as she did so.

He didn't know it yet, she told herself, but she was going to wear him down and win him over. He was the ultimate challenge and she had no intention of it going unanswered. A takeover really was in the hospital's best interest. It would put the hospital in line for advancements and most definitely for several lucrative study grants.

Right now, Walnut River General was just a quaint hospital, the only one in Walnut River, and while it had been nurtured to its present state by James Wilder and now had Peter Wilder overseeing it, what happened when the day came that there were no Wilders to render their services, to be the kindly country doctors that the hospital's reputation thrived on? Then what?

It took very little imagination on her part to envision conditions degenerating within the hospital to the point where it wouldn't be able to attract any physicians of high standing to join their staff. In the blink of an eye, Walnut River General could easily turn into a mediocre hospital staffed with mediocre physicians.

If NHC oversaw its management, that sort of thing wouldn't happen.

Besides, Bethany thought as she finished the last of her latte, these days no one fought city hall and won. That kind of thing just didn't happen anymore. If, indeed, it ever had.

She placed the empty container on her tray and carried both to the nearest conveyor belt. Stepping away, she dusted off her hands. Ready for round two.

It was damn time for Dr. Peter Wilder to realize that he had to stop standing in the way of progress before he and his precious hospital were left behind in the dust. The sooner she got him to acknowledge that, the sooner they could all move on.

Chapter Five

The reading of the will that evening at his house held no surprises. Fred arrived at seven, with Ella there a few minutes earlier, and it went as Peter had expected. All of his father's worldly possessions, the house, the small bank account, were to be divided equally among the children. James Wilder had no living siblings, no distant people he felt honor-bound to reach out to beyond the grave. A few mementos went to friends, worth more in sentimental value than they were monetarily, but most items were part of the very small estate that was to be divvied up equally.

His father had left the execution of it entirely in Peter's hands.

"Short and sweet," Fred declared. Finished, he placed the will on the mahogany desk and rose to his feet. He snapped the locks back down on his black leather briefcase. "Still, it's a shame that David and Anna couldn't have stayed one more day to hear the reading of the will for themselves."

Peter knew that Ella felt the same way the lawyer did: that David and Anna should have remained out of respect for their father. In her own way, Ella was very protective of her father and his memory. But he knew that no disrespect had been intended by his siblings. Both excuses they'd given were thin, veiling the different demons David and, to an extent, Anna, had to wrestle with. Nothing anyone in the room could say would change that.

So he played down their absence and responded to Fred's comment with a half shrug.

"They each thought that there wouldn't be anything unusual about it," he said. "And pressing circumstances called them away."

Fred's expression said he would have expected more from the children of his close friend. He nodded toward Ella as he circumvented Peter's desk. "Lovely seeing you again, Ella. I hope the next time we meet, it will be under happier circumstances."

"Yes," she murmured softly with feeling, "so do I."

Peter saw fresh tears glistening in her eyes. It was going to take her a while to get over this, he thought. In the meantime, he could give her her privacy.

Placing himself between Fred and his sister, he volunteered, "I'll walk you out."

"Speaking of unusual…" Fred picked up the thread of their earlier exchange as they left the room. "Have you, um, you know—"

Peter shook his head. "No, I haven't 'um, you know' yet."

Fred eyed him as they walked slowly to the front of the house. "Afraid it might be something bad?"

Afraid. Maybe that was the right word after all, he thought. Something about the presence of the envelope made him uneasy. He didn't want anything changing his image of his father and he was afraid that whatever was in the envelope might do just that.

"Well, it can't be something good, now, can it? If it was, there wouldn't be this aura of mystery surrounding it. My father wasn't the to-be-read-after-my-death kind of person. Or at least," he sighed, shoving his hands into his pockets as he walked, "I wouldn't have said he was." *Until now.*

Fred looked at him, a sympathetic expression on his round face. "Only one way to find out."

Peter glanced toward the living room as he passed it on his way to the front door. The thick envelope was still resting on the mantelpiece, where he'd placed it after the reception. And where it was going to stay until he was ready to deal with it.

"Yes, I know. I'll get to it," he promised. He stopped at the door. The overhead fixture hanging down from the vaulted ceiling was on high, casting more light through the area than it ordinarily did. The added brightness only marginally negated the somber atmosphere and mood.

Fred's eyes met his and the man said, "Be sure to let me know when you do."

Peter didn't feel comfortable with that. "Whatever it is, it's my father's secret."

Fred laughed softly to himself. "And I was your father's lawyer—and his friend. He had no secrets from me," Fred told him significantly.

Peter looked at him sharply. "Then you know what's in the envelope?"

It was obvious that Fred was not about to say yes—or no. "I have my suspicions," he admitted.

If that was true, what was all this cloak-and-dagger stuff about? And if Fred knew, what, exactly, did he want to be informed about after the envelope was finally opened and its contents read?

"Then why—"

"Lawyer-client confidentiality," Fred was quick to cite the standard, one-size-fits-all defense. Fred patted Peter's arm. "Keep an open mind," he advised. "Remember, you're the son James trusted."

Peter thought of the envelope that contained a secret his father had all but taken to his grave. The secret that James Wilder hadn't shared with him in life. "Apparently not."

The look in Fred's brown eyes told him that he could all but read his thoughts.

"Think of it as not burdening you until he absolutely had to." Fred glanced at his watch and looked surprised at the hour. "Well, I need to go. Selma is holding dinner for me." He laughed, patting his ample stomach. "Sometimes, I wish she was a worse cook than she is. Then I wouldn't have this—" he searched for a descriptive word that wasn't entirely unflattering "—robust physique. 'Bye, Ella," he called out, raising his voice. "And let me know once you break the seal," Fred said again, lowering his voice so that it wouldn't carry.

Fred let himself out and closed the door behind him. The next moment, Ella was entering the foyer.

"What was all that about?" she asked.

Turning around, Peter saw that she had managed to pull herself together. Ella was good at rallying. He had to stop thinking of her as his baby sister. She was a grown woman and a doctor to boot. That meant she could handle her own battles.

Still, something had him saying evasively, "Just lawyer talk."

"I thought Fred was finished with all that in your study."

"You know lawyers, they never stop." He could see that Ella wanted details, so he embellished a little, elaborating on what had actually been on his mind earlier. "He wanted me to draw up a will, now that I'm head of the family."

Ella drew in a breath, as if that could protect her from what she was thinking. She shook her head vehemently. "You're not going anywhere for a very long time, big brother." Peter was eleven years older than she was, which made him half brother, half father as far as she was concerned. And she intended to hang on to both halves. "I absolutely forbid it."

Peter laughed, amused. "I'll let Fred know."

Ella tucked her arm through his. "You do that," she agreed. "Meanwhile, let's go out to dinner. My treat."

He glanced at his watch. It was getting late. "Aren't you on call?"

She'd drawn the graveyard shift. "Not for another few hours."

He smiled fondly at Ella. He'd decided to open

the envelope after she went home. But there was no hurry. The envelope wasn't going anywhere. "Then you're on. And I warn you, I have expensive taste."

"Sky's the limit," she declared with a nonchalant wave of her hand. "As long as the sky's hovering somewhere in the ten dollar neighborhood," she added, her eyes twinkling.

He laughed. "I'll get the coats, Rockefeller."

"NHC is sending a man to negotiate with us at the end of the month," Bethany announced without preamble as she walked into the small, cluttered office within an office where Peter retreated when he wasn't either making hospital rounds or seeing patients in either the exam room or the E.R.

It was barely eight o'clock in the morning. His patients didn't start coming in until nine-thirty and he had yet to make his rounds of the three that he currently had staying at the hospital.

Looking up from the medical journal he was reading, Peter frowned ever so slightly. He was going to have to remember to lock his doors until his hours began officially. Not even Eva, his nurse/receptionist was here yet.

He looked at the redhead for a long moment. "Don't you have someplace else to be?"

Determined to break through his resistance, Bethany gave him a very complacent smile. "Not anyplace more important."

So much for catching up on his reading before making his rounds, Peter thought. Putting a bookmark into the medical magazine, he let the pages flip closed and rose to his feet. "Well, you might not have anywhere else you need to be, but I do."

She shifted to block his way. Other people at the hospital might think of Peter Wilder as a kind, gentle man, but at the moment, she thought of him as a stubborn jackass. A sexy jackass, but a jackass none the less. "That's what you said yesterday in the cafeteria."

He looked undaunted. "And it's still true. I'm not a hundred percent certain what it is that some of the other members of the board of directors do with their time, but mine is better spent doing what I was meant to do—doctoring."

It wasn't exactly true. He knew that four of the members were doctors, just like he was. Senior members of the staff, they had full agendas to follow even when they weren't seated around the table, reviewing tedious budgets and constricting overall policy. He knew she was an efficiency expert, whatever that actually meant.

"I have hospital rounds to make," he told her, heading for the same door that she had breached a minute ago. "So, unless you want to spend the greater part of the next hour standing in the hospital corridor, waiting for me to finish seeing my patients, I suggest you get back to whatever it is you're supposed to be doing."

And with that, Peter made his second escape from the woman in as many days.

"What do you know about Bethany Holloway?"

Finished with his rounds, his office hours still more than half an hour away, Peter decided to swing by the chief administrator's office to get a little information that might ultimately help him outsmart the attractive board member.

Henry Weisfield looked up from a travel brochure he'd been wistfully perusing and pushed his bifocals up his long, straight nose to look at the doctor he still thought of as "James Wilder's boy."

He smiled, letting his mind wander for a second. "That if I were thirty years younger, I'd be actively pursuing her. Why?" Henry slid his thin frame forward on his chair, his gray eyes momentarily bright with questions. "Are you interested?"

You would think that by the time a man hit forty, people would stop trying to pair him up with someone. Peter had been badly disappointed with that route once, and had more important things to do than spend time risking a part of his being that modern medicine had not come up with a way to heal.

"Only in so far as wanting to know where she comes from and why she's here," he answered after a beat.

Leaning back again, Henry told him what he knew. "The woman has not one but two business degrees. Graduated with top honors from Princeton and is a real go-getter. Wallace is very taken with her," he added.

Peter thought of the way the chairman had fawned over Bethany yesterday. "I'm sure that's a hit with Wallace's wife."

"Your father thought she had potential, too," Henry remembered.

Not if he'd known that the woman would back a takeover by one of the larger HMO companies, Peter thought. "If she's so brilliant, why isn't she sitting on the board of some big-name organization? Why has she graced us with her presence here?"

"Good question." Henry nodded more to himself than to him. "My best guess is that it has something to do with not wanting to be a little fish in a big pond."

That made sense, he supposed. Peter wandered over to the window and looked down the four stories to the back parking lot. It was beginning to fill up. Employees were reporting for the morning shift; visitors were beginning to make their pilgrimages to see friends and loved ones in hospital rooms and outpatients were coming in for tests they most likely didn't want to take.

They were doing fine just as they were, Peter thought. They didn't need some bloated conglomerate coming in, telling them what to do.

Fisting his hands, he leaned his knuckles against the windowsill. "So she's taken over our pond and is trying to make a name for herself here, is that it?"

Henry thought before answering. "Sounds about right." And then he chuckled to himself. "I hear that you walked out on her in mid-sentence at the board meeting yesterday."

Peter turned around to look at him. "I had patients waiting."

Henry's smile told him he knew better. "No, you didn't. I checked your schedule. You left a full half hour before your first appointment."

Peter thought that was rather an odd thing for Henry to do, but then Henry had always been one to move to the tune of a different drummer. Eccentric, he was still an excellent administrator, able to find ways to cover expenses at the last minute time and again. Henry was one of a kind and Peter was fond of him.

So he leveled with the man. "I didn't want to lose my temper."

"Lose your temper?" Henry echoed with a short laugh of disbelief. "I would have paid good money to see that. I didn't know you even had a temper. Most of the staff thinks of you as patience personified."

Peter felt himself chafing a little. Yesterday, Bethany had referred to him as a saint. Henry was telling him that the people at the hospital thought of him as the soul of patience. Deep down, he knew he was neither. He was just a man trying to do the best that he could at any given time.

Peter sighed. "I am what I need to be at the moment."

Henry leaned forward and peered at him through the bottom of his glasses. "And right now, you seem a little—" Feigning surprise, he splayed his somewhat gnarled hand across his chest. "My God, you're a little annoyed." And then he smiled. "And this has to do with Ms. Holloway?"

Peter nodded. He had no idea why she rubbed him the wrong way so hard. Ordinarily, he took annoying people in stride. "The woman is a cheer-leader for Northeastern Healthcare."

Henry sobered a little, but looked at Peter sternly. "Northeastern Healthcare is not the devil, you know."

Peter looked at him in surprise. He'd expected to find an ally in Henry of all people. "Henry, you don't mean that."

Rather than retract or retreat, Henry shook his head. His expression mirrored the confusion Peter felt inside. "Oh, I don't know," the older man said with a sigh. "Maybe I do. Maybe we're looking at the face of progress and by digging in against it, we might be turning our backs on something really worthwhile."

He had no idea what might have caused Henry to say that, but he knew in his soul that the man couldn't possibly mean it.

"What's worthwhile is good patient care. You know that, Henry. You don't have to be a doctor to know how going the extra mile can mean the difference between saving a patient and over-looking symptoms in the interest of the almighty profit margin."

Whether Henry was playing devil's advocate or had been brainwashed, Peter had no way of knowing when the administrator said, "The doctors at NHC aren't all soulless creatures."

Peter was willing to make a concession only up to a point. "Maybe not, but the organization that they work for won't allow them to access that part of themselves." He blew out a frustrated breath, feeling the base he was counting on eroding right beneath his feet. "Let them go take over some other hospital. We're small— barely a blip on their radar. Why the interest all of a sudden?"

Henry looked surprised by the question. "Don't underestimate what your father accomplished here. How hard he worked to make sure that Walnut River General was not just up to par, but above and beyond that in every possible way. Before James came on board, this was just 'a blip' as you called it. But not anymore. Definitely not anymore."

But Peter saw it another way. "If we were all that good, David would be here instead of practicing on the West coast."

"David's not here because he and your father came to loggerheads and they never patched up their differences," Henry reminded him. "And besides, maybe we're just less vain than the patients he finds in Los Angeles." Henry glanced at the latest quarterly bulletin that the hospital had released. On the front was a list of names of the physicians on staff. "We have excellent cardiologists, excellent orthopedic surgeons and even an oncologist who graduated from Yale."

Would those same doctors remain if the NHC took over? Peter had his doubts. "Then why would we need NHC?"

It was a tired voice that answered him. "Because we need new equipment." Henry sighed. "We need a lot of things."

Peter looked at him incredulously, still unable to believe what he was hearing. "So you're advocating the takeover?"

Henry shrugged. His head hurt. He'd been thinking of nothing else and waffling ever since the rumors had begun. "I'm advocating retirement. Mine," he clarified.

It was the last thing Peter had expected, or wanted, to hear. "Henry, no."

"Yes," Henry said gently. "I'm old, Peter. Older than your father was." A lot older, he thought. "And I'm tired. Tired of wrestling with hospital policies, tired of wondering how we're going to be able to fund this program or that—"

Peter cut in. "You've always done a fantastic job. We all thought you were part magician."

"It's time for someone else to pull a rabbit out of a hat," Henry said wearily. He loved the hospital, loved the people who were there, but his health wasn't what it used to be and it was suffering. He couldn't do as good a job as he had been doing and he refused to be in a position where the board voted to release him from his contract. "To struggle and lose sleep over ends that just refuse to meet."

Peter looked at the man closely. Henry did look tired. And there had been that late-onset diabetes that he knew Henry felt confident no one knew about. But he did. That was why he didn't press, even though he wanted to.

Still, he had to ask, "Your mind's made up?"

"About the retirement? Yes. About everything else? No." Henry shook his head again. "In theory, I agree that NHC should keep its sticky fingers off us. But we're not going to do anyone much good if we have to close our doors because the funding's not there to keep us going. Doesn't matter how good our reputation is if we can't get supplies because there's no money. Even when we don't charge some of the poorer patients who can't afford us, the services aren't really free, you know. Somebody has to pay for everything from a swab to a suture to everything else. Every department wants more and I just can't find a way to get it."

Peter squared his shoulders, as if ready to do battle with some invisible force. "I refuse to believe that HMOs are the only answer."

"Maybe they're not," Henry gladly conceded. "But I for one don't have any other answer." He rocked back in his chair. "Except to retire."

Resigned to the inevitable, Peter asked, "So, how soon?"

Henry glanced at the calendar on his desk and flipped a few pages. He was grateful that Peter wasn't calling him a coward and accusing him of running away from the battle. "April, maybe May. I've already half been scouting around for a replacement."

Whoever came wouldn't be nearly as good, Peter thought sadly. "Won't be the same without you."

Henry smiled, appreciating the kind words but knowing better. "You'll manage, Peter. You're a Wilder. The Wilders always manage."

The man's words echoed in Peter's head long after he'd left Henry's office. He knew his father had felt that way, as had his grandfather. He only wished he could feel half as confident about it as they had.

Chapter Six

It was hard not to fidget. Even harder not to let his eyes shut.

Peter couldn't help thinking he had more important things to do than sit here, trapped in this airless room, held prisoner by what felt like an endless board meeting.

For the better part of the week, his schedule had been entirely filled with patients. The rest of the time Peter found himself looking over his shoulder in an attempt—successful for the most part—to duck the very woman that fate now had him sitting next to in this so-called official meeting of the board of directors.

Larry Simpson, the current board secretary, had all but put him to sleep, reading the minutes in a voice that could, hands down, easily replace the leading medication for insomnia.

Part of the reason he was struggling to keep his eyes open was because he'd put in an extra long day yesterday. It had actually extended into the wee hours of the next morning—today. Too exhausted to drive home, he'd slept in his office. It had seemed like a good idea at the time, but the misshapen sofa was not the last word in comfort. He was now paying for his impulsive choice with a stiff neck, not to mention the various other parts of his body that felt less than flexible today.

After Larry had finished droning on, the first order of business had been the formal announcement of what he was already privy to: Henry Weisfield's pending retirement. That led to an impromptu testimonial by Wallace during which he listed Henry's skills and accomplishments.

"He's going to be a hard man to replace," Wallace predicted, using the exact words he had employed when he'd spoken about the passing of James Wilder. "But I charge each and every one of

you to keep your eye out for a suitable candidate
to at least partially fill Henry's position."

"We could try offering Henry more money,"
suggested Gladys Cooper, a fifteen-year veteran
of the board.

"Not everything is solved with money." The
words slipped out of Peter's mouth before he
realized he was actually saying them aloud rather
than just thinking them.

"No," the redhead at his elbow agreed. "But it
certainly does help pave the road and make things
a lot easier."

Not wanting to get caught up in another confrontation with Bethany, Peter replied, "Can't
argue with that."

"Oh, I'm sure you can," she countered with a
smile he couldn't begin to fathom.

Damn, but he wished she'd stop wearing that
perfume. It wasn't overpowering. It was very light,
actually, but it left behind just enough scent to stealth-
ily slip into his senses, blurring things for him.

He had opened his mouth to respond when the
sound of a cell phone playing a shrill samba rever-
berated through the room. The next second,
Wallace's wide hand covered his jacket breast
pocket.

"Sorry," he apologized with a sheepish expression. "Forgot to turn off my phone." But when he took it out to shut off, he looked at the number on the tiny screen. His expression turned to one of curiosity. He held up his hand as if to beg an indulgence. "I need to take this. Why don't we just take a break for a few minutes?" he suggested. Not waiting for the members to agree, he quickly left the room.

Everyone around them rose from their chairs, taking the opportunity to stretch their legs. Bethany watched the man at her left for a cue. Now that she had him in her sights, she intended to follow his lead in order to finally be able to say more than a handful of words to him regarding the takeover.

Peter remained seated. So did she.

"You didn't go home last night, did you?" Bethany asked quietly.

The question caught him off guard. But then, he thought, it really shouldn't have, given the fact that she had been popping up all over since Monday. "Are you stalking me, Ms. Holloway?"

She maintained a mild expression, as if tracking him down had never even crossed her mind. "No, I just noticed where you were parked when I left last night." She didn't add that she'd waited a quarter of an hour, hoping he would appear, since it was already after-hours. But sitting in her car on a cold January evening was her limit. "It snowed last night."

Where was she going with this, he wondered. And why did she have to look so damn attractive going there? "So I hear."

"You car had snow all around it this morning— as if it hadn't been moved," she said, explaining how she'd come to her conclusion.

"Very observant." Peter looked at her for a long moment, wondering whether to be amused or annoyed.

She smiled and something definitely responded within him. He vaguely recognized what was going on. This wasn't good, he thought.

"Look, Dr. Wilder, let's talk openly. What will it take to get you to listen to arguments for the other side?"

All around the table, people had begun to return to their seats, drawn in by the verbal duel.

He tried to make it as clear to her as he could. "You can't possibly tell me anything about NHC's motives that I don't already know."

Oh yes she could, Bethany thought. She had access to the latest studies, something she highly doubted this throwback bothered with. "There are statistics, Dr. Wilder."

He waved her words away with an impatient hand. "I deal in patients, Ms. Holloway, not statistics."

"Patients *make up* the statistics, Doctor," she insisted, and felt color rising in her cheeks. "Where do you think they come from?"

He banked down his impatience. The woman probably didn't know any better. Wiser people than she had been led astray by the hocus-pocus of numbers if they were juggled just right.

"Ms. Holloway," he began in a patient, quiet voice, "statistics are very flexible. In the hands of someone clever, they can be bent to support almost anything. The good done by a bloated, fat-cat conglomerate, for instance."

Her eyes blazed, reminding him, he suddenly realized, of Lisa. Of the woman he'd once thought—no, knew—he'd been in love with. The one he'd made plans to spend the rest of his life with. The one who'd left him in his senior year for a medical student who was "a better prospect" because once *Steven* graduated, he was slated to join his father's lucrative Manhattan practice.

A chill worked its way down his spine as the realization took root. Bethany Holloway had the same coloring, the same full lips, the same slender figure.

And the same take-no-prisoners ambition, he thought.

"Everyone I know at the hospital thinks that you're this kind, gentle, understanding man," she retorted. "So far, I'm not convinced they're right."

At that moment, the silence in the room was almost deafening.

And then Peter said quietly and with no emotion, "I have no desire to convince you about anything that has to do with me, Ms. Holloway."

But he knew it was a lie. What people thought of him did matter to him. He didn't like being thought of in a bad light. It bothered him.

Bothered him, too, that the sensual fragrance she always wore was really filling up his head, undermining his senses. It gave her an unfair advantage because it made him think of her during the course of the day when his mind was supposed to be on other things. And then his mind would wander. Wander in directions he was determined not to take. Not with her.

Where was all this coming from? Peter silently demanded. He was arguing to preserve the hospital, not fantasizing about his opponent. He wanted to save the place that had been a second home to James Wilder. Walnut River General was his father's legacy. And if NHC came into the picture, that legacy would be changed, if not eradicated entirely.

And Peter needed to do everything he could to keep that from happening.

"Sorry, sorry," Wallace announced, coming back into the room. He made a show of turning off his phone. "I hope you all got to stretch your legs for a moment, before we launch into part two of our agenda this morning." He chuckled at some joke he thought he'd made, then paused, waiting for the stragglers to be seated. Moments later, he began again. "First up, I'm told that the radiology department desperately needs a new MRI machine. The old one, according to Mrs. Fitzpatrick, the department's head technician, has been down more than it's been up in the last few months. Any ideas?" he asked, looking around the table as he threw open the matter for discussion.

He no sooner asked the question than Bethany's hand went up. The chairman nodded toward her. "Yes, Ms. Holloway?"

"If we take NHC up on their offer when they formally present it, we won't have to worry about how to pay for the new MRI machine. The money—" she slanted a look in Peter's direction "—would come from them."

"Yes, but at what price?" Peter countered, struggling to keep his temper in check. This should have been a no-brainer, if not for her, because of lack of experience, then for everyone else seated at this table. They all knew what HMOs, no matter what they called themselves, were like.

Obviously trying to keep the peace, Wallace asked him, "What do you mean?"

Was the man playing dumb for Bethany's sake? Heaven help him—maybe it was the lack of sleep talking—but he had no patience with that. "You know what I mean, Wallace. We've all heard horror stories about HMOs—"

"Yes, but those are all from the nineties and earlier," Bethany cut in. "Things have changed since then."

"Have they?" Peter challenged. "Instead of sitting around, waiting for NHC to come sniffing around, why don't we investigate some of the other hospitals that have become part of their conglomerate in, oh, say the last five years or so? See what they've become in comparison to the way they were."

Wallace cleared his throat uncomfortably. "Our resources are limited, Peter," he protested. "We can't afford to do that."

Didn't the man understand? If he was going to actually entertain this proposition, then he needed to know what might happen to Walnut River General.

"We can't afford not to," Peter insisted. "Now,

as for the new MRI machine—" he knew how costly those could be "—why don't you have Henry Weisfield put together one of his fund-raisers? He's still not leaving for another three months or so. He could do it easily."

"That's your answer?" Bethany demanded, her voice rising. "A fund-raiser?"

The angrier she seemed to get, the calmer he became. "It's worked so far."

"And when we need to modernize the operating rooms?" she posed. "What then? *Another* fund-raiser? Just how many of these things do you think we can swing before we wind up losing donors altogether?" she asked.

"We'll tackle that when it comes," he said, smiling.

Was he laughing at her? "If NHC oversaw us, we wouldn't have to tackle anything. We would just make the request in writing."

He looked at her, stunned, not really sure she believed what she was saying. Was she just saying it to convince the others?

"Are you really that naive? Don't you realize that a company big enough to give you *everything*, is also big enough to take everything away if you don't dance to the tune they play?" He was tired of this. He was beginning to understand why

Henry felt the way he did, why he wanted to retire. "If I'm going to have my strings pulled, I want to be able to see who's pulling them." He addressed his words to Wallace, not Bethany. With Wallace he had some hope of getting through. "Not having some conglomerate versed in buck-passing doing it."

Just then, his pager went off. Glancing down at the device clipped to his belt, Peter angled it so that he could read the message that had just come in. "Sorry, Wallace." He rose to his feet. "There's been a car accident. I'm wanted in the E.R."

Wallace nodded. "Of course."

As he left, Peter couldn't help thinking that the chairman sounded rather relieved to see him go.

"Talk to me," Peter urged the E.R.'s head nurse, Simone Garner, a slender woman with brown hair and a ready smile, when he arrived in the emergency room several minutes later. As he questioned Simone, one of the other nurses helped him on with the disposable yellow paper gowns they all donned in an effort to minimize the risk of spreading infections amid the E.R. trauma patients.

The paramedics had left less than two minutes before, so Simone quickly recited the vital signs for the three patients, then added, "It was a two-car collision. The police said the brakes failed on the SUV and it plowed into the other car at an intersection."

"Where did it happen?" he asked as he took out his stethoscope.

"Less than two miles away. The paramedics got them here quickly. Those two were the drivers." She indicated the first two gurneys. "The little boy was a passenger. Sitting in the front, I gather." The little boy was crying loudly. She pushed her hair out of her eyes with the back of her wrist and leaned in closer. "It's going to be all right, honey," she told him, then raised her eyes to Peter's face. "No child seat in the car," she said. It was obvious what she thought of the driver's negligence. "I think the little guy got the worst of it. He's pretty banged up. There might be internal bleeding."

"Get him to X-ray as fast as you can," Peter instructed. She motioned to an orderly and, between them, they took the gurney away.

Peter turned his attention to the other two victims. Before he could say anything, the man on the gurney closest to him grabbed his forearm.

"My little boy," the man implored hoarsely.

Peter looked down into a face that was badly cut up and bruised. One of the man's eyes was swollen shut and he looked as if he was barely able to see with his other one.

"Your son's going to be all right," he said with the conviction he knew the patient needed to hear. Long ago he'd been told not to make promises he might not be able to keep, but he knew the good a positive frame of mind could do. "Now let's make sure that you are." He pointed to the first empty bed he saw. "Put him in trauma room two."

He'd had to remove the boy's spleen. Then he'd gone back to the boy's father to explain at length everything that had been done. It had taken a lot to make the man believe his son was going to make a full recovery. Peter had never seen such concern, such guilt, displayed by anyone the way it was by Ned Farmer.

Farmer, a self-employed auto mechanic and former racer, berated himself over and over again for being so busy working on other people's cars that he'd neglected to check out his own.

"My fault, my fault, it's all my fault," Farmer kept saying over and over again, working himself up almost into a frenzy. It got to the point that Peter finally authorized an injection of diazepam be given in order to calm Farmer down.

The other driver, it turned out, had some traumatic bruising to his spine. So much so that the swelling was pinching his spinal cord, causing his lower extremities to become numb and unresponsive.

He called Ella and asked her to come down for a consultation. He thought his sister's soft voice and gentle manner might help quell the second driver's fears. She was there within the quarter hour.

The last he'd seen, Ella was at the man's bedside, calmly reassuring him. "In ninety-nine cases out of a hundred, the victim walks as soon as the swelling on his spine subsides. You just have to be patient."

The man looked anything but that. "But I'll walk again?"

"Most likely, as soon as the swelling there goes down," she repeated.

"But what if it doesn't?" he pressed nervously. "What if it doesn't go down?"

She took his hand in hers and said without wavering. "We'll do everything we can."

Peter smiled to himself and thought how proud his father would be if he could see her.

NHC, Peter was certain, would never approve of all this handholding on the part of their doctors. The patient would be swiftly examined, given his diagnosis and then sent home to recuperate. And to nurse fears of never being able to walk again. Who knew how much damage that would ultimately create?

It made him more determined than ever to block the takeover.

All in all, Peter thought as he changed back into his street clothes in his dimly lit office, this had been one of the worst Januarys he'd ever experienced.

He remembered Bethany saying it had snowed, and wondered if he was going to have to shovel his driveway when he got home that night. It wasn't a heartening thought. Despite having lived in Walnut River his whole life, Peter was definitely not a fan of the white stuff.

He paused just long enough to locate some lab and radiology reports and place them in his brief-case. When he stepped into the elevator car, it was empty. He continued to have it to himself all the way down. The doors opened again on the first floor and he walked out, then made his way down the corridor leading to the parking lot.

As he opened one of the double doors and emerged into the frigid night air, he was in time to hear a woman exclaim, "Oh damn," and then see Bethany Holloway suddenly disappear from view as she slid down the icy stairs.

Chapter Seven

Working triage in the E.R. had honed Peter's reflexes. Instinct just took over.

Holding on to the banister, he sailed down the steps and grabbed Bethany's arm just before her body came in ungraceful contact with the icy ground.

With her feet sliding in one direction and her body being jerked in another, Bethany overcompensated. In an effort to regain her balance, she threw her weight forward.

The next second, instead of keeping her steady, Peter found himself going down. He landed flat on his back. Since he was still holding on to her arm, he wound up pulling her down as well.

Right on top of him.

The air knocked out of her, she stared down at his face, stunned. He thought she'd indignantly scramble to her feet—or try to. Instead, she started to laugh. Her laugh, low, melodic and sensual, was highly infectious, not to mention that he could actually feel her laughing.

Picturing how absurd this had to look to anyone passing by—mercifully, there was no one—Peter started laughing, too. He laughed so hard, he became practically helpless and moisture began forming in the corners of his eyes.

Moving with the rhythm of laughter, their bodies rubbed lightly against each other.

Slowly, the laughter died away.

Caught between amusement and concern, Bethany struggled to regulate her breathing. "I don't think that this is what you had in mind."

Looking up at her, Peter found himself fighting an urge that hadn't come over him in a very long time. So long that he could barely remember the last time. The pace he'd kept up these past ten years had left very little time for him to even attempt to nurture a private life. Even if that was partly by choice.

Right at this moment, with her breath drifting down along his face and their bodies pressed together, he was acutely aware of what had been missing from his life. What *was* missing.

So aware that he wasn't conscious of anything but the tightening of his groin, the long, warm tongues of desire traveling through his body, heating it.

Making him yearn.

The look in her eyes told him he wasn't alone here. For whatever reasons, Bethany was experiencing the very same thing. The same attraction, the same electricity.

He wasn't a reckless man by nature. Acting on impulse was something other men did, not him.

Until now.

In one unguarded moment, Peter reached up and framed her face with his gloved hands. He brought her face down to his.

If having her body on top of his had set off a series of sharp, demanding electric shocks, kissing Bethany multiplied the sensations tenfold. She tasted of fresh strawberries and spring, both equally far removed from the moment.

He lost himself in the sensation.

For one brief shining second, he wasn't Dr. Peter Wilder, highly respected internist, keeper of his father's flame. He was just Peter, a flesh-and-blood man who longed for companionship, for someone to be there for him at the end of the day, for someone with whom he could share his thoughts, his plans. His love.

He remembered other dreams he'd once had.

Her head was spinning so badly Bethany thought maybe she'd hit it when Peter had accidentally pulled her down. But she'd landed on top of him and, though his body felt solid and hard, she knew for a fact that her head hadn't made contact with him.

Her pulse accelerating, she could almost feel her blood, exhilarated, surging through her veins.

Bethany deepened the kiss.

The second their bodies had come in contact, it'd felt as if something had just come undone within her.

But if she didn't draw back, if she let him continue even for another moment, Bethany was sincerely afraid of what that might do to her resolve, to the walls she'd been building up around herself for longer then she could remember. She only knew that they had been forged to keep the hurt back. If she let no one in, then she would never be hurt, it was as simple as that. She'd be invulnerable, the way she wanted to be.

She wasn't invulnerable now, she realized. She

was shaking. Inside *and* out. Any second now, it was going to occur to him that the cold weather had nothing to do with her reaction.

Her mind scattered in all directions, searching for something plausible to say in order to throw his attention off.

"So." The single word swooped out of her mouth on a breath that was all but spent the moment she drew her head back. And then she smiled down at him. "About that takeover."

She felt the laughter rumble in his chest before it burst from his lips. The up-and-down movement was soothing and erotic at the same time. So he did have a sense of humor, she thought, relieved. Thank God for small favors.

"One takeover is about all I can handle right now," he told her amicably. It was obvious that he wasn't talking about NHC—he was referring to what had just happened between them.

Confusion, enhanced by nerves, echoed in her head. The only thing she was certain of was that she wanted to kiss him again. She was even more certain that she shouldn't.

Placing his hands on her arms, Peter gently moved her back so he could sit up. When he did, he drew in a long, deep breath, then exhaled. Slanting a look at her, he apologized. It seemed like the thing to do.

"I'm sorry about that."

"Are you?" Was he sorry that he'd kissed her? The second she thought that, she felt this odd pin-pricking sensation around her heart. What *was* that? Rather than deliberate over it, she struggled to block it.

Peter's eyes held hers. "The fall," he clarified.

Her breath had stopped in her throat and she had to force it back out again, had to consciously make herself breathe.

"And the kiss?" she asked softly.

Peter slowly moved his head from side to side. "I'm not sorry about that."

She looked at him for a long moment. He wasn't lying, she realized. An unexpected wave of happiness suddenly drenched her.

"I'm not, either," she confided. And then she smiled at him, really smiled. "Finally, something we can agree on." Was it her imagination, or had his smile just deepened?

"I have something else we can agree on," Peter told her.

A leeriness slipped in again. She reminded herself that this was the man who opposed her ideas, whom she had to win over. She knew he was no pushover.

"Oh?"

He nodded. "That we should get up before someone comes by and sees us."

A wave of regret came and went. She couldn't begin to understand it. "Right."

Bethany was about to spring to her feet, but he was faster. Standing up, Peter extended his hand to her. She looked at it, then raised her eyes to his face.

"Isn't this what got us in trouble in the first place?" she reminded him.

He continued holding his hand out. "Lightning rarely strikes in the same place twice."

She had a wealth of extraneous knowledge in her head, retaining everything she'd ever read, even in passing. "That's a fallacy, you know. Lightning's been known to strike twice in the same place. Sometimes even three times."

"I said 'rarely,'" Peter pointed out, trying to keep a straight face, "not 'never.'"

"Good enough." Wrapping her long, slender fingers around his hand, Bethany held on tightly as she rose unsteadily to her feet. Once up, she took a step and felt her feet begin to slide dangerously beneath her. Instantly her hand tightened on his. She wasn't pleased about coming off like some damsel in need of rescuing. "This is what I get for not wearing my boots," she murmured under her breath.

"I'll walk you to your car," he offered. "I'm not in any hurry." *For once*, he added silently.

She had an independent streak that was a mile wide and she considered it one of her chief sources of pride. It almost made her turn him down. But she also possessed more than her share of common sense and, in this case, common sense trumped independence.

So Bethany murmured, "Thank you," and then tried to make light of the situation by adding, "I've always depended on the kindness of strangers."

He looked at her and she could all but feel his eyes delving into her. He was probably wondering what she was talking about, she thought. And then he surprised her by commenting, "*Streetcar Named Desire*. You're a lot younger than Blanche DuBois."

She nodded, impressed. "You're familiar with the play?"

The corners of his mouth curved in amusement. "We're not entirely backward here. Town's got a library with books on the shelves and everything."

She hadn't meant to insult him, or be patronizing. It was just that she wasn't accustomed to people who were versed in the arts. Her world had always revolved around business and she'd naturally assumed that his did the same around medicine.

A pink hue overtook her cheeks as Bethany pointed out her vehicle. "The car's right over there."

He gave her his arm to hang on to. They proceeded carefully. His shoes were rubber soled and he was far more sure-footed than she was, but he took small steps to match her pace. The snow crunched beneath their feet as they went.

"Is it true?" he asked, breaking the silence just as they reached her sedan.

She wasn't sure what he was asking about. "That it's my car?"

They'd reached their intended destination, but he was in no hurry to reclaim his arm. He rather liked the way she held on to it. "That you've always depended on the kindness of strangers."

Maybe that had been giving too much of herself away, even though it had sounded like a flippant remark. "Well, I've moved around a bit, so most of the people I interact with are strangers."

Which brought up another question in his mind. "Why did you move around so much? Army brat?"

The question made her laugh. Her father in a uniform, now there was an image. "Hardly. Both my parents made their mark in the corporate world." Nannies had raised her and her older sister because her parents put in ten-, twelve-hour days, seduced by the promise of success, then working even harder once it came. "For the most part, I lived in New York until I went away to college."

"And afterward?"

"Afterward, I moved around."

"Which brings us back to why?" He looked into her eyes. "Unless you think it's none of my business."

It wasn't, but she answered him anyway. "I was looking for the right fit," she replied, and then asked a question of her own. "Is this part of some psychological workup, Dr. Wilder?"

He shook his head. "Not my department." And then he looked down into her eyes. "We've kissed in the snow, Bethany. I think we can dispense with the formalities, don't you?"

She shrugged, looking away. The parking lot had thinned out a great deal. What was left had a layer of snow on it. "I guess maybe we can. Does this mean you're going to use my first name when you growl at me at the next meeting?"

"I didn't growl," he protested. "I just raised my voice a little."

She smirked at him.

Peter blew out a breath. She was right, he'd let his anger get the better of him. "If I growled, I apologize. For the sound, not the sentiment," he emphasized, wanting to be honest with her.

Bethany inclined her head. They'd made a little

progress, she supposed. "Fair enough. Does this mean that you're willing to listen to the positive side of NHC taking over the hospital?"

She asked the question with a smile that he found very difficult to resist. He supposed that he could listen. That didn't mean she could convince him, because some things were written in stone. But to refuse to listen made him out to be irrationally stubborn and he didn't want her thinking of him that way. Not after what had just happened between them.

"I might be willing to listen," he allowed, enunciating each word.

"But?" she pressed, sensing that the word was hovering about, waiting to emerge from his lips.

"No 'but,'" he assured her. "Just a condition."

"A condition," she echoed. "What condition?"

She was looking at him warily. It amused him. No one had ever thought of him as someone to be wary of. "If you let me buy you a cup of coffee, I let you talk."

He expected her to be relieved, and perhaps a little embarrassed for being so suspicious. She appeared to be neither.

"Is this going to be like the last time you bought me coffee? You walked out on me in mid-sentence," she reminded him when he looked at her quizzically.

"No, it won't," he said with a warm smile. "This isn't going to be like the last time. You can finish your sentence and I'll finish my coffee." He turned to his right. "There's a coffee shop two blocks down. It's open late. Is that out of your way?"

"No, it's not."

Maybe he wasn't quite the stick-in-the-mud she had thought he was. Lord knows he didn't kiss like a stick-in-the-mud. He kissed like a man who knew his way around women. But then, she didn't have much experience in that area.

Bethany smiled up at him and nodded. "Okay, you're on." She glanced over toward his car. "I can drive," she suggested. "Since your car looks like it's gone into hibernation for the winter."

"No, I think I should dig it out." The sooner he got it running again, the better. "Don't go anywhere," he cautioned.

"And miss the chance of engaging in another argument with the chief of staff?" she teased. "I think not."

He stopped. "Temporary chief of staff," he reminded her.

"You could be chief permanently if you wanted the position."

She said it with such certainty, he almost believed that she meant it. He wanted to set her straight before things got too complicated. Peter shook his head. "I don't want it."

Bethany stared at him. He wasn't being modest, she realized—he was serious. He didn't want to be chief. She couldn't understand that. Couldn't understand not wanting to advance, not being driven to strive ever further. She couldn't understand a man who wasn't goal oriented, who didn't want to climb to the top of the mountain just to claim it. Her whole life had been filled with personal challenges, with pushing herself to the next goal, the next finish line. It was all she'd ever known.

"Why not?" she asked, mystified.

The answer was simple. "Because I'm busy enough. Because being chief of staff or chairman of the board of directors or holding down any official position that has to do with the hospital, takes time away from doing what I was meant to do, what I love doing. I love being a doctor. I love helping people."

"You could help them more in a position of power," Bethany insisted. "You could dictate policy if you were the chairman."

He decided that she must have known far more influential chairmen than the one who ran the hospital's board. "No, I couldn't. I could make suggestions and have them up for a vote, during which time I would spend my time arguing with a bright up-and-coming Princeton MBA graduate."

She smiled. "And this is different from the present situation how?"

He grinned. "Well, right now I have more time to devote to my patients than I would if I were tangled up in all the paperwork and demands on my time that either position ultimately requires."

Peter saw her nod her head, whether in agreement or because she was just giving up, he didn't know. But for now, it was enough.

He turned away from her and began to walk to his vehicle. The dark blue sedan was half-submerged in snow, just as she had pointed out. Mentally, he crossed his fingers and hoped the engine would start once he turned the key in the ignition.

"Peter!" she called to him. As he turned around, he heard her yell, "Think fast!"

He didn't think fast enough.

A snowball came flying at him, hitting him in the face. He heard her laughing gleefully. Without pausing, he squatted down and scooped up a handful of snow, packing it quickly with the expertise he'd acquired living in Massachusetts and growing up with three siblings.

He let it loose, getting her on the chin.

Bethany shrieked with laughter as snow found its way under her coat, drizzling down along her throat.

"Oh God, that's cold," she cried, shivering as she brushed away the snow.

He was already prepared to fire off another salvo, but he stopped, his arm raised behind his head. "Give up?" he challenged.

It went against her grain to give up, even when it came to something as simple as a snowball fight. But she had a feeling that pitted against him in this sort of contest, she'd lose. It was better to do it now—before she got any colder—than later.

"For now," she conceded.

There was something in her tone alerting him that this really wasn't over. Dropping the snowball to the ground, he brushed the remnants of the snow off his overcoat.

"Does that mean I should be on my guard?"

Her eyes reflected her amusement and what he could only describe as a delighted wickedness.

"Maybe," she laughed. "Consider yourself warned, Dr. Wilder."

"Peter," he corrected.

"Peter," she echoed.

"I will," he responded. "But that warning works both ways," he added.

It gave her pause.

Without quite turning his back on her, Peter hurriedly brushed off some of the snow that had settled on top of the hood of his car before getting in. He turned the key in the ignition. The car made a futile-sounding noise, as if it were coughing, then suddenly fell stone-cold silent.

He tried again. This time there wasn't even a hint of a sound.

On his third try, the car cautiously came to life. Relieved, he let the engine run for a couple of minutes, wanting the vehicle to warm up before he took it out of park.

Waiting, he got out for a moment and called to her. "Want me to lead the way?"

"I know where it is," she assured him. "I'll lead the way."

With that, she got into her car. After a couple of false starts, it came to life and she peeled out of the parking lot. Snow flew away from both sides of her vehicle as the tires made their way through the lot.

"Of course you will," Peter murmured under his breath. He got back in behind the wheel. Closing his door, he threw the car into Drive and took off after her.

The woman drove like she kissed, he thought. Fast and hard.

Peter pressed down hard on the accelerator. He was determined to keep up.

Chapter Eight

Peter arrived in the parking lot some five minutes after Bethany did. He'd been harnessed by such little things as obedience to speed limits and not flying through yellow lights that were turning red. Because of the hour and the weather, the tiny lot was all but empty.

Peter parked his car beside hers. When he got out, so did she. She looked rather satisfied with herself, he thought. "This wasn't a race, you know."

She had the good grace to look somewhat contrite. "Sorry, I'm always in a hurry to get where I'm going."

"I noticed that." She appeared set to dash up the two steps leading to the coffee shop door. "Hold it."

She looked at him, puzzled. Was there a lecture in the wings? "What?"

"You have snow in your hair." He brushed it aside with his fingertips. "Makes you look like an ice princess." The moment he said the words, he saw her eyes cloud. "What?" he wanted to know. "What did I say?"

"Nothing." Bethany turned away and walked up to the entrance. The snow on the shop's roof made it look almost quaint.

Moving ahead of her, Peter opened the door and held it. The warm air within the shop instantly brushed over her face, making the cold a thing of the past. She took a breath.

Silly to act that way, she upbraided herself. It had been years since she'd heard the taunting term applied to her and she knew that Wilder didn't mean it in the same way. Just an unfortunate choice of words, that's all, she thought.

The shop was empty except for one person sitting alone at a table near the front counter. About to walk over to a table, Peter curbed his impulse. Instead, he let Bethany choose one, sensing that she'd prefer it that way.

"You don't want to talk about it," he guessed.

Stopping by a table in the middle of the shop, she unbuttoned her coat and draped it over the back of the chair before sitting down. "No."

Peter followed suit, sliding into his chair after leaving his overcoat on the back. The waitress came over, an old-fashioned order pad in her hand. He found that oddly reassuring, given that orders were now electronically taken and submitted in some of the more upscale restaurants in Walnut River.

He waited until the young woman retreated before leaning across the table and responding to Bethany's answer. "Fair enough. I won't push."

She knew what he was saying. That he respected her desire not to discuss the matter while she'd continued to push for a lengthy discussion of the blessings involved in Northeastern Healthcare's possible takeover.

Well, he was wrong here, too, she thought. "Apples and oranges, Peter. One subject's personal, the other is very, very public."

"Patient care should be personal." His voice was mild, his feeling wasn't.

In a perfect world, he'd be right, she thought. But the world was far from perfect. They had to do the best they could and make use of every opportunity that came up. And being taken under NHC's wing was a genuine opportunity.

"It's a noble sentiment," she allowed. "But it really is no longer possible."

He nodded at the waitress as the woman returned with two cups of coffee and the Danish he'd convinced Bethany to split between them.

"Well, it isn't if we all just give up and focus on a paycheck," he said, once the waitress had left their table again.

Bethany gave him the benefit of the doubt, since he seemed to be so impassioned about the subject. Maybe the man was too close to see the big picture. "Medicine is specialized now."

That would presuppose that what NHC offered was special and, as far as he was concerned, the HMO route detracted from medicine, it didn't add to it.

Raising his cup to his lips, he took a swallow and let the black, bitter brew wind through his system. "Working for an HMO is too compartmentalized. I don't treat a left pinkie or a right toe, I treat—"

She sighed wearily. "The whole patient, yes, I know. So you said. But in the time you've spent with that one *whole* patient, you could have helped three."

She was still thinking assembly line. That didn't work in this case. People brought nuances, shades of gray, individuality, to the table. They weren't all the same. "Or missed important symptoms for all three because I was moving so fast."

She stirred in cream and raised her eyes to his. "No, you wouldn't."

All right, he'd bite, Peter thought. "And why wouldn't I?"

"Because you're good," she said simply. "You're experienced."

Gotcha. The woman had just made his argument for him, Peter thought. "I got that experience one patient at a time."

They were going around in circles. "In your grandfather's day, doctors could do that—make house calls, be devoted to their patients like he was—"

"You've been looking into my background?" he interrupted, surprised. He hadn't mentioned that his grandfather had been a doctor.

When it became clear that he was going to be a stumbling block, she'd made it her mission to learn as much as she could about Peter Wilder. She liked to know what she was dealing with. With the possible exception of when he'd just kissed her, she really didn't like surprises. "I like being thorough—"

He was quick to feed her words back to her. "So do I, that's my point."

He was fast when he wanted to be, she'd give

him that, Bethany thought. But she was just as sharp, if not sharper. "And my point is that medicine has made an awful lot of wonderful strides and breakthroughs in the last couple of decades, things your grandfather wouldn't have dreamed of."

He broke off a piece of the Danish. Glazed sugar drizzled down from his fingers just before he popped the piece into his mouth. It didn't take a clairvoyant to see where she was going with this. "And you're saying these breakthroughs wouldn't have been possible without the backing of conglomerates like NHC."

He noticed that there was a small, triumphant toss of her head accompanying the single enthusiastic word. "Exactly." Before he could respond, she held up her hand, stopping what she knew was going to be an onslaught of information.

"I'm not saying that medicine was in the Dark Ages before managed care came along, but you have to admit that progress has definitely sped up since it came on the scene. By operating efficiently, HMOs like NHC can fund research projects, secure the latest equipment for their clinics and hospitals—"

Peter cut in, feeling that he knew a little more about that situation than she did, no matter what she professed to the contrary. "Equipment that a physician has to plead with the powers that be to use because usage is so expensive," he reminded her.

She looked down at the pastry in her fingers, uncomfortable with the fact he'd just tossed at her. She couldn't, in good conscience, tell him he was wrong. "Sometimes," she conceded.

"A lot of times," Peter countered. Placing his hand on hers, he claimed another small piece of the pastry.

Bethany drew back her hand self-consciously. "Look, I—"

He'd had enough of this confounding dance during work hours. Right now, all he wanted was to share a cup of coffee and a few unnecessary calories with a woman who, heaven help him, stirred him in a way he hadn't been stirred in a very long time.

"Bethany," he began quietly, his eyes pinning hers, "why don't we just call a truce for now and enjoy our coffee?"

Why did that make her more nervous than discussing the takeover? She tried to bank down the odd flutter in her stomach. "And talk about what? The weather?"

He laughed in response and looked out the window that faced the parking lot. It had started snowing again. "Beats being out in it."

She followed his gaze and groaned. She could

feel her feet getting cold already. "Well, we'll have to be soon enough."

But right now, they were warm and dry. "Do you always take the pessimistic view of everything?"

"It's not pessimistic," she informed him, her chin raising defensively. "It's realistic."

She was an overachiever, he thought. An over-achiever used to being in charge. But somewhere along the line, the woman had obviously forgotten the reason she was trying so hard. She'd gotten caught up in the race and forgotten the reason.

He studied her thoughtfully, peering at her over his coffee cup. "I bet you got straight A's in school."

Where had that come from? "Not that it has anything to do with anything, but yes, I did."

It had a lot to do with things, Peter thought. It told him the kind of person she was. Determined. Relentless. And probably very hard on herself if she fell short.

"Your parents must have been really proud."

She made a small, disparaging sound. "If they were, they never let on." She saw the interest that instantly entered his eyes and silently chastised herself. What was she thinking, letting that slip out?

"They were too busy to notice?" he asked.

She bristled at the sympathy she heard in his voice. God, but she didn't want any pity from him. She'd done just fine. Successful people didn't need pity.

"They had—have," she corrected herself, "important positions. There was a lot of demand on their time," she explained. She was making excuses for her parents, she realized. The words felt awkward in her mouth. "They were trying to give my sister and me a quality life."

Peter read between the lines. It wasn't that uncommon a story. "And they wound up skimping on the quantity, didn't they?" he guessed.

He saw her squaring her shoulders and wondered if she was conscious of the action. Was she gearing up for a fight?

"We had the best education, a beautiful penthouse apartment, everything we could ask for," she said proudly.

"Bedtime stories?"

Her mind came to a skidding halt. She couldn't have heard him correctly. "What?"

"Bedtime stories," he repeated, breaking off yet another piece from the swiftly dwindling pastry. The portion that was left was small. He pushed the plate toward her. "Did your parents read you and your sister bedtime stories?"

"No." They were rarely home when she and her sister were young. "I didn't need bedtime stories," she informed him, then finished the last of the Danish.

"Every child needs that," he said with gentle authority.

She sighed. He was making her feel as if she had been denied something important. She didn't like being made to feel that way. "Is that what you want to do, Peter?" she asked sarcastically. "Read your patients bedtime stories?"

He smiled and shook his head. "No, I can bond without that." Taking a napkin, he wiped his fingers carefully as he regarded her with interest. "Do you see her often?"

She needed a map to keep track of this conversation. "Who?"

"Your sister."

"Belinda? No," she replied, "not often." Bethany could see that Wilder was going to push this. She nipped it in the bud. "She's living in London, has been for three years." She shrugged slightly. "Some fantastic job for an international banking firm." And their parents were proud of her, she added silently. Belinda had been the older one, the one who did things first. Anything Bethany achieved had to be bigger and better or it wouldn't be noticed.

But she'd made her peace with that, she insisted silently. *Right?*

"So your sister has an MBA, too."

"From Yale," she told him. That trumped hers from Princeton. The thought always rose in her mind when she told anyone about her sister. Needing to take out her frustrations on someone, she glared at Peter. "You make it sound as if getting an MBA is like coming down with some kind of a disease."

That wasn't his doing—she'd come up with that all on her own, he thought. "Only if the degree robs you of your sense of humanity."

She shook her head. "Tell me, do you leave your halo and wings in your office, or do you take them home every night so you can polish them?"

The woman was working up a full head of steam, he thought. The best defense was a good offense. It was one of the rare sports analogies that he was familiar with.

The cell phone belonging to the man at the far end of the floor rang as if on cue. Peter smiled. "I think we're supposed to go back to our corners, now."

Since he'd mentioned it, this *was* a little like a boxing match. And that, she thought, was probably her fault. She doubted that he would have initiated a conversation about NHC on his own.

Not that it seemed to be getting her anywhere. She was tired and not at her best. "Why don't we table this for the night?" she suggested.

He was more than happy to accommodate her. "Fine with me. I'd rather talk about you, anyway."

They weren't going that route, either. "And I would rather go to bed." No sooner were they uttered than her words came back to her. One second before her cheeks turned an electrifying shade of pink, bordering on red.

"I mean my bed." That still sounded like an invitation, she thought, embarrassed. "Alone. To sleep," she added with an almost desperate note in her voice.

Laughing, he took pity on her and let her off the hook. "Relax, Bethany. I didn't take that to be an invitation."

She was relieved, and yet there was a small part—a very small part, she qualified—that wasn't so relieved. That was insulted.

Memories of being the butt of everyone's jokes in elementary school and junior high came rushing back to her with such a force, they all but stole her breath.

Was he being insulting? After kissing her? Or maybe *because* he'd kissed her.

"Why not?" she demanded. "Do you find me that unattractive?"

Seemingly bemused, he looked at her. "Do you even own a mirror?" he asked. "Because if you do, I suggest you look into it more often. If anyone could pull me out of my workaholic state, it would be you—" he paused "—as long as you promised not to launch into another debate in the middle of a heated embrace."

Flustered, yet at the same time warmly pleased, Bethany was at a loss as to what to say. She didn't want to encourage him, and yet, if she were being totally honest with herself, she didn't want to completely discourage him, either.

The upshot was, she didn't know what to say in response. She had no practice here, no experience to draw on. For her, flirtation, or whatever this was, constituted uncharted waters.

And then he came to her rescue. "I think we should call it a night."

She grasped the excuse with both hands. "Yes, so do I."

He smiled, pretending not to notice how relieved she looked. "We agree on something. That's a good sign. Maybe I'll bring you around yet."

She'd been so intent these past few days on getting him to change his mind and thinking of him as being incredibly stubborn, it had never occurred to her that he might be trying to change her mind, as well. This put everything in a slightly different light. Made the verbal tennis game a little trickier.

"Don't count on it," she told him.

"Counting" on it wouldn't have been the way he would have put it. Still, one thing was certain. His outlook. "Oh, but I'm an optimist, remember?"

How could he hem her in so effectively when the words were of her own choosing? "I—"

Whatever she was about to say was cut short by the sound of squealing brakes and the screech of tires. A bone-jarring crash followed, as the sound of metal twisting and entangling itself about the obstacle it had just disastrously met echoed through the coffee shop.

Peter was on his feet instantly, forgetting his overcoat behind him.

Stunned, Bethany's mouth dropped open as she watched him fly out the front door. She felt the blast of cold air from the open door.

"Peter, wait," she called. "You forgot your coat."

But the door was already shutting, separating them. Leaving her inside the warm shop while he braved the cold without any regard for himself.

Hastily throwing on her own coat, she grabbed his and hurried out the door.

The cold threw its skeletal arms around her, locking her in a frigid embrace. As the warmth of the shop swiftly faded, Bethany initially had trouble focusing.

And then she saw the accident.

She didn't have far to look. The car she'd heard screeching had crashed into a utility pole so hard, two-thirds of it had folded up into itself, forming a grotesque metal accordion. Luckily for the driver, his car had spun around and it was the rear of the vehicle that was compressed.

Had it been the front, there was no way the teenager would have survived the impact.

By the time she reached Peter, he had managed to pull the teenager free of the wreckage.

The windshield had shattered, as had one of the side windows. His attention never leaving the victim, Peter pointed that out to her.

"Call 911," he instructed.

She nodded, already pulling her cell phone from her coat pocket. "You forgot your coat." She handed Peter the garment and then quickly hit the three crucial numbers on her phone's keypad.

Someone picked up immediately.

As she spoke to the dispatcher on the other end of the line, Bethany watched Peter drape his coat over the driver in an effort to keep the teenager warm.

But not before he began ripping a strip of the lining out.

"What are you doing?" she cried.

The lining resisted but finally separated from the coat. "Trying to stop the bleeding."

"With the lining from your overcoat?" she asked incredulously.

"It's not the most hygienic way to go," he agreed, "but it's all I've got unless I use my shirt." Even as he wrapped the material around the young man's arm, he could feel Bethany staring at him. "What?" he finally asked.

"Did it ever occur to you that if something goes wrong, this guy you're working over might just turn around and sue you? And if he doesn't, maybe his parents will?"

Peter shook his head. He couldn't think about things like that now. It wasn't the way he operated. "Frankly, no," he admitted freely. "I have people like you for that."

Chapter Nine

The police and paramedics arrived less than ten minutes after Bethany had placed the 911 call. The sounds of their approaching sirens created a chilling cacophony of noise.

Peter gave as much information as he could to both the paramedics and the fresh-faced officer who looked as if he was only minutes out of the academy. In the case of the latter, Peter began by saying that he didn't really have much to offer. He hadn't witnessed the accident and he wasn't acquainted with the victim, who was still unconscious. The officer clearly wished he had more information.

The paramedic appeared pleased with not only Peter's recitation of vital signs, but what he had done while waiting for the ambulance to arrive. Bethany realized that the two knew each other by the way the paramedic spoke.

"Nice work, Doc. If you hadn't been here to stop the bleeding, we'd be taking this kid down to the morgue instead of to the hospital." As carefully as possible, he and his partner transferred the teenager from the ground to the gurney they'd taken from the back of the ambulance.

Stepping out of their way, Peter brushed away the compliment. At this point in his career, saving lives was second nature to him.

He nodded back toward the parking lot. "I'll get my car and follow you in," he said to the lead paramedic, then bent over to retrieve his bloodstained and rumpled overcoat.

"See you there," the paramedic told Peter just before he closed and secured the rear doors of the ambulance. Walking to the front of the vehicle, he opened the driver's side and got into the cab.

Bethany looked at Peter. "You're going back to the hospital?"

Peter brushed off as much snow as he could before putting his overcoat back on. She sounded surprised, he thought, trying to gauge her tone. "Yes."

She wanted to dissuade him. His hours were over. The man wasn't a robot. "Whoever's on call at the E.R. can take care of him."

It didn't matter who was on call. The teenager had become his patient the moment he'd applied the makeshift bandage to his wound. "I started this, I might as well finish it."

He actually meant that. He was willing to give up his evening, his free time, for a stranger. She looked at him for a long moment. Everything he'd said before wasn't just lip service or arguing for argument's sake. Though she tried not to be, Bethany had to admit she was impressed.

"You really are as dedicated as they say, aren't you?"

He shrugged. "I have no idea what *they* say." He didn't do things based on what someone else might or might not say or think. He did things because they were the right things to do. "So I can't answer that." To his surprise, instead of saying anything, Bethany placed herself in front of him, blocking his path to his car, and began unbuttoning his overcoat. What was this all about? "What are you doing?"

"You mis-buttoned your coat," she said, beginning to rebutton the overcoat correctly. "Not that putting the right button into the right hole really matters. You still look like a homeless person," she declared. Stepping back, she shook her head. His coat was a mess. "You're not going to be able to get that blood out."

Peter glanced down at his coat. She was probably right. "Small price to pay for saving a man's life," he commented.

She tried to picture her father saying that with any kind of true feeling and couldn't. Her parents had a completely different set of sensibilities than Wilder obviously did. And there was something almost hypnotically fascinating about his world.

About him.

The unbidden, fleeting thought jarred Bethany right down to the roots of her teeth.

Maybe hypothermia was setting in and she was hallucinating. She really wasn't sure of anything anymore. Especially not since he'd kissed her.

Peter paused for a moment. "You'll be okay going home?" Because if she felt uneasy for some reason, then he'd follow her home before going to the hospital.

What a strange question, she thought. The man was a roving, card-carrying knight in shining armor.

"I have been up to now," she assured him. She had no idea why she added, "So I guess the cup of coffee is over."

He'd begun to walk to his car and stopped to look at her. A strange pang nipped at his stomach. Peter realized that he didn't want it to be over. But of course it was, and after all, it had only been a cup of coffee, not an actual date. Not even a preliminary meeting to set up a date.

But it could have been.

And then an impulse burst over him. "That fund-raiser Henry's throwing together, the one to raise money for the new MRI machine…"

Bethany bristled slightly. Wilder made the reference as if she wouldn't be aware of what the fund-raiser was for without his sidebar. He didn't think much of her, did he? As the efficiency expert, she was very aware of everything that was going on in the hospital. Maybe even more aware of things than he was. She was in the business of knowing everything about the hospital's operation.

"What about it?" she asked formally.

"Are you going?"

Why? Didn't he think she'd attend a fund-raiser? "Yes."

He almost stopped, thinking it wiser to keep his next question to himself. But that same impulse he'd had a moment ago experienced a fresh surge and he heard himself ask, "With anyone?"

"No." That was the honest answer. The next

moment, she backtracked. "I mean—" This was where she pulled a name out of a hat to cover herself. To make it seem that she wasn't the social loner she actually was. Why she felt her lips moving and heard her voice repeating "No," she had no idea. The only answer seemed to be that she was turning on herself.

Caught up in her own unraveling, she certainly didn't expect to hear him say the next words.

"If you're not going with anyone, would you mind if I took you?"

Stunned, she recovered fast. "No, I wouldn't mind." Bethany felt her mouth curving in response. "Are you asking me out, Dr. Wilder—um, Peter?"

He grinned. "I guess I am."

Say yes. What've you got to lose? She took a deep breath. "All right."

"All right?" he echoed quizzically. He didn't know if she was agreeing with what he'd just said, or if she was agreeing to go to the fundraiser with him. This woman, above all others, should have come with a set of instructions or some kind of manual.

"All right," she repeated. "I'll go to this fundraiser with you. Since we're both going," she added. After a slight pause, she added more. "We can economize and use one car. Less gas—"

His eyes met hers. "Bethany."

His eyes seemed to pin her in place. She stopped in mid-sentence. "What?"

He smiled at her. "You don't have to justify your decision to me."

"I'm not," she said. Lowering her eyes, she addressed her shoes. "I'm justifying it to me."

"Oh." Turning the key, he started his car. It instantly hummed to life. "I'll see you in the morning."

She nodded, rooted to the spot, watching him drive away. Was that a throwaway phrase he'd just uttered, or was he planning on actually seeing her tomorrow? Except for the board meetings and when she deliberately went out of her way to look for him, they didn't see each other ordinarily.

Her body was tingling when she turned away, whether from the cold or anticipation, she couldn't decide. She was hoping for the former.

Turning away, she went to her own car a few steps away. She knew what she needed—to make her mind a blank, to think about nothing and no one.

That wasn't the easiest thing to do, especially not after he'd kissed her.

He'd kissed her.

The thought vividly brought back the sensation. Instantly, she became warm. So much so that for a moment, she simply sat in her car, frozen in the moment. Enjoying the moment.

And then she became disgusted with herself. She was pathetic, Bethany silently chided. Most women her age fantasized about the lovers they'd had; they didn't go on and on about a single kiss no matter how good, how toe-curling it was.

Enough!

Bethany started up her car and headed toward the residential development where she lived. What she needed, she told herself, was some hot soup and a diverting program on TV.

That's not what you need, a soft voice whispered in her head.

Maybe not, she countered, banking her thoughts down before they got any more out of hand. But hot soup and TV was what she was going to get.

Peter walked into his house and turned on the light. He stomped his feet on the small scatter rug just inside the threshold, trying to knock as much snow as possible off his shoes.

It had been a long evening. He'd put in another two hours at the E.R., but the teenager, Matthew Sayers, was going to be all right. His parents had all but flown to the hospital the second the police had called them about their son's car accident. Both had expressed overwhelming gratitude to Peter for coming to Matthew's aid and for "saving our boy," as Matthew's mother had sobbed.

It turned out that the Sayers were quite well-to-do. Matthew's father was a top-level magazine executive and his mother was an heiress. They had only recently bought their house in Walnut River. They also owned a condo in Manhattan. The senior Sayers wanted to show his appreciation for having his son tended to.

After being enthusiastically pressed several times, Peter had finally made a suggestion to the man, which was how Walnut River General got its first donation toward the MRI machine.

A sense of satisfaction pervaded him.

All in all, it had been a very productive evening. He'd saved a boy and gotten Henry a sizable donation to kick-start the fund-raiser.

He'd also kissed an angel.

The stray thought made him smile. Memory of the kiss had been moved temporarily to the back of the line because of the urgent situation he'd had to deal with, but now it had reappeared at the front, swiftly growing in proportion.

Despite the time that had lapsed, he could still taste her on his lips. Still taste the subtle flavor of ripened strawberries.

The overhead light dimmed for a second, then returned full strength.

Probably the work of the storm, he thought. Outside, the wind was howling and the snow was falling harder. Perfect conditions for a power outage. It wouldn't hurt to keep a flashlight handy, he decided. Just in case.

He kept a couple of flashlights on the bottom shelf of his anemically stocked pantry. Shrugging out of his overcoat, he left it draped over the first piece of furniture he came to—the sofa.

Bethany was right, he thought, glancing at the coat. It looked like something a homeless man would wear. One particularly down on his luck. He was going to have to see about buying another one. He certainly didn't want the woman to be embarrassed to be seen with him.

The thought that had just floated through his head bemused him. When, other than at the gala, would that be happening? And why would her feelings about his appearance even come into play? Assuming she *had* any feelings about his appearance.

His thoughts were definitely going in strange, uncharted directions. Peter pushed the question and its accompanying thoughts away. He had no desire to get emotionally involved with anyone again. He was too weary and too wired at the same time to properly tackle anything right now.

As he walked through the room to reach the kitchen, his eyes were drawn to the envelope that was still lying on the mantelpiece. The envelope with his father's handwriting on it.

The one he still hadn't opened.

Haven't had the time, Peter thought defensively.

Was that it? Was a lack of time the reason he hadn't opened the envelope, or was it really more of a lack of nerve? Was he afraid of what he might read, what he might discover?

He shook off the thought.

This was ridiculous. He was a grown man, a doctor for God's sake. He'd had his hand inside a patient's stomach, dealing with a perforated ulcer, had to face a grieving wife to give her the gut-wrenching news that her husband was gone. Had had to summon the courage to step, at least partially, into his father's shoes. Those kinds of actions weren't the actions of a man who lacked nerve.

So why was an envelope causing perspiration to pop out all over his brow?

What was it that he was afraid of?

And then he knew. He was afraid of finding out that rather than a saint, his father had just been a man. Fallible.

Ridiculous. Stop stalling, Wilder.

With determination, Peter walked into his kitchen. Crossing to the pantry, he opened it. The flashlights were just where he'd left them, on the bottom shelf. The pantry contained very little else. A box of matches, a collection of napkins in the corner. Containers of salt, pepper and sugar and one opened box of stale cereal.

Taking the larger of the two flashlights, he checked to see if it worked—it did—and then walked back into the living room. To confront the monster hiding in the closet.

Or lying on the mantelpiece, as it were.

Peter set the flashlight facedown on the mantel and picked up the envelope. After taking a deep breath and then letting it out, he ripped open the envelope. His fingers felt ever so slightly icy.

Inside the envelope was a letter and another, thinner envelope. This one was addressed to Anna.

Was this some kind of a game? Like the little gaily painted wooden Russian dolls, the ones where when you opened one up, exposed another, smaller doll inside, and then another, and another until there were six or more lined up, each one smaller than the last?

Were there other envelopes, addressed to David

and Ella, inside this one? Was this some strange inside joke from the grave?

There was only one way to find out.

Bracing himself even as he silently argued that there was no reason to feel this kind of apprehension, Peter decided it might be prudent to sit down before he began to read.

He perched rather than sat on the sofa, tension taking less than subtle possession of his body. The air felt almost brittle as he drew it in.

The letter was handwritten, and reading was slow going. While not illegible, his father's handwriting was a challenge at times.

"To my son Peter,
From the first moment you drew breath, I have always thought of you as my successor. Not just at the hospital, but with the family as well. I am very proud of the man that you have become. You are so much more than I ever was or could hope to be."

Peter frowned. What did *that* mean? An uneasiness continued to build within him. He forced himself to continue reading.

"I don't want to burden you with this. But you are the only one I can ask to make this decision. You are the only one I can trust with this secret.

By now you've noticed that there is a second letter, addressed to Anna. I am leaving it up to you to decide whether or not she would be better off knowing. Knowing what, you may ask. Or perhaps, since you were always so bright, so intuitive, you already know. Your mother always suspected but never asked. I think she was afraid of the truth.

Anna is not your adopted sister, she is your half sister. Her mother was an E.R. nurse who was very kind to me during that period when your mother and I were having such a difficult time together. You were nine at the time so perhaps you don't remember. Your mother had been suffering from depression, and had retreated to her own world. A world she later emerged from, thank God. But while it was happening, it was terrible for both of us.

I had my work, and you boys, but I felt lost and, in a moment of weakness, I gave in and accepted the comfort of another woman. Anna is the result of that single liaison. Her mother, Monica, knew she wasn't going to be able to raise her and give her the things she would need to succeed in this life so she gave her up. We agreed that she would leave the baby on the steps of the hospital and that I would "find" her there.

Not long afterward, Monica died in a plane crash. I've debated taking this secret to my grave, but part of me felt that Anna should know the truth. That she was always my daughter—and your sibling—in every way. However, if you think that she would be better off not knowing, then burn this letter, and hers as well.

Please don't think any less of me because of my transgression. I am still your father and I love each of you—and your late mother—very much.

Forgive me,

Your loving father, James."

Peter sat, holding the letter in his hands and staring at it, his mind completely numb, for a very long time.

Chapter Ten

Peter wasn't sure exactly how long he sat there. When he finally managed to rouse himself, he felt the bitter taste of betrayal in his mouth as he slowly tucked the letter and the other envelope back inside the original one.

Taking a breath, he could feel, awakening inside him, a whole host of emotions warring with one another. Most prominent of all was disappointment, mixed with confusion.

He wished he'd never read the letter, had never been given this burden to deal with.

Never been robbed.

Because that was what it was—robbery, pure and simple. His father's confession had robbed him of the image that, until this evening, he had carried around with him.

Yes, he knew the man was not a saint, that he was flesh and blood and human, capable of making mistakes. But he'd always assumed that those mistakes would be tied in with judgment calls about his patients. Maybe an occasional failure to diagnose a particularly elusive illness properly.

Never in his wildest dreams would he have believed that his father would be guilty of personal misconduct. He would have gone so far as to swear on a stack of Bibles that his father had never strayed, never cheated on his mother, never been anything but loyal and faithful to everyone he knew, especially to the people in his immediate family.

Instead, James Wilder had betrayed his wife and, in a way, Anna.

No—all of them, Peter thought, trying in vain to bank down the hurt he felt.

This showed him another side to his father, a far more human side than he was willing to cope with at the moment. If his father had done something like this, had hidden a secret of this magnitude, were there other secrets that James Wilder *hadn't* admitted to?

Here he was, trying to preserve his father's legacy and maybe it was all just a huge sham, illusions created by smoke and mirrors to hide the actual man.

Maybe he really didn't know his father at all.

Who knew, maybe his father would have jumped at the opportunity to have the hospital taken over by an HMO, to have someone pocket all the expenses, pay for everything and ultimately remove the responsibility for judgment calls from his hands.

Maybe…

No. Discovering that his father had had a relationship—and a child—with another woman while married to his mother, didn't change the things that mattered. The basic things. And it sure as hell didn't change the man that *he* was, Peter thought angrily.

He hadn't based his feelings, his position, on the fact that his father would have done it this way. That his father would have approved of the stand he was taking. Believing that had only served as reinforcement. He, Dr. Peter Wilder, *believed* in what he'd said to Bethany and to the board. Believed that, when it came to the hospital, the old ways *were* the best and that Walnut River General would be much better off *not* being swallowed up whole by a soulless, unemotional conglomerate, no matter *what* kind of promises were made.

Rising to his feet, he sighed heavily and shook his head. He felt drained and exhausted beyond words.

Peter put the envelope back on the mantelpiece, not wanting to touch it any more right now. Wishing he could wipe its existence from his mind. But he wouldn't be able to do that, even if he threw his letter and Anna's into the fire.

"I wish you hadn't told me this, Dad. I wish you hadn't passed the burden on to me," he whispered, aching.

Everything fell into place now. It all made sense to him.

This was why his father always seemed to go out of his way for Anna, treat her differently, share more time with her than he did with the rest of them. It wasn't because he was trying to make up for her feeling like an outsider. He was doing it because he'd felt guilty about her very existence. Guiltier still because he didn't tell her she was his real daughter. He had let her go on thinking she'd been abandoned when just the reverse was true. She could have been put up for adoption. Instead, he'd taken her into his family rather than let her go to someone else's—and have the secret go with her.

His first instinct was to preserve his father's memory for the others. Because this didn't just affect Anna, but David and Ella as well. It was a package deal. If he passed this letter on to Anna, once she read it, the others needed to know, too. They needed to know that the family dynamics had changed.

No, Peter thought as he walked up the stairs to his bedroom, that was for Anna to decide. If he told her, it would be her secret to share or keep.

He laughed shortly. Who would have ever thought that he would be aligning himself with Anna against his brother and sister?

An ironic smile curved his mouth. That wasn't altogether right now, was it? Anna was his sister, too.

His sister. His *real* sister.

Well, that explained why she seemed to have his father's eyes. Because they *were* his father's eyes.

Just when he thought there were no surprises left, he mused, shaking his head sadly.

The letter was no longer on his mantelpiece.

Early this morning, he'd gotten up and decided to leave the thick envelope in his study, in the middle drawer of his desk until he decided what to do with it.

Meanwhile, he was still a doctor with patients, still the chief of staff, albeit temporarily, faced with a supreme dilemma: how to make the rest of the board of directors vote his way regarding the NHC takeover.

Because all options needed to be explored, someone from the grasping conglomerate would be coming at the end of the month to look them over. Supposedly to observe how they functioned, but in likelihood, to attempt to sway them with promises.

If he came out staunchly opposed to the NHC executive's visit, it would seem to the board that he was afraid of the challenge or the potential changes. Afraid that Walnut River General couldn't withstand an in-depth comparison to the way hospitals beneath NHC's massive banner were run.

He had too much on his mind to deal with the burden of his father's request right now.

But the discovery hung over him heavily and made him far more serious than usual. A couple of his patients remarked on it, as did Eva, his nurse. All of them attributed the change in mood to his father's passing.

He said nothing to correct them. This was *not* something he wanted to discuss even if he were free to do so.

The morning went on endlessly until the last patient was finally gone at twelve-thirty. It had taken Eva less than two minutes to grab her purse and run off to lunch.

"Want me to bring you back anything?" she offered just before she slipped out.

"No, I'm fine. I brought lunch." It was a lie, but his appetite had deserted him last night, making no reappearance this morning. Food was the last thing on his mind.

"Okay, I'll be back soon," she promised, exiting.

He heard the outer office door close and turned his attention back to the work he'd spread out on his desk. There were several files he wanted to review before signing off on them.

Something else he probably wouldn't be able to do soon if NHC came in, he thought. They were pushing for paperless offices. All the files would be on computer, on some nebulous server located in the middle of the country.

And what would everyone do if there was a power spike? Or a blackout. What then? What would happen to all the information that was stored?

Give me paper any day, he thought, opening the first folder he came to.

Forcing himself to focus, he was immersed in the file—and the patient—within seconds.

Preoccupied, he didn't hear the knock on his inner office door, and was startled a bit when Bethany walked in. He sighed inwardly. Any other time he'd have been glad to see her. Now, the last thing he needed was another frontal assault about the virtues of NHC.

He felt his temper shortening already. "I'm in the middle of something," he told her, then looked back at what he'd been reading.

"I won't take up much of your time," she promised. "I just came to give you this."

Curious, he looked up in time to see her place a bottle of wine, tied with a bright red ribbon, on his desk.

He eyed it for a long moment. He was familiar enough with wine to know that this was not an inexpensive bottle hastily purchased at the nearest supermarket. This brand took a bit of hunting.

Why was she bringing it to him? She couldn't possibly be trying to bribe him. Or could she? He leaned back. His eyes never left her face. "What's this?"

This was not easy for her. But she had always prided herself on being fair. "An apology."

That was the last thing he'd expected from her. Especially since he wasn't quite sure what she was referring to. "For?"

She took a breath before answering. This was going to be a little tricky, but he'd impressed her a great deal last night. "For thinking that you're an arrogant jerk who doesn't see past his own ego."

Instead of taking offense, he laughed. At least she was being honest and, after the surprise he'd received, being honest was a very good thing. "I thought you said you thought I was a saint."

She felt relieved that he was taking this in the spirit it was intended. "No, I said *other* people thought you were a saint. To be honest, I thought that maybe you were using that image to make people see things your way."

He supposed he could understand her feeling that way, especially considering the world she came from. Big-business dealings were hardly ever without some kind of backroom dealings.

"And now you've suddenly changed your mind about me because—"

She knotted her hands before her. "Because I watched you in action. Because you didn't stop to worry about being sued if something went wrong." Even though she had deliberately pointed it out to him last night. "Because you just got in there and helped that boy simply because he was a human being in trouble." She had to admit, if only to herself, that she'd felt a certain thrill watching him rush to the rescue like some modern-day hero. "You almost make me yearn for the 'good old days.'"

He laughed, shaking his head. "You're much too

young to have been around for the good old days."
He said it as if he were far more than merely nine
years older than she. Peter indicated the bottle of
wine. "Apology accepted." Taking it in hand, he held
the bottle out to her, implying that she was free to take
it back. "But you really don't have to do this."

She made no move to accept the wine. It was
clear she was disappointed that he seemed not to
want the peace offering.

"We don't seem to agree on anything, do we?"

Not wanting to offend her, Peter put the bottle
down again. "Well, I do remember us being in
agreement at one point last night." He looked at her
significantly, a hint of a smile on his lips.

Bethany could feel heat rising in her cheeks.

"Perhaps one," she allowed.

"Maybe there's more where that came from," he
speculated. Then, in case she thought he was suggesting something a little more personal, he added,
"Agreements, I mean."

Her eyes met his. "Maybe," she echoed softly.
She wasn't talking about being in agreement, only
in concert. She could feel her face growing yet
warmer. So much for poise. Bethany cleared her
throat. "I'd better get out of your way."

"You're not in my way," he said. And suddenly,
as much as he had wanted to be alone before, he

didn't anymore. His father's revelation had left him in a strange, vulnerable place. He'd always felt so sure about everything, so confident. Now he wasn't. It was as if he was back in college again, just after Lisa had abruptly left him. "Stay for a minute," he urged. "Unless there's somewhere else you need to be."

He gave her a way out, but she didn't want to take it, not just yet. So she edged back toward his desk and sat down in the chair opposite his desk. "Aren't you busy?" she asked, nodding at the files.

"It's nothing that won't keep." He closed the top folder but left it where it was. "Just paperwork I thought I'd catch up on. It's a losing battle," he added with a slight, disparaging sigh. "There never seems to be enough time to catch up on it all. Besides, no one ever died saying 'I wish I'd had the chance to catch up on all my paperwork.'"

"What *would* they regret?" What would *he* regret, she couldn't help wondering.

"Not spending enough time smelling the roses." It was something he sincerely advocated but hardly ever did. The closest he came was to urge his patients to do it. "Or take in the beauty that's around them." He was looking directly at her as he said it. Her cheeks began to take on color again. "You're growing pinker," he commented, amused.

She'd give anything for a good, solid tan right now, but given the weather, it would have been rust, not tan. "The room is warm," Bethany murmured. She lowered her eyes. "If that compliment was intended for me, Peter, you might think about having your eyes checked."

This wasn't false modesty, he realized. She really meant what she was saying. "Hasn't anyone ever told you that you're beautiful before?"

Not once, she thought. Not ever. And when she was growing up, the exact opposite was true. Kids were cruel and her parents didn't provide a haven for her where she could lick her wounds. Looking back, she supposed that was a toughening device on its own.

Since he was obviously waiting for an answer, she told him the truth. "You'd be the first."

He couldn't believe that. "Where did you grow up, in a swamp covered with mud?"

The sincerity in his voice delighted her. "No, just with people who had twenty-twenty vision." Her parents, especially her mother, could be trusted to point out her flaws, but never comment on any of her attributes. They expected her to be a high achiever. Anything less was not acceptable. And there was always Belinda to live up to.

"Unlike yours." A self-deprecating smile played on her lips. "I was the original ugly duckling."

"You remember the rest of the story, don't you?" he asked. "That so-called ugly duckling became a beautiful swan."

She shrugged, looking away. "I haven't reached that part yet."

If asked, he would have said that Bethany Holloway did not lack confidence, but obviously, he would have been wrong. "Not only have you reached it, Bethany, you've surpassed it."

When she looked at him, there was something enigmatic in his expression. "What?"

Peter was silent for a long moment, debating whether or not to say anything or just shrug away her question. But she'd taken the first step and held her hand out in a truce. He couldn't be any less of a man than she was.

The second he'd thought it, he realized that it was a sexist thought, but he hadn't meant it that way. "It's my turn to offer you an apology."

"For what?" Was he apologizing for walking out on her in the cafeteria, or something else?

"For thinking you were like someone else I once knew." Maybe that was why he'd reacted so strongly against her when she put forth her arguments. "You're not a thing like her."

"Like who?" she asked. "And why do you think would I be insulted if I'd known you were comparing us?"

"Lisa Dandridge." He saw the next question in her eyes. "Someone I once knew in college. Someone who didn't turn out to be who I thought she was. At first glance, you look a lot like her."

There were things he wasn't saying. Before she got carried away, reading between the lines, she decided to get it straight from the horse's mouth. "This Lisa, was she important to you?"

"For a while, yes." For a while, she was the moon and the stars to him. Until he'd suffered an eclipse.

"How important?" she pressed.

Well, he'd started this. He had no one to blame but himself for her question. To withdraw now wouldn't be fair. "Engaged-to-be-married important."

Bethany fell silent for a second. She hadn't expected him to say that. "Oh." There was no follow-up from him. "Well, don't leave me hanging," she prompted. "What happened?"

"We got unengaged."

She hadn't gotten to where she was by being a shrinking violet. "And that happened because…?"

Because. It was an all-purpose word that

covered so much territory. "Because she found someone else."

Her mouth dropped open. "She cheated on you?" How could any woman in her right mind cheat on someone who looked like Peter? Who was obviously as decent as he was? There was no doubt in her mind that he was better off without this Lisa person.

He'd never known whether Lisa had slept with Steven Wilson, the medical student she'd left him for. He never wanted to let his thoughts go that far. It was enough that she'd left him for the reasons she'd cited.

He shrugged, looking out the window. More snow. Just what they needed, he thought. "We never got into that."

"Then why did you two break up?" He struck her as the type of man who didn't easily give up on a woman he professed to love.

Her question brought the past vividly back to him. "The 'other man' had 'more potential' than I had. He was going into his father's prestigious practice in New York and I was coming back here, to work with *my* father in a place that was far less lucrative and upscale. Lisa didn't see herself living in Walnut River. She saw herself shopping on Fifth Avenue."

"What an awful woman." The words just came out before she could stop them.

"No, Lisa just knew her limitations. Knew what would make her happy. And obviously, it wasn't going to be me."

Bethany frowned. "Well, you were better off without someone like that." She paused, thinking. "And you think I look like her?"

Peter laughed softly. "At first glance, perhaps. But you're far more beautiful than she ever was."

Bethany felt her breath backing up in her lungs. "Really?" she whispered.

"Really."

He was looking at her lips. She felt herself getting warm again. "I think I'd better get back to my office," she murmured.

He nodded. "Maybe you'd better do that," he agreed. Before he went with the demands inside him that were beginning to grow insistent. "And thanks for the wine. I'll save it until I have something to celebrate." He looked at her as she edged her way to the door. "Maybe we'll even share it together."

He was referring to the board's vote regarding the possible takeover. Did he think because she'd brought him a peace offering that she was throwing her vote in with his? Or was that his way of saying he might reconsider his own stand?

She didn't want to ask and risk spoiling the

moment. So she inclined her head in agreement. "Maybe we will," she agreed as she slipped out.

He found himself smiling as he returned to his files.

Chapter Eleven

Though she told herself she wasn't, the truth of it was Bethany was looking forward to the fund-raiser. However, none of the reasons she'd cited to herself regarding why it was important to attend the function were responsible for creating that warm, nervous feeling in the pit of her stomach. There was only one reason for that.

She was going with the man who had literally made the world fade away when he'd kissed her.

Okay, so he'd kissed her and she'd liked it. *Really* liked it. But there was no reason, she told herself, to believe anything of that nature was going to happen again. It was an aberration, a once-in-a-lifetime occurrence. Peter Wilder was a healer, not a lover, even though he had a lethal mouth that had melted her like drawn butter.

Professional, she silently insisted—it was all going to be strictly professional. If there was anything she was, it was professional.

She was still silently clinging to this belief, repeating it over and over again like some kind of mantra, as she went shopping for "the right dress."

It turned out to be a gown, a gown like no other she'd ever owned. The moment she saw it on the alabaster mannequin, she'd fallen in love with the gleaming creation.

Because the gown wasn't her.

It was the kind of gown that belonged on a socialite, a jet-setter, someone who was accustomed to frequenting parties on both coasts and collecting heady, over-the-top compliments.

Depending on the light, the gown, suspended on two thin gossamerlike straps, was either silver or gray-blue, and when she put it on, it adhered to every curve she had. Moreover, it somehow miraculously awarded her more cleavage than she was accustomed to having and the material swayed provocatively with every step she took. Simultaneously, the material played peekaboo with the slit that ran from her ankle to halfway up her thigh, drawing the beholder's attention to the fact that whatever other attributes she might possess, Bethany Holloway, former card-carrying ugly duckling, had stunning, killer legs that seemed to go on forever.

Because she was ordinarily governed by more than her share of logic, Bethany put the gown back on the rack three separate times before she finally snatched it up and fairly trotted to the register.

In most cases, the purchase price of the designer gown would have been prohibitive for someone earning the kind of salary she did. But money had never been a problem for Bethany, never the bottom line that proved to be a deciding factor. What her family lacked in warmth and nurturing attributes it made up for with money. Specifically, a trust fund that was passed on through her mother's family. Martha Royce, her mother's mother, had been obscenely wealthy. The woman believed in giving her descendents a sizable jumpstart in life, not out of any sort of affection but because she believed her lineage was better than anyone else's and should be rewarded for that.

Her grandmother died the year before Bethany graduated from college. At the funeral, which included both her parents and Belinda, she was the only one who shed any tears at the woman's passing.

As she looked at herself now in her wardrobe mirror, Bethany couldn't help wondering what her grandmother would have said if she'd seen her in this gown.

You go, girl.

Bethany smiled to herself, pressing her hand to her unsettled stomach. If the stories she'd heard about the woman's youth, mostly through relatives other than her parents, were true, Grandmother had been a rebel and a hell-raiser. She only wished she had inherited a little more of the woman's spirit instead of her money.

Then, at the very least, she wouldn't feel as nervous as she did about wearing this gown.

Really, darling, this kind of a gown should be worn by someone who can carry it off, don't you think?

This time it was her mother's voice that had popped into her head to haunt her. Her mother who, even when she was seemingly praising her always made Bethany feel as if she were lacking.

Bethany set her jaw, deliberately shutting her mother's perpetually condescending voice out. She really liked the gown, liked the way she looked in it. She looked, she thought, like someone special.

She fervently hoped she wasn't just deluding herself.

The doorbell rang, breaking into her thoughts. The next second, she could feel her stomach seizing up and her heart beginning to race.

Maybe this was a mistake. What was she trying to prove? This backless, almost strapless silvery revelry wasn't her. She belonged in subdued colors, quiet shades that didn't call attention to all the things she lacked. Her nerves spiked to incredible highs as she looked toward her closet.

But it was too late to change, too late to surrender to second thoughts on their third pass-through. She was going to have to wear this.

Here goes nothing.

Taking a deep breath, Bethany walked out of her bedroom and to the front door on legs she willed to be steady.

Opening the door, she summoned her brightest, most carefree smile—or some reasonable facsimile thereof.

And then she saw him. Peter was wearing a formal tux. God, but he looked handsome.

"Hi," she heard herself murmur through lips that felt frozen in place.

The next moment, she saw Peter's dark eyes

slowly travel down the length of her before returning to her face. Unable to tell what he was thinking,
she held her breath, waiting for the verdict.

He already knew, even if she professed not to,
that Bethany was beautiful. But in this dress, she
transcended anything that had come before. The
word *vision* didn't even begin to cover it, but it was
the only word his numbed brain would come up
with.

Realizing that he was staring, Peter cleared his
throat. He was stalling, searching for his voice.
There was a very real danger of it emerging in a
squeak. She did take his breath away.

When he smiled, she could feel warmth spreading all through her.

"I should have brought my portable defibulator,"
he murmured. When she raised a quizzical eyebrow,
he explained, "I think my heart just stopped."

Was he teasing her? Telling her it was inappropriate? Rather than become defensive, she bowed
to his experience. This was her first fund-raiser at
Walnut River General and she didn't want to look
out of place.

Bethany looked down at her dress. "You think
it's too much?"

He laughed at the innocent question. "On the
contrary, I don't think it's enough." He saw the un-

easiness enter her eyes and quickly added, "I mean, it's fine with me, but I'm not sure I'm up on my dueling techniques."

"Dueling techniques?" she repeated, confused.

He nodded. "The way I see it, I might be called upon several times this evening to defend your honor."

He *was* teasing, but in a nice way. Pleasure whispered through her.

Bethany caught her lower lip between her teeth in an unselfconscious, endearing way that just further evaporated his breath. At this rate, he was going to need an oxygen tank before they reached the hotel ballroom.

"I could change," she offered.

He didn't see that as an option. She was almost too beautiful to bear. "And break the hearts of every single male over the age of eight within ten miles? I think not."

So what was he telling her? That he liked the way she looked? Or was he trying to say something else? Bemused, she shook her head. "You certainly know how to confuse a girl with a compliment."

He couldn't help but laugh at the word she'd used. He would have thought that the term "girl" would have offended her. She was more reasonable than he'd given her credit for. He liked that.

"Trust me, Bethany," he assured her. "You might still feel like a girl inside, but outside, you are all woman."

She felt her cheeks warming. This was getting to be a habit around him. She tried to divert his attention from the deepening hue of her skin. "When did you learn to be so charming?"

"About two minutes ago, when you opened the door."

It wasn't the answer she was expecting. He definitely wasn't the stiff, humorless man she'd initially taken him for. Bethany picked up her coat and her purse from the sofa where she'd placed them earlier. "You really are full of surprises, aren't you?"

Peter took the long black coat out of her hands and helped her into it. "The same can be said of you. Those two-piece business suits you wear at the hospital don't begin to adequately convey what's beneath."

She tried her best not to glow at the compliment, but it wasn't easy. "Nice to see you out of a lab coat, too." Turning around, she looked at him again. His overcoat was open, giving her a full view of the tuxedo he wore. She noticed something else, as well. "You look younger."

"That could be because tonight, I don't have the

weight of the world on my shoulders." With his hand at the small of her back, he escorted her out the door. Bethany paused to lock her door. Turning, she took hold of his arm before she realized what she was doing. It just seemed like the natural thing to do. He smiled, completing his thought. "Just a beautiful woman on my arm."

The cold wind carried the scent of another impending snowfall, whipping around, chilling any exposed area it could find.

"About that vision test…" she began playfully as she took small, careful steps to the curb where he had parked his vehicle.

"You should schedule to have one immediately," he agreed. "You're obviously not seeing how beautiful you really are."

Blushing, she slid into the passenger seat and waited for him to round the hood and get in on his side. When he did, she said, "Uncle."

Seat belt in his hand, he stopped mid-motion and looked at her quizzically. "Excuse me?"

"Isn't that what you cry when you know you're outmatched?" Bethany asked. She vaguely remembered hearing that once. "Uncle?"

Peter turned the key in the ignition. After a second, the car started up. He was going to have to remember to check his antifreeze level, he told himself. "Yes, but why—"

She sat back in her seat as they pulled out of the driveway. "I didn't think that such a person existed, but you can clearly outtalk me."

He spared Bethany a glance and smiled at her warmly. "Nice to know."

Just as he'd expected, everyone in the ballroom turned their way when they walked in. Bethany looked far too stunning tonight for people to nonchalantly absorb her into the group without first appreciating every sensual inch of her.

The first to approach them, with the other members of the board not to far behind, was the chairman. The expression on Wallace's moonlike face was that of extreme pride, as if he'd had a hand in inventing Bethany.

Wallace hadn't even been the one to hire her. That had been his father's doing, in order to get the hospital to run more smoothly, Peter thought. At least he could thank his father for something.

An odd sensation undulated through him. It took Peter several moments before he recognized it for what it was: possessiveness.

What was that all about? he demanded silently.

This was just a casual date. No commitments involved. There was nothing for him to feel possessive about.

Yet there it was, this feeling nibbling away at him, leaving tiny grooves in its wake.

As if to prove to himself that this was absurd, that he felt no such attachment, Peter began to step back. To his surprise, Bethany tightened her hold on his arm, forcing him to remain where he was.

This was a new turn of events, he thought. A couple of weeks ago, she would have been relieved to have him go.

"Would you like something to eat?" He leaned forward, whispering the question in her ear.

It was only through the greatest control that Bethany managed to stifle the shiver that shimmied up and down her bare spine in response to the feel of his breath along the side of her neck.

"That would be very nice," she murmured. Any second now, her heart was going to pound right out of her chest.

He continued to linger, to draw in the subtle scent of perfume in her hair and along her skin. "Anything in particular you'd like?"

She turned to face him. "Surprise me."

Damn but he'd like to. He'd probably surprise all of them if he gave in and did what he wanted to: whisk her out of here and back to his house.

Back to his bed.

Lord, when was the last time that he'd even

thought like this? Like some knuckle-dragging Neanderthal?

Like a man who longed for a woman?

Peter inclined his head. "All right," he promised.

He really did need to start socializing more, Peter thought as he made his way over to the buffet table that ran along one wall.

The affair was being catered by a company that was doing it all at cost. It was their donation to the institution that had long treated most members of the owner's family.

Ella was standing at the far end of the table, contemplating her choices. Despite the clusters of people scattered along the perimeter doing the same thing, for all intents and purposes, Ella appeared to be alone.

Since their father's death, she'd withdrawn into herself, working at the hospital and then slipping home, spending most of her time alone. Though he would have never pushed her toward it, Peter was glad she'd decided to attend the fund-raiser.

Taking a plate, he queued up behind her. "How are you doing, kiddo?" he asked quietly.

Preoccupied, Ella seemed a little startled as she turned around to look at him. "Oh, Peter, hi." His question played itself back in her head. "I'm fine," she replied, keeping her voice light. "I had a slightly tricky procedure today, but I think I handled myself well. It turned out all right in the end. Patient's doing very well…"

"I don't mean professionally," Peter said, cutting in. He deliberately looked down into her eyes. "How are *you* doing?"

Ella's shrug was vague and, for a moment, she looked away. She knew what he was asking. Taking the protective covering from her wounds was difficult. But this was Peter, so she forced herself to do it. Because he'd asked.

"It's hard for me to believe that I'm not going to run into him somewhere in the hospital. That Dad's not going to come walking around the corner at any minute." She sighed, making choices from the buffet without really paying attention to the canapés she placed on her plate. "He was bigger than life, you know?"

A few days ago, it would have taken no effort on his part to agree with her because he'd shared that opinion. But now…now it took a bit of doing for him to keep the truth from surfacing. It took effort to nod his head and say, "Yes, I know what you mean."

Another sigh escaped her lips and she nodded, as if in response to something she'd hypothesized in her mind. "I guess it's going to take time before things are back to normal for us."

Here he couldn't flatly agree. Wouldn't be able to face himself in the mirror come morning if he didn't contradict her, because nothing was ever going to be the same again. Not for him. Not for the rest of them if he decided to share the secret.

But this was Ella and his instinctive need to protect her had him tempering his response. "I doubt," he told her slowly, "that things are going to get back to normal anytime soon."

Because the hospital staff was all speculating about the possible takeover by NHC, Ella thought he was talking about that. She knew how he felt about it without having to ask.

Ella placed her hand on his and squeezed, offering comfort. He seemed surprised. "Don't worry, Peter. Northeastern Healthcare isn't going to come and gobble us up."

It was on the tip of his tongue to say he wasn't referring to that, but then he stopped. It was better this way, better for her to think he was preoccupied about the takeover and not what he'd learned about their father. "What makes you so sure?"

She flashed what he'd always referred to as her thousand-watt smile. "Because we have the great Dr. Peter Wilder fighting our fight for us," she told him with affection, patting his cheek. "And you're not going to let anything happen to Dad's hospital."

Right now, he couldn't bring himself to think of the hospital in those terms. "The hospital belongs to all of us—and to the town."

"Right," she agreed. "And that's the way Dad saw it, but I still can't help thinking of it as his baby."

"Whether he meant to or not." The words had just slipped out.

She stared at him, confused. "Excuse me?"

Damn, he was going to have to exercise better control over himself than that, Peter silently chided. "Sorry, my mind wandered for a moment."

The light of understanding entered her eyes as Ella looked over her shoulder toward Bethany and the circle formed by some of the other board members who were attempting to engage her in conversation.

"I can't blame you," Ella said. "She is really a knockout." And then her gaze returned to her brother. She regarded him with unabashed curiosity. "Are the two of you, you know, involved?"

That was all he needed, for a rumor to get started. He didn't want that pushing them together. He was already having enough trouble standing on level ground.

"Only in keeping Walnut River General an excellent hospital," he answered. "The problem is, we have two very different opinions on how that might be accomplished."

"So I've heard." And then she smiled. "Well, if anyone can change her mind, Peter, it'll be you."

She was giving him far too much credit, he thought. "I'm not a knight in shining armor, Ella."

"Next best thing—a doctor in a brilliant white lab coat." Ella paused to kiss her big brother's cheek. "Don't ever stop being who you are, Peter. I couldn't stand it if you suddenly changed."

And how, he wondered, would Ella take the news that her beloved father had changed from an angel to a man with feet of clay? Or, at the very least, that he'd had one fall from grace and then compounded it a thousandfold by never owning up to the truth?

Again he felt the weight of his father's secret all but bending his back. At that moment, he found himself resenting his father.

"Whoops," Ella declared, looking toward a far-off corner of the room, "there's Ben Crawford. I've been trying to get a hold of him all day for a consult. Excuse me, Peter, but I've got to corner him before he gets away again." And with that, she made her way across the ballroom.

"You look pensive," Bethany said, coming up beside him. "Ella all right?" And then she added,

"You were taking your time with the food and I thought it might be easier if I came to get my own."

"Right." He handed her a plate, feeling slightly guilty that he'd forgotten all about bringing her back something to eat the way he'd promised. Talking to Ella had steered his thoughts in another direction. "Ella's doing as well as can be expected."

She picked up two stuffed mushrooms, placing them side by side on her plate. "You two seem to have a good relationship. I was watching," she confessed. "You're lucky. Both of you."

The way she said it had him reading between the lines again. "You don't have a good relationship with your sister?"

"I don't have any relationship at all," she admitted. It wasn't something she was proud of. "We competed as children. After college, we went our separate ways. It's been more than a year since we spoke."

He recalled that she'd mentioned her sister worked at a bank in England. "They don't have telephones in England?"

"Yes." She put two tiny popovers onto her plate. "And she doesn't call."

The woman was too bright to miss the obvious, he thought. But he said it anyway. "Last I checked, phone lines worked both ways. Sometimes all it takes to start the healing process is taking the first step."

It would take more than that, she thought. "You moonlight as an advice columnist?"

He laughed, then deposited a couple more canapés on her plate before taking some for himself. "All part of being a doctor."

He meant that. Not for the first time she thought to herself that Peter Wilder was really a very rare man. And, not for the first time, she felt an accompanying little flutter in the pit of her stomach as she thought it. Except that the flutter was getting bigger each time. She was going to have to watch that.

Chapter Twelve

Observing people had always been a hobby for Peter. At a very young age, he'd discovered he could tell a lot by the way people interacted with one another. For the most part, people fascinated him.

But tonight, watching the different board members cluster around Bethany—not to mention studying more than a handful of the male physicians buzzing around her like so many bees who had lost their navigational system—caused a mild irritation to rise up within him. Irritation, and—he conceded—perhaps a minor case of jealousy as well. He didn't like it. He'd always believed that jealousy was a useless, demeaning emotion.

So why did he feel like separating Bethany from her admiring throng and keeping her all to himself?

Where the hell were all these primitive feelings coming from? Moreover, where were they going to lead him? He wasn't all that certain he wanted to know.

When the orchestra began to play after dinner, Peter decided that maybe it was time to stop trying to figure out what was going on internally and just make the most of the moment.

Coming up behind her chair, Peter bent down until his lips were next to her ear and asked, "Would you care to dance?"

Bethany abruptly ended her conversation with the neurologist who had been monopolizing her for the past ten minutes and looked at Peter quizzically. She seemed surprised. "You dance?"

He inclined his head in silent assent. "That would be what my question implies, yes."

Bethany had trouble wrapping her mind around the concept. She thought of Peter as intelligent, capable, generous and kind. Fluid and graceful, however, did not enter the picture.

"Funny," she said, rising. "I never thought of you as someone who would enjoy dancing."

"How *did* you think of me?" Taking her hand, he led her to the dance floor. "Besides the obvious." When he turned to face her, he smiled, prodding her memory. "I believe you said something about my being a stick-in-the-mud?"

Bethany's smile was rueful. "I was wrong," she admitted freely. Then, as anticipation flared within her veins, she added in a quieter voice, "About a lot of things."

Taking her hand, he tucked it against his shoulder, then placed his other hand at the small of her back. His palm came in contact with her bare skin. He'd forgotten that there was no material there. Desire shot out to the foreground.

"Such as?" he prodded gently after a beat.

They were swaying to the music, their bodies all but merging. All sorts of feelings were swarming inside of her, feelings that hadn't visited before—except perhaps since he'd kissed her.

She found herself aching for a repeat performance. Aching for a great many things. Everyone around them began to fade away.

Raising her head, Bethany looked up into his eyes. "Some things are better left unsaid."

"I can appreciate boundaries," he told her indulgently.

Until just now, he'd thought that his own were

fairly well defined and in place. But now, suddenly, they felt as if they were crumbling. Holding her to him like this, feeling the heat of her body mingling with his, he could feel those barriers shattering like so much glass being struck by a stone. When she leaned her head on his shoulder, her hair brushing against his chin, he could feel everything within him tightening as heat traveled up and down his body, making him aware of every single inch of hers.

As they continued to dance, he tried not to breathe in the scent of her hair, tried not to let his mind wander down paths that would ultimately lead nowhere, but his thoughts refused to be bridled.

When the musicians stopped playing, Peter and Bethany were still dancing, their bodies moving in time to a melody all their own.

Bethany laughed, then covered her mouth to lock in the sound. It was late and all the lights of the houses that surrounded hers were off. The neighborhood was asleep.

It might be asleep, but she felt wide-awake. Wide-awake and ready to go. Anticipation pulsed all through her like a horse at the starting gate.

"We could buy two MRI machines with the money that was raised tonight," she declared.

Peter had driven her home and she was now vainly searching for her keys in a purse that should have given her no trouble because of its minute size. She still couldn't locate them.

"I had no idea there were that many well-off people in Walnut River. Walnut River," she repeated. Another infectious laugh, quieter this time, escaped. "That sounds like a quaint town that should be down the road from *Little House On The Prairie*." She looked at him to see if he agreed, then went back to swishing her fingers around the bottom of her purse, seeking to come in contact with metal.

"Henry knows a lot of people." Amusement curved his lips as he watched her rummage. The lady, he thought, had had a few too many. Uninhibited, she was adorable. "People who like to feel good about themselves because they give to good causes. By the way, that was a sizable donation you offered," he pointed out. She'd made the pledge after having her second or third glass of wine. She was new at this sort of thing, he judged. People who didn't ordinarily drink tended to be a little reckless when they did imbibe. "At the risk of being indelicate—"

Her head shot up. Was that hope in her eyes? Couldn't be.

"Yes?"

He didn't want to see her embarrassed when it came time to make good on the pledges. "Can you actually afford it?"

God, but he was proper. She'd thought he was about to say something a lot more personal, a lot more intimate, than ask about her financial state.

"Sure. I'm rich." And it had been more of a burden than a boon most of the time, she thought sadly. "Didn't you know that? Got a trust fund and everything. But it's a secret." To underscore the point, Bethany placed her forefinger to her lips, as if to seal in the sound of her words.

He wasn't quite following her and wondered if the wine was jumbling up her thoughts. "Your trust fund's a secret?"

Still searching through her purse, she nodded. "Don't want anyone to know," Bethany said, then sighed. "People don't believe you're serious about your work if they know you're well-off. They think you're just slumming, amusing yourself," she announced, saying it as if it was the latest cause that needed to be taken up. And then her eyes brightened. "Ah, here it is."

Triumphantly, she pulled the key ring from her purse and held it up.

Getting said key into the lock proved to be yet

another challenge. Bethany missed the opening twice, hitting the door instead. On her third attempt, she dropped the key ring altogether.

She looked down at the keys as if they'd escaped. "Oops."

Peter bent down and retrieved her key chain. Rather than hand it to her, he decided it would be simpler if he just unlocked her door, so he did. Turning the knob, he opened the door, pushing it so that she could walk in first.

He followed her into the house, then placed the key on the small table next to the door. She swayed a little as she turned around to face him. He caught her by the shoulders to steady her. "I think you had a little too much wine."

Unfazed, she looked up at him and said, "I did."

She made it sound as if she'd done it on purpose. He couldn't fathom her reasoning. "Why?"

She took a heartening breath before answering. "Because if I hadn't, I wouldn't be able to do this."

"This" turned out to be wrapping her arms around his neck and sealing both her lips and her body to his as if her very life depended on it.

Caught off guard, Peter's initial reaction was to tighten his arms around Bethany's waist, kissing her back with as much fervor as she was exuding.

An urgency traveled through his body, making

demands he knew he couldn't, in all good conscience, follow through on.

So after allowing himself a heady, breathless moment, he summoned a surge of strength—not exactly as easily as he would have liked—and placed his hands on the inviting swell of her hips. Rather than give in and mold her to him the way he really wanted to, Peter gently pushed her back, away from him.

Bethany blinked, dazed, surprised and bewildered. Why had he stopped? "What's wrong?"

The innocent question squeezed his heart. "Nothing." He tried to make her understand his reason for backing away, wishing that either she was clearheaded or he had no conscience. But neither was true. "Bethany, you're tipsy."

Her smile was quick, sinking him like a stone. "We've already established that." But as she tried to drape her arms around his neck again, he stopped her. His hands on hers, he lightly disengaged her hold. "What?" she cried. Didn't he want her?

Peter shook his head. This nobility was killing him. "I can't take advantage of you like this."

"You're not taking advantage," she pointed out, frustrated. "You're just standing still. I'm the one taking advantage." Standing on her toes, she laced her fingers together behind his head.

"So stop giving me an argument and let me do it, damn it."

He laughed. He'd always sensed she was aggressive, but not in this vein. It would take so little to give in, to stop trying to talk her out of it and just enjoy what was happening. It had been a long time since he'd been with a woman and she was the first one who had aroused him in eons. It felt as if there was lighting in his veins.

"Bethany," he protested, knowing he had to protect her from herself, "this isn't you."

"Well, it should be," she insisted, pouting so adorably he was sorely tempted to nibble on the lower lip she stuck out. "The sober Bethany is repressed. She's afraid to feel anything because once she opens up those doors, she knows she can also feel pain. Feel the hurt when others talk about her." She lowered her eyes and he thought he saw tears shimmering in them. "Feel inadequate because she's always falling short."

She got to him. The sad look in her eyes, the heartwrenching downward twist of her mouth, it all got to him. Slipping one arm around her shoulders, Peter lightly ran the back of his hand along her cheek, her mouth.

"There's nothing for you to feel inadequate about, Bethany," he told her softly.

"Then why won't you kiss me?" she cried. "Don't you want to?"

So badly that it hurts. "You have no idea how much I want to."

"Then why won't you do it?"

He could feel her breath along his skin, could feel himself capitulating even as he struggled to hold on to his control.

"Because if I kiss you, it won't stop there." He moved a soft curl back from her forehead. "And I don't want you waking up tomorrow morning, regretting what you did."

"I won't," she insisted.

He almost believed her. Almost. He'd never known what temptation meant until this very moment. "You have no way of knowing that. You're not in any position to make that kind of decision."

She shook her head, feathering her fingers through his hair. Shaking up his soul. "You sound like me. Weighing, measuring, debating and, ultimately, doing nothing." She turned up her face to his, imploring him to not turn away from her. "I don't want to be that way anymore. I want to ring the bell, reach for the stars." She took a breath and said it. "I want you to make love with me."

Did she have any idea what she was doing to him? "Bethany…"

A smile moved the corners of her mouth. "Unless, of course, you're some kind of alien and this is going to lead to your secret identity being uncovered."

Where did she get this kind of stuff? Serious one second, adorably silly the next? He was losing ground and he couldn't hold out much longer, noble thoughts or no noble thoughts. "I'm not an alien."

She nodded her head a bit too hard. "Good, because I wouldn't have been up for that."

"You're not up for this, either." He was going to have to carry her up the stairs, he thought. She just wasn't steady on her feet. "Go on to bed, Bethany. You'll thank me in the morning."

Rather than turn toward the staircase, Bethany latched onto his lapels and yanked, drawing him down closer to her level.

"Only if you're in the bed with me," she breathed. And then, before he had the opportunity to say anything else, to turn her down again, Bethany raised her mouth to his.

She caught his lower lip between her teeth and ran her tongue along it. When she heard the low moan escape, she knew she'd won.

Peter knew he damn well should have been stronger than this. He wasn't one of those men who went from conquest to conquest, thinking of sex as the greatest indoor sport ever invented. He *had* no love life to speak of and, other than an occasional moment of loneliness, he was fine with the path he'd chosen.

But this was different. *She* was different and, try as he might to resist her, he couldn't help himself.

There'd been electricity humming between them, possibly from the first moment they'd stood on opposite sides of the takeover. He liked the way her eyes flashed when she talked and the way every fiber of her being seemed to be brought into the argument, even if he ultimately did disagree with her.

Her passion stirred him then and it was certainly doing a number on him now. Any reserve he thought he had went completely out the proverbial window.

Especially when he felt her hands tugging his jacket off his arms, her fingers fumbling with the buttons on his shirt.

In comparison to her, he was wearing much too much in the way of clothing.

Still kissing her, he began helping Bethany remove the various cloth barriers that kept her soft, tempting flesh from his. Shucking out of his trousers, flinging off his shirt and the cummerbund that made his attire so formal.

His body thrilled to her touch, to the feel of her fingers against his skin. It was with great self control that he refrained from working her free of the shimmering gown until the very end.

It was the prize at the end of the rainbow.

She had no idea where this frenzy was coming from. It was as if something inside of her, something that had been waiting patiently and quietly to be set free had just taken over.

When he pressed his lips to the hollow of her throat, she moaned, her knees all but buckling. The next moment, she felt the shadow-thin straps of her gown being coaxed in unison from her shoulders. Within a heartbeat, the gown had left her breasts, sinking seductively to her waist. Instead of material, his hands covered her, igniting a fire within.

Bethany kissed him over and over again, unable to get enough, afraid to stop because she was afraid that she might disintegrate into a million little pieces if she did.

Her breath seemed to back up in her lungs as Peter slid the gown from her hips, leaving her standing only in the whisper of a thong she'd bought this afternoon, a last-minute purchase to go with her gown.

Bethany felt the urgency of his body as it hardened against hers. And then suddenly she was airborne. Peter lifted her into his arms and brought her over to the sofa, carrying her as if she were some precious treasure he'd been entrusted with.

His lips whispered along her body, warming her, generating huge waves of desire, leaving her begging for more.

Over and over again he kissed her, with feeling, with restraint, with fervor, all the while continuing to melt her.

When his mouth just barely grazed the skin along her belly, Bethany felt everything within her quickening. Felt desire take her prisoner, demanding things she'd never experienced before.

He made her head spin, her blood rush in her veins and her breath all but evaporate. She twisted and turned beneath his hands as they caressed and explored, beneath his warm mouth as he drew the woman she wanted to be to the surface.

His tongue teased, aroused and nearly drove her over the edge.

It was agony. It was ecstasy. And she desperately wanted more, wanted to be his in every conceivable way possible.

Never in her wildest dreams had she thought it could ever, *ever*, be this wonderful, being with a man. Making love with a man.

Bethany was arching against him, tearing the last shreds of restraint out of his fingers. He'd wanted her from the moment she'd kissed him. It had been only through the greatest effort that he held back, determined to pleasure her, to make as sure as he was able that she wouldn't regret this in a few hours.

Working his way up along her slender body, he paused for a moment as he pivoted above her, just looking at her face. He had been so certain that he'd never feel the kind of desire that would bring him to this point, would never want a woman this much again, and yet, here he was, a smoldering cauldron of emotions and feelings.

Bringing his mouth down to hers, Peter moved her legs apart with his knee and thrust his hips forward, trying to move slowly.

Bethany locked her arms around his neck and pulled him closer, and Peter was helpless to resist. Desire flamed, stronger than ever. He drove himself into her, taking what she offered so urgently.

Chapter Thirteen

Bethany had never felt such peace, never been quite as happy, as she was during those precious moments in Peter's arms.

The heavy breathing slowed and became regular, both his and hers. She was aware of Peter shifting his weight, moving off her until he lay beside her. Aware, too, of the silence that was becoming all-pervasive and almost deafening.

She could only interpret it one way. She felt sadness elbowing its way in.

She had to ask.

"Disappointed?"

As she uttered the word, Bethany struggled to steel herself for what she felt was the inevitable answer. Refusing to look his way, to see the answer, or worse, pity, in his face, in his eyes, she stared at the ceiling instead.

Her question seemed to come out of nowhere and it caught him off guard. He took a minute to think about his answer.

"With myself? Yes. With you?" he guessed when she didn't say anything. He turned to look at her quizzically. How could she possibly even think that? "How could I be?"

She ran her tongue along her lips. They felt as dry as dust, not to mention that her throat felt as if it was constricting.

She didn't believe him.

All her inadequacies, all the criticisms she'd endured through her adolescence, came flying back to her. How could she have been so stupid as to think he could feel something for her? That he could enjoy himself a fraction as much as she had. What had possessed her to push so hard? If there had been something between them, something to be nurtured, she'd just destroyed it.

He was looking at her, she could feel it, waiting for her to answer. Bethany forced the words out.

They scraped along her dried lips. "Because I'm not exactly all that experienced."

She heard him laugh softly to himself. Was he laughing at her? Oh God, she couldn't stand that. "There's such a thing as a born natural, Bethany," he finally said. "*You,*" he emphasized, "fall into that category."

"You don't have to be nice." Although she was grateful for it, she thought. The very tight knot in her stomach loosened just a little.

He raised himself up on his elbow to look down at her. The thought that there hadn't been a parade of men through her life pleased him. "*Nice* has nothing to do with it," he assured her. "I'm being truthful."

Her eyes slanted toward him, and then, summoning her courage, she slowly turned her face to him as well. "Then it was all right? You enjoyed yourself?" she asked in a hesitant, low whisper.

He ran his hand lightly along her cheek, wondering what sort of things were going on in her head. Could a woman as beautiful, as poised as she was really be plagued by such insecurities?

"Despite the fact that I just did a terrible thing, yes," he said, "I did. And *enjoy* is a very small, inadequate word in this case."

She took heart in his second sentence, but it

was his first one that confused her. "What terrible thing?"

"Made love with you even though you weren't thinking clearly and even though you were…" His voice trailed off for a moment, looking for a delicate enough way to say what he wanted to say without having her feel insecure all over again.

"Tipsy?" she supplied.

Peter nodded. "A man and a woman's first time together should be special."

She turned so that her body brushed up against his. Her eyes were large, luminous. They peered into him, drawing him in all over again.

"What makes you think it wasn't?" she breathed.

He touched her face. "I think there's something between us, Bethany. If I hadn't made love to you here tonight, it would have happened in the not-too-distant-future." He smiled at her, truly sorry for what he'd robbed her of. "It would have been a night for you to remember."

Placing her hands on his chest, she leaned her head on them and raised her eyes to his face. Again, she asked,"What makes you think it isn't?"

Cupping the back of her head, Peter brought her down to him and kissed her mouth.

Within moments, the lyrical dance began all over again, this time in a slower, richer tempo.

This time, Peter felt he was making love with a woman he was certain wanted exactly the same thing he did. Guilt was no longer an uninvited guest at the proceedings.

Dawn hadn't yet arrived when music suddenly splintered the stillness and Bethany's rhythmic breathing.

Beethoven's *Fifth Symphony*?

Where was *that* coming from?

Prying her eyes open, trying to make sense of the sound which was half in her dream, half in her waking consciousness, Bethany heard the music stop, replaced by a voice.

A male voice.

In her bedroom.

Her thought process imploded, collapsing completely in on itself and demanding to be restructured. Now.

Stunned surprise gave way to memories. Last night came flooding back to her in vivid color and wide-screen. With a start, she bolted upright, then belatedly grabbed the sheet that had pooled around her waist. She yanked it back up to where it could do some good.

Peter was sitting up, talking on the phone. His back was to her.

They were in her bedroom, in her bed, and it was obvious that they had both fallen asleep after they'd made love that third time.

The fog left her brain just in time for her to hear Peter say, "I'll be right there."

Holding the sheet, she drew her knees up to her chest and dragged her hand through her hair. Wishing she could drag her brain into place as easily.

She cleared her throat, doing her best to sound as if everything was normal when right now, everything was anything *but*.

"Be right where?" she echoed.

Shutting the cell phone that had awakened her, Peter placed it back on the nightstand and shifted around in order to look at her. "The hospital."

"The hospital?" she repeated as if saying what he said would somehow clear everything up for her. But it didn't. "You're going to the hospital at—" she looked at the clock on her side of the bed "—four-thirty in the morning?"

"Emergencies don't happen on schedule," he said lightly.

God, but he didn't want to leave her. She looked incredibly enticing with sleep still whispering along her eyes. His hand swept along her throat, tilting her head back a little. He allowed himself only a moment to brush his lips over hers.

This could become an intoxicating habit, he caught himself thinking.

"I was going to make you breakfast, but I'm afraid I'm going to have to give you a rain check, instead."

"You cook?" she asked in disbelief. She barely knew how not to burn water.

He got out of bed and quickly slipped on his underwear and trousers, then put on his shirt. There would be amused comments about his formal attire at the hospital, but he could handle that.

"Cook, dance, I can actually sew on a button in a pinch," he told her, "but I don't like admitting that."

He looked at her just before he began buttoning up his shirt. His fingers froze in place. The sheet was molded to her, but his imagination was vivid enough to do away with the barrier and remember her as she'd been last night. Fluid. Golden. And all his.

The shirt remained hanging open as he leaned over the bed to kiss her one last time. "And, just in case there are any doubts still lingering this morning, you were magnificent," he assured her.

Breaking away, he made it all the way to the door before he impulsively retraced his steps to the bed and swept her into his arms to kiss her one last—last time.

He sighed as he drew his head back. "You know,

this is going to make it very hard to argue in the boardroom," he surmised. "I'll keep picturing you just the way you are right now."

Bethany blushed. "I know," she whispered, agreeing with his first statement. Arguing—debating about *anything*—was the furthest thing from her mind right now. She could feel her body aching, her hunger returning. She knew it was selfish, but she didn't want him to go. "Are you sure that emergency has your name on it?"

Her very tone was coaxing him to remain. But he had to resist. He had his oath to honor. "'Fraid so. The patient's wife specifically asked for me when they brought him in."

"Oh." She'd learned that he had legions of patients, people who swore by him and didn't want to have anyone else touch them. She could understand that. If she had something wrong, she'd want him to be her doctor.

With a sigh, she gave up her claim to him. For now. "Then I guess you'd better ride to the rescue." She gathered the sheet around her again. "How long do you think it'll take?"

He shook his head. There was no way he could tell right now. It wasn't like an oil change on a car. "I don't even know what's wrong yet."

Wearing the sheet like a toga, trying not to trip

on the hem, she followed him to the doorway. "Will you come back after you're finished?"

He didn't want her curtailing her schedule and waiting, especially when he didn't know when he'd be finished. "Depends on the time."

That wasn't what she wanted to hear. But rather than retreat, she made a bid for his time. "It shouldn't." She waved her hand around vaguely. "It's Sunday, supposedly a day of rest. You can come back here whenever you're finished. To rest." A mischievous grin curved her mouth before entering her eyes. "Or whatever."

He looked at her, amused. "To rest?" There damn well wouldn't be any resting done and she knew it. She'd all but wiped him out as it was. He was going to need this emergency just to recharge.

"Or whatever," she repeated, her smile now positively wicked.

He liked the sound of that.

Peter laughed, shaking his head. He needed to be on his way, and yet he couldn't help lingering a second longer. It took all the resolve he had not to tug away the sheet she was clutching to her.

"I didn't know the real you, did I?" he speculated. There was so much more to her than he'd initially believed.

"Neither did I," she confessed. She stepped

back, allowing him to cross the threshold. To leave her. "Hurry," she urged as he turned away.

"As fast as I'm able," he promised.

And still do a good job. That part he'd left unsaid, but having come to know the man the way she did in these past few weeks, Bethany knew that was what he meant. The man probably was incapable of doing anything less than his best.

She had no idea where the sense of pride that suddenly washed over her came from. After all, the man really wasn't hers. There was no joint bond between them, nothing to suggest that his triumphs were also hers by proxy. And yet she knew that if someone said something positive about him, she'd be the one to feel the pride. Probably more than he.

With a sigh, rather than abandon the sheet and face the day, she made her way back to bed and got in. She could almost, if she tried very hard, still feel the warmth on his side of the bed.

For a second, she splayed her hand out, absorbing it. She closed her eyes, envisioning him still there. But that led her nowhere.

Holding her knees close to her, wrapping her arms around them, she stared off into the darkness, thinking of Peter.

* * *

She was dressed and all the things that had wound up scattered over the floor last night had been picked up, cleaned up and put back in their rightful places by the time Peter finally returned to her house later that day. It was just past one in the afternoon and he had been gone a full eight hours.

The moment he rang the bell, she flew to the door, opening it before the last chimes faded away.

He could probably see that she'd rushed to the door, she thought. So much for playing hard-to-get.

"I'd pretty much given up hope," she confessed as she stepped back, holding the door open wide.

She banked down a very strong urge to throw her arms around his neck and lose herself in a soul-melting kiss. No point in frightening the man off.

That was how it was done, right? If she behaved as if they belonged together, as if he was the half of her soul that had always been missing, she'd scare him off. The guy would most likely be on the first flight out of town, destination: anyplace but here.

So she went back to restraint, something that had always governed her actions up until last night.

"I had to wait for the lab results to come back," he told her. Damn, but she looked good enough to eat. "And there's only a skeleton crew on Sundays."

"People aren't supposed to be sick on a Sunday," she said lightly. "I think it's a law that's written down somewhere."

"Too bad Gerald Muffet hadn't read that particular law," he said, referring to the man who he'd been ministering to since he'd left her bed.

His tone was weary and he looked a little tired. She didn't know how to interpret that. Had he come back out of a sense of obligation, because he'd said he would? Or was he here because he really wanted to be?

She fell back on what she knew. "Did you have breakfast?" There were waffles in the freezer and a toaster on the counter. She could manage that.

When she moved like that, reaching for the toaster and bringing it closer, he could see her breasts straining against the thin white blouse she had on. He stopped being tired.

"Coffee and something out of the vending machine," he recalled vaguely, then shrugged, trying hard not to stare at her. "I don't know what."

"Sounds delicious," she said, glancing at her watch. "It's too late for brunch. Would you settle for plain old lunch?"

That wasn't the appetite that had surfaced the moment he'd begun to walk up the driveway. Certainly not the one that was ricocheting through him right now. But he didn't want her thinking of him as some rutting pig preoccupied with sex.

"Plain old lunch sounds wonderful," he assured Bethany.

She took the freshly sliced roast beef she'd dashed out to get earlier and placed it on the counter. "So what was the big emergency that couldn't be handled without dragging you out of bed?" Rolls joined the deli meat, as did a jar of mayonnaise, romaine lettuce and a green pepper.

"Man came into Walnut River General looking like death after being confined to Hilldale Memorial in the next town for almost two weeks."

She cut four slices of pepper, wrapped up the rest and returned it to the refrigerator, then sliced the rolls. "Was he a transfer?"

Sometimes a hospital would send one of their patients to Walnut River, but that was admittedly rare.

He frowned. Just thinking about it made him angry. "No, actually, they gave him a clean bill of health and sent him home, saying it was all in his head."

She deposited meat on the cut rolls and turned to look at him. "And was it?"

Peter shook his head. "Turned out to be all in his belly." Breaking off a tiny piece of the pepper, he munched on it as he watched her work. And let his mind take over. "Man had a bleeding ulcer and he'd lost approximately forty percent of his blood before he ever got to us. If his wife hadn't nagged him into coming to Walnut River General, he would have been dead by tomorrow. Probably sooner."

"I guess then in this case—" she grinned "—nagging served a purpose." Depositing a leaf of lettuce on top of the mayonnaise-slathered roast beef, she paused, playing back the facts he'd given her. "How could that other hospital have missed the fact that the man's blood supply was down by forty percent?"

He couldn't resist saying, "They were probably trying to be cost effective and skimped on the tests." Couldn't resist, because it was the truth. "Either that, or their lab tech made a mistake. It has been known to happen—far more than we'd like," he added, wishing it could be otherwise.

She put the top of the bun on top of each opened sandwich and then cut both sandwiches in half. "How did they happen to come in asking for the great Dr. Peter Wilder?" she teased.

He paused for a second, wanting to get the

order right. "His wife's sister's husband is a patient of mine."

The man has a fan base, she thought with a grin. "Six degrees of separation, huh?"

He took that literally. "More like four, but in the end, all that matters is that the guy came to Walnut River and that we found the problem. With any luck, he will probably be on his way home by Tuesday."

"That's great, Peter," she said.

He'd used the word *we* but he was the one who had spearheaded everything and they both knew it. Modest on top of good. Not to mention damn sexy. Hell of a combination, she thought.

After all these years of being alone, could she finally have gotten lucky?

Turning from the counter, she impulsively ran her hand along his chest. She could feel his heart beating a little faster in response. It spurred her on to raise herself up on her toes and kiss him.

It was meant to be just a light, passing kiss. A fond expression of affection.

But it deepened the moment contact was made. So much so that neither of them came up for air until a good two minutes later.

"So," she said, trying to sound as if every molecule in her body hadn't come apart and then resurrected itself again. "What would you like to have served with your lunch? Soup? Salad? The soup's out of a can and the salad came ready-made," she qualified in case he had any concerns that her culinary attempts might make him ill.

He didn't seem to be interested in food. "How about a side order of you?" Wrapping his arms around her again, he nibbled on her ear and sent flashes of heat dancing all through her. "Better yet," he proposed, "how about you as the main course?"

She glanced at the sandwiches on the counter. "You're not hungry?"

He didn't take his eyes off her. "Starved," he contradicted.

Her mouth began to curve as anticipation took hold. "But not for food," she guessed.

He didn't say anything at first. Instead, he grinned in response and then lifted her into his arms the way he had last night. He was picking up where he'd left off this morning.

"Not for food," he confirmed just before he lowered his mouth to hers.

Chapter Fourteen

Peter's anger toward his father was slowly dissipating. In its place was empathy. It was hard to fathom how the man, as chief of staff *and* chairman of the board, not to mention being a practicing physician, ever found even five seconds to rub together. It was a wonder the man had come home at all.

Granted, Peter himself wasn't the chairman, only a member, but even that took a chunk out of his time. And he was the acting chief of staff until a permanent one could be found. Keeping everyone happy and everything running smoothly was *really* time-consuming. He was beginning to see why, in the midst of turmoil, his father might have turned to a sympathetic ear, a kindly attitude and, in a moment of weakness, allowed one thing to lead to another.

He was walking the proverbial mile in his father's shoes and beginning to think a little differently than he had before.

Right now, those shoes, after having been confined to the E.R. for the past hour, acting as a consultant for one of the other doctors, were headed in Bethany's direction. And he couldn't suppress the eagerness he was experiencing—nor did he really want to try. This was a new feeling and he wanted to savor it, to enjoy it and make it last.

He couldn't help wondering if it had been like this for his father when he'd begun seeing Anna's mother. The excitement, the anticipation that it brought into an otherwise overburdened life. He was beginning to understand his father's action a lot better. Understand and forgive.

In addition, whenever he'd had the opportunity this past month, he'd begun to sort through his father's legal papers. There was a lot to be learned about the man there, too. All good. Still, he hadn't made up his mind what to do about the letter that had started it all. The longer he waited, the harder it would be…

He didn't want to think about that, not right now.

Preoccupied, he didn't even see Henry Weisfield until he was almost on top of the hospital administrator. Henry said his name twice before he even heard the man.

"Sorry," he apologized. "I've got a few things on my mind."

The man cocked his head, studying Peter as if he hadn't seen him before. "Is it my imagination, or is there this extra—" he gesticulated in the air, searching for the right word "—spring in young Dr. Wilder's step?"

Peter avoided Harry's inquisitive gray eyes. "I don't know what you mean." He deliberately kept his voice as vague as possible. He also slowed his pace to practically nil. He had no intention of leading Henry to his ultimate destination.

Henry laughed to himself. "Peter, you're a wonderful doctor, a great humanitarian. If I had a ruptured appendix or had only one person to choose to be stranded with on a desert island, it would be you because you always come through." He allowed the compliments to sink in before he continued. "But with all your attributes, you do have one failing."

Henry did like to build up to things and, ordinarily, Peter didn't mind. But right now, he was in a hurry. "And that is?" Peter coaxed.

"You're a lousy actor. I would think that a man with all your burdens—" and he proceeded to enumerate them "—temporary acting chief of staff, newly appointed member to the board of directors, plus the recent passing of your father, a man you admired and respected, not to mention loved, *and* the prospect of the hospital changing hands and being absorbed into the NHC stable—"

He was about to urge Henry on to his point, but the last phrase waved red flags in front of him, the way it always did. "Not going to happen," Peter told him with feeling.

"Don't be too sure," Henry commented before finally getting back on track and to his original point. "I would think that a man with all that weighing so heavily on his shoulders wouldn't look as if he's about to break into song, or at least start whistling and clicking up his heels at any moment."

Peter tried to summon a scowl, but he couldn't. He was feeling too good. Way too good. And Bethany was the reason.

"I've been reading people longer than you've been breathing," Henry was saying. "What's changed in your life?"

There was no denying it. Henry's assessment was correct. Everything the man had just mentioned should, by all rights, make him feel as if he had the weight of the world on his shoulders. Heaven knows he was still wrestling with his conscience about whether or not to shake up Anna's world by giving her their father's letter; still coming to grips with the discovery that his father had harbored dark secrets and wasn't the plain, open, selfless man everyone believed him to be. Still struggling with how to make the board reject the takeover proposition, although that was showing promise, especially since he felt he'd opened Bethany's eyes. But somehow, everything had slipped into the shadows. Eclipsed by the feeling that was generated by being with Bethany. By sharing his nights, his bed with her these past few days.

"Only one thing I know of that can do that to a man," Henry concluded. The older man's eyes narrowed beneath his bushy eyebrows. He pushed his rimless glasses up his nose and peered more closely at him, as if he were studying a slide through a powerful microscope. "Peter," he asked suddenly, his voice lowered in utter surprise, "are you seeing someone?"

Peter smiled to himself. Seeing someone. It was a very old-fashioned term, in keeping with what his life had been like up until now. But Lord knows that despite the fact that the feelings being with

Bethany created inside of him were as old as time, he felt reborn. Not unlike a gangly adolescent on the uplifting path of his first love.

Love?

There, he'd said it. Or at least finally allowed himself to think it. And doing that shook him down to his very core. But there it was.

Love.

That's what he felt for the woman who had brought light into his darkening life. Something he never thought he'd experience again. And it made all the difference in the world to him, filled him with an optimism that he could barely contain.

Still, his common sense remained intact and that meant, at least for now, Henry wasn't going to be privy to any of this.

So he winked and smiled and said, "A gentleman never tells, Henry."

Henry cleared his throat and fixed him with a look that might have pinned a younger, less confident man to the wall.

"On the contrary. A gentleman can *always* tell Henry." When nothing was forthcoming, Henry nudged him with his elbow. "I'd all but given up on you, you know. Everyone thinks you're married to this place." The second he said it, his small eyes widened as a realization hit him. "Is it someone here?" And then he laughed at himself. "What am I saying—of course it has to be someone here. You never go anywhere else."

Peter knew exactly what the man was trying to do and he shook his head. "Talk all you want, Henry. We're not adolescent boys, hanging around a gym locker, swapping stories."

"That we are not," Henry agreed, but not for the reasons that Peter had. Both men stepped to the side, out of the way, as several nurses walked by then, going toward the elevators. "Ever since my Mildred passed on, I haven't had a story to swap.

"So who is it?" Henry asked, not about to give up. "Not Simone," he concluded, mentioning the day-shift head nurse in the E.R. "She's got eyes for that paramedic. What's-his-name, the one who has all that really dark hair."

It amazed Peter that Henry, with all his duties and responsibilities, could still take in these extraneous details. He mentioned the first paramedic that came to mind. "Mike O'Rourke?"

Henry pointed his index finger at him, as if he'd won some sort of prize by guessing correctly. "That's the one."

Peter laughed, shaking his head. "What are you, Henry, the hospital gossip?"

Henry shrugged his thin shoulders beneath his

jacket. "I just pay attention to what goes on around me."

"Right." Peter knew better. "Pay attention and pass it on. And you actually expect me to tell you my secrets?"

Henry heard what he wanted to hear. "Aha, so there is someone. And, by the way," he corrected with a small, insulted sniff, "I'd rather think of myself as the relayer of interdepartmental news, not a gossip." He uttered the label disdainfully.

It was Peter's turn to shrug. He tried not to be too obvious as he glanced at his watch.

Henry was undaunted, but, began to head for the elevators. "I'll find out soon enough, you know."

Peter was relieved they were parting company. "There's nothing to find out."

"Like I said," Henry called after him, "you're a lousy actor."

Peter merely smiled to himself as he kept walking down the corridor. That was all he had to do, admit to Henry that he was "seeing" Bethany Holloway. Henry would have the news telegraphed throughout the hospital in record time. Neither he nor Bethany needed that kind of attention.

This thing, whatever "it" was, between the two of them was still new, still fresh, still without a name to define it and he was afraid that if he examined it too closely, shed too much light on it, it would fall to pieces, unable to sustain itself beneath the attention. It needed time to root, to take hold.

You called it love.

That he had. Maybe it was, maybe it wasn't. All he knew was that he hadn't felt this happy, this content, in years. His work was his life and he was completely dedicated to it, but there was no denying that even when it took up every waking minute of his day, there was still an emptiness inside him that his work couldn't fill.

Not the way being with Bethany could.

It was lunchtime and he was hurrying to one of the small enclosures that was laughingly referred to as an office. Currently, it was Bethany's office. He was going to surprise her by stopping in to see if she wanted to have lunch with him.

He knew it would catch her off guard because ordinarily, she was the one who swung by his office and extended the offer. She'd been doing it for the last few days. Days in which they saw each other every day, sometimes for just a few minutes, sometimes for longer.

And sometimes, especially lately, all through the night.

He was grateful for this, grateful for the lightness he felt inside because of it. Otherwise, he seriously doubted he would be equal to everything else that was going on.

Like most people, he could handle one or two problems, or even three. But somehow, of late, he felt as if everything was conspiring to band together and crush him. He *needed* what was happening between him and Bethany.

Her door was open. He might have thought that unusual but the heating was on the blink again and doors were open all along the floor in a desperate attempt to share warmth.

He had his own ideas about how to share warmth, he thought, smiling to himself.

About to knock despite the open door, Peter heard her voice. She was talking to someone. Because there were no audible responses and she still carried on a conversation, he assumed she was on the phone. Not wanting to interrupt her, he stood there and waited until she was finished.

Looking back later, he would have been better off if he'd gone ahead and knocked rather than waited outside her door—and listened against his will.

"No, no, don't worry," she assured whoever she was talking to on the other end of the line. "I've got the man practically eating out of the palm of my hand."

Peter straightened, alert now. He didn't believe in eavesdropping, but she was talking about him, he was certain of it. What other man could she be referring to? Her tone unnerved him. Was she just amusing herself at his expense?

"Right," she was saying. "Yes, yes, when the time comes, he'll see things my way. I'm good at this kind of thing, don't worry," she repeated. "I can persuade him one way or another."

Peter felt something inside his chest twist and freeze.

So that was it. That was why a beautiful woman was making all the first moves. She was playing him. Manipulating him so that "when the time comes" in her words, he'd be so taken with her, so completely mesmerized and captivated by her, he'd vote her way for the takeover instead of following his beliefs.

Damn, what was the matter with him? Hadn't his time with Lisa taught him anything? He should have realized that a woman as upscale and classy as Bethany Holloway wouldn't even notice someone like him unless there was a specific reason.

How could he have been so stupid? So willing to believe she felt things for him? No woman looked at him romantically.

He should have realized that Bethany wouldn't,

either. What he'd mistaken for electricity between them was only the static variety, brought on by dry air, not full hearts.

What Bethany hadn't been able to do using logic, she was hoping to accomplish using her body.

Angry, he felt like confronting her, calling her out on this. But he wasn't the kind to shout, to air his feelings or grievances in any place remotely public.

Instead, he turned on his heel and walked away.

He was nearly at the end of the corridor, about to make a turn around the corner when he heard his name being called.

"Peter!"

Bethany had obviously emerged from her office, more than likely to come over to his. Although he stopped, he made no effort to turn around. He didn't trust himself to be civil quite yet. His anger wasn't fully harnessed yet.

He dug his nails into his palms, forming fists, his back to her. "Yes?"

"I was just coming to see you. Are you up for lunch?" she asked, her voice bright and cheery. The very same voice that had moments ago bragged about holding him in the palm of her hand.

He heard her closing her door, undoubtedly confident of what his answer was going to be. But he couldn't look at her right now. Couldn't sit across from her in the cafeteria or the small coffee shop down the block and pretend that nothing was wrong. Pretend that she hadn't just ripped his heart out of his chest. Within three minutes of their being together, there was no way she wouldn't figure out that he'd overheard her.

As Henry had pointed out, he was a lousy actor.

"No, I'm afraid not," he answered, his voice devoid of any emotion. "I'm busy." And with that, he picked up his pace and walked away as fast as he could without breaking into a run.

Bethany stood there, stunned as she watched his back disappear down the hall.

That wasn't like Peter. Even when he was swamped, he was polite and lately, he'd been making time for her even when he was drowning in work. He'd never just brushed her off, not even that first time in the cafeteria when she'd tried to argue him around to her point of view.

She was making too much of it, she told herself. The man wasn't a superman, he couldn't be upbeat *all* the time. Besides, he was still terribly concerned about NHC's push for a takeover. That, added to Peter's already full-to-the-bursting-point day, undoubtedly put a strain on his good humor.

Still, she couldn't help feeling he'd just abandoned her.

A small voice, sounding a great deal like her mother, whispered, *Told you it was too good to last.*

Clenching her fists at her sides, she blocked out the voice, blocked out what it was proposing. Because she couldn't bear to think about it.

With a sigh, Bethany turned back and unlocked her office door. She wasn't hungry anymore. Her appetite had evaporated.

He wasn't taking her calls.

It was two days later and every time she called Peter's office, his nurse said he was with a patient and too busy to come to the phone. The woman mechanically assured her he would call her back later.

But he never did.

Just as he wouldn't answer his cell phone whenever she called. Bethany damned call waiting for identifying her number to him, foiling any possibility of actually getting him to pick up and talk to her.

Why was he avoiding her?

Something had definitely changed and she didn't know why or what. She tried her best to sit tight, hoping that whatever it was would pass, that it had nothing to do with her but just the workload he was staggering beneath.

But the sinking feeling in her stomach as she

watched Peter walk in for the board meeting at the end of the week told her she was wrong on both counts.

It had everything to do with her. Whatever "it" was.

When he crossed the threshold, the last to arrive, Peter didn't look her way. Instead of sitting beside her as he had done the other meetings, he chose one of the other two empty chairs, sitting down in the one that was farthest away from her.

That stung. Part of her wanted to ignore Peter, to show him that if he wanted to withdraw from her, that was fine with her. She didn't need him.

But the other half told her that she did. That since she'd been with him, she'd felt more self-confident, more alive. Happier. Being with Peter had made her feel like a complete woman.

A woman who, for some mysterious, whimsical reason, he'd decided to fling aside, ignore and be downright rude to.

Well, she damn well wasn't going to stand for it.

Bethany could feel herself fidgeting inside as Larry Simpson droned on, reading the minutes of the last meeting, a meeting that had been as exciting as watching paint dry the first time around. Listening to it rehashed for a second time was excruciatingly boring. Especially when all she wanted was for the meeting to be over so that she could confront Peter in person since she'd been unable to do it these past few days. Wherever she was, he was always somewhere else.

It was almost as if he were intentionally playing a game of hide-and-seek with her. A game she was in the process of losing.

She didn't like to lose. She liked feeling empty even less.

The meeting dragged on. Neither she, nor Peter she noted, had any of the food that Wallace had brought in. It was the chairman's way of trying to make up for the fact that the board meeting was taking place during their regular lunch hour.

Peter looked ready to flee at any second, she could tell by his body language. Whatever was being discussed wasn't even registering—not with her and not, she suspected, with him. She vaguely heard that Wallace said something about a J.D. Sumner arriving later today. Sumner, she gathered, was from NHC.

She saw the veins in Peter's neck stand out, but he said nothing.

And then Wallace dropped a bombshell. "And there might have to be an investigation to verify if these allegations of insurance fraud are indeed true."

"Insurance fraud?" Bethany echoed, startled.

Wallace looked a little perturbed, but whether it was with her for speaking out of turn or with the situation in general she had no way of knowing.

"Yes." Anger creased Wallace's normally cheerful face. "Apparently two or more of our doctors are suspected of some sort of wrongdoing. Nothing is clear yet, but this is obviously muddying the waters."

Peter scowled. She could almost hear the rumble of thunder as his eyes darkened.

"It's a set-up," he replied in a low, hard voice. All eyes turned in his direction. "Engineered by NHC to get Walnut River to capitulate. They assume that we'd be eager to get out from under this about-to-break scandal and accept any offer they make." And Bethany saw him turn to look at her for the first time that morning. He aimed the words directly at her. "They couldn't be more wrong."

Chapter Fifteen

The second the meeting was over, Peter was up and out the door. Bethany followed suit, bolting from her chair and taking off after him.

"Bethany, a word," Wallace called to her.

"I'll be right back, Wallace," she promised as she hurried out the door. She had no intention of losing this opportunity to talk to Peter. If he was going to ostracize her for something, she was damn well going to find out what it was.

Drawing in her breath, she fell into step beside him, lengthening her stride considerably to stay abreast. She'd never realized precisely how long his legs were until this moment. "I have to talk to you."

He didn't bother sparing her a look. There was still a soft spot in his heart for her and he wasn't about to allow that to undermine his resolve. "Sorry, but I'm afraid I'm busy."

God, but he made her angry. "You've been *busy* a lot lately," she said sarcastically.

"Well, you know how it goes. Running an anti-quated hospital like this takes up a good deal of time. For those of us living in the Dark Ages, it requires more effort than most expect."

His response, not to mention his somewhere-below-freezing tone, left her stunned and tempo-rarily speechless. She almost stopped trying to keep up.

Maybe this was the real man and the other had been a fleeting illusion, someone who really didn't exist. Maybe instead of the saint that everyone claimed Peter Wilder to be, he was actually just a colossal, boorish, self-centered jerk.

But he'd been a kind and gentle lover, she reminded herself. Could a man who was thought-ful in bed *be* that much of a jerk out of it?

No, damn it, Bethany thought. She was tired of rationalizing, tired of trying to pretend this didn't hurt like hell and that all Peter needed was a little space so things would get back to where they'd been a few weeks ago.

No more making up excuses for him. She wanted answers and she wanted them *now*.

Determined, Bethany picked up her pace and hurried after him again.

She managed to catch up to Peter just as he got on the elevator—bound for the next saints convention for all she knew. She stuck her hand in between the shutting steel doors. They came in contact with her fingers, then bounced back.

Getting on, she glared at him. "I said I needed to talk to you."

If he was surprised by her relentless determination, he gave no indication. What he did, staring straight forward, was repeat his response. "And I said that I was busy."

"I don't care," she snapped back. That finally surprised him, she noted with triumph. "Your ears are free for the next few seconds."

Peter looked at her, his eyes cutting her off at the knees. "You're going to need a lot more than just a few seconds," he informed her.

Finally, he was opening up. It was about time. "Then there *is* something wrong."

He faced the doors again, infuriating her. "There's a great deal wrong."

The doors opened on the third floor and three people got on. Their presence abruptly cut the conversation short.

Bethany pressed her lips together. There was no point in dragging out their confrontation in front of strangers, although, if she was forced to, she was willing to go that route. The bottom line was if Peter was going to treat her as if she'd suddenly developed leprosy, she wanted to know why.

When the doors opened on the first floor, Peter got out. Bethany was beside him like a shot, muttering apologies as she elbowed her way past the other occupants on the elevator who were obviously bound for the basement and the cafeteria.

"Would you care to elaborate on that?" she demanded, picking up the thread of the conversation that had been dropped. She kept her voice as low as she could, given the amount of emotion that was throbbing in it. For most of her life, she'd lived with one form of personal rejection or another. Her parents, the students at school, even her sister. Being with Peter, making love with him physically *and* mentally, had turned all that around for her. She was damned if she was going to lose that without knowing why.

She shadowed him step for step until they came to the entrance to the emergency room.

Stopping just before the inner doors that led to the treatment area, Peter looked at her coldly and answered her request with a single word. It drove a spear right through her heart. "No."

And with that, he walked through the swinging double doors, leaving her standing, dumbfound and crushed, in the hallway.

Tears, created out of equal parts anger and hurt, sprang to her eyes. Drawing in a deep breath, struggling for control, she valiantly tried to suppress them, to make them go back. She was too old to hurt like this. Too old to stagger beneath the oppressive weight of rejection.

She'd endured that all through elementary school, through high school. She was supposed to have left it behind her, be her own person by now, content to live in semi-isolation because she'd convinced herself she didn't need anyone to complete her. And then he'd come into her life, lighting up the very sky, and she'd realized just how wrong she was.

Was that all she was going to have? All that she was entitled to? A few weeks of happiness and now she had to go back to her cave?

Well, she didn't want to. At the very least, she

didn't want to without first finding out what had gone wrong.

Did it matter? she asked herself, turning away from the E.R. doors. It was clearly over. This had been merely a fling, something women her age had all the time. A fling. Brief and exciting. To be enjoyed and then forgotten about. If she'd had more of them, if she'd lived like a normal woman, this wouldn't have been such a big deal for her. It would have been merely business as usual.

No, damn it, she thought angrily, it *hadn't* been simply a fling, not for her. And not, from everything she'd gathered about the man, for Peter.

There was something between them, something strong. He'd made her into a different person, maybe a better person or maybe her real self, she didn't know. All she knew was that she didn't want that person to go away. She didn't want *him* to go away.

Bethany turned back and burst through the E.R.'s swinging doors, Bethany stopped the first nurse she saw. "Where's Dr. Wilder?"

"Ella?" the woman asked.

She'd forgotten there were two of them. "No, Peter. The chief of staff," she added for good measure.

The vague look on the woman's heart-shaped

face didn't inspire confidence. "In his office, probably. He's not on today."

So he'd walked into the E.R. just to get away from her. For a second, her stomach sank. But then she rallied. She was going to get to the bottom of this if it killed her.

Muttering a thank-you, she turned on her heel and hurried back to the tower elevators.

You're not going to get away from me that easily, Peter Wilder, she vowed.

J.D. Sumner turned up his collar as he stepped outside Walnut River General's front entrance. The wind whipped around him, chilling him to the bone as it brought fresh snow flurries with it. It was late. The moon was hiding behind one of the clouds.

It was too dark for him. He was accustomed to the ever-present glow of the city, 24/7.

He'd put in what he felt was a full day, trying to get on the good side of the hospital staff. More than a full day, he thought wearily. It had been a tough, uphill battle.

He had his work cut out for him, that was for sure.

While the members of the board had all been basically polite, he could feel the waves of hostility just beneath the surface. Especially from Wilder, the son of the founder. He supposed the man felt he had a personal stake in all this and J.D. was, after all, he thought with an ironic smile, the enemy.

While he was used to that, he had to admit there were times, like now, when it was wearing. He preferred to think of himself as a representative of the future, not the enemy. It was the only way he could continue doing what he did. He was the one the conglomerate sent out to smooth the way for NHC's inevitable takeover.

He wished there was no resistance. Didn't these people realize this was progress? The way things were going to be from now on, not just here but everywhere? Big was in, little was out. No more mom-and-pop shops, be they grocery stores, video shops or hospitals. Corporations were going to run everything and, in the long run, that was a good thing.

Or so he told himself.

The wind continued blowing, stirring up gusts, swirling the snow. He turned his face to the side as he continued walking.

And that was when it happened.

One moment he was walking, albeit taking baby steps, toward his partially buried car, the next moment his feet were no longer on the ground. They were airborne and so, for a split second, was he.

Trying to break his fall with his gloved hands,

J.D. came down hard when he landed. The jarring sensation traveled all the way up, rattling his teeth, hurting the top of his head. Pain shot through one of his legs. The one twisted beneath his body.

It wasn't the kind of pain that bruising brought. It was definitely sharper, more excruciating.

Something had twisted unnaturally as his full weight came down on it, despite his attempts to distribute it. Was his leg broken?

More pain shot through him as he tried, unsuccessfully, to get up.

He called for help. The wind whipped the sound of his voice away, sending it toward the near-empty lot.

God, but he hated this insignificant little town.

The door to Peter's outer office was locked. Determined, Bethany circled around to the side door, which led directly to his small, inner office. When she tried to turn the doorknob, she was rather surprised that it gave. Unlike the one in the hallway, this door was unlocked.

Did that mean he was expecting her, or just that he was being absentminded?

No, she reminded herself, she wasn't going to overanalyze this. Whenever she did that, she only got in her own way.

With a quick knock, she swung the door open. Peter was at his desk, making notes in a file and cross-referencing them onto the computer. Surprised to see her, he recovered nicely.

Bethany pushed the door shut behind her. "You weren't on duty in the E.R." It was an accusation, not a statement.

He shrugged and went back to looking at the top file. "Slipped my mind. I thought I was."

Crossing to his desk, she moved the file, silently demanding his undivided attention. "Lying doesn't become you."

She couldn't read the expression in his eyes when he looked up. "I could say the same thing about you—except that it does. You looked beautiful, lying."

His words completely floored her. She had no idea what he was talking about. "When did I lie?"

The laugh was short and without a drop of humor. "When didn't you?"

She wanted a clear, direct answer. "I'm not in the mood for riddles."

He leaned back in his chair, mainly to put distance between them. She was too close and he could feel himself responding despite his anger at being duped. "And I'm not in the mood for any of your elaborate charades. I guess that makes us even."

"No," she contradicted heatedly, "because only one of us knows what you're talking about and it sure as hell isn't me."

He looked away, toward the window. It killed him to do so when, despite everything, all he wanted was to take her in his arms and kiss her. What kind of a fool did that make him?

Bethany deliberately moved so that she was in front of him again, giving him no choice but to look at her. She had a panicky certainty, growing disproportionately by the moment, that if she let this misunderstanding between them mushroom, she was going to lose the best chance she'd ever had at happiness.

She meant to do or say whatever it took to unscramble this mess. "Look, I'm new at this, at trying to correct whatever it is I did, or you think I did. Help me out here," she said, "because right now, I'm in the dark."

He almost believed her, almost believed that she meant what she said. But then, she was good. She'd bragged as much to whoever she'd been talking to the day he overheard her. "There's no point."

"There is *every* point," she insisted desperately. "You can't make me fall in love with you and then just walk off into the sunset like some John Wayne wannabe. Not without some kind of explanation."

She was pleading now and she knew it. But she was in too deep to care about her pride.

Peter looked at her, completely stunned. "You're in love with me?"

"Yes," she snapped. She could feel tears forming again and it made her angry to be that helpless in the face of her emotions. This wasn't fair. She didn't want to cry in front of him. She was risking everything and he was just sitting there, unaffected, damn him. "And it's all your fault."

He shook his head. He'd never wanted to believe anyone so much in his life. But he'd heard what he heard, the unguarded truth, said when she thought no one was around to hear her.

"Are you that desperate to get me to vote for the takeover?" he asked.

For a second, she was speechless and dumbfounded. This was coming out of nowhere. "What in heaven's name are you talking about?"

He sighed. She was good, denying everything until the very end. "Don't play dumb, Bethany. It's not like you."

She squared her shoulders, the walking wounded refusing to succumb to her injuries and fall. "I've always been proud of my intelligence. It's all I had and I never thought I would *ever* say this, but I am not playing dumb. I *am* dumb, ignorant of whatever it is I was supposed to have done that set you off this way."

He was tired of going around in circles. If she wouldn't give him the courtesy of owning up to it, he was going to have to tell her. "I heard you."

"Probably the whole fourth floor has heard me," she acknowledged, lowering her voice. "I'm not accustomed to yelling."

The woman was incredible. She was going to go down fighting. If it wasn't that she'd skewered his heart, he could almost admire her grit. "No, I mean I heard you when you were on the phone on Monday."

He was ringing no bells. She shook her head, not following him.

It almost physically hurt to say the words. "You were telling whoever you were talking to that you had me in the palm of your hand. That you could get me to see things your way. *Now* do you remember?" he demanded. Frustrated, he got up, turning his back on her and looking out the window.

"I never—" And then it hit her. Like the proverbial ton of bricks. She understood everything. Her hands flew to her mouth, as if to contain the shock. "Oh my God."

He turned around. She looked as if she was in shock. He supposed losing didn't agree with her.

Well, winning this time didn't agree with him. He would have given anything if he hadn't overheard her, if he could have just continued the way he was, ignorant of her real objective.

"Coming back to you now, is it?" he asked sarcastically.

"Yes, it's coming back to me." Incensed that he would think this of her, she fired straight from the hip. "I was talking to someone about taking over Henry's job. Since he's considering retiring in a couple of months, the person I was talking to has the right qualifications. I told him that if he applied and really wanted it, I could probably convince Henry to see things his way—my way," she amended, using the phrase he'd said he overheard. "Henry's a dear and we get along rather well."

The anger vanished so quickly it left him almost breathless. He felt like a fool. "*He's* the one you have in the palm of your hand?"

She shrugged. "It wasn't the nicest thing to say, but I had my reasons. I exaggerated because the person I want to hire tends to need a fire lit under him before he makes a move."

Someone she cared for? Someone who was less of an idiot than he was? "This person—"

Bethany could almost see the questions forming in his head. She was quick to get in front of them.

"—Is my cousin. Distant cousin," she emphasized. Now it was her turn to be indignant. "How can you possibly think that I'd try to manipulate you after you and I—after we've—" She was so overwhelmed she couldn't get herself to finish the sentence. "Don't you realize that I think you're the most honorable man I've ever met? That I think it's wonderful that you're willing to stick to your principles even when that's not the popular stance to take?"

She looked into his eyes, searching for a sign that he understood how she really felt. Searching for the man she'd fallen in love with.

"I wouldn't want to change you even if I could. I like the fact that you stand up to me. I like the fact that you're you." And since she was being honest, she added, "I *don't* like the fact that you can turn me inside out like this."

The smile inside of him had been growing from the moment he'd realized what a mistake he'd made in not trusting her. From the moment he'd realized he hadn't made a mistake falling for her.

It curved his lips now. "Are you going to stop talking anytime soon?"

She was out of breath anyway. "Yes." Her eyes narrowed. "Why?"

He put his hands on her waist. The moment he

did, he realized just how much he'd missed touching her these past few awful, agonizing days.

"So that I can apologize for being an ass." He drew her closer. "I am sorry, Bethany. Sorry I didn't give you a chance to explain. It's just that you're not the only one who's being turned inside out here." It occurred to him that she still might not know how he felt about her. "And you're not the only one who's in love, either."

"I'm not?" she asked in a whisper.

"Not by a long shot." He framed her face in his hands. "I love you, Bethany." His eyes held hers. "So what are we going to do about it?"

She grinned. "I hear that make-up sex is really great."

He had something more in mind. A lot more. And he had a hunch that she did, too. "Is that all you want?"

She looked into his eyes. And saw everything. "You know it's not."

"Me, neither," he confessed sincerely. "Marry me, Bethany."

He took her breath away again. The proposal was unvarnished. And perfect. "Just like that?"

"No, not just like that." She loved him, he thought. She actually loved him. He might never stop smiling again. "I've been waiting for you to come into my life for forty years."

Now that she was here, she had no intentions of ever leaving. "You're not going to be able to get me out with a crowbar."

After his terrible mistake, he didn't want to assume anything. "Is that a yes?"

"That's a yes." She slipped her hands around his neck. "Now can we have make-up sex?"

Peter smiled and said, "You took the words right out of my head," before he lowered his mouth to hers.

* * * * *

FIRST-TIME
VALENTINE

BY

MARY J. FORBES

Mary J. Forbes grew up on a farm amid horses, cattle, crisp hay and broad blue skies. As a child, she drew and wrote of her surroundings and in sixth grade composed her first story about a little lame pony. Years later, she worked as an accountant, then as a reporter-photographer for a small-town newspaper, before attaining an honors degree in education to become a teacher. She has also written and published short fiction stories.

A romantic by nature, Mary loves walking along the ocean shoreline, sitting by the fire on snowy or rainy evenings and two-stepping around the dance floor to a good country song—all with her own real-life hero, of course. Mary would love to hear from her readers at www.maryjforbes.com.

Chapter One

J.D. opened his eyes to a murky dawn.

For a moment, he was at a loss with his surroundings. Oh, yeah. Back in Walnut River, Massachusetts, his hometown—and the hospital of his birth.

He groaned as memories of a long night of pain and fitful dreams rushed together. He lay in a hospital bed. IV attached to his vein. His right knee…

He did not want to consider the mess there.

Outside his room, the hospital woke. In his head, memories tumbled. The board meeting last night. The snowstorm. His knee popping like a firecracker as he slipped on those damned icy steps. And then…*oh, man*…the killing pain.

Had he blacked out? He couldn't remember. Just the crazy pain.

He should've had his knee fixed years ago. Hadn't he learned back in high school playing basketball? When the doctor told him about "jumper's knee"? Had he taken the man's advice? No. Instead, he'd ignored every recommendation and for years depended on over-the-counter painkillers. And then he'd defied fate seven years ago by joining the Northeastern HealthCare basketball team when the company hired his ambitious mind.

Arrogant jackass is what you were.

J.D. grunted. Damn this February weather. Damn the ice and snow, and why he'd returned yesterday to this armpit dot on the Massachusetts map. And damn the fact that he was now doomed to wait for surgery by the esteemed Dr. Ella Wilder, another one of the family of Wilders he'd come to lock horns with—well, not lock horns, to wine and dine and sway to realize that NHC's contemporary model of practicing medicine was the way of the future. A model second-to-none in efficiency. A model favoring corporate-run medicine, not the old-fashioned methods prevalent in this quaint little hospital.

If he did his job right, Walnut River General would be brought under NHC's generous umbrella in a matter of months, a move that would benefit patients and doctors with some modernity—with a capital *M*.

But first he needed to get out of here. Fast.

Six hours later and still waiting for his surgery, he realized fast was not a key part of this hospital's policy and his apprehension had mushroomed into full-blown anxiety. Okay, they'd told him the E.R. was having a chaotic day. But he hadn't seen the doctor—any doctor—since he'd been there.

Stop worrying, J.D. Your gurney is third in line for the O.R. Won't be long now. Which did not calm him at all.

Goddammit. Didn't they know he hated Walnut River General? His mother—Grace Sumner—had died here. Died of a blood clot in her brain—as a result of the C-section at his birth, or so Pops maintained.

You go to the hospital to die. End of story. As far back as J.D. remembered the old man's words had been a slogan in their house.

Yes, Grace was the reason J.D. had avoided getting his knee repaired years ago. Nobody was cutting into him, causing blood clots. Last night, however, he knew he could no longer dodge surgery. It was either that or end up walking with a cane for the rest of his life, *plus* attracting arthritis before he was forty.

So, where was the female Wilder? He hated to admit it, but the way she touched him, spoke, smiled last night in the E.R....

"Mr. Sumner," she had said upon entering his curtained cubicle. "I'm Dr. Ella Wilder. I hear you fell on some steps and banged up your knee." Against the collar of her white lab coat hung a hot-pink stethoscope.

"Should sue the hospital," he'd ground out, gazing at her through half-closed eyes. He hadn't expected a woman doctor. Nor one resembling a French fashion model.

"Suing won't heal your knee, sir," she informed him, dipping her head to examine his exposed leg.

The paramedic—Mike O'Rourke was it?—had found J.D. sprawled across the snowy steps by the hospital parking lot. In the E.R., the man had cut away the expensive cloth from his right pant leg, easier for radiology to take X-rays.

Ella Wilder snapped on a pair of surgical gloves and tested the wounded area gently. "Tell me when it hurts."

He winced; she nodded. "I'm sending you for an MRI."

"Think I broke something?" He tried to lift up on his elbows.

"According to the X-rays, no. However, I'd like more information about the soft tissues around and under your kneecap. We'll also do some blood work to see if there's a sign of arthritis."

"Arthritis?" He bit his bottom lip as she gently probed the distended knee. "You saying—" a pained grunt "—I'm getting *old*?"

"Not at all." The dark bob of her hair swung along the line of her jaw as she removed the gloves. "Arthritis can happen at any age."

"Terrific. Worst-case scenario?"

"Let's see what the MRI brings. If it's what I suspect, we'll do surgery tomorrow once the swelling subsides." She offered a smile and it blew through his pain like a breeze on the Cayman coast. "Meantime, we'll keep you off your feet tonight and get some pills into you."

"Don't need pills," he mumbled. "Don't wanna stay here."

She patted his hand. "Trust me, the pills will help

while we wait for the injury to settle and the throbbing to lessen."

In spite of his pain, a corner of his mouth lifted. "You going to be my doctor?"

"If your injury is what I suspect, then yes, I will be."

His eyes closed. "Good. I like the idea of throbbing for you."

God almighty. Were you delusional last night, J.D., or just a total jerk? He couldn't believe he'd actually uttered those words. To a doctor, no less. He owed her an apology, preferably before the operation. The last thing he needed was for her to cut into him with payback on her mind.

Across the O.R.'s inpatient waiting bay, an old guy hacked as if his lungs were full of gravel. From out of nowhere a nurse hurried to raise the guy's head, asking how he was holding out, and if anyone sat with his wife and did his son still work at the paper? J.D. groaned. The old home-week chitchat he could do without.

He checked the wall clock. 12:23 p.m. Eighteen hours since he'd tumbled down those steps that led to the parking lot across the hospital's entrance lane.

Never in his life had he been this idle. Okay, admittedly the care so far had been excellent. Nurses, doctors and technicians were gentle and promptly got him whatever he asked for: magazines, water, juice…everything except an early surgery slot.

New York, that's where he should be, in his plush office with its cherrywood desk and his proficient secretary. Hell, he hadn't scratched and clawed his way to the rung of executive for Northeastern HealthCare by stopping to smell the Mayflowers.

He grunted. He'd be hard-pressed to find any flower in the concrete jungle where he worked.

"Hello, Mr. Sumner," a soft female voice said before blue scrubs and *her* face came into view.

God, she was one appealing woman. And those dark eyes… A brown he couldn't quite describe—until he thought of the fancy bag of hazelnuts his secretary had bought him last Christmas.

"How are you feeling?" Ella Wilder asked, unaware of where his thoughts traveled. This afternoon the bell of her pink stethoscope was tucked into a breast pocket.

"Bored as hell," he grumbled.

She offered a quick smile. "Won't be much longer. I have one surgery ahead of you which will take about thirty minutes." Moving down to his iced knee, she marked the spot where she would do her work. "The swelling has decreased. That's good."

Her hair, he saw now, was a study of browns and blacks. Today she'd clipped the thick locks behind her ears.

She asked several more questions about his injury, ensured he was Jared Devlin Sumner, and had he taken his meds?

"I gave all that info to the nurse," he said, annoyed as hell that through everything he couldn't stop taking inventory of her body.

"We like to double check. It's standard procedure." She jotted a few extra notes on his chart. "Do you have family here, Mr. Sumner?"

"No." Well, he did, but his old man was no one's business. "This isn't a big deal, is it?" He would never admit it, but the notion of having his flesh divided by a knife scared him witless.

Her expressive eyes held his. "Everything should go fine."

"Should? Not sure I like the sound of that." He tried to swallow past the fist in his throat.

Again the smile. He liked her mouth. The cute little body, the shape of her eyes…that great mouth…. Hell, he liked everything he saw.

"You'll be fine, Mr. Sumner."

"Maybe I'll take legal action. Those stairs should've been de-iced." All right, he sounded like one of his dad's scratched records, constantly playing the same line over again.

One dark brow curved. "Were you wearing snow boots?"

"I had proper footwear."

The brow remained high. "Not from what I saw last night."

When he was wearing his five hundred dollar pair of Gucci loafers. "Fine. You've made your point," he grouched.

She patted his hand. "You wouldn't be the first to misjudge our weather."

"I grew up here." Now why mention that?

This time both eyebrows sprang. "Oh?"

"Long time ago."

"And no doubt well before my time."

He grinned. "I'm not much older than you, Doc."

Going with the years in med school, he estimated she was in her early thirties.

"According to your chart you're seven years older." Her cheeks flushed and she looked away. "See you in the O.R."

"Hold on—you're twenty-nine? Are you a real doctor?"

Her nostrils flared. "I finished my residency last year."

"Should I trust you with my knee?" The flip tone contained his thread of worry, he knew.

"You can trust me."

"Where have I heard that before?"

"I'll see you in surgery, Mr. Sumner." She walked away, tidy in her blue scrubs—determination in her eyes.

J.D. swallowed. He'd offended her twice in less than twenty-four hours and he was going under the knife. *Her* knife.

And he'd forgotten to apologize.

Should I trust you with my knee? The words plagued Ella's mind as she scrubbed in for his surgery.

Lord, she thought, *if he only knew how close his question struck.* Well, she wouldn't think of it. She would not. Instead, she inhaled slowly and checked the equipment tray readied by the scrub nurse. *Interning is behind you. You're a doctor now. With excellent surgical talent. You know what to do.*

Her counselor's mantra, calming her pounding heart and the jitters edging into her fingers. *One more deep breath....*

They wheeled Sumner in and she saw he was calm and slightly drowsy from the sedative administered twenty minutes before.

Shelly, the circulating nurse, went through the preoperative checklist again, ensuring he was the correct patient via his armband, X-rays, consent forms, lab results. Next Brad, Ella's anesthesiologist, explained his role to her patient.

The pain will be gone soon, she told him mentally. On the monitor, she scanned Sumner's vitals.

"Good to go," Brad informed her. Patient was out.

"Let's get started then."

An hour later, Ella pulled off her soiled surgical gloves and tossed them in the disposable bin. She had repaired his damaged cartilage. He'd been lucky—the kneecap hadn't shifted, and while the soft tissue had bruised, it hadn't sustained severe injury. However, the fall had wreaked havoc on his right meniscus—torn the cartilage from its mooring—and after studying the X-rays last night and the MRI this morning, Ella had known J.D.'s repair would entail the arthroscopic surgery she had just performed.

Now he was on his way to recovery. She'd check on him in fifteen minutes, but first she needed a drink of water. Surgeries with their intense lights and stress always dehydrated her. In the small doctor's lounge down the hall she found her internist brother, Peter, sitting at one of the two small tables reading several pages of a letter, a coffee at his right hand.

"Hey, Peter." Ella reached into the fridge for the liter of Evian she'd brought that morning from home.

He gave her a glance. "El."

She sat across from him, stretched her legs, took a long pull on the water and jutted her chin at the pages. "What's up?"

"More crap from the state medical board. They're claiming we're unethical in our methods, that we're focusing too much on coddling—their word—patients and not enough on speed of recovery and effectiveness of treatment." He gathered the pages into the big brown folder marked Dr. P. Wilder, Chief of Staff. The word *confidential* had been typed above his name.

"Should you be telling me this?" she asked, hoping he would say no. She had no time or interest in crazy allegations, especially when they alluded to a political agenda. Having already heard the rumors and innuendos, she simply tried to focus on her work.

Undoubtedly some of those rumors had evolved from the tug-of-war between Peter and his fiancée, Bethany Holloway—before they'd fallen in love. As a newcomer to Walnut River and the hospital board, Bethany had initially advocated Northeastern HealthCare's takeover of Walnut River General. Until Peter convinced her NHC's financial "support" would disintegrate the heart of the hospital.

Now, he shrugged his big shoulders. "You know the most of it already," he said.

"I don't want to," Ella said honestly. "I was never any good at political science."

He gave her a smile. "Aw, El. You were the brains of the family. We all knew that the minute you turned two and told Mom she'd made an extra cookie for Anna."

Their sister who had estranged herself from the family almost ten years ago. Ella rubbed her forehead. "I wish…"

"What?"

"That Anna believed in our love."

"She's got to work it out herself, Ella."

Momentarily they remained silent, the hospital's sounds drifting through the open door: a medicine cart's squeaky wheels in the hallway, the beep of someone's pager, the jingle of a maintenance staffer's keys. Sounds that had soothed Ella since she'd first toddled down the wide, polished corridors with her daddy, Dr. James Wilder.

Oh! Sometimes missing him would hit her so hard she had to catch her breath.

She thought of the man whose knee she'd repaired. Of course she'd recognized him last night. J. D. Sumner, executive of Northeastern HealthCare had arrived two days ago from New York City to woo the hospital board. A man with an agenda that, according to Peter, would uproot her father's legacy and the principles of Walnut River General.

A man who had the greenest eyes—like moss on a forest tree….

Moss on a tree? Sheesh, Ella. Have you lost it?

Shoving the silly analogy aside, she said, "Sumner's surgery went well, although he'll be using crutches for a few days." Her lips twitched. "I wouldn't put it past him to show up in the boardroom with his butt hanging out of a hospital gown."

Peter flashed a grin. "I'll tell Beth. She's doing some digging on who's feeding the wolves." He tapped the folder.

"Speaking of which, I need to check the one in my recovery."

With a last gulp of water, she deposited the empty bottle into the recycle bin and headed down the hallway.

She still couldn't believe she'd given Sumner that tidbit about her age and experience. Thank goodness, she hadn't blurted out anything else—such as *I have confidence issues in the O.R. and am seeing a psychologist in Springfield.*

God forbid.

Walking into recovery, she saw that consciousness wove through her patient's mind, a sunbeam eliminating shadows.

"Hey, Doc," he mumbled, those green eyes braving the light before drifting closed again.

Wolf or not, J. D. Sumner was a patient whose knee had been carved into by her scalpel. Her compassionate heart—the same one Peter had inherited—softened.

She laid a cool hand across Sumner's forehead; found his pulse on the big freckled wrist resting on the blanket. Good—regular and strong. Skin a little warm but that was expected fresh out of the O.R.

Thank God. Another win.

Stop thinking like an intern! Focus on your patient.

She did. And saw he was a big man, long and lean and honed in all the muscled regions. She knew the human anatomy inside and out. Eleven years of school, orthopedic studies and her residency had garnered her that knowledge. Sumner was the epitome of health.

"The surgery was a success," she told him quietly, her hand slipping upward to stroke back his hair.

He had wonderfully thick hair, McDreamy-shaggy and a dark auburn hue she'd sell a kidney for. Rich was all she could think. The color was rich as a forest of oaks in autumn.

Forests again. What was the matter with her? She wasn't even an outdoor kind of gal.

"Feels good, Doc." His words came less slurred; his eyes slowly zeroed on her. "Your fingers are nice and cool."

God, what *was* she doing? She snatched back her hand, but not before his lips curved in a slight smile and a current landed in her abdomen. "The nurses will take you to your room in about fifteen minutes," she told him. "You'll need to wear the knee brace for a few days to keep the leg straight. I also want you to use crutches until you can put pressure on the leg without pain."

He was having trouble keeping his eyes open. "Can I have some water? Mouth feels dry as Arizona."

"The recovery nurse will give you a few sips." For anyone else she would have complied. But there was something about J. D. Sumner that confused her, sent tingles up her arms wherever she touched him. The moment he'd come into the E.R., snow-covered and biting his lip, she had felt that electricity. Thankfully, during surgery her focus had been too intense.

"No, you," he said. "I want you to—"

"Yolanda can—"

"Please." He caught her hand in a shocked move. "You."

"Mr. Sumner, I have other patients."

"J.D. It's…J.D."

In his eyes she saw that same flicker of apprehension she'd noticed before the operation. For some reason NHC's top man was afraid. But of what—hospitals in general? Was that why he hadn't had his knee fixed years ago? Oh, yes, she'd noted the old damage, the 'jumper's knee.' Why had he ignored the problem so long?

Again, her heart responded. While fear often accompanied patients and families into the hospital, Ella worked hard to ease their situations. J. D. Sumner was no different.

"All right," she said and nodded to the nurse tucking a warming blanket around his feet. Within seconds, Yolanda handed Ella a plastic water bottle and straw.

Gently she slid her hand beneath his head—fingers automatically weaving through the density of his hair—and lifted him to the flexible straw. His lips were well-shaped, though dehydrated from the anesthetic. Dark whiskers covered his top lip and obstinate jaw, and flowed down his neck to his Adam's apple.

As a kid he would've had freckles across his cheeks.

Sipping slowly, he watched her watch him and again she felt that prickle in her belly. Gold dusted his irises, but most surprising were his lashes: black and long, curvy as a seashell. To achieve what he grew naturally, she'd need extra-lash mascara.

"Thank you," he said hoarsely.

She slipped her hand free of his head, set the bottle on the rolling tray. "You're welcome. Yolanda will look after you now."

"Will I see you again?"

"In about an hour. Meantime, try and sleep." She gave him what she hoped was a reassuring smile. "You'll be up before you know it."

She turned to go.

"Doc? I'm sorry for last night. What I said. About the throbbing."

"No offense taken. Sometimes pain will make people say strange things." Which was true.

"You're Peter Wilder's sister."

"I am."

His dry lips worked up a semi-smile. "Much prettier to look at. But…this won't stop me from moving NHC's agenda forward."

Of course it wouldn't. "Mr. Sumner. I have larger issues to worry about than what's up your sleeve."

His gaze touched her bare arm. "Cute arm up *your* sleeve."

"Later," she said. But his look felt like a touch of his big hand.

"The pretty lady blushes."

Shaking her head, she left recovery vexed he could knot her tongue with less than a handful of words. With just a look. *Get ahold of yourself, Ella. You're a doctor and he's…he's a patient!*

And the most virile man she'd seen in years.

Lord, the mere length of his eyelashes had her heart in arrhythmia. Oh, yes. One look from him and her palms sweated as though she sat behind the hottest boy in ninth grade—instead of being the accomplished doctor she was and a woman of almost thirty.

And still a virgin, Ella. Let's not forget that.

The thought of celebrating her next birthday in another maiden voyage had her shuddering.

Dammit. Four years ago she should have worked harder to coax Tyler out of his issues of impotency and away from thinking he wasn't a "whole" man because he sat in a wheelchair. However, she'd been so busy interning she'd let them fall into a platonic relationship. Which in itself was a revelation. She hadn't truly loved Tyler as a woman should. She'd loved him as a friend.

Perhaps, if they'd had sex… Who was she kidding? She'd chosen him as a safety net—one that kept her focused on her honors status rather than her status as a woman.

Still, had they had some form of sex she'd be more suave today, more adept around the J.D.'s of the world.

Pretty. His word swirled in her mind. She'd never considered herself pretty. Anna, her sister, was the pretty one. No, the *beautiful* one with the white-blond hair and lovely blue eyes.

If J. D. Sumner saw Anna, he wouldn't look a second time at Ella with her plain brown eyes, the straight dark hair she hacked off the instant it closed in on the collar of her lab coat.

Be grateful for what you've got Ella.

And she was grateful. For many things. Her siblings. This hospital, founded on the ethics and standards of her late father. Her family's resources to send her to university. Her intelligence.

So…why couldn't she be grateful *and* pretty?

She gave herself an inner shake. She didn't have time for this—this silly vanity. She'd taken the Hippocratic oath, for God's sake. Nothing mattered but her skill. She

had no time to think about J.D. and the experiences he
had with beautiful women.

So she told herself…every spare second of her shift.

Chapter Two

At 8:00 p.m. that night she pulled her Yaris into her garage from the back alley and shut off the ignition. Bone-tired, she sat listening to the engine tick. The car had been her father's last birthday gift, a month before his retirement—and untimely death.

She remembered the massive red ribbon on the hood, the gigantic card with *Happy 29th, Ella! Love always, Dad* on the driver's seat.

Her eyes stung. Never again would she see her barrel-chested daddy, hear his kind voice, feel his big bear-paw hands stroke her hair or rub her shoulder affectionately.

That birthday had been the best. Sometime during the night, he'd driven the car into her garage and had her beatup Chevy removed. Then he'd rung her doorbell at five in the morning, an hour before her shift at the hospital. He'd stood there on her little porch with a cup of Starbucks in one hand and *The Boston Globe* in the other. And the biggest grin.

The early morning sun dappling his gray hair, he'd led her through her little backyard, with its grand old maples, to the garage, saying he needed a ride to the hospital because he'd cabbed it to her house to wish her a happy birthday.

And there sat the little blue Yaris.

Ah, Daddy. I hope you know I miss you like crazy.

Sighing, she hit the remote for the garage door before climbing from the car with a sack with homemade clam chowder from Prudy's Menu, a deli she frequented when she worked overtime.

Tugging her wool-lined coat tight around her, she headed across the snowy, moonlit backyard for the rear door of her small Cape Cod house, the one her maternal grandmother had lived in for sixty-two years and bequeathed to Ella and Anna three years ago. From the start, Anna hadn't wanted the house, but Ella vowed to buy out her half by setting up an account and depositing monthly increments in her sister's name.

As she stepped inside her quaint country kitchen, a squeaky meow greeted her before a three-legged bundle of gray fur came around the corner. A year ago, Ella had found the wounded kitten on the side of a highway, and brought her home to heal.

"Hey, Miss Molly." She cuddled the animal close. "Smell the soup, do you? Let's find you some nice tuna instead."

At nine, she turned out the kitchen lights and headed down the hall to take a bath. Oh, but she was tired.

Today had been a grueling one. Ice on the highways resulted in two traffic accidents, causing broken legs, a shattered shoulder and a fractured spine. Then there was the man shoveling snow off his roof who'd fallen to a cement patio, smashing both heels.

And of course, J. D. Sumner with his damaged knee.

She had popped into his room before leaving the hospital. Why she'd left him until last on her evening rounds, she couldn't say. Normally, she checked each patient room-by-room, ward-by-ward.

But she'd gone to check the roof faller first before backtracking to room 239—one of only three private rooms in the hospital.

Nothing but the best for the executive of Northeastern HealthCare, she thought wryly.

Eyes on the small muted TV, cell phone attached to an ear, he'd been resting comfortably when she entered the room.

Finally, I get some attention, he'd grumbled after ending the call. His sensual lips quirked and between his lashes there lay a gleam. *Heard you in the corridor,* he'd gone on. *Either you were afraid to come into my room or I'm your favorite patient and you saved the best till last.*

At that, she laughed. She couldn't help it. Despite his helplessness in that hospital bed, the man had an impossible ego. She explained that his room was near the exit— at which he'd chuckled and called her a fibber.

The banter continued for several moments before she

examined his surgery, checked his blood pressure, pulse and temperature. And then he asked, *Why are you doing the nurse's job?*

Why, indeed? she thought now, letting herself slide beneath the steamy water for a moment before rinsing out her hair.

How could she characterize her father's legacy to a man geared to implementing the type of corporate practices armed to decimate the care of WRG? Practices that filed a patient under a number rather than a name, that sent patients home with little more than a fare-thee-well.

So the rumors went.

James Wilder was the reason she'd gone into medicine. His compassionate teachings were entrenched in Ella. She would not give them up. Not even if the hospital board decided to accept NHC's takeover bid, should it come to that. Which she desperately hoped would never happen.

The water grew cool and she pulled herself lethargically out of the tub. Molly offered a squinty-eyed look from the mat by the sink.

Ella laughed. "Yeah, I know. Nothing riveting." No, Anna was the family beauty queen. Elegant, lovely and gifted. *Oh, Anna. I miss you.*

With a sigh, Ella pulled the tub's drain. Maybe one day they would be close again—as sisters should be.

The phone rang. The nightstand clock read nine twenty-eight and caller ID indicated the hospital. Although she wasn't on call, she became immediately alert, and lifted the receiver. "Dr. Wilder."

"It's Lindsey, Doctor."

The night nurse.

"Your patient, Mr. Sumner, is reacting to the Demerol, I believe. Heart's pounding, sweats, woozy."

She climbed from the bed, reached for her clothes. The symptoms definitely sounded like a reaction. "Temp and BP?"

"Fifty-two, and seventy over sixty. Feels as if he's about to pass out."

Damn. His admission form hadn't signified any allergies. "Get two liters of saline into him, flush it out. Now. And get Doctor Roycroft in to check his stats." Roycroft was on night call. "I'll be there in a few minutes."

She hung up, rushed into her jeans and a sweatshirt. She didn't stop to think why she needed to race to his bedside. The nurses and on-call doctors were there.

They're competent, Ella. You're not dealing with an alcoholic nurse who wouldn't acknowledge her own problems.

Still, she couldn't take the chance. This time *she* was responsible, not a scrub nurse. *She* had prescribed the meds.

In her car, she shivered, although the vents blasted hot air. At the hospital, she half-jogged up the stairs to the second floor.

A male nurse inputting computer data sat behind the counter of the floor station. "Is Lindsey with Mr. Sumner?" she asked.

The man glanced up from the screen. "No, but the patient is okay, Doctor. We got him settled. Changed his nightshirt and the sheets. Sponged down his skin."

Ella scanned Sumner's chart. Heart and blood pressure back to normal. Saline doing its work. "Thank you. I'll check on him while I'm here." She headed down to the room.

A nightlight glowed from the opposite wall, casting a dim hue across the bed and J.D.'s form under the blankets. His leg had been propped on several pillows. He was still awake.

"Hey, Doc," he said, voice deep and raspy. "You come all the way back just to see me?"

Sick as he'd been, she heard the grin in the tone, pictured his grass-green eyes in the dark.

"How are you feeling?" she asked, automatically checking the pulse along the arch of his elevated foot for circulation. *Steady.*

"Wasn't feeling so hot a while ago."

"You reacted to the Demerol. Were you aware about the symptoms before, by chance?"

"No. Never bother with meds unless it's aspirin or some such. Don't like taking prescription meds. Don't need 'em."

She wanted to ask about his jumper's knee. He hadn't gone without pain at some point in his life. But he was drowsy and he'd been through enough for one night. "You may need a medical alert bracelet for the Demerol." Setting a palm against his forehead, she noted the coolness of his skin. He was okay.

"Get some rest, Mr. Sumner."

"I wish..." His eyes drooped. "I wish you'd call me J.D."

She ignored the request. J.D. was far too personal. It gave him an edge she wasn't prepared to relinquish.

"Sleep, sir. It's best for your injury. Let the saline and the medication do its job."

"They gave me Tylenol 3."

"It'll help with the pain." And the fever. "I'll see you in the morning."

"What time?"

"Around seven."

"I pressed the call button right away," he said, as if reluctant to let her go. "Was surprised someone attended so fast."

"That's how our hospital works. No calls go unnoticed or unattended. Here, patient care is first and foremost."

"Good." His breathing slowed, his eyes drifted closed. "Wish you were on call. I hate…hospitals."

"Well," she said softly, "I hope you won't hate ours too much."

"'Ni', Doc."

"Goodnight."

She left his room, returned to the nurses' station and wrote her observations on his chart. Several minutes later she was heading home, hands gripping the steering wheel. Would she ever get past the horrifying repercussions of that surgery in Boston?

One day at a time, the counselor had told her.

God help her if something had gone wrong with J. D. Sumner.

He's already scared. The thought popped up like a weed.

Oh, he had a cocky attitude, but an underlying current of apprehension rode his voice from the moment Mike

O'Rourke, one of the hospital's paramedics, brought him into the E.R. Which, she supposed, was understandable, but still…

In her mind she backtracked the past two days. His constant questions, the hint of anxiety. His need for her at his side. And it was more than simple attraction. He saw her as his lifeline. Why?

Why was J. D. Sumner, executive of one of the largest health care corporations, leery of hospitals?

Or was it just *her* hospital?

J.D. woke in a cold and drenching sweat.

The hospital gown stuck to his clammy skin and for a moment his brain didn't register his surroundings. And then his eyes focused.

He lay in the hospital, a place he had not spent one night—never mind two—since his birth. The clock radio read 12:03 a.m. He'd been asleep less than two hours. His mouth tasted of dryer lint. He reached for the water, took a sip. The ice had long since melted.

Someone had placed the call button within reach, tying it to the guardrail near his hand. He pressed the red glow light of the tiny plastic knob—one, two, three. Shudders rolled through his body.

Within ten seconds, a soft tread came down the corridor. A woman entered his room.

"Doc?" J.D. rasped, eyes blurry.

"It's Lindsey," the woman said. "The night nurse. Are you okay, Mr. Sumner?"

"I'm soaked." His teeth rattled. He tried to focus, but

she stood etched in the dim glow from the hallway. "Need the doc," he slurred.

At his bedside, the nurse ran gentle fingers down his arms, took his cold hands between her palms. "I'll get you a clean gown and some extra blankets," she said, then disappeared.

J.D. shivered. He hadn't been this cold since he'd been a kid and had to shovel his dad's truck out of a ditch one bitter winter night when the old man hit an icy patch and plowed into the snowdrift along the shoulder of the road. *I'm frozen,* he'd told his dad.

You're not shoveling hard enough, Pops had retorted.

Another shudder rushed through J.D.'s body.

Lindsey returned with blankets in her arms, a fresh water bottle in her hand and the male nurse on her heels.

"We'll get you comfy in no time, Mr. Sumner," she said.

Gently, they assisted him from bed to a chair. And while Lindsey changed the linens, the man changed J.D.'s nightshirt. Minutes later he lay snug and dry under the covers. His knee throbbed like a son of a bitch.

While he sipped water, Lindsey took his pulse and inserted an ear thermometer. She had calm hands and a soothing voice. He'd always imagined hospitals as semi drug-induced prisons where the injured were at the mercy of emotionless medical staff who pretty much wanted you out of the way and not holding up the assembly line.

The type of hospitals NHC praised. For some reason, tonight the standard felt false.

Checking his stats, Lindsey asked, "How's the knee?"

"Feels like it's been run over by a truck."

"We'll give you some more Tylenol."

His breathing eased. "Is the doc coming?"

"We've called her, but it's just the Demerol working itself out of your system."

After he'd taken the pills, the nurse tucked him in as if he were a child. "You'll sleep now," she said kindly.

He damn near expected her to kiss him goodnight on his forehead, but she stepped back and drew up the guard-rail. "Good night," she whispered.

He was too tired to respond. Already the pills were spreading their smooth serenity into his raw knee and his last thought was that he couldn't remember anyone ever tucking him in at night.

Definitely not his old man.

The wind had died down by the time Ella drove through the cold dawn to the hospital the next morning. All night, between bouts of sleep, she'd worried about Sumner. Considering Lindsey would have notified her if something had gone awry, forfeiting sleep had been silly and foolish. *Sheesh.* If she thought of the thousands of lost nights during her studies and internship....

Pulling into her parking spot, she inhaled hard. If she hadn't been so driven, so fevered over getting her medical degree, maybe there would have been someone after Tyler....

Oh, God. The last thing she needed was to remember Tyler. Dear Tyler with his brilliant medical mind. His broken body after his skiing accident in their first year of internship. Tyler whom she had loved, but hadn't been *in love* with. Until he was gone, dead of acute pneumonia, and she cried and despaired and regretted.

More for him or for you, Ella?

The thought stopped her cold at the door of the change room.

Be honest. Tyler hadn't wanted to live. He hadn't been able to surrender his dreams of neurosurgery.

All right. The tears were more for me.

Her conscience shaken, she pushed into the room. As always, changing into her scrubs and lab coat made her a doctor once more. No time for regrets or moaning over lost chances.

She walked to the nurses' station and collected her charts, scanning each of the seven patients requiring her attention. J.D., she noted, hadn't slept well initially according to Lindsey: *Cold sweats, shivers, dry mouth. 9:35—Changed Demerol to T3. 24:03, paged Dr. E.W.—Changed bedding/gown. Patient repeatedly asked for Dr. E.W.*

That his temperature rose a half degree after a restless night was normal. His vitals overall were good. She reread *repeatedly asked for*, glanced down the hallway to 239 and her heartbeat quickened. He was okay. The remainder of the night had been uneventful. She wondered if he was awake, if he'd eaten breakfast, if he waited for her.

She began her rounds. Each patient received her personal attention, each received encouragement for healing. These were the ethics her father had taught that made WRG a hospital where patients could heal in comfort and ease. *Patients are people*. She could almost hear her father's voice. *They have faces and names. They are not medical terms.*

She walked into J.D.'s room with her dad smiling over her shoulder. "How are we this morning, Mr. Sumner?"

He was sitting up in bed, knee raised by pillows, his hair falling endearingly over his forehead—and with a sex appeal that seared like a flame.

God, he was a striking man. All the studying, all those late, late nights when she'd propped her eyes open with toothpicks and drank coffee until her back teeth floated…none of it prepared her for *this*. For J. D. Sumner.

Her next breath snagged at the flash of his smile. "Hey, there, Doc. Can you get me out of here this morning?"

On the pretense of checking his chart, she walked to his side. "You had a bit of a tough night."

"Nothing I couldn't handle."

"Mm-hm." She pressed two fingers against his wide, warm wrist. Heart rate steady, strong and slower than yesterday. "Do you exercise regularly, Mr. Sumner?" she asked, examining his knee for discoloration and swelling.

It took her a moment to realize he hadn't replied. Ella lifted her head. Eyes dark and deep as jungle pools stared back.

"Why won't you call me by my first name?" he asked quietly.

"It's better this way." *First names are too close and personal.*

A chuckle. "Ah…got it. Better for *you*. Interesting."

"Not interesting, professional."

At that he laughed. "Now there's a fun word coming from one of this hospital's finest. In my world, professional comes with proficiency and competence."

"And we're not?" she asked mildly.

"Oh, you're professional, don't get me wrong. You just need to speed things up a little. Not do so much hand-holding."

She ignored his critique. "Hold as still as possible, I want to change the bandages. Then later this morning we'll get you up and around for a few minutes. And for your information, professionalism is at the top of our agenda, particularly when it comes to patient care." She shot him a stern look. "Which your company doesn't seem to understand, from what I hear."

"My company understands you would do well to update equipment, move into the modern world. Why work with old tools, old standards, if new ones are at your fingertips?"

She tossed the bandages in the trash bin by his bed. "God forbid, I ever need medical care in an NHC-run hospital. I'd be a faceless, nameless entity."

"You'd be cared for in the most resourceful, sophisticated way possible."

Ella paused, her eyes locking on his. "Have you received any *un*sophisticated medical attention since you were admitted, J.D.?"

She realized her error the instant his name left her tongue and his grin bloomed big as a kid's on the last day of school.

"Now, *that* sounds perfect," he said, much too brash for her liking. "A little culture, a little smokiness, a little se—"

"Stop right there."

"I was going to say—"

"Do not go there."

"—sensitivity." Another broad grin. "Ah. You thought I had something else on my mind."

Despite his injury, the man was relentless. And he read her too well. "What you have on your mind is not my concern."

"That a fact?"

"Absolutely. My interest in you, Mr. Sumner, falls into one category. You are my patient. Nothing else."

He sighed with flair. "You break my heart, Ella."

Oh, boy. She had to force herself to remember that he'd been in the board meeting the other night representing Northeastern HealthCare. He could possibly eradicate everything Walnut River General stood for. Which meant he could not, in any way, be trusted.

His flirtations were a guise, a smoke screen to obtain information to sink her hospital. The hospital her father had worked all his life to uphold with integrity and dedication—and above all—class-A skills and leadership. Shifting the subject, she placed her fingers on his knee and hiked her chin toward the S-shaped birthmark on the inside of his thigh. "Who gave you the birthmark?"

"Probably some ancient ancestor."

"Do you have family in Walnut River?" She moved her fingers around his kneecap.

"Why?"

"I have another patient with the same birthmark."

His leg jerked. "Take it easy," he breathed.

Concerned, she touched the area where her fingers had been. "This hurt?"

"It's sensitive."

Leaning closer, she examined the region below the knee. "Hmm. It shouldn't be. It's too far from the incision." Beyond the small line of stitches, his knee appeared normal in its healing. No signs of blood poisoning, thankfully.

Ella pressed the call button. "I'll prescribe a topical cream."

"Now?" J.D. asked, suddenly serious. His gaze searched his injury, his Adam's apple bobbed.

For a moment Ella was tempted to reverse her call to the nurses' desk and ease the nervousness his tone carried. "Everything's fine, but a nurse will finish up here so I can continue my rounds."

"Will you be back later?"

June Agger, a twenty-year veteran with the hospital, entered the room. "Dr. Wilder?"

"Could you finish dressing Mr. Sumner's surgery for me, June? Thanks." To J.D., she said, "I'll be back when I do rounds tonight. We're going to keep you an extra day to monitor your meds, make sure nothing else causes you fever and nausea. If you need me for anything concerning your knee, June will know where to find me. Meantime, Ashley, our physiotherapist, will begin some passive and very mild ambulatory exercises. Don't overdo it, though."

"Doc," he called before she made it out the door. "The day can't go fast enough."

Until she returned to him.

She headed down the hallway, convinced danger was spelled J.D.

Except for the octogenarian dozing at the tiny desk near the door, the hospital library was empty at three in the afternoon.

Dressed in a blue terry robe and using the crutches the physiotherapist prescribed, J.D. quietly thumped his way across the hardwood floor. The library was elementary-sized. Ten inner shelves were stacked with fiction and two walls held reference, research and an assortment of current magazines.

Situated in the northwest corner of the hospital's ground floor, the library had a cozy nook facing two corner windows where patients could enjoy the hospital gardens now under three feet of snow.

Gingerly, he sank into a cushiony chair. Beyond the glass, a variety of trees—elm, oak and maple, New England's finest—were scattered across the gardens. He'd read about them in a brochure at the information desk four hours before he busted up his knee. Which at the moment throbbed like an insane drum behind the brace.

Too much damn walking, he thought. Hadn't she told him not to overdo it? Mercy, but he wanted out of here. He wanted to get back to his job, back to New York. He wanted out of Walnut River.

Barely loud enough to be discerned, the PA system called "Dr. Ella Wilder, recovery three. Dr. Ella Wilder, recovery three."

He pictured her hurrying to the patient, her pink Nikes quick and quiet on the tiled floor, a worry line between her fine dark brows. He imagined her slim hands on the patient's forehead, taking his pulse, her voice—the one with smoke and sex rolled into its vowels—a balm to distressed nerves.

J.D. smiled. Oh, yeah. *Sex.* She'd read him well this morning. She, with the keen mind, perceptive eyes and beautiful face. Ella Wilder had a sensuality that shot a man's testosterone sky-high.

Unfortunately, such women were out of his league. The type he attracted was brash and bold. Women who knew how to have a good time, if not for a long time. Women who knew how to let him take what he needed, what he wanted. Without frills. Without obligations and assurances and emotional morasses.

A deep disillusionment crept in. Out over the gardens a soft fall of snow had begun and he felt it burying what he'd always known. No matter how hard he scraped and clawed his way through the maze of life, the ghosts of his blue-collar past would forever haze his heels.

And a woman like Ella Wilder, with her culture and sophistication, with her background smacking of old money, heritage and long lines of tradition would see him as a mere speck on her chart.

Well, dammit, maybe it was time to make some alterations to that speck. And maybe, just maybe, it was time for him to be a different kind of man.

One the good doctor would appreciate.

Chapter Three

Whenever she could, Ella took lunch at home. The quiet of those sixty minutes helped her reenergize and refocus. Today was one of those days. She hadn't been able to get J.D. out of her head. The man dominated her thoughts during every lapsed moment. When she took a ten-minute water break. When she changed her scrubs from one surgery to the next. Thank God, the second she began scrubbing in her mind zeroed on her task.

This afternoon she had a single surgery scheduled. Eighty-year-old Mrs. Shipmen needed the radial head on her right elbow repaired. Ella looked forward to the surgery. She did not look forward to its completion. The afternoon would leave too much room for thoughts of J. D. Sumner.

Molly greeted her at the back door, purring happily as she twined around Ella's ankles.

She was standing at the window over the sink, eating the tomato and chicken salad sandwich she'd thrown together and musing about the snow she needed to clear from her walkway before dark, when her neighbor across the alley stepped out of his house and began sweeping his back stoop.

And suddenly it struck.

Jared Sumner. Best known for his gardening skills around Walnut River. Not only had he maintained the hospital's gardens, last summer she'd hired him to care for and nurture her property.

Six months before, she'd observed him limping around his backyard with a cane, so she had gone across the alley to inquire about his health. The old man had shrugged off her questions—until unbearable pain drove him to see her.

Last October she replaced his left hip. And asked about the birthmark on his inner thigh.

The S-shaped birthmark she queried J.D. about this morning.

Who gave you the birthmark?

Probably some ancient ancestor.

And then he'd felt pain. In a spot that should not have been painful. Surely, it hadn't been a ruse to sidetrack her?

Over the sink, she brushed the crumbs from her hands. "Wait here, Molly-girl. I'll be right back."

Ella shrugged into her coat, then headed out the back door. The cold air bit her lungs as she half-ran, half-strode, coat flying behind her, across the alley, through Mr. Sumner's back gate and across his tiny yard, a yard that in summer was an Eden.

A yard J.D. had played in—if the man on the stoop with the bristly outdoors broom was whom she believed.

The old gent raised his head as she came up the walkway he had yet to clear. "Hello, Mr. Sumner," she called.

"Doc." He straightened to his full height, a height equaling J.D.'s. and, leaning on the broom's handle, waited for her to halt below the stoop's four narrow steps. "Ya done for the day?" he asked, his Boston accent thick as the snow in his yard.

"I go back in about twenty minutes." She glanced at the broom. "Thought one of the high school kids was clearing your walks and steps." If she sounded exasperated it was because she could well imagine the old guy flying off those steps, arms and legs windmilling.

Like J.D. had.

"Huh," he grunted. "Damn kid doesn't know what the hell he's doin' half the time. Leaves the snow piled so close to the walk, all it does is slide back down."

She went up the stairs. "Give me that broom, please, and go on inside where I know you won't fall on your keester."

"Don't you mean my ass?" he grumped, though a smile lay in his voice.

"Whatever." She took the broom, and waved him toward the door. "I'll see you shortly."

"What for?"

"I have some questions to ask. Now, are you going to let me finish this or are you going to stand in the way?"

"Huh," he said again. "I've a mind to lock you out. Don't need a li'l mite like you naggin' my head off."

"I don't nag. It's called TLC. But you wouldn't know what that means, would you?"

"Fresh-mouthed doctor, is what you are," he griped, shutting the door in her face.

She swept the stoop and stairs, then grabbed the snow shovel parked against the house and tackled the walkway.

The door opened. "Do a good job—or I won't let you do it again." The door slammed shut.

Old coot, she thought, unable to resist the affectionate laugh that erupted. He'd been her neighbor since she moved into her grandmother's house a week after she finished her residency last year. After her grandmother's death three years before, renters had lived in the place— and neglected the property.

Mr. Sumner Senior had jumped at the chance to fix up her "pig sty," as he termed it. His labor didn't come cheap, but then a first-class groundskeeper was worth every penny she put in his pocket.

Finished with the walkway, she set the shovel in its spot and climbed the steps. She had all of five minutes.

After brushing the snow from the hem of her long woolen coat, she knocked once. As though he'd been waiting on the other side, he flung open the door.

"Thank you." Ella strode in. The kitchen's warmth stung her cold cheeks. She looked past the man to the interior and saw a small tidy room. He was as meticulous here as he was with the outdoors.

"I thought you had people to dice," he grumped,

gripping his carved wooden cane. "You're takin' up my afternoon."

"And you're welcome for the walkway."

A grunt.

She shoved her cold hands into the deep pockets of her coat and studied him a moment. Except for his height and thick silver hair, he looked nothing like J.D. Could she be mistaken? Oh, she understood that by asking specific questions she'd be digging into a part of their lives that was not her business. She was both men's doctor. Not their priest, psychologist or social worker.

But there was that birthmark.

And the last name—as well as the first—marking father to son.

She stared into the old man's blue eyes. "I'll make this short, Mr. Sumner. Do you have family?"

He was taken aback. "What the hell concern is that of yours? First you come here bitchin' about my shovelin', then you storm into my house and now you're askin' questions that got nothin' to do with patient care."

She wouldn't back down. "Do you?"

"If you're askin' if I have kids the answer is no."

"No children?"

"Ya deaf, Doc?"

The tension ran from her shoulders and settled in her gut. The old man was lying. "I have a patient in the hospital right now. His name is J. D. Sumner from New York City—"

"Don't know nobody in New Yawk." Cane in hand, he turned away and shuffled to the kitchen table, a small sixties chrome-and-Formica affair with two red vinyl chairs.

Had J.D. sat there once?

Hanging the cane over the back of a chair, the old gent lowered himself into the one facing the window that overlooked his backyard, and it startled Ella that her own kitchen table mirrored an identical arrangement.

He said, "Go back to your hospital, Doc. I'm gonna take a nap, if you don't mind." Staring out at his snowy world, he began massaging his hip.

She stepped forward. "Are you in pain?"

"Nothin' I can't handle."

J.D.'s words.

"You're due for another checkup next week. I'll expect to see you in my office."

He turned suspicious eyes on her; eyes that had her thinking of J.D. when he lay on the stretcher in Emerge and asked what she planned for his knee.

"If I need pills, I'll call you."

Stubborn old cuss. "You do that," she said. She should leave well enough alone. But she couldn't. Her heart could not stand by without trying. "And if you're curious about my other patient…he's mid-thirties, has dark auburn hair. And," she said, pausing for effect, "brown eyes."

No reaction. The old gent continued his vigilance on the yard.

"All right," she said. "I'll go now." However, as she opened the door she heard him whisper a word. Had it been *green*? She slanted a look over her shoulder to be sure, but he sat in profile, his jaw pointing toward the winter landscape, his lashes unblinking.

Ella released a small sigh. "See you later, Mr. Sumner."

He remained motionless.

Stepping outside, she softly shut the door, and smiled. In profile, Jared Sumner was the image of his son.

J.D.'s skin was on fire one minute, the next like he'd been dunked in the North Atlantic, his teeth chattered so hard. What the hell was going on with his body? He'd done the exercises the therapist told him to do and he'd walked the corridor most of the day, resting whenever the pain got a little touchy.

He glanced at the plate the dinner staff had brought, the chicken congealing in the gravy. It smelled good ten minutes ago, before a wave of heat swept his body and a migraine set up camp in his brain.

Pulling the covers to his neck, he let his eyes drift shut. Maybe if he slept for a bit he'd be okay.

Another shudder shook his body. *Dammit.* What the hell was the matter with him? All he'd done was a little damage to his knee, for Christ's sake. Nothing major.

Except his body had switched into betrayal mode.

A stickler for health—he watched what he ate, exercised daily, drank in moderation, had sex regularly—the fact he had no control over his anatomy's behavior at the moment did not endear J.D. to the hospital. Had *she* made an error during surgery? The way that quack doctor had with his mom? Had Dr. Ella gone into the wrong area? Used an unsterilized scalpel? He'd read of such things.

Your imagination is running amuck, J.D. You know she

did her job. The incision was neat and tidy. Hadn't he viewed that thin, red line each time she redressed it?

Tomorrow couldn't come fast enough. Tomorrow he was leaving, whether she liked it or not. He couldn't recall ever staying more than a couple of hours in a hospital. Now here he was again, heading toward his second day with his temperature a rising tide.

Maybe he should call a nurse.

Where was the call button?

God, he was cold....

"Dr. Ella Wilder, line one, Dr. Ella Wilder, line one." She punched her office intercom.

"It's Lindsey from floor two, doctor."

The night nurse began her shift at five o'clock. Ella glanced at the slim-banded watch on her wrist. Six-thirteen. She'd been at her desk almost an hour and a half. No wonder her shoulders ached.

Lindsey continued, "Mr. Sumner in 239 has a mild fever again. Fluctuates between chills and sweats. My guess is he worked the leg too much today, but he won't admit it."

"Swelling?"

"There's some distension and redness. Temperature's one hundred. He's asking for you."

"I'll be there as soon as I can. Put the leg on pillows and pack the area in ice. Also, increase the antibiotics by ten milligrams. Has he eaten?"

"Said he wasn't hungry."

"Let's get the fever down. Then we'll get some food into him. Thanks, Lindsey."

"Anytime, Doctor. Um…" Pause. "He's quite adamant about seeing you."

Her heart kicked. "Did he say why?"

"No. He just seems a little agitated, like he's nervous about being here."

"Here, or hospitals in general?"

"He didn't say."

"All right, I'll finish ASAP and come down."

Ella ended the call. It wasn't that often a patient of hers ran a fever that high. She'd bet he'd gone overboard with the exercising. Routinely, at noon and four o'clock, if she wasn't in surgery, she checked with the nurses' station to see how her patients fared. J.D., she knew, was determined to leave tonight after her rounds.

Well, J.D. It seems you'll be with me another night.

The thought had no more entered her mind than she glanced around her office as though she'd spoken aloud. Lord, she needed to go home, soak in a hot bath and—

Oh, Ella. You can't win with those double entendres. Grabbing another patient file, she set to work. Fifteen minutes later, she took the stairwell down to the second floor; stopped at the desk.

"Is he sleeping, Lindsey?" she asked the nurse.

"No, but he's adamant about speaking with you." A glint entered the woman's eyes. "I think he has a crush on you."

Ella sighed. "It's the meds."

"Maybe we should cut back, considering the number of questions he asks about you." She winked.

One thing about hospitals, Ella realized early in her career, their gossip mills loved information about their medical personnel. Her brother Peter had been fighting off rumors since he and Bethany butted heads and then locked lips.

That gossip mill was why Ella chose a counselor who practiced in Springfield, twenty miles away. The last thing she needed was her past—those dreaded few days during her years of internship in Boston—sifting down WRG's corridors. Not even her family knew of the deep-seated guilt Ella harbored due to that one incident, or of the nightmares that still galloped into her sleep. Yes, she understood the fault of the incident was not hers. That the scrub nurse with her in the O.R. had been an alcoholic, had neglected to sanitize one of the instruments. And, yes, the woman lost her job over the whole awful situation.

But a little boy nearly died as a result of that nurse's disregard—a child under Ella's care, and on whom she'd operated with an instrument she trusted and believed to be sterile.

And though she still fought to regain the confidence she'd once possessed as a doctor, it *was* returning, growing stronger day by day within the walls of her beloved Walnut River General.

Picking up J.D.'s chart and ignoring Lindsey's comments, Ella headed for 239.

His glassy green eyes fastened on her the instant she stepped around the door. "Finally," he said.

Taking the ophthalmoscope from her pocket, she went to his side, turned his face toward her, checked his pupils. "You're not my only patient, J.D."

"You called me J.D. again."

"Isn't that what you wanted?"

"There's a lot I want."

She ignored his look as she reached for the blood-pressure cuff hooked on the wall above his head.

"And," he added, voice indistinct with fever, "I usually get it."

Ella pumped the cuff. "Not all of us are so lucky."

A corner of his mouth worked. "We talking about the same thing, Doc?"

Oh, she understood precisely what he meant. What surprised her was his ability to tease while a fever warred inside his body. He was a determined man. "Well, there's one thing you won't get," she said, releasing the cuff.

"You?"

"Since you've elevated your blood pressure and contracted a second fever, there will be no discharge until tomorrow."

His mouth sobered. "You're keeping me another night?"

Ella curled her hands around the guardrail and pulled it up. "How many times did you exercise today?"

"A few."

"More than the physiotherapist's recommendation?"

He looked askance; she noticed his chapped lips. "J.D.," she said, offering the bottle of ice water to him, "do you know what it means to rest?"

"'Course. I do that at night."

"Not just at night. During the day, too. After any surgery your body needs time to heal, to redefine itself, so to speak. There's a lot going on inside you that requires your patience—and rest. In other words, I want you to empty your mind of work and whatever else is on your BlackBerry. While exercising prevents clots—" his eyes, she noticed, sharpened "—going beyond the recommended sessions has aggravated your injury. It's not going to get you back to your office quicker. And while your fever isn't off the charts, it is high enough to tell me your body has put up a red flag. So, until we get it down and stabilized for at least twenty-four hours, I can't discharge you."

During her speech, he sipped the water.

"Do you understand?" she asked.

He handed her the bottle. "I understand."

"Good." She set the water on the table and picked up the lip balm. "Keep your lips lubricated," she said, handing him the tube.

Fevered as his eyes were, the lightheartedness returned.

"To keep them from bleeding," she informed him, removing the ice packs. The swelling was there, more than she liked, but not as bad as she'd envisioned. By morning, he should be on the mend.

She assessed his circulation on the arch of his long narrow foot, and behind his anklebone where his skin was hairless and smooth and vulnerable.

"What's the rate?" he asked when she was done.

"Eighty-eight—normal with a fever."

"My resting pulse is fifty-four," he lamented.

"It'll be back once your temp decreases and you're healing." She gave him a smile. "You're in excellent shape." And he was. His calves were defined, his shoulders broad and solid. She'd noted the muscles in his forearms and biceps. No doubt another gym advocate. *Juice monkey* was Peter's description.

"Are you a member of a gym?" she asked.

"Hate gyms. I run, hike and row in the summer, snowshoe in the winter." He frowned at his leg. "I'd hoped to do some trails around here, maybe follow the river a few miles."

"No other sport injuries?"

"Nope." His eyes kept hers. "Maybe I *should* sue," he added, smearing his lips with the balm she'd given him. "For lack of viable fitness and fresh air—never mind my more, um, basic needs—all of which I'll sorely miss this month." His brows jumped twice and Ella suppressed the urge to roll her eyes.

"You are one predictable patient, Mr. Sumner."

He hissed. "Doc, Doc. How'm I to rescue my self-esteem after that comment?"

"I'm sure your self-esteem will hold out. I'll get Lindsey to change these ice packs in thirty minutes and then redress your leg."

From a narrow cupboard in the corner of the room, she retrieved a fresh, plump pillow.

"Meanwhile, I'll send up some soup so you'll have something in your stomach for the night. Lift up on your elbows." When he did, she removed the old pillow and tucked in the laundered one. "Better?" she asked when he'd resettled.

Something grazed his expression—like a butterfly's fleeting touch to a flower—and it curled around her heart the way the pillow she held wrapped his body's warmth around her hands. "I'll see you in the morning, J.D."

"Ella." Her name was soft on his chapped lips. "Thank you."

She touched the big hand resting on his chest. "You're welcome." Before she could draw away he gripped her fingers. "Can I see you?"

She pretended to misunderstand. "I need to finish my rounds."

"I meant after. Once I've left the hospital."

Carefully, she withdrew her hand from his clasp. "I seldom go to New York."

"I'll be staying in Walnut River for a couple weeks."

"Oh? So you do have family here?" Would he admit it now?

"Trying to get me offtrack, Doc? I'm asking if you'll have dinner with me once I'm discharged."

"Not offtrack. We just want to ensure—"

"Will you?" he asked, his throat so raspy she handed him the water bottle again.

"Let me think about it."

"Better than no, I suppose." He took a sip of liquid, eyed her. "I'll call you tonight." He flashed a smile. "You're in the phone book. I checked."

She shook her head. "I wonder how many other female nurses and doctors you've wooed." *For NHC.*

He didn't blink. "Not a one."

She huffed a laugh. "And I'll bet not for lack of trying."

"Don't have to try, Doc."

"Ah. Women drop like flies at your feet, then?"

A wicked grin. "Something like that."

"Good to know. Well, then." She lifted her chin. "Don't let me get in their way."

His laughter followed her out the door.

Chapter Four

J.D. checked his watch. Twenty minutes till nine.

Would Ella be up or in bed? While he liked the idea of her in bed, he hadn't liked the idea of her thinking he was shallow about women. Okay, he dated noncommittal types, those driven and married to their jobs, and he didn't savor that behavior in himself. But he had no clue how to act otherwise. He'd been raised to keep his emotions tightly reined.

Yes, by some stroke of luck, somewhere in his childhood he must have felt cared for, maybe even loved. Whatever smidgen he'd encountered, it stuck with him, gave him a lighter view of life, one in which he teased and cajoled and made goofy remarks.

And dumb-ass ones,

Women drop like flies at your feet, then?
Something like that.

As if she gave a damn about women fawning at his feet. Her dark eyes had laughed at him. Not with him, *at* him.

And he'd felt like the village idiot, pure and simple.

She was class through and through. Intelligent, lovely and most of all, a doctor who cared about her patients, and he'd treated her like one of his bar meets after a long board meeting.

He owed her an apology.

Dialing her number on his BlackBerry, he waited for the ring. One…two…three…four. She wasn't home—

"Hello?" A little breathless. As if she'd been rushing from the bath or from making a cup of tea or having sex—

"Hello?" she repeated, a hint of sharpness in her tone.

"It—" He cleared his raspy throat. "It's me."

"J.D." His name slipped like a breath into his ear and for a second he couldn't speak. "Are you okay?"

"I'm good," he assured, though his leg ached like hell, even with the painkillers she'd prescribed. "I wanted to apologize for my behavior earlier."

"Your behavior?"

She'd forgotten him. God, he *was* a fool. As if she had time to think of him. "When you came to check on my fever. I acted like an idiot." He gusted a breath of relief she hadn't hung up. "I'm not used to…" How to explain what he felt her, these…*emotions*? "I'm not accustomed to doctors giving such thorough care," he finished lamely.

Not at all what he meant, but then every time he was

in her proximity his brain cells scattered like dandelion fluff in a spring breeze.

"You've never been in a hospital before, have you?"

"A few years back I cracked my elbow playing basketball."

"Thought you had no other sport injuries."

He chuckled. "I lied."

"Do you do that often?"

"What, play sports?"

"Lie."

The word punched. "No," he said. "Never."

"So you're honest as the day is long when you say things like not having to try around women."

He sputtered a laugh. "You don't forget much, do you, Doc? Guess I'd best watch what I say."

"Excellent idea," she said and he detected a hint of humor. "Women can read you like a book, Mr. Sumner. You're on page thirty-three."

"Ouch and ouch."

"Mm-hm. And here's a little tip. Don't tell a woman she looks pretty when in reality she looks like roadkill."

"Yikes. Is that worse than a bad-hair day?"

"Far worse."

"And you've known women who looked like roadkill?"

"I've *been* a woman who's looked like roadkill."

"Unbelievable. Cannot picture it."

"You haven't seen me after a seven-hour surgery."

"I'd give anything to see you after *any* surgery." And he meant it. She fascinated him.

She laughed, and he imagined those dark eyes soft in

the lamplight. "Not in this lifetime. Besides, if your fever stays down tomorrow, you'll be discharged, and on your way back to New York."

"I'm not returning to New York. Not right away," he added. "I'm taking a couple weeks off, staying in Walnut River."

"Oh?"

"*Oh*? How about, 'Oh, J.D. I'm so glad because I look forward to seeing more of you'?" he teased.

"If I see more of you," she retorted, "it would mean you're back in the hospital. And that would mean I didn't do my job right."

He glanced at his elevated leg, which nurse Lindsey had redressed after removing the ice packs. "You've done your job perfectly. The swelling is down." He hesitated. "I want to see you on a personal level, Ella. Have dinner with you."

"J.D., I'm your doctor, not your next conquest."

Her notion of him dug into a nerve. "Who the hell said anything about conquests? I'm asking you to sit across a table and have a meal and a bottle of wine with me. That's it."

"Can't happen."

"Can't or won't?"

"Both. Now I need to get some sleep and so do you. 'Night."

"Ella—dammit, wait!"

When he didn't hear the dial tone, his eyes closed in relief. "Thank you," he said quietly. "Look, I'll get to the point. I told you I don't lie and I don't. I'm attracted to you, all right? And I think it's there for you, too. Now, maybe I'm presumptuous, but I don't think so. I feel it every time you look at me. I'm familiar with a woman's response and—don't hang up because I'm not being arrogant. You treat me differently than other patients. You're reserved, you look away when our eyes meet, which intrigues me, Ella. You make me wonder. I've never wondered about a woman." Pressing a finger and thumb against his eyes, he said, "And I can't believe I'm making an absolute ass out of myself but there you have it."

Lungs laboring as though he'd run hurdles, he gripped the phone so hard his hand shook. *Hell*, he'd never been so nervous around a woman in his life. What was the matter with him?

For five slow heartbeats, silence. Had she hung up after all?

Then, "I'm not saying yes and I'm not saying no. I understand you want an answer tonight, but I can't give it."

"Okay." He could deal with that. After the litany he'd given, a *maybe* was more than he had expected. Maybe had possibility. Reams of possibility.

"However," she went on, "we will not discuss this again until the day of your discharge. Agreed?"

Which could be tomorrow. "Agreed."

"And J.D.?"

"Yeah?"

"What you just said?" Pause. "You're right." She hung up.

His smile was slow but strong. That maybe had just ballooned into a yes. And tomorrow was a whole new day.

* * *

He was eating breakfast when his BlackBerry indicated a text message from NHC. Grabbing the device from the side table, he snorted. Took his boss long enough. It had been three days since J.D. called the man and left a voice mail about his knee surgery.

Opening the message, he noted its subject: "Congratulations." J.D. frowned, read:

You've got the inside track. Perfect opportunity to observe hospital staff. Talk to administrator. He's easy to convince. Present case Feb. 26. –FJS

"Well, Frank Jerry Sorenson," J.D. muttered, closing the BlackBerry and picturing the bull-necked senior executive chairing the thirty-seat mahogany table in the New York boardroom like a kingpin. "Thanks for the heartfelt commiseration about my knee."

Should it surprise him?

'Course not. Frank was all business. If one of his grunts—which, even with his recent promotion, included J.D.—fell ill or caused a ripple in NHC's ever-widening pool of conquests, that grunt was either fired or demoted. J.D. could thank his fairy godmother that Frank considered his wrecked knee an opportunity. On the bright side, he'd keep his promotion and his position. And, seven years of slaving wouldn't be in the toilet.

Appetite lost, he pushed his breakfast tray aside and thought about the message he would return to Frank. *Sound enthusiastic. Don't let him think you're in pain or having a problem.*

"Problems" meant your fingers got squashed as the guy behind you took a giant step upward on the ladder of success. FJS hated problems. In other words, kiss butt—and imagine a raise.

He flicked open the BlackBerry, clicked Reply. *Done* he wrote. Frank drooled over cryptic notes that said precisely what he wanted to hear. J.D. closed the device just as Ella walked into his room, a smile on her pretty lips. His heart leapt.

"How's my patient this morning?" she asked, going straight for his foot, and pressing two fingers against his pedal pulse.

If she said *my* patient again, his tongue wouldn't work for a week. As it was he barely mumbled, "Much better, thanks."

"Good." She wrote her findings on his chart and he realized she wore her white lab coat over jeans this morning. "Rest and relaxation today, okay? No strenuous exercises. I don't want that fever back. And then tomorrow you're home free."

"You mean I'm in bed all day?"

She smiled. "All day."

"Doc, that sounds like a hell—heck—of an idea if it involved a woman, but—Whoa, the lady blushes. Now there's a unique sight."

A little laugh erupted. "Yes, I imagine it is for you."

"What's that supposed to mean?"

"It means…" She leaned forward, shone the eye gizmo in his left pupil; he could smell this morning's shower on her skin, in her hair. "That you're beyond redemption."

He clapped his chest. "You injure my sensibilities."

"Hmm." She looked into his right eye, but he caught

the hint of a grin—and damn near kissed it before she straightened to write on his chart. As she reached for the blood pressure cuff, he noticed her long, slim fingers, imagined them around other parts of his anatomy. For a moment, he closed his eyes.

"Hurt?" she asked.

He snapped to attention. "Huh?"

"Do you need a painkiller?"

Yeah, but not the kind she meant. "You available?"

Her eyes locked on his. Again a corner of her mouth twitched. She was laughing at him. He was in pain and she was laughing. "It's not funny," he grumbled.

"Let's have a peek at the knee, shall we?"

"Let's not." He squirmed under the covers, not wanting her to look at the spot on his leg barely twelve inches from his arousal….

Both her dark brows lifted. "Something wrong, Mr. Sumner?"

Oh, yeah, there was *something* all right. His erection. "J.D.?"

"Look, can we do it later?" *Great word choice, J.D.*

"Fine, I'll get June to redress your leg. When you're ready."

He caught her hand. "I want you." *No good, no good.*

She studied his fingers curled around her wrist and he forced himself to let go.

"That won't be possible," she said, as though the texture of her skin hadn't etched itself onto his palm. "This is actually my day off. Once I've finished rounds I'm heading back home."

"You're leaving me here all day—alone?" he asked, at last understanding why she wore jeans under that lab coat.

"I am."

His heart kicked into his throat. She was his lifeline. Knowing she was in the hospital made his day bearable. At night, she was less than twelve hours away. And if he called her that time was sliced to six hours. But an entire twenty-four hours while he had no idea of her whereabouts…?

"Ella, I…" *Hate hospitals. My dad hated hospitals. My mother died here. It's stupid, I know, but hospitals scare the hell out of me.*

"You'll be okay." She touched his hand, that quick re-assuring touch. Just as swift, he caught her fingers again.

"Don't—" *Don't leave me alone.* His chest burned with shame. Talk about instant deflation. He was a coward of the first degree. A wimp in a man's body. He wished he could control his fears. He hoped she wouldn't tell her colleagues. If FJS found out…

For a weighty moment, she let her hand remain under his. "J.D., is something wrong?"

Holding her gaze, he shook his head once.

Her hand slid from his. "Sure?"

"I'm fine." He mustered a grin. "Don't miss me too much, okay?"

A small bark of laughter escaped. "Don't consider yourself so important." At the door she hesitated, a soft smile on her lips. "You know, humility is a virtue I admire very much." Then she was gone.

J.D. stared at the empty doorway as the sounds of the

hospital returned—a trolley clattering with breakfast dishes; a page for Dr. Mason; nurses in the corridor, discussing an upcoming surgery…

Humility, she'd said. He was doomed. Humility wasn't in his repertoire of emotions. You didn't get to the top of the achievement ladder carrying a briefcase of humility.

Okay, she wanted him to be humble. Fine. Hadn't he decided to be a different man?

So if he gave it some thought he could, he supposed, reach a compromise, take that step toward change, toward…God help him…*humility*.

Feeling more at ease, he chuckled quietly. Of all the women he'd known—and he'd been familiar with a few—Ella was a puzzle he had absolutely no clue how to piece together.

He couldn't decide if that was bad or good.

Chapter Five

A light snow had begun to fall from slate-gray skies when Ella pulled into the church parking lot an hour before lunch. Already a small group hovered under the overhang of the side doors opening to the basement stairs. Below, the soup kitchen for Walnut River's homeless was in full swing.

After completing her residency at Massachusetts General Hospital in Boston, then returning to her hometown last summer, she'd been involved with the soup kitchen and its clientele. A number of the homeless were elderly, some intellectually disabled. Some had been on the streets for years, sleeping on sidewalks or in Dumpsters—sometimes through bitter winter nights—and prowling the city for handouts and drugs.

The church's minister, Rev. Oliver Blackwell, had referred Ella's first "street" patient two weeks after she began her practice at the hospital's medical clinic. Freddie Meikle was seventy-eight, an intellectually disabled man who had lived the streets for nearly thirty years. He had no family. Walnut River's sidewalks were home, the church's kitchen his dining table.

Ella had treated the old guy for severe arthritis in his knees and hands at Rev. Blackwell's request. The church offered a small stipend from their budget to cover some of the costs, but she'd refused. Instead, she had taken the case to Peter, who brought it to the board of directors. Two months later, with the aid of the hospital's Sunshine Fund, Ella capped Freddie's knees with plates.

Shutting off the car's motor, she saw the old guy wave and rush into the parking lot. His booted feet shuffled on the trampled snow and his thin shoulders drooped under his oversized army jacket.

"Hiya, Doctor Wilder," he called in his sweet, high voice. "You comin' to eat with us?"

"Sure am, Freddie. Do you know what's on the menu?"

"Uh-huh. Beef barley soup. It smells *goood*. I think Mrs. T made it."

Mrs. T. was Prudy Tavish, another of Ella's across-the-alley neighbors. Prudy lived next to Jared Sumner and, in partnership with her daughter, owned the delightful little deli called Prudy's Menu on Lexington Avenue, the main street of Walnut River. Each Sunday, she brought the day's homemade specialty to Rev. Blackwell's kitchen, and from the scent drifting through the side

vents, Freddie was right. Today she'd brought her wonderfully thick and tasty beef barley.

"Then I'm in luck," she said. "I'm starved as a bear."

Guffawing, Freddie fell into step beside Ella. "Ain't no
bears out now, Dr. W. They's hibernatin' in the mountains."

"Well, then." She smiled. "Guess I'm hungry as a
squirrel."

Another hoot. "Squirrels most likely in holes now, too.

They had reached the side entrance where several
other men and one woman she recognized stood, rubbing
their gloved hands and blowing white puffy breaths.

"Can we go in now, Dr. W?" Freddie's voice escalated
to a whine. "'S cold out."

"Hold on." She rang the buzzer.

"Hello?" the minister's voice came through the intercom.

"It's Ella Wilder, Reverend. May we come in?"

"Sure thing, Doc. How many so far?"

The question was the same every Sunday when she
rang the basement bell.

"Seven."

"Come on in, then."

A second later, the door buzzed. Ella waited for the
early birds to clomp down the stairs and line up at the end
of the kitchen counter where the food would be distrib-
uted within the next twenty minutes.

"Freddie," she called to the old gent clutching the stair
railing. "How are your fingers these days?" He continued to suffer from chronic arthritic joint pain, so Ella administered his medication via his long-time pal Rev.
Blackwell, whom Freddie saw twice a week.

"They're fine, Doc. No more pain."

They went into the spacious basement with its long tables and stacking chairs, ready for the lunch crowd.

"May I see?" she asked. "Just need to check for swelling."

Like a child, he stopped and removed his gloves, shoving them into his coat pockets. "See," he said, pointing to the twisted joint of his left middle finger and pinky. "Ain't near so bad no more."

She took his gnarled hands and examined each bony finger. The nails had grown unkempt over the past two weeks and grime lined the cuticles. She felt each knuckle, pressing gently, working her way across his hand and palm and probing the ulna bones in his dirt-rimmed wrists. He hadn't flinched and she was satisfied.

"I told you," he said, his grin wide and showing several gaps where teeth had once been.

She nodded. "You did, Freddie. Now, go wash your hands before you eat, okay?"

"Okay." He shuffled toward the rear of the basement and the washrooms.

Ella watched him go. He'd been one of her first patients as a licensed and certified doctor. For the rest of her life, she would remember him with tenderness in her heart.

Reverend Blackwell walked over. "Looks like we're getting a good crowd again."

"I wish we wouldn't," she said, watching more people come through the doors. "Because then we'd know they were kicking their drug addictions or were cared for by their families."

"Or dead," he said.

She smiled sadly. "That's not my option."

"Nor mine, Ella. How's Freddie?"

"Good. Fingers are actually starting to look normal again. The meds are helping. Did he get that coat from you?"

Oliver shook his head. "Prudy gave it to him. Was her husband's from the army."

Ella's cell phone rang. "Excuse me a moment." She pulled the phone from her shoulder purse. "Dr. Wilder."

"Ella." It was Peter. "Did you come in this morning?"

"Just to do a quick round. Why?"

"How many times have I told you to take time off when you *have* time off?"

"Did you call to check up on me again, big brother?" A grin tugged her lips.

"Not on your life." She heard him sigh. "Actually, I called to ask if you spoke with your patient, Mr. Sumner, this morning."

Immediately, she strode to the back of the room, to the women's washroom and the quiet there. "I checked his vitals. What's wrong?"

"Henry Weisfield came to see me."

Henry was the hospital administrator, the CEO of the institution's business and legalities, the man who oversaw all that went on in the belly of the medical community. He was also retiring in a few months—and he semi-favored NHC's takeover proposition. Scuttlebutt, however, indicated he lacked the faculties to make coherent decisions anymore and simply wanted to spend his last remaining years fishing, gardening and golfing. Not necessarily in that order.

"What did he want?" Ella asked, pushing through the door of the washroom. Thankfully, it was empty.

"He's given permission for one of NHC's people to observe the hospital's workings. Can you believe it?" He groaned. "Having NHC snooping around will be suicide."

"How so?" She checked her face in the mirror. The collar of her black, woolen coat nudged the hem of her hair. Time for a cut. She turned away and leaned her fanny against the sink's counter. "We don't have anything to hide. Let the guy check around for a day or two. All he'll see is a great hospital with a fantastic staff."

"The whole thing smells of rat dung."

"Paranoia doesn't look good on you, Peter. Give a little. What's Bethany say?"

"Says Weisman doesn't much give a damn and why should he? In a couple months, he'll be hitting the golf course. Meantime, he's not rocking the boat. Plus, he's half in favor of NHC taking over."

So she'd heard, but hadn't had the time to really sit down and analyze the hospital administrator's viewpoints. "Who are they sending?" she asked.

"The pigeon's already in place."

A chill ran up her spine. Only one fitted the bill. "J. D. Sumner."

"Correct."

"But you knew about his proposal—or NHC's—four days ago. And his knee injury was not done on purpose, Peter. I can't believe you'd think that way."

"Of course not. The injury was an accident, but I don't think he was sent here on a whim. He's been recently promoted and they want to see what kind of bacon he can bring home."

Ella hated slotting J.D. in that role. He seemed like a nice person, funny—albeit a little stuck on himself where women were concerned. But… "How can you be so sure?" she asked Peter. "Is that what Weisfield said?"

"I did some digging."

She didn't want to know what his digging had uncovered or who had helped. Or why he'd dug into J.D.'s history in the first place.

"I hear he likes you," her brother said offhandedly.

"I hope most of my patients like me," she shot back.

"I meant as a woman."

"Then you're listening to hospital gossip."

"So it's true?"

She laughed, but it sounded hollow and…a little cross. "Come on, Peter. You know better than to listen to the grapevine."

"There's never smoke where there isn't fire," he countered.

"Now you're quoting Mom." Their mother had died five years ago of cancer. Ella felt her loss still; some nights she mourned her parents and longed for the days when they had laughed and joked and sat at Christmas and Thanksgiving dinners, when each offered wisdom in their own way. Alice Wilder had loved quotes.

Peter said, "She had a point. Just be careful, Ella. That's all I'm saying."

"Fine, you've said it."

"Okay. I'll let you get back to the soup kitchen. Holler if you need another pair of hands down there."

"We're good. See you later." They hung up.

The washroom door swung open and a young woman, bundled in two coats and a knitted red hat, entered. Recognizing her, Ella smiled and turned on the sink's tap to wash her hands. "Getting crowded out there, Mavis?"

"'Bout fifty, maybe more."

"Have you decided to try detox?" she asked without preamble, knowing addicts could vanish in a blink of an eye.

The woman cast a furtive glance at the door. "Maybe."

"I know someone who can get you help," Ella went on casually.

"Okay." Clearly Mavis wanted to escape, either into a stall or out the door.

"Her name is Isobel Suarez." Ella turned on the hand dryer. "She's a friend of mine and a really nice person."

Mavis shifted from one foot to the other.

"If you want me to introduce you, tell Reverend Blackwell."

Mavis slipped into a stall. The conversation was done. "Bye, Mavis," Ella said.

No response.

Maybe one day, but not today.

Don't hope too much, Ella.

She returned to the noisy, crowded soup kitchen— and wondered how much more the church could do if corporations such as NHC had a vested interest in helping people like Freddie and Mavis.

Most of all, she wondered what J.D. would say. If she asked. Which she wouldn't. The less J.D. knew of her work, the less she'd need to keep from him.

J.D. lay a long time without moving, pretending to sleep.

God almighty, his father had come to visit him. He'd known the instant the old man sat down in the chair next to the bed. Pops had brought the smell of snow with him and a hint of the house of J.D.'s childhood, that light musty scent of aged hardwood floors and water leaks and decades of boots at the back door.

Truth was, long ago J.D. had loved the old house with its tiny, boxed rooms and gingerbread eaves and massive spruce on the thumbprint-sized front lawn.

Face it, J.D., you loved that house on Birch Avenue far better than your sleek condo in Manhattan. The condo half the size of his daddy's home and costing twenty years of the old man's pay.

With a long, slow breath, he opened his eyes and looked at the empty chair where his father had sat. Why hadn't he let the old man know he was awake? Why hadn't he said, *Hey, Pops. How you doing? Good to see you. It's been too long.*

Because J.D. didn't know how to connect with his father.

Was it any wonder he shied away from getting too serious in a relationship with a woman? Oh, he'd tried a couple of times to go the distance, but each time the relationship had ended. He hadn't been able to tell the woman he loved her. He hadn't needed, wanted, yearned the way he supposed a man should if he loved a woman. Without a qualm, he could put her out of his mind.

Ella Wilder was his doctor, his single link to the outside. He *had* to think of her. That would end tomorrow upon discharge. Once he got back to the Walnut River Inn and his laptop, he had no doubt the sweet-voiced doctor would be a distant memory.

Liar. You can't wait until she's back on shift so you can see her, talk to her. J.D. frowned. All right, he admitted she was easy on the eyes, but she could never be in his picture. She was small town; he'd become a city boy. She was family oriented—working with her brother was proof; J.D. was a loner. His gut crimped. *Your dad came to see you, jerk, and you pretended to be asleep. You don't have to be alone. It's what you choose.*

And there it was. Once again, he was listing reasons not to smell the roses—as the adage went. Yeah, he was a regular class act.

So why did he feel so damned disillusioned?

Because, had he opened his eyes, looked at his old man, they would have had nothing to say to each other.

Nothing at all.

Same as always.

Chapter Six

She wouldn't rush to his room first. She would do her rounds in order this time. No favorites.

But she couldn't wait to see him and wondered if he felt the same, if he had this crazy yearning to lock eyes, this need to hear her voice, her words. Was he waiting for her hands on his skin?

Don't miss me too much, okay?

Twenty-four hours, and he'd been right. She missed him, and it was…strange and thrilling. And when she rose at dawn, dressed, ate her bowl of oatmeal, excitement had run through her.

She tried not to glance out her kitchen window and across the alley to the house where J.D. had been raised. Yesterday afternoon when she'd called the nurses' desk to

obtain a quick update on her patients, she'd been told of
J.D.'s visitor. June had recognized the old man; after all,
he had been in Ella's care four months ago, lying in the
room across the hall from where J.D. was recovering.

"What's wrong with me, Molly?" she asked the cat
twining around her ankles. "It's like I'm sex starved." At
that she sighed. It wasn't possible to be sex starved when
you'd never feasted at the banquet. *Jeez.* How was she
coming up with this drivel?

"I won't deny it," she muttered, setting out a fresh
bowl of water for Molly. "I've had *it* on the brain since
he came into my care."

And then there were the dreams and fantasies. With
J.D. naked and her naked and bed sheets and pillows and
kisses and hands here and fingers there and…

Sheesh, Ella! Enough already!

Wishing she'd booked a two-week vacation and gone
to California to visit her brother David, she slung on her
coat, grabbed her keys and trudged out the back door.

A vacation would've prevented her from treating
J. D. Sumner.

At 6:58 a.m. she began her rounds. First was a teenager
with a broken shoulder, next was a seventy-year-old woman
who'd need spinal surgery. Ella worked down the list, deliberately slowing her pace as she treated her patients, conscious the distance to J.D.'s room shrunk with each step.

And then he was next. "Good morning," she sang,
sailing through the open doorway.

He lay on his side facing her. Ashley, the physiotherapist, worked J.D.'s leg.

"It's not *that* good," he grumbled through white lips.

"Problems?" Ella asked the woman.

J.D. answered, "I'm out of here, Doc, whether you say so or not. I'm not staying another day."

She stood beside Ashley, who paused the exercise so Ella could see the area of concern. "Looks fine. The swelling is gone, the incision is healing nicely." She checked his heart rate for ten seconds. "Pulse is normal. Good circulation." Scanning his chart, she saw his BP reading an hour ago was one-ten over seventy. Excellent. "All right," she said. "You can go any time after eleven."

"Why not now?"

"Because," she said as Ashley gathered her tools and left the room, "I instruct my patients with home care before they leave."

J.D. frowned. "So do it now."

"I don't have time now." She moved toward the door.

"Then later. I'll call you from the inn."

"Won't you be staying with your father?"

His eyes narrowed. "News does travel fast."

She gave him an encouraging smile, but he looked away.

"I won't be staying with him," he said.

Something in his tone, the turn of his mouth, had her returning to the bed. "Is everything okay, J.D.?"

He drew a hard breath. "As to be expected." Cynicism flicked across his eyes. "My father and I aren't on the best of terms. That okay enough for you?"

For several seconds she studied him. "Want to talk about it?"

His lips lifted imperceptibly. "You my confessor now, Doc?"

"We can be good sounding boards if necessary."

"Doctor-patient confidentiality and all that?"

"Exclusively."

He pinched the bridge of his nose. "Look. Pops and I haven't talked in, I don't know, five years or more. We're not the communicative kind. He does his thing, I do mine. Why he came yesterday is beyond me. I didn't call him or ask him to come."

"You're his son," she said simply.

He stared. "You're kidding, right?"

"Not at all. Fathers are funny. They may not seem like they care, but most often it's that they care too much." She thought of her own dad, whom she missed more than she could describe. What she wouldn't give to have one more minute—heck, thirty more seconds with him. J.D. was luckier than he realized.

"Caring wasn't on my old man's agenda," he said. "Pops couldn't wait for me to leave home. Know what he said when I turned eighteen? 'If you're gonna get a life, get a damned good one. End of story.' He loved staying that. 'End of story.'" With an abrupt grin the darkness left his eyes. "There you go, Doc. Got some jeez for my whine?"

Ella couldn't help laughing. "Okay—jeez," she repeated, glad to see that sexy smile again. "And for your effort I'll drive you back to the inn." She strode for the door.

"Wait a sec," he called before she could escape. "You don't drop an offer like that and go."

Ella paused in the doorway. "Our policy is we don't leave our patients stranded."

"That's going a bit above and beyond, isn't it?" His eyes bored into hers. "What's in it for you?"

"In it for me?" For a moment, she stared at him before realizing he saw it as some kind of payoff. Anger struck. "There is nothing in it for me, Mr. Sumner. Our hospital may not have everything your company can offer, but there is one thing we do have and that's heart. Our doctors and nurses care for our patients, not just in here, but when they leave the premises. We want them to heal, which means following their treatment to the end. We don't want them back here."

His eyes softened. "Okay," he said. "You've convinced me."

"I'll see you at eleven."

"Ella."

Again, she waited.

"I'm glad you're my doctor," he said quietly.

She did not return his smile. Nodding once, she left. What on earth had she gotten herself into?

Oh, Ella, you are in such deep, deep water with this man.

For the first time in twenty years, she had no idea how to swim.

Stomach in a knot—which she blamed on too much caffeine—she returned to his room at eleven. It was empty, tidy, the bed linens changed and pulled to military standards. His cell phone, water bottle, watch—all that was his—were gone from the night table. She turned and went to the nurses' station.

"Mr. Sumner check out, June?" she asked the nurse sitting at one of the computers.

"He left about ten minutes ago."

"Did someone pick him up?"

"Not that I saw. He told us he was leaving and that he'd catch a cab. Didi assisted him downstairs. She was taking her lunch break afterward so you'll probably find her in the cafeteria."

"Thank you." Ella took the stairs to the main floor.

Between a pair of crutches, J.D. stood at the big windows beside the entrance doors with Didi at his side. Both looked toward the access lane and parking lot where people, bundled in winter wear, came and went.

"You were supposed to wait," Ella murmured coming to stand beside J.D.

"Hey, Dr. Wilder," Didi greeted from J.D.'s other side. "Cab shouldn't be much longer."

"Thanks, Didi. Go have your lunch. I'll wait with Mr. Sumner."

The nurse nodded, understanding Ella's need to have a moment with her patient. She handed over a plastic sack.

When they were alone, Ella gazed out at the gray day. This morning's skiff covered most vehicles' hoods and roofs. A taxi drove up and stopped in front of the doors and a nurse waiting with an elderly woman using a walker hurried out to speak to the driver. Seconds later, the woman eased her patient into the front seat, then climbed into the rear and the cab drove away.

"That standard around here?" J.D. asked. "Medical staff taking patients home?"

"Only if the patient has no family or someone to pick them up. We don't put people in cabs and say *sayonara* after having surgery. Too much can go wrong. A nurse will ensure the patient is secure and comfortable in their home before leaving the premises."

"Are these special nurses you've hired for the job?"

"They're home-care nurses who work out of the hospital."

"You going to tuck me into my room?"

No, but I want to. Shoving the thought aside, she jingled the sack Didi had given over. "These your things?"

"Yeah. The rest are at the Walnut River Inn." He hobbled forward. "Changed my mind, Doc. I decided on a cab after all."

"And I told you I needed to give you some home-care instruction, then I'd drive you to where you wanted to go."

"Don't you have patients to cut into?"

"Not until this afternoon. It's my lunch break now and I take that at home when I can. Today I can."

An eyebrow lifted. "You want to take me to *your* home? Hell, why didn't you say? I would've waited in your car."

Just like that tension rolled from her shoulders. Her lips twitched. "You never miss a beat, do you?"

"Not when I can pull a smile from you."

Briefly, those green eyes between their pitch lashes

flashed and held her hypnotized. Mentally, she shook free. *Duty, Ella.* "My car is in the staff lot behind the hospital."

"Cab company's not going to appreciate losing a fare," he said and maneuvered his crutches around.

"There are always people needing rides from here," she said. "He'll earn his dollar, don't worry."

They walked slowly down the hallway leading to the rear of the building. When they'd reached the exit, she said, "I'll bring the car up so you don't have to go through the snow," then ran across the parking lot. While the motor warmed, she brushed off the thin coat of snow. Two minutes later, her Yaris sat parked beside the door and she hurried into the building.

"I'm not a complete invalid, Doc," J.D. muttered as she took his arm and assisted him to the passenger door.

"It's a safety measure. I don't want anything happening to that knee ever again."

"What about me?"

"What about you?" They'd reached the car and she lifted his right leg carefully as he positioned himself onto the seat.

This close she saw he'd missed a tiny spot shaving, right next to his ear lobe. Had he been in a hurry? Anxious to leave? Anxious about her offer to drop him at the hotel?

The scent of the hospital's soap on his skin shot pheromones into her veins.

"You're staring, Doc," he whispered.

Ella jerked back, bumping her head on the rim of the door.

J.D. winced, caught her hand. "Hurt?"

"A little. My fault."

He grinned. "Nah, it's mine. I have that effect on—"

She slammed the door shut. The man was impossible. And she was crazy to be taking him back to his room when Didi could have done the job as well.

She rounded the car, climbed behind the wheel.

"You okay?" he asked as she drove down the lane to a side street.

"Just peachy."

He shot her a grin. "A little touchy after the bump, are we?"

"Not at all. Hardly felt it."

At that he grunted. She drove through town. The snowplow had cleared most of the main arteries to the hospital and other public-service venues. Turning north, Ella headed down the long winding street toward the Walnut River Inn.

The B and B–styled hotel was one of Walnut River's first notable structures dating back to 1850 and located on a wooded acre fringing the town's outskirts. Through barren branches of ancient maples fronting the white clapboard three-story, a wide front porch with cane-backed rockers currently covered against winter, welcomed guests and visitors.

She pulled up along the curb near a wrought-iron street lamp advertising the inn's name. While she knew of the Inn, Ella had never ventured inside or met the owners.

J.D. gazed up the curved swept walkway sprinkled with sand. "It'll be damned good to eat a home-cooked meal again," he remarked. "All right. I'm out of here." He swung open the door.

"Hang on." Ella was out of the car and at his side in seconds.

"I can manage, Doc. I had knee surgery, not an amputation. At least not the last time I looked."

"Smart aleck," she said, handing him the crutches.

"How long do I have to use these?"

"A day or two, then I'd like you to use a cane." She took his arm. "For a few more days, until you can stand on the leg without pain. Ashley has booked you into PT for the rest of this week. Do you know where it's located?"

"Main floor. Opposite the library and solarium."

Slowly they went up the walk. "Next week you can attend the clinic across the street from the hospital. Keep with the antibiotics for seven days. Then I want to see you again." They had reached the Inn's front door.

J.D. held her in place, his long, hard fingers covering hers on his arm. "And I want to see you again, Ella."

Her name in that deep voice caught her breath. "I've sched—"

"I mean personally. Outside the hospital and my medical care."

She shook her head. "As I've said before, you're a patient."

Several heartbeats passed. He said, "We'll talk in a couple days. When I come to observe you and your floor."

Apprehension skipped up her spine; she recalled Peter's words about Henry Weisfield cutting deals with Northeastern HealthCare. "Just so you know, I'm not in favor of Mr. Weisfield's decision."

"Even if it meant a new CAT or bone-density scanner?"

"Ours work fine, J.D." She had to stand behind Peter, who knew more about the situation than Ella. As temporary chief of staff, Peter had an excellent finger on the budget pulse and the hospital's necessities.

"But new ones would be nice." His smile went into his eyes and she relaxed. Perhaps the company's agenda was only to assist small hospitals, not take them over. Perhaps she and Peter and everyone else had read their intentions wrong….

No. She couldn't lose sight of J.D.'s reason for being in Walnut River in the first place. Or NHC's takeover bid.

"Of course. State-of-the-art equipment is always on a hospital's wish list," she said smoothly, "but that doesn't mean we need to throw out our current equipment if it gives the data we require. That's excessive spending."

A cold wind whipped around the corner of the porch and cut through her jacket. They'd stood outside too long. Not wanting him to get cold, she pushed open the front door.

Immediately, the smell of baking had her stomach grumbling.

J.D. chuckled. "Greta's afternoon cookies. Come back at four when she sets a plate out in the parlor for the guests and I guarantee you'll be drooling like Pavlov's dog."

"I've never drooled," Ella replied, though her stomach rebelled. And she wouldn't be back here. At all.

J.D. leaned in close. "Oh, come on. Not even in high school when the class jock walked by?"

She snorted. "Especially not when he walked by. If your room is on another floor, I hope this place has an elevator."

"It's on the main." He bounced his eyebrows. "We could order in and have a quiet lunch together."

"I'll pass. I need to feed my cat. Take care, J.D." Now that she was leaving and wouldn't be seeing him again, except once more for a checkup, sadness slipped into her heart. He was a good man who made her laugh when most of her days were serious.

On impulse, she hugged him, meaning it to be quick and sisterly. But his left arm closed around her and held her against his body for several beats longer than appropriate.

Oh, but he felt wonderful, all hard angles and long, lean bones and with her nose pressed against his jacket, his scent filled her lungs. Her heart trembled. Had he kissed her hair?

"I'll miss you," he said, voice sandy.

She stepped from the warmth of his clasp. "Bye."

Outside, she welcomed the biting wind on her hot cheeks.

He's your patient, Ella. There are ethics involved, don't forget.

Never mind that he worked for the wrong company.

Thirty minutes later, J.D. sat on his bed and opened the chicken sandwich he'd had delivered from Prudy's Menu. Greta, the Inn's owner, had recommended the place for the best sandwiches in town. Prudy. Jeez, she'd brought him home-baked cookies from her shop when he was a kid. Some things never changed.

And some things had. They were changing whether he liked it or not. His dad's silent visit, for example. What had it meant? The old man never went out of his way to see J.D., to communicate. But the minute he got laid up, Pops appeared like a shadow on the wall.

Then there was Dr. Ella. When had a woman consumed his mind the way she did? All she had to do was walk past him and he wanted to take her to bed. And that hug in the foyer? He'd damn near sunk his tongue into the wet warmth of her mouth. Damn near dragged her into the bedroom, slammed the door and sunk into her other parts.

His heart thudded in his chest, his groin pulsed to the beat. The woman was driving him crazy. He wished to hell NHC hadn't demanded he tour the hospital for the next week or so. He wished he could avoid physio-therapy tomorrow.

He did not want to see her again.

He couldn't wait to see her again.

The sandwich sat on the night table, forgotten. Was she back at the hospital, treating her patients? Was she prepar-ing for surgery, going over vitals, charts, records, asking questions? Was the patient young, old, male, female?

He envied the person hearing her voice, feeling the warm, gentle touch of her hands.

J.D. scrubbed his palms down his cheeks. He was a jerk. Those patients were in pain, otherwise they wouldn't be having surgery. How could he envy that?

Because you're letting a woman control your emotions.

At that he almost laughed. "Like you have any

emotions *to* control," he muttered. Popping a painkiller, he realized a truth. Ella Wilder had cracked the corroded lock on his heart.

Two days and she hadn't seen him, not on the main floor, heading for physio, not wandering the second floor on an "observation" hunt for his employer.

What had she expected?

Nothing. He was a patient, one leaving Walnut River in a couple of weeks. Then why on earth had she expected…*something*? She asked herself the question again while standing at the big stainless steel sinks and scrubbing for the arthroscopy she would perform on a forty-year-old woman experiencing early signs of arthritis.

You need a life, Ella. You need to go to a bar, have a couple of margaritas, sit beside some hunk on a stool and let the cards fall where they will. Or go shopping, buy a bikini and fly to some beach where sweaty guys played volleyball in the sand. Any of the above won't lead to expectations. They'll lead to…to…

Sex. Plain and simple.

Sex without conditions.

Sex without commitment.

Sex, sex, sex.

"Patient is ready, Doctor," the circulating nurse called from the O.R. doorway.

"Be right there, Shelly."

Get your mind on task, Ella, or you're going to regret ever meeting J. D. Sumner. You are not a sex-starved woman. You are a doctor. Breathing deep, she stepped away from the tub. *Okay. Count backward. Ten, nine, eight, seven... All right. You're good to go.*

Water dripping, she walked to the hot-air dryer, punched it on with an elbow. Keeping her hands aloft, she pushed butt first through the doors of the O.R. where the scrub nurse tugged a pair of surgical gloves over Ella's fingers. She pushed back the flutter of nerves as she surveyed the instruments placed on the stainless steel trays. "How's Wanda doing?" she asked the anesthesiologist.

"Out."

"All right. Let's make her a new knee."

Two hours later, surgery complete, Ella headed for her examination offices on the fourth floor. Rounding the corner of the corridor leading to the bank of elevators, she gasped when a big body blocked her way and a hand gripped her arm. "J.D.!"

"Hey, Doc, where's the fire?"

The crutches were gone, the cane in place—which he leaned on while he released her slowly, amusement in his eyes. Navy flannel pants outlined the contours of the knee brace and a gray sweater contoured his impressive shoulders.

She brushed at her bangs. "What are you doing here?"

"Working on my report."

Ella's mind blanked when she caught sight of his full bottom lip. His mouth hitched; her gaze shot up. Green eyes glinted.

"Sorry I can't chat," she said, feeling abashment creep along her neck. "I have patients waiting."

"What about this patient?"

She headed down the hall. "You're healing very fast, I see." He followed with barely a limp.

"Have dinner with me, Ella."

She had no time for this. "Are you asking because I'm your doctor and you want information about the hospital?"

He scowled. "I'm asking because I like you. Because—as I've said before—I'm attracted to you."

"Which is why we can't have dinner." Darn, the elevator car was stopping at every floor. She should have taken the stairs. "I don't date patients."

"First, no offense, but I've switched doctors. I have an appointment with Dr. Taggart in Pittsfield for my follow-ups. Second, I'm staying till the end of the month. I've decided to take vacation time after my assignment with WRG is finished."

Panic. Excitement. She squelched both. "J.D., this is not—"

"Please, Ella."

The *please* streamed through her, warm as melted chocolate.

Ding. The car had arrived, the doors slid open. She stepped inside, turned.

He stood with both hands stacked on the handle of the cane, his expression as serious as she'd ever seen. "Will you?"

The doors began to close. "All right," she said quickly. Before the door shut him out, before she could analyze her response.

"Tonight," he called. "I'll call you."

And then she was alone.

She leaned against the wall, hung her head.

Lord. Her brain cells went AWOL when it came to J. D. Sumner. The man was her patient. *Had been* her patient—an act he'd accomplished with deliberate purpose, she was certain. Worse, he worked for a company proposing to take over her hospital.

Don't let Peter find out about J.D.'s personal intentions, was all she could think.

Chapter Seven

Standing in her kitchen, cuddling Molly into her neck and stroking the cat's satiny head, Ella listened to J.D. on the answering machine. He wanted her to call him at the Inn.

Again, she hit Play. Again, his deep voice traveled along the nerves under her skin. If she closed her eyes and imagined…

He stood right behind her, his arms wound around her waist, his hands were on her breasts—

She blinked against the bright kitchen lights. *Fool!*

Setting the cat on the floor, she decided to phone and renege with some excuse. She couldn't *not* call him.

He picked up on the second ring. "I'm sorry, J.D.," she said without preliminaries. "But I can't make dinner tonight. I just got in and I need to go over some notes. I have an early morning meeting."

"It's only dinner, Ella. Not the entire night. Much as I'd like it to be."

She sighed. "I've never met a more persistent man."

"Good. How long will it take you to get here?"

She glanced at the clock. 6:45 p.m. "Half hour." She replaced the receiver before he could respond.

Naturally, he phoned back. "Yes?"

"You pick the place, but make it somewhere nice. And wear a dress." The phone buzzed in her ear.

She looked at Molly, hobbling away, tail flicking the air as if to say, *Fine. Go with him. Don't think of me being home alone.*

Ella swooped up the cat and hurried down the hall. "Oh, Mol." She kissed the animal's head. "You're my special someone."

In the bedroom, she dropped the cat on the quilt and turned for the closet. Forty minutes later, dressed in a brown skirt and an ochre sweater, she was late, excited and nervous. And she gloried in the emotions. It had been so long, so very long since a man had her head in a tizzy and her blood humming.

He stood waiting under the Inn's mellow porch light.

Oh my oh my, but he was beautifully male. Ten years she had examined people, living and deceased, and none had appeared as fit and hale and rugged as J.D. standing on that porch in the semi-darkness of winter. Tall and elegantly dressed in black boots and a long black trench coat, he conveyed a blend of sophistication and danger.

"Where is your cane?" she asked, coming up the walkway.

"Don't need it." He waited until she stood on the bottom step. "I have you." And then he smiled.

If the words *I have you* hadn't sent her to the ground in a puddle, the smile had her gripping the newel post for support.

Soon, she thought. *You will have me. If you wish.* And she saw by his eyes that he did wish…very much.

She went up the stairs, latched onto his arm to assist him down the snowy walkway.

"You are definitely irredeemable, Mr. Sumner. And brash. And, I suspect, unrepentant."

He chortled. "How are you, Doc? By the way, you look fantastic in a skirt. Nice change from those scrubs. Not that I don't like the scrubs, but I don't get to see your lovely legs in them."

Her stomach did a slow twirl. "If you must know, I didn't have time to shave them. Just saying." The non-shave had been deliberate, done to prevent her from doing anything too risqué. Like undressing for him.

"Shaved legs are overrated."

Scoffing mildly, she started them toward the car. "You wouldn't say that if you saw me—" *Naked.*

"Without any clothes?" His eyes were ripe with humor. "Good. Can't wait to get whisker burn."

Her blood went thick. "Hmph."

As she had done three days before, she assisted him into her car. Tonight, however, she did not look into his eyes or pause to sniff the scent on his clothes and hair. Rather, she tucked in his wounded leg and closed the door.

Behind the wheel, she said, "If you don't mind, I'd like to eat in Pittsfield. There's an excellent restaurant called the Dakota that serves the best steaks and seafood you've ever eaten."

"I know the place," he said.

Yes, she thought. Walnut River was his childhood home after all. She pulled from the curb.

They headed out of town and, within minutes, were on the highway leading west. In the CD player Jann Arden sang her poignant *Greatest Hurts.* For the next ten minutes Ella couldn't think of a thing to say—but, oy—she could feel him sitting a foot away, big and invincible, crowding the dash-illuminated confines of her little car. The light swiped the blade of his nose, the perimeter of his cheekbones, the camber of his lips. And whenever he turned his head she felt his glance sear into her flesh. She flicked off the vents, aching for a cold wind.

At last they reached the restaurant and she stepped from the car into the wintry night, relieved to be free of the silence and tension that had increased with every mile.

J.D. waited at the curb until she'd hooked her arm through his and they went inside the rustic restaurant with its hunting-cabin decor of canoes and elk and moose heads mounted from rafters and walls. In a cozy booth they sat across from each other and, under the soft shine of a wall lamp, scanned the menu. Ella ordered the wood-grilled chicken, no rice, extra vegetables, J.D. the filet mignon, medium rare. Neither ordered alcohol. She was the designated driver and he had a week's worth of anti-biotics to finish.

After ordering, Ella looked at J.D. An edge of his mouth lifted in a quiet smile. "You haven't said more than ten words since we drove out of town," he said.

"I was thinking."

"About?" Intensity darkened his eyes.

Her shoulders sagged a little. "Too much, I'm afraid."

"Things at work?"

She shook her head slowly, her eyes on his face. "Me." *You.*

For a moment he watched her. "I think about you, too. A lot. Maybe too much." He reached across the table. "Let me hold your hands, Ella."

"Why?" To the outsider the gesture would appear as if they were in a relationship. As if they were lovers.

"I'm betting they're cold."

She had the urge to take her clenched hands from her lap and shove them under her thighs for warmth, to hide. *Juvenile behavior.*

"Come on," he coaxed. "We're in Pittsfield. The like-lihood of someone recognizing us is remote. That's why we're here, isn't it?"

Oh, she was in trouble. The man understood her far too well. "My hands are chapped," she said swerving from his implication that she wanted to keep their outing a secret. "Too many scrubbings."

"They're the gentlest, most beautiful hands I've seen. They can hold a scalpel and scrape an eyelash off a gnat, they're so steady." Smiling, he held out his palms. "Let me, Ella."

She hadn't gotten past "most beautiful." He was too charming, too magnetic. Entranced, she slid her hands over the wooden surface of the table and he curled his fingers around her, warm as a flame.

"You're like ice." And then he bent his head over their joined hands, blowing a soft gust of air against her fingers, his mouth brushing her thumbs.

Oh, my. Such a simple, sensual act and with a thousand tingling responses!

"J.D.," she whispered, amazed her voice still worked.

"Don't be nervous. It's just me."

"*That's* the problem."

He peered up; stroked his thumbs over the surface of her hands. "What am I going to do with you, Doc?" he asked, though she felt the question was more a self-analysis. Straightening, he set her free. "You are a puzzle. I can't figure you out. Do you know this is a first?"

"What is?" Back in her lap her fingers slid into the opposite sleeves of her light-knit sweater, sealing in the warmth from his body.

"That a woman has my head in a mess."

She forced a laugh. "Once you're back in New York your head will be fine. You'll be back to work, doing activities you're accustomed to." *Dating women who won't muddle your brain.*

"Have you ever thought of working in a bigger hospital?"

"Not once." Before she could explain, the waitress arrived with the bottles of sparkling water they had ordered, and when they were alone again Ella said, "I obtained my degree at Harvard and did my residency at Mass General. But I've always wanted to return home, back to Walnut River General. It's where I grew up and first learned about medicine. I owe that place my life." Smiling, she cupped her water glass. "My dad loved that hospital. He was a good and kind man and he taught me that medicine is an art defined by caring."

As she spoke, J.D. drew closer, setting an elbow on the edge of the table and propping a fist on his thigh.

"Sorry," she said, suddenly conscious of his scrutiny. "I tend to get on a bandwagon sometimes. What about you? What got you into health care?"

He leaned back, as if her question meant nothing, except his posture told a different story and a mask fell across his face. "I grew up believing hospitals weren't good or kind." He frowned and she sensed memories warred within his mind.

He went on. "My dad had a bad experience long ago. My mother died in childbirth." His eyes hardened. "Mine."

"Oh, J.D.... I don't know what to say. Your father must have suffered deeply." *And J.D.*, she thought. Subconsciously, he would have suffered a loss no child should ever experience—that abiding, nurturing love only a mother could give. Then, remembering Prudy at Jared's bedside last fall, Ella took a chance. "Did he ever remarry?"

"Nope. Been a widower for thirty-six years."

That made the situation seem sadder. She imagined the little boy J.D. had been so long ago without a mother to come home to, without a mother to hear humming somewhere in the house—the way it had been with Ella's mother baking cookies. And her sweet-scented hugs. Alice had grown jasmine in her flower-beds and placed sachets among her clothes. It was the thing Ella recalled best, that lovely, light scent on her mother's skin.

Indeed, J.D. had missed a great deal.

The waitress arrived with steaming plates of chicken and filet mignon, fresh salads and seasonal vegetables. Suddenly, Ella realized she hadn't eaten since eleven-thirty that morning.

"Bon appetit," J.D. said with a wink.

For several moments they savored their meals. She was grateful he had suggested dining out; barring hospital food, she hadn't eaten a prepared meal since last summer. Which said something about her personal life. It didn't exist. *One day, Ella, you'll wake up an old maid facing menopause.*

The notion burned in her throat; she reached for her glass of water. Caught in the lamplight, fire stroked J.D.'s hair. From the moment she'd seen him in the E.R., that dark auburn color had attracted her. A color unusual on a man, yet on J.D., it pronounced his knife-keen cheek-bones and square jaw, his dark brows.

Black lashes lifting, his eyes immobilized her across the table. Her every cell stood alert, sensitized.

"Dollar for your thoughts," he said in that deep, raspy Sam Elliot voice.

"I love the color of your hair. I'd give my left kidney for it. Well, not really—" she sipped her water "—but I'd give it some serious consideration. Who'd you inherit it from, your dad or your mom?"

"My mother."

"She must have been very beautiful."

"My dad thought so."

"And you?"

"I concur. From the photos I've seen."

"I'm sorry you never got to know her, J.D."

A nonchalant shrug. "You don't miss what you don't know."

Ella disagreed. She suspected he had missed a mother's love far more than he would acknowledge. "I'll miss my parents forever. They were a very big part of my life." She could not imagine growing up without a mother—or a father, for that matter.

A rueful smile touched J.D.'s mouth. "You were lucky."

"I was," she admitted. "My mom used to read us bedtime stories when we were little, and my dad would come in and tickle our toes. Of course, that would get us all excited, and then we wouldn't want to go to bed at all. Mom would fuss and fume at my dad, but she'd be laughing while she shook her finger at him."

J.D. cut into his steak. "Pops wasn't a story reader. Never had the time." At Ella's frown he shrugged. "No big deal. Besides, he always said he'd read to me later. Good thing I learned to like reading on my own."

An awkward pause descended. Ella wanted his grin, his sexy grin, back, but the way he tilted his head, the relentless line of his mouth… A long-forgotten memory played across her mind.

She said, "I think you and I knew each other when I was a little girl. Well, not really knew each other…" She waggled her head. "Sort of were *aware* of each other."

As she hoped, J.D. laughed. "Now you're making stuff up." He lifted a forkful of mashed potatoes to his mouth.

"Actually, no." Pushing a lock of hair behind one ear, Ella shot him a grin. "My grandmother lived across the alley from your dad. Mom took my sister and me to visit once a week. The year I was in first grade, I saw a red-haired boy—" her gaze skimmed his hair again "—practicing on a skateboard down the cement walkway in Jared's back yard. Grandma said the boy had just gotten the board the day before. Anyway, it was summertime and I remember being fascinated by that skateboard and how the boy could ride like a pro. Then he started practicing in the back alley and I went to the gate and watched through the wooden slats for a long time."

He sat back on the bench. "Unbelievable."

"It is, considering I'd forgotten it myself until just now." Ella took a bite of chicken.

His smile was slow, striking. "So, Doc, we have a history."

A giggle she couldn't hold erupted. "I was six, J.D. Your skateboarding techniques and claim to fame lasted all of fifteen minutes at most before I got bored and went inside."

"Uh-uh, you can't reinvent the story here. You said you were fascinated, not bored."

"I take the fifth. We're talking a six-year-old's attention span."

He cut another piece of steak, dipped it into the extra gravy he'd ordered. "I was your first boyfriend."

"You were no such thing," she retorted.

"You remembered my red hair."

"Who wouldn't? In the sun it blazed like fire."

Whimsy danced over his features. "Like fire, huh?"

"Oh, for heaven's sake," she sputtered. "It's an analogy."

"I know what it is, Doc. I'm just pointing out that you've had me in your memory banks most of your life. Which means—"

"Absolutely nothing."

"—that I was your first boyfriend."

Laughing, she shook her head and pushed her fork into the final piece of chicken. "All depends on whose point of view."

"All right." He set his cutlery on his plate, pushed it aside. "How about this? While I'm in town I'm your boyfriend. Or if that's too tweenish, your significant other."

She studied his eyes, saw a glimmer of something deeper and more substantial.

"J.D.—"

The waitress interrupted to take their plates. J.D. ordered the seasonal fruit crisp for dessert. "One order, two spoons." His gaze was on Ella. "We're sharing tonight."

The words, the mood, *his look* pooled low and hot in her abdomen and she wondered if she'd ever breathe again. Then he looked around the room, said, "I like your style, Doc," and the spell was broken.

The discussion led to safer topics: his love of snowshoeing and hiking, her love of running. She surprised him by enjoying hard-hitting movies like *Blood Diamond*. Most women he knew, he told her, went for light comedies and chick flicks. Her taste in music varied, though she favored songs that spoke to the heart. And he surprised her by his preference for country music.

She ate only three bites of the crisp. Enough to let the sweetness alert her taste buds, and to have him dip his spoon in her area of the bowl, have metal click on metal while his expression specified he knew exactly what he was doing: sharing intimacies reserved for couples that were in each other's soul.

On the drive back to Walnut River, they spoke little, listening to a CD of twenty favorites from her collection at home. Roberta Flack's haunting voice about a woman seeing the face of a special man for the first time filled the dark interior. Although three decades old, the hit trembled through Ella in a way it hadn't before. It was as if the lyrics were hers, as if the singer saw J.D. through Ella's eyes.

She glanced across at the man in the next seat.

He had turned his head and his absorption was entirely on *her* face. Heart jamming her throat, she refocused on the headlights channeling the snow-shouldered highway.

"Just to let you know," he said quietly, "I'm going to kiss you when we get back to the Inn."

Heat shot through her. "Just to let *you* know, that will be my decision to make."

"Agreed. You can decide how hot it'll be."

She clenched the steering wheel to keep from driving off the road. "What if I don't want you to kiss me?"

"You do." His voice was soft sand, the tropical kind that burned your bare toes.

"You're awful sure of yourself." But she heard a quiver of excitement in her voice. She toughened her resolve. "Not every woman you meet wants to jump your bones, J.D."

"Nor do I. Want to jump the bones of every woman I meet."

She chuckled. "Wow. You have standards?"

He was silent for several miles. She drove through the winter darkness, aware her remark had ruined a lovely evening, shame replacing the heat his anticipated kiss had caused.

She stopped in front of the inn's sign, expecting him to throw open the door and climb out as fast as his injured knee would allow in order to get away from her and the chaos of their date.

Instead, he turned. "Yes," he said, threading a hand into the hair at her nape and tugging her gently across the console. "I do have standards. But you've broken them all."

And then he put his mouth on hers.

On initial contact she had thought he might be a devouring kind of guy but he surprised her yet again.

Soft, slow, tender. And everywhere she yearned for more and more and more.

She drank him; she inhaled him.

His fingers wove deeper into her hair, touched her face, trailed the line of her neck. Warm and flavored of fruit, his breath wisped her chin, whispered at her ears. Her eyelids fluttered shut and she rode the sensation, followed his lead, fell into his kiss—into *him*.

J.D. The thought emerged through the dizziness, the want, the need, like a bright, lone star at midnight.

Her hands found the fabric of his shirt, slipped upward along hard muscle and bone, crept around his neck. And hung on.

Was it a moment? She wanted forever.

At last, he lifted away, a finger's width. "Hello, Ella," he whispered and she felt his air caress her tender mouth.

"Hi," she whispered in return.

He kissed her again, a hint of lip to lip. "I need to go in," he said. "Before something…happens."

She didn't need to ask what. She was a doctor. She knew how a man's body functioned in passion. She knew how a woman's body responded and hers was already on fire, ready, willing to consume, *to be consumed.* Carefully, he eased back until he was on his side of the car again and their bodies no longer touched.

"I'll find my way in," he said.

She shook her head. "No, I don't want you slipping on the ice."

She got out to stand beside him on the sidewalk, gripping his arm. They walked to the porch, up the steps, to the door where she released him. "Good night, J.D.," she said. As if she hadn't had the lips kissed off her face two minutes ago.

"How long before you're home?"

"Ten minutes."

"I'll call then, make sure you're okay."

Under the light, she saw that his face held no humor. "I'll be fine, J.D. Thank you for a very enjoyable evening."

She trotted down the steps, strode for her car, welcoming the freezing night air against her swollen mouth, welcoming back wisdom and logic into her head. What she'd done in her little blue Yaris had neither wisdom nor logic, because she'd almost climbed into a man's lap and had sex for the first time and right in the middle of the street. She couldn't get home fast enough. She needed the shelter and safety of her house.

By the time she arrived and put the car in the garage, she was calmer, her body in sync to mind and emotion.

Until she opened the kitchen door and heard the phone playing its "Here Comes the Sun" ringtone.

Chapter Eight

J.D. listened to the fourth ring. She should've been in her house; she'd been gone fifteen minutes, five more than she'd estimated.

Sitting in his skivvies on the four-poster king-sized bed, he stared at the phone in his hand. What was the matter with him that he needed to know she was okay, that he needed to hear her voice again?

He moved to disconnect the cordless when he heard a faint "Hello?" and snatched the phone to his ear.

"You're home," he said unnecessarily.

"Sleep well, J.D."

"I had a great time tonight," he interjected before she clicked off. "I wanted to tell you, but you took off before I got a word out." *Argh.* He sounded like a petulant kid.

Silence. Then, "I'm on E.R. rotation this weekend, so late nights are not an option."

All right, he wouldn't quibble over two extra minutes. "When can I see you again?"

Tonight, he'd barely scraped the surface of Ella Wilder, but what he saw under those meager scuffs beckoned him like a starved man. He didn't understand why he felt the way he did. What he knew was that he'd been empty, heart and soul, for years, maybe all his life and Ella…Ella was a pool of warm water filling up a deep and parched well.

Jeez, why not write some painful teenage poetry, J.D.? I'm sure that *would impress her.* He gave himself a mental shake.

"—and a very busy week ahead," she was saying.

He'd missed half her conversation with all his mooning. "How about coffee then? At the hospital? Ten minutes—"

"Don't you have reports to write? An agenda to meet for NHC?"

"I do, but I also take breaks. Listen," he said, feeling her pull away as if tonight had never happened. "I was serious when I said I'll be your man while I'm in town. We can have a little fun—"

"And I'll be your woman so you get the info you need? That about right?" Her tone was cooler than he'd yet heard.

"Work won't enter the picture. Unless you want it to. Deal?" He scraped at his hair, waiting for her response. When it didn't come he said, "Ella, I just want to see you again. That's it. No hidden agenda. I like you. More than I want to admit, even to myself. You bewitch me. God knows why. I mean I do know why. You're gorgeous, intelligent, witty, sophisticated. Hell." Again a frustrated hand pawed through his hair. "I've never had this happen before."

"This," she said and her voice had softened. "As in wanting a relationship with someone you don't want a relationship with?"

"Yeah. No. Sort of. It's difficult to explain. That kiss tonight…Look, short of sounding like a teenage jock, you do something to me."

The line went quiet. God, he'd offended her with all his idiotic rhetoric. Phone still attached to his ear, he lifted his aching leg onto the bed, sank against the pillows. "Ella?"

"You do something to me, too," came her whisper.

Tiredly, he closed his eyes. "Thank you."

"We'll talk later. Meantime, go visit your father, J.D. He needs you." And then she hung up.

Exhaling slowly, he pressed End. Ten minutes—or was it longer?—he stared at the ceiling with its intricate scrolls and swirls.

She had known of their family since she was six, when J.D. hadn't known a thing about hers until a week ago. Until he met her brother in a boardroom and Ella in the E.R., in the building where his mother had died, the building his dad had hated for more than three decades.

He needs you, she said, minutes ago.

And I need him. The thought startled J.D. For twenty years the bond between he and his old man had steadily eroded. *Not too late to remedy that while you're here.*

Who was he kidding? Pops wasn't a warm, fuzzy kind of guy. And neither was J.D. The old man wouldn't give a rat's ass if his son showed up on his doorstep. Hell, he'd probably tell J.D. he deserved a banged-up knee for not paying attention and slipping on those steps.

He came to see you in the hospital. And that was the crux of it. Old Jared had sought out his son, came to offer support not censure. He'd sat at the side of the bed, still as stone, not opening his mouth once. In those minutes, J.D. sensed a difference in his dad, an unfamiliar difference, one that bordered…heartbreak. Could it be?

Confused, he crawled under the covers.

He'd think about it in the morning, when daylight brought a clearer head and a better attitude.

Weekend rotations during the winter months were often crazy. The weather did not mix well with the townsfolk. They broke ankles, wrists, legs, fractured elbows, injured rotator cuffs, dislocated shoulders. Most injuries were the result of icy traffic accidents, winter sports, shoveling snowy roofs and walkways, disconnecting strings of Christmas lights.

This Saturday, Ella's waiting room was already packed when she read the chart of her first patient, Florence MacGregor, the elderly mother of West MacGregor, who managed the hospital's budget. Last October, when Ella operated on her hip, Florence had shown signs of Alzheimer's.

Now, entering the room with the set of recent X-rays she'd ordered from radiology, she saw the white-haired woman on the examination table, wringing her hands. "Hello, Florence," she greeted.

"Hi, Dr. Wilder. West—he's my son—he wants to talk to you after. He's in the…the…kitchen." Briefly her blue eyes went blank before memory returned. "He's in the waiting room."

Ella nodded. "I'll have a chat with him when we're done. Now, let's have a peek at those hips of yours." She shoved the first X-ray onto the light box. "Right hip looks fabulous, Florence. How's the physio going?"

"I like it," she said. "West is such a good boy. He takes me all the time and helps around the house. He doesn't mean to be overprotective. It's just that he's got so much on his plate, y'know?"

Ella smiled. She wished more children would be as concerned about their aging parents as West was about Florence. "Sometimes overprotection is a good thing."

"Mm-hm." Florence stared at the next X-ray Ella put up. "Does my hip need a…replace…replacement?"

Ella rolled her stool closer and took the old lady's gnarled hand. "We talked about this last fall, Florence. Remember? I wanted your right hip to heal completely before we did the left one."

"It hurts when I walk and…and…and…."

"I know," Ella said gently. "That's why I've scheduled you for surgery on May second. I'll tell West, okay?"

Florence bobbed her head. "West is a good boy. He doesn't want me to worry about the cars." A frown. "I mean the cooking."

"Nor should you," Ella said as though nothing was

amiss. Giving the woman's hand a gentle squeeze, she rose from the stool. "Now let's have a little peek at your new hip. Can you lie down for me?" Keeping her voice soft, she carefully assisted Florence into position.

Ten minutes later, Ella left her patient to dress, then instructed the nurse to send West to her office at the end of the hallway.

"You wanted to see me, Doctor?" a voice asked as she was updating Florence's file. West stood in the doorway of her tiny office. As always he wore a classy dark suit, and his thin face held no smile.

"Hi, West. Take a seat."

She summarized his mother's case. "Don't be alarmed if she's in the hospital longer this time. It'll be her second surgery in a little more than six months, which can set back healing a few weeks."

"Guess it's to be expected," he said. "She is seventy-five."

"Yes. However, there are seniors who've healed more rapidly, but generally those people have maintained a routine of exercise."

West bounced a knee. "And Mom hasn't."

"No. Last fall she admitted she hates exercising. Most people do, so she's not alone. That's why I'd like you to get her involved in a group exercise program along with her physio. Thirty minutes of gentle exercise four or five times a week will help a lot. For now."

"For now?"

Ella considered. The man was Florence's primary care-taker, as well as hospital staff. "I'll be frank, West. Last fall, I mentioned that your mother is heading into dementia. I know it's not an easy thing to hear about a parent, but I strongly urge you to have her tested. For your sake and hers. I know the name of a great doctor who would—"

"No, that's okay." West shook his head and stood. "I'll look into it. Thanks." Pausing at the door, he said, "By the way, that NHC fellow, J. D. Sumner? He's a patient of yours, right?"

Surprised at his turn of topic, Ella said, "You know I can't divulge that information."

"Sure. Just thought you should know he's asking people all kinds of questions. What certain floors need equipment-wise, what doctors want to see upgraded, that sort of thing. I'm wondering why he requires all that info."

A prickle ran up her spine. While she was aware of the situation, she didn't care for West's tone or conjecture. "I'm sure it's something he and the board have discussed," she said calmly, though her heart booted her ribs.

He shrugged. "Interesting, though, don't you think? He comes to town, and suddenly the hospital is notified by the state investigator's office of patients being charged transportation costs by the hospital because there's no one to pick them up after surgery. They've also claimed doctors keep patients longer than necessary. Meantime, this guy's tallying lists for NHC." Another shrug. "Hope Peter knows what he's doing, is all." Then he was gone.

Ella stared at the empty doorway. She knew Peter had been reviewing a notice from the state investigator's office the morning of J.D.'s surgery. But did it relate to her patient?

It doesn't, a small inner voice said.

Then why had West implied J.D. was behind these notifications? And…had her hormone overload around the man blinded her?

Peter sat on the board as temporary chief of staff. He would safeguard the hospital's interests.

She picked up her pen. *Focus on your patients. They come first.*

Still, the unpleasant niggle West had planted lurked in her mind for the remainder of her shift. After all, *she* had insisted J.D. stay in the hospital an extra day.

J.D. stood in the hospital library overlooking the snowy gardens Pops had landscaped a lifetime ago. He recalled his dad cussing about needing the money that came with prettying up the place where his young wife had met her fate. Thing was, when the gardens were that job, Grace was still alive and J.D. a mere twinkle in the old man's eye.

Right. As if the old man's eyes ever twinkled. Well, maybe they had once—around Grace.

This morning, when he'd showered and shaved, J.D. had a certain gleam in *his* eyes. He'd woken on the ebbing tide of an erotic dream about Ella.

He massaged the back of his neck. The woman was in his blood and he had to get her out. But how, dammit? How did you stop thinking, wondering, *feeling?* Feeling, for God's sake. When the hell had he wanted more than sex from a woman?

Bracing a hand on the window frame, he studied the

gardens and pictured his dad digging in the soil. Had he brought Grace around, showed her the result, his pride palpable? J.D. imagined her telling Jared, *I love what your hands have done.*

Your hands.

Last night at the Dakota, hadn't he said virtually the same words to Ella? Marveled at the skill of her nimble fingers?

She'd cut open a part of his body—something more intimate than anything he'd dealt with in bed—and healed him.

So where are you going with this, J.D.? What does the old man and his gardens have to do with your attraction to Ella? On the economic spectrum, never mind the intellectual one, they're ten thousand miles apart.

And so was he. She came from a family of doctors and he spawned from a family of dirt diggers. He had no business lusting after her, yet the thought of leaving her staggered him.

She would not leave this town or this hospital; she'd told him so last night, though heaven only knew why he'd broached the subject in the first place.

Which meant…what? That he should stay?

Would that be so bad? a rascal on his shoulder asked.

Hell, yes!

He had no intention of relocating. He had a career in New York. He had money in New York. Dozens of women. A kick-ass condo. Why the hell would he want to move back to Walnut River?

Because she's here. Because your old man is here.

Because you're thirty-six years old and when it comes right down to it, that condo, those women, that career won't visit you in the old folks home. And they sure as hell won't stand at your gravesite one day, mourning your loss. He wasn't fool enough to think it for a second.

So, where did that leave him?

Frustrated, he turned from the snowy gardens, and limped out of the library. There were several more people to interview for his business bulletin. At least in this he had a goal. He could do something worthwhile for the hospital.

And her.

Tired to the bone, Ella locked her office at 5:20 p.m. and headed for the elevator. She couldn't wait to get inside her little house, run a hot bath, cuddle in her flannel pajamas on the sofa with Molly and dig into some Chinese takeout. Healthy or not, greasy chicken dumplings sounded perfect as long as a stove and dishes weren't involved.

On the way down to the main floor, she wondered if J.D. liked takeout. *Good grief. You're barely done at work and he's on your mind again.*

In truth, he'd been in her mind since West MacGregor dumped that information two hours ago. The J.D. she'd come to know—yes, it had been only a week—made her laugh and feel and think about things outside her work. Above all, he tangled up her emotions. No man had done that before.

But did she *really* know him?

Last night he thought she could do better than Walnut River General. Had his questions meant NHC's plans were already in place for her hospital, and he would rather she wasn't here to experience them?

Somehow, the two didn't mesh. J.D. might be business through and through, but he wasn't a user. His interest in her was purely hormonal.

Are you sure?

No, dammit, she wasn't, but right this minute she was too tired to go through a long, weary analysis. One thing was certain, and her heart ached at the thought. If she was this confused, she needed to take a break from him.

Hurrying toward the rear exit and staff parking on the main floor, she caught sight of chestnut hair peeping above the back of a cushiony chair in the solarium at the end of the corridor. She'd recognize that color anywhere. Heart tripping, she approached the open doors. Except for J.D., the room was empty. Silently, she walked forward.

He was asleep.

A knot filled her throat. During his hospitalization she had not seen him so relaxed—or so vulnerable.

Carefully, she perched on the edge of an adjacent chair. His head had fallen slightly to the right; the lines between his black brows lay quiet, peaceful. The corners of his mouth were innocent as a napping toddler's—that mouth she had kissed, which had kissed her. With passion and tenderness.

She fancied herself leaning over him, setting her lips there again, waking him with nibbles and caresses and sighs. She imagined cupping his bristly cheeks, threading her fingers through that thick, lustrous hair that hooked the light from an end-table lamp.

A triangle of white cotton lay in the V of his navy sweater and the sight of that bit of cloth, that *masculinity*, sent a hot spear into her belly. From that tiny point her gaze traveled his body: big, strong hands linked loosely across his abdomen, tailored black slacks, the bent left knee, the stretched right leg, the expensive black boots. Then back the same long route, up to his square chin, his beautiful mouth…and his watchful green eyes.

That quick she was seized by a wave of hunger and desire.

Drawing a deep breath, she broke the spell. "You looked so peaceful, I didn't want to wake you."

"How long…?" His voice was gruff from sleep.

"Few minutes."

He tugged himself up into the chair, checked his watch. "Seems I lost an hour."

"Evidently, you needed it. How's the knee holding up?"

"Holding." A hint of a smile.

"Did you cab it here?"

"Why? Are you offering to drive me home again?"

"Actually, I came to talk about last night." Gathering courage, she glanced at her hands clasped between her knees, took another breath. "Last night was lovely. But," she raised her eyes, "we can't do it again. I mean, we can't go out again. Together. Your employer is a company that might take over this hospital. Therefore, our association would be a conflict of interest."

An unreadable element flickered in his eyes. "By

whose standards, Ella? Yours or the hospital's? Way I see it, unless there's a legal aspect to all this, the hospital and for damn sure my employer have no business dictating who I *associate* with. Nor do they control your social calendar. That leaves you and me. Getting back to last night, you're right—it *was* great. And I want to do it again."

"J.D.—"

"Don't say it." Moving to the edge of his chair, he caught her hands and brought her forward so their faces were a foot apart. "I can't explain it either, but I need to see you. Why do you think I'm prowling the corridors of this hospital?" Before she could respond, he continued. "Yes, I'm here for my company, but it's more than that. I'm seeing things I'm not familiar with, ways and techniques I know don't exist in larger centers anymore. There's camaraderie among staff members, a dedication toward patients. Doctors and nurses don't rush people to heal. And—" his smile touched his eyes "—I like it. I think if I make my case right, NHC could reduce some of the administrative overhead and implement a stronger front where care is crucial. In other words, enhance Walnut River General's community base."

He jiggled their hands. "I've seen you work in that community, Ella. I've *been* part of that work." His eyes darkened. "You make me want to do better, to be a better man. Give us a chance."

"But you're leaving soon," she said and her voice squeaked. His words had opened her heart like a bloom in springtime. He wasn't the ogre MacGregor had insinuated.

"Not for a couple of weeks. By then…who knows? New York isn't so far away. A seventy-five minute flight to Hartford and a thirty minute drive here." He flashed a grin. "For me."

"A long distance relationship?" She couldn't help her disappointment. The first time a man had her insides churning and he was asking her to live for weekends. She got to her feet. "I really need to go home." *To think.*

Gripping the chair's arms, he rose gingerly to tower over her. "Have you eaten?"

"I'm picking up a couple boxes of takeout."

"Chinese?" One dark brow slanted upward.

"Yes. And no," she said on a laugh. "You are not invited. I need to have an early night."

"Tomorrow, then?"

Tomorrow was Sunday and she was still on call. "Sorry."

"Monday?"

Too close, he stood too close with those sparkling eyes, that kissable mouth, the scent of him swirling around her head. "That's three days away. I don't know what I'll be doing then."

"Good. Pencil me in."

Exasperated, she gave in. "Fine. Monday night." She moved out of the nook of comfortable chairs and soft lamp-light that sent shadows dancing across the ridges of his face.

"What would you like me to bring?" he called as she walked toward the exit.

"Just yourself. I'll cook."

"What?"

Over her shoulder she repeated, "I'll cook."

"No, I mean *what* will you cook?"

She paused. He stood where she'd left him, tall and lean, hands in the pockets of his trousers, his honed body archetypical of the genuine red-blooded American male.

"Are you allergic to something?"

"Only Demerol." His grin curled her toes. "No food. Just like to know what's on tap in your kitchen."

"At this point I haven't a clue. You'll need to wait, and be surprised." She strode through the doors, already counting the hours.

Chapter Nine

He was surprised.

Surprised to get her call after three days of silence. Surprised she offered to pick him up at the inn after work. And surprised where she was taking him for the meal she promised to create.

Dark as it was at five-thirty, the energy-saving street lamps provided enough clarity for J.D. to recognize the neighborhood the moment Ella's car headed east to the residential area known to locals as "down by the river." Riverdale, an offshoot suburb near Walnut River established in the forties by blue-collar workers living in shanties which, in later years, had been renovated by their offspring.

Like J.D.'s father, who had inherited land and house from *his* dad.

The moment she turned down the darkened back alley, he couldn't keep calm. Where the hell was she taking him? Had she planned to take him to his dad's house all along?

Rubbing damp palms on his cargo pants, he asked, "You playing a game with me, Doc?"

Her head turned. "Game?"

"What're we doing down by the river?"

"This is where I live, J.D. In my grandmother's house." Slowing, she hit a garage door opener clipped to the sun visor, then pulled into the garage, turned off the ignition and, briefcase in hand, stepped out of the car. "My grandmother left the house to my sister and me. It's my home."

She took his arm as they left the garage. "I haven't cleared the walkway today, so watch your step. Sometimes there are icy patches."

J.D. glanced through her barren trees toward his former home across the alleyway. Night enveloped the building. When was the last time he'd been inside? Five years? Six? He couldn't recall exactly; the stay had been short. One day and a night, before he left angry and disappointed he and the old man hadn't connected, *again*.

Inside her house, a gray, three-legged cat purred greetings and butted their legs.

Ella lifted the feline. "This is Molly. Not allergic?"

"Nope." Pets hadn't been a part of his childhood.

"Good." Without removing her burgundy jacket, Ella went into the kitchen to fill a pair of stainless steel bowls with water and refrigerated meat; she set the bowls on the floor beside the stove.

J.D. removed his boots on the mat by the door. Purposely leaving his coat on, he went to stand by the sink to gaze out the window at the house where he'd grown up. The kitchen was lit, a shadow passed by the curtained window. Pops?

"Who lives there?" he asked, needing to be sure.

Ella came beside him. Their arms bumped. "Don't you know?" Her head turned and he felt the heat of her gaze.

"Few years ago, it was still my dad."

He felt her shift toward the window. "When was the last time you talked to him, J.D.?"

"Too long."

A heavy silence fell. Behind them the cat ate her meal, in another room a clock tick-tocked away the minutes. To the right, the refrigerator droned softly.

She said, "If you need to talk…"

"I don't." The top of her head was level with his shoulder. Her hair shone sleek and dark. Cut to an inch below her jaw, the length swung like a mini-veil when she looked up at him.

She dipped her head and the veil shielded her profile. "I'm not trying to pry, J.D., but bottling this up isn't good for you."

Deliberately, he turned, backed against the counter, arms folded. "You playing shrink, Doc? 'Cause if you are, I'm out of here. I'm hellaciously attracted to you, but my old man is off-limits."

Sadness shaded her eyes. "We're not so different, you know. What you're doing with your dad, I'm doing with my sister. We barely talk and when we do, it's all superficial. We rarely get together anymore. She lives in

New York, I'm here and," a shrug, "life goes on. It breaks my heart."

"Were you close?"

"Very. She's a year older, but it was like we were twins conceived at the same moment. She was my best friend. My dad used to say we were 'old soul friends'."

"What happened between you?"

Ella shrugged. "Things fell apart in college. I've never been able to figure out why, exactly. I think when she couldn't stand the blood and guts of medicine, she felt guilty. Here she was, part of a family of doctors and not able to *be* one. I think it affected her confidence. Which is stupid to the outsider, but not to the person it's happening to." She sighed. "I miss our friendship."

J.D. stared for a moment at the floor. "You were lucky to have that kind of relationship. The old man and I…" He huffed a laugh, pushed from the counter. "I don't want to talk about it." A half smile. "I know what you're doing, Doc. It isn't going to work."

She frowned. "Excuse me?"

"You share, then I share, that sort of thing?"

Her eyes flashed. "You think I told you about my sister to get you to talk about your family?" She walked across the kitchen, flung around. "I told you about her because I *wanted* to, J.D. Not because I thought you'd feel obligated to disclose your family history. I thought we had something here, at least that's what you keep insisting. Two days ago you were jumping all over a long-distance relationship. Seems I misinterpreted *long distance*. You meant emotions, not miles." Pulling out her keys, she headed for the back door. "Know what? I don't feel like cooking after all. I'll take you back to the hotel."

He was in front of her in three long strides, biting back the sharp sting in his knee. "Look, I'm sorry, okay? I'll tell you whatever you want to know."

"Oh, J.D." Her shoulders sagged. "That's not how it's done."

"Sure it is. I'm offering to talk about my dad. Isn't that what you wanted?"

"You don't get it, do you? It's not what *I* want, it's what *you* want. Sharing personal histories is part of a relationship. It's part of taking off the scabs on your heart for another person. Willingly. Without pressure to do so by anyone. It's not a game of If You Show Me Yours, I'll Show You Mine." She stepped away from him to open the door. "Come on. I'll drive you home."

I am home, he wanted to say. *Here in your kitchen is home.* The room's warmth, the hum of the fridge, the plants on the sink's windowsill, the welcome mat at the back door, the old cupboards, the little wooden table, the yellow walls, the cat curling around her legs...

Home.

Where he couldn't stay.

He followed her back into the winter night.

She was in bed, reading, when her phone rang. A glance told her it was J.D. She had expected his call. On returning to the inn not a word had passed between them. When she pulled to the hotel's curbside, he'd told her that he could manage the pathway alone. And she had let him go, then waited while he walked up the porch steps and into the building. Heart heavy, she drove away.

Before it began, it was done.

How silly of her to have imagined more. *To have let your heart get involved.*

Again.

Relationships were not her thing. *Best get used to your destiny.* Work was her love, her marriage, her baby. What made her think she had time for a man?

But, oh, he was *such* a man. And, if she could admit it, she might have felt a little more than attraction to him. She might have begun, just a little, to fall in love.

The phone was on its final refrain before her voice mail would click in; she grabbed the receiver. "Hello, J.D."

"Sometimes," he said, his voice deep in her ear, "I hate caller ID. I thought you'd let it ring because it was me. Ella, I'm a sorry ass. The way I handled tonight… If you don't want to talk to me again… Hell." She envisioned him pinching the bridge of his nose, running a hand through that lush hair.

"I shouldn't have pushed," she said, trying to find balance with her own emotions. "It wasn't fair." *Considering I barely know you.*

"Can we start over?"

And there it was, the question begging a yes or no that could alter her life's path. If she said yes where would he lead her? If she said no, where would she lead herself?

Already she knew the answer to the second question and it sent a chill across her heart. Saying no would confirm having no life outside of her work and her patients.

There's no one at WRG who remotely interests you.

And in a town the size of Walnut River, with its aging population, how great were her opportunities? J.D. offered a chance at a bit of freedom and fun and excitement.

And more…if she let herself romanticize.

"We can start over," she agreed slowly.

"Great." His relief was audible. "I've decided to follow your recommendation. I'm seeing my father tomorrow."

"Don't do it for me, J.D."

"I know. Do it for myself. And I am. It's time. I had a wake-up call tonight at your house—which, by the way, I'd really like to see beyond the back door."

Though he couldn't see it, she smiled. "You will and you'll be okay tomorrow."

"I hope so."

"Just be yourself. The way you are with me," she added.

At that he chuckled. "If I acted *that* way around him, he'd see me out the door with a shotgun. Ella?"

"Yes?"

"I think we've had our first fight. I've never had a first fight with a woman before."

"Really?"

"I'm ashamed to admit it, but I just didn't care enough to have one. With you it's…" Sigh. "You scare me."

A little jolt hit her stomach. "Ditto."

"Yeah?"

"Don't let it go to your head."

He laughed. "I could take that another way."

"But you won't. Good night, J.D."

"'Night, babe."

For a long while she lay awake, thinking. The days since she had met him in the E.R. were a string of pearls she touched and retouched, turned and rolled in the palm of her memory. She went over conversations, the way he looked at her and she at him.

Until she was back to tonight's phone call—and the fact he wanted to begin again.

J.D. took a cab to his childhood home. *We can start over.* Her voice, soft in his mind. Words he also planned for him and Pops.

The cement driveway had been cleared and sanded. The old man might not be home, but out with his cronies, drinking a beer at the Crab Shack along the river.

Careful with his cane, J.D. took his time to the front door. Sometime in the past five years the house had been painted gold, the shutters dark brown. Near his old bedroom, the red maple reached its stark branches above the roofline; beside the front stoop the hydrangeas outdistanced his own six-three height.

He rang the doorbell, something he'd begun to do when he left and returned that first year.

A long minute later, the door opened. And there was his father's craggy face.

Here the changes were more dramatic. Half a decade could do that to a man's eyes and mouth and hair, his posture. Jared Sumner no longer stood straight and tall. Instead, he leaned on a cane similar to J.D.'s, his bony shoulders sagging in a blue plaid shirt.

But his eyes were still keen as a Fourth of July sky.

"Hey, Pops."

"J.D."

"How you doing?"

"Fine. You're up an' walkin', I see."

"Yeah. Heard you came to the hospital." *Are you going to invite me in, Pops?*

"I did. You were sleepin'."

"Should've woke me."

"Maybe." For several seconds Jared studied J.D.

"Pops? We gonna stand out here in the cold and talk or are you going to let me in?"

The old man jerked. "Oh, yeah. 'Course. Come in." He stepped back, pulling the door wider.

J.D. entered the small foyer, automatically turning left to the coat closet. "Mind if I stay awhile? Or do you have plans?"

"No plans. Hang up your coat." Leaving J.D. to do just that, his dad walked to the kitchen. "Want some coffee, tea? Don't know what you drink anymore."

"Coffee's fine." J.D. shrugged off his coat.

The living room furniture he'd sat on as a kid had been replaced, the TV upgraded to a sixty-inch wall unit. The kitchen, however, astonished him. Quaker cupboards, fresh green paint, new sink, yellow-patterned linoleum.

"Wow, when did you renovate?"

"Couple years ago. Got tired of the dark colors."

"Looks great. Nice and bright."

Jared turned from the counter, eyes full of something

J.D. hadn't seen in a long while, maybe never: pleasure. "Think so?"

"Yeah," he said, meaning it.

"It was Prue's idea."

"Prue? You mean…" J.D. jerked his head left.

"Yup. The same. She's got an eye for things."

J.D. wondered what else she had an eye for. His old man, maybe? "She still live next door?"

"Yup. Husband passed on four years ago."

"Still has the bakeshop, right?"

"Bakeshop and deli now. Belle manages it."

Prudy's daughter, and old classmate of J.D.'s.

He walked to the window opposite a table for two. Across snowy yards was Ella's house. Last night, he'd stood at *her* window viewing his dad's place—and now, here he was. Without thinking, he asked, "Do you know your neighbor across the alley?"

Pops set cloth placemats on the table. Another of Prudy's influences? "Doc Wilder. She's the one who gave me my new hip. Damn fine woman, that one."

J.D. remained at the window. Except for the cat, her house was empty. Ella would be at the hospital, likely in surgery, working those long fingers around someone's distressed bones or joints. The way she had on him. And, evidently, his old man.

No wonder she'd been full of questions. She had recognized similarities. The birthmark on his inner thigh.

"I was wrong, you know." Pops broke into J.D.'s reverie.

Turning, he met the old man's eyes. "In what way?"

"Making you believe hospitals are bad, that they end

your life. I was wrong to put those thoughts in your head when you were a kid, J.D. I knew it when I took you into the clinic with that double ear infection when you were five, an' you cried an' cried that you didn't want to die. I knew then I'd done wrong."

J.D. shrugged. "I got over it." But he hadn't really.

A week ago he'd sweated through bizarre dreams and anxiety. Believing he could die any moment. Die quick like his mother, without warning.

No, he hadn't gotten over it. However, in Ella's care he'd recognized a difference.

Pops pulled out a chair. "I wanted to tell you when I came to see you in the hospital."

J.D. noticed his father's hand shake pouring cream into his mug. He wanted to put a hand on the old man's shoulder. Instead, he pulled out the opposite chair. "You're telling me now, Pops. Better late than never, right?"

Jared stirred his coffee. "S'pose. It's a good hospital. Lotta folks come for miles to get care. There are lineups for elective surgeries, y'know." He eyed J.D. "Wouldn't want to see that change."

J.D. held back his surprise. "Why would it change?"

"That's what you're here for, ain't it? To amalgamate Walnut River General into a bunch of hospitals. You're wrong, is all I'm sayin'. Walnut River should care for this town in its own way. Leave it alone, son."

J.D. snorted. As always, his dad was telling him what to do. Why had he thought today would be different?

Tamping back disillusionment he said, "NHC could make the hospital more effective with increased surgeries per day, for example. Maybe implement a graveyard shift for elective surgeries. *That's* what I'm trying to help with."

His dad shook his head. "Call it what you want. Rumors fly. Prudy hears 'em when she stocks sandwiches in the docters' lounge."

Prudy again. J.D. considered. If he told his father his intentions, good old Prudy could take *those* back to the staff lounge as well.

"Look. Pops. I'm not a bad guy. Walnut River is great, better than great. But there are areas they could improve with updated equipment." *Ours is working just fine,* he could hear Ella scoff. *Why waste money?* Resolutely, he went on, "Furthermore, the hospital could lobby for funding, gain a larger professional base to draw from when they need relief staff. Done with the hospital's current qualities in mind, that could add to it, not detract."

Jared shook his gray head. "Son, you do what you have to do. But this ain't right. You'll be ruinin' a good hospital and makin' a lot of people unhappy, includin' that sweet gal across the way there."

J.D. glanced at Ella's house. *Would* he be ruining her place of work? He reflected on the hospitals NHC had bought out. Efficient institutions today, with little overhead and exceptional equipment. Dammit, Ella *could* use another bone-density scanner. With two, she'd assist more patients, accelerate services.

Suddenly Jared's hand covered J.D.'s. "All I'm asking, J.D., is when you talk to people, listen to what they say. Really listen. Before you put in your report. Will you do that?"

J.D. gazed at his father's work-hardened hand, the knuckles thick and twisted, the veins high and round. A working man's hand.

Shame rose to his throat. "All right. I'll give it a shot."

The doorbell rang. Jared rose and limped from the kitchen. J.D. remained seated. *Jeez.* He thought he'd had the old man pegged all these years. Seemed he didn't know his dad at all.

As a kid, a punk, *could* he have misread Pops?

Murmurs drifted through the house. A woman, a child.

His dad entered. Behind him walked a woman dressed in slacks and a blue sweater that fit her trim body and a little girl, with gold curls to her shoulders, wearing pink overalls. The woman carried a cloth-covered plate.

J.D. stood. He caught Jared's pride at his ingrained manners.

"Remember Mrs. Tavish, son?"

Prudy. "How are you, Mrs. T? It's been a long time."

"It has," she agreed. "But let's forget the formalities, okay? You're no longer a boy and I prefer Prudy." Her smile was honest, happy. "And this…" She brought the child forward. "My granddaughter, Shay. We've been baking all afternoon because today is teachers' in-service and Shay has a day off school. We thought Jared—" Something tender passed between them. "Well, we wanted to share our goodies," she ended, placing the plate on the counter.

"Shay is the best baker." Pops ran a hand over the child's hair and winked. "Aren't you, pint?"

J.D. stared at his dad. Had the old man once winked at him like that? And when had he touched J.D. with such protective care?

A few minutes ago at the table, or did you forget already?

The thought shook J.D.

Pops *had* reached out, there was no denying that handgrip. What else had J.D. forgotten over the years? Had he squelched the good memories because, in his eyes, Pops hadn't acted like the fathers of his school buddies?

Smiling, Jared led the girl to the table. Prudy dug orange juice from the fridge as if it was the most natural thing to do in another person's house.

"Sit, Prue." Pops pointed to the chair J.D. had vacated. "Wanna grab another mug an' the coffeepot, son?"

J.D. did as asked. He couldn't recall Jared ever having a woman to his table. Occasionally, he'd let J.D. have school pals over, and sometimes his cronies from work, but never a woman. To J.D. his old man had been a hard-ass without a soft bone in his body.

After retrieving the coffeepot, he excused himself and went down the hallway to his old bedroom. The door stood open.

Here, nothing had changed. His football jersey still hung on the wall above the bed, his baseball cap sat on the dresser. Track-and-field medals and mystery novels lined the shelves. The bed was the narrow twin mattress he had slept in since he turned two. Why hadn't the old man changed his room when he'd renovated the rest of the house?

"You came home so seldom."

J.D. startled. Pops had followed him into the room. "I

wanted to keep a little part of you with me. Stupid, I know. I shoulda packed up your stuff, put it in the attic."

"I'm glad you didn't," J.D. said hoarsely.

"Yeah?"

"Yeah." And suddenly a waterfall of history he'd forgotten streamed through his mind….

Playing baseball, his dad standing on the sidelines, encouragement in his eyes. Scoring a touchdown and Jared in the bleachers, yelling his name. His old man's hands, his gardener's hands, reaching around J.D.'s ten-year-old shoulders, helping cast a line into the river on a summer's afternoon.

Pain lodged in his chest.

The old man loved him.

It was on his face and in the memories tethered to this room.

He had to get out of here, to reassess God-knew-what. "Look," he said. "I gotta head back to the Inn."

"So soon? You just got here."

"Need to finish some work." His business case waited.

"If you wanna stay in your old room…"

J.D. shook his head. "Can't, Pops."

Stepping around his dad, he walked out of the room.

A minute later, he was outside, buttoning up against a sudden cold wind that bit his face.

Chapter Ten

J.D. sat on the edge of his bed at the inn, cell phone in hand. He'd been mulling over what happened on Birch Avenue for an hour. *If you wanna stay in your old room…* The emotion behind the old man's words tumbled hard through J.D.'s chest.

They had connected in that room. On some level they had connected. Pops wasn't the badass J.D. had always assumed he was. He was a man who had tried to make a home for his kid the only way he knew how.

A man who loved that kid deeper than J.D. had believed.

Before he changed his mind and hooked his cell phone to his belt, he punched in the familiar number.

His father picked up immediately—as if he'd been sitting right by the phone, waiting. "'Lo."

J.D. swallowed. "Hey, Pops."

"Son. Glad you called."

"You alone?"

"Yeah. Prue and Shay left right after you."

Probably because Prudy thought she'd interrupted a father-son bonding moment. J.D. closed his eyes. "Sorry," he said. "Didn't mean for them to run out on you." *Like I did.*

"They didn't. Prue understands things."

No doubt better than J.D. "Look," he said and his throat constricted. "I'm glad we got together, you know? It was nice."

The line was quiet for several beats before Pops said, "You're taller than I was at your age, bigger in the shoulders."

J.D. released a small laugh. "Must be all those New York steaks."

"Got your mother's hair…the way it whipped in the wind. Sun catches it the same, too. Guess you hadn't expected me to keep your room the same, huh?"

"No, Pops. It surprised me." After all the reno work throughout the house.

"Shoulda been a better father when I had the chance," Jared remarked. "Been kinder, gentler. Like I am with Shay."

"Dad—"

"Let me finish. I made us strangers with nothin' in common 'cept our names. I ain't making excuses 'cause I was the adult, the role model." He grunted. "Some role model."

J.D. pressed his fingers to his eyes. "Don't punish yourself."

"Didn't teach you what I shoulda. You're thirty-six years old, a good-lookin' kid, yet you ain't married. So I'm bettin' you're scared to get in deep with a woman. Scared of what might happen to her."

J.D. swallowed. Pops was paring back layers he hadn't recognized. Could it be possible?

Gruffly, Jared continued, "If I'da showed you more affection the way a dad should…"

"You did, Pops. You showed me in a lot of ways. You may not have said the words, but you showed me. Go look at that stuff in my room, and think about the memories."

"I do. Every day."

J.D. was silent. What could he say to take away the guilt in his father's voice? "Pops, listen. There comes a time a kid has to take responsibility, teach himself the ways of life."

"When Gracie died," his dad continued, on a mission now. "When she died, part of my heart died with her. I'd look into your face, see those same green eyes, and it scared the hell out of me. I had no idea how to raise you alone. My old man—" Jared cleared his throat. "He taught me never to show my feelings when things got tough. A man persevered. He shut his mouth, got the job done. I did that with you and it wasn't right. Wasn't right at all."

J.D briefly closed his eyes. Three-and-a-half decades and he'd never heard his father speak with so much emotion. "Pops, you don't need to do this." *You don't need to tear out your guts for me.*

A ragged sigh drifted through the phone. "Yeah, son, I do. I owe you an explanation that's been way too long in coming."

J.D.'s heart banged his ribs. "Maybe we could start fresh."

"I'd like that," Pops said slowly. "I'd like that a lot."

The grin stretching across J.D.'s face hurt. "It's a deal."

After their last botched dinner two days ago, Ella wondered if he'd decided to go back to New York, after all. Twice she'd been tempted to call Ashley, see if he still attended physio, but she didn't want to appear interested—either to J.D. or the hospital staff.

She stayed up until eleven every night telling herself she wasn't waiting for his call, but catching up on her reading. Then one night, lying under the quilt, propped by pillows, *The New England Journal of Medicine* in her lap, she realized she'd read the same paragraph about chronic osteomyelitis a dozen times.

Late in the afternoon on the third day, she sat in her car at the intersection of Lexington and River Road, waiting for the light to change—and debating. Should she turn left, pass the inn? Or continue straight to her side of town?

The light flashed green. Though traffic was slower because of the snowfall that began an hour earlier, Ella pushed the accelerator, intent on home, but halfway through the intersection, she swung left.

Hands tight on the steering wheel, she drove down the road with its big trees, until the inn's lamppost came into view. No gray rental stood in the guest parking. Had he checked out? Or was he still at the hospital, gathering names, slumbering in the solarium? She hadn't ventured near that room since...

Eyes on the road, she drove past the inn.

Pathetic, Ella. He's probably in New York and here you are, driving by like a teenager wanting a glimpse of the school hottie.

She so needed a life.

And groceries.

Pulling into the New England Ranch Market at the next light, she caught sight of Simone Garner, their top E.R. nurse, heading for her vehicle, a sack in each hand.

"Simone," Ella called, stepping from her car.

The nurse had worked at WRG for fifteen years and her kindness and skill was renowned throughout the community. Ella regarded her as a good friend.

Suddenly, she missed her sister Anna fiercely. She missed their camaraderie and girl talks. She missed being able to say *Tell me what to do about J.D.* Seeing Simone sent a sharp spear of yearning through Ella for that kinship with another woman.

Abruptly, she hugged the nurse. "How are you?" she asked, stepping back quickly, embarrassed by her display. "I haven't seen you in a while." Her rotation and Simone's often went in opposite directions for weeks.

Simone's brown eyes smiled. "I've had extra shifts, which my dog has not enjoyed in the least. But—" She chuckled. "Today I'm off, so he's happy. You?"

Ella brushed at her bangs. "Crazy busy. Can't seem to get ahead of the lineup some days."

"Don't tell Sumner, that rep prowling the hospital. He'll take it to NHC's bank and we'll find ourselves sold to the highest bidder."

"J.D.'s not like that."

Simone blinked. "Ella, he may be your patient, but he's also a snitch for that corporation."

"Snitch? That's an awfully strong word."

But a niggle of doubt hovered. Was Simone right? Could there be more to that discussion at the Dakota last week? Intentions that, perhaps, weren't as on par as Ella had thought? Argh. She was so confused about the man. "I have to go," she said, starting for the electronic doors of the store.

Simone caught her arm. "Ella, I'm sorry, but—"

"Look, I'm just tired and want to get home." *Where I can think and put some sense to all this.*

"If you need to talk, I'm here."

"I know. Thanks, Simone, but I'm okay. See you later." She hurried across the parking lot, through falling flakes that, in the lamplight, materialized big as the cotton ball in her throat.

By the time she walked into the back door of her cozy little house on Cedar Avenue, her kitchen clock read 6:45 p.m., and Molly leaned against her legs. "Hey, my little fan. I love you, too." She hauled the cat into her arms.

Ten minutes later, the groceries put away, Molly fed and the cat box cleaned, Ella stood in the bathroom, washing her hands. The mirror revealed dark circles under her eyes. When her stomach growled, she realized breakfast had been her last meal.

"If you're not careful, you'll be the one in a hospital bed," she muttered to her reflection.

Would J.D. care?

J.D.'s gone.

Deflated, she dried her hands and returned to the kitchen to heat a plate of leftover lasagna and toss a small salad.

The dishes cleared and cleaned after her meal, she loaded the washing machine and ironed a blouse for tomorrow. By the time she crawled under the covers it was almost ten.

About to turn out the light, the family photo on her dresser caught her eye. Taken twelve years ago in her parents' backyard, she remembered the moment as if she had just stepped into the cluster of her family and her mom had just put an arm around her waist. Ella, Alice, James and Anna stood in the first row, with David and Peter behind.

David had one hand on Ella's shoulder and one on their mother's. Beside Alice stood James, patriarch of both family and Walnut River General. Ella could see the tips of his fingers around Anna's waist; Peter's hands clasped her shoulder and their father's.

A day of celebration for Peter's completed internship, the photographer had taken a dozen group photos, each with family members trading places. Ella loved this photo because her mother had hugged her close and given her a little squeeze and David had teased in her ear, *Smile so we know how much you love pictures,* just before the camera had clicked its shot. Ella's lips tugged. At seventeen she'd hated having her photo taken. Back then, her glasses, braces and near-flat chest cried out *nerd.*

Anna, on the other hand, looked like a Scandinavian goddess with her lovely white-blond hair and sky-blue eyes. At eighteen she had the figure of a siren. Full breasts, tiny waist, long, shapely legs.

Anna, whom James and Alice adopted before Ella was born, had been the closest to Ella—even through their sibling rivalry and those catcalls of loser and bitch.

Such teenage drama, she thought, her gaze falling on Anna's Mona Lisa smile. Not for the first time, Ella wondered what had been going through her sister's mind in that photo.

Smiling at the camera, had Anna known then medicine wasn't her gig? *Oh, Anna. There's so much I want to share with you.*

Except those days were done. She and Anna hadn't talked, really talked, in almost ten years. Not since her sister's first year of med school when she marched into Ella's bedroom and shouted, *I'm not doctor material. I don't have that kind of rhino skin. Why can't anyone get that?* Then she'd stormed out of the house and driven to a friend's place. A week later she moved to New York.

Aw, Anna. You always got woozy at the sight of your own scrapes and cuts, and cried when you saw an animal in pain. Poor dad. He thought you'd outgrow it.

Worse were the family gatherings. James, Peter, David—*and me,* she admitted—talking shop: hospitals, patients, medicine. Standing apart, Anna would wait for someone to notice her, to say, *Hey, what's going on with you in the Big Apple, sis?*

Was it any wonder her sister rarely came home anymore?

Ella glanced at her phone. *Call her*, a tiny voice whispered. *Take the first step, start making things right.* The way she had with J.D. and his dad.

"What do you think, Molly?" Squinty yellow eyes blinked and a mouth full of tiny, sharp teeth yawned widely. "Right. It's up to me."

Quickly she dialed her sister's number. "Anna?" Ella began when her sister answered.

"Hi."

One word, hanging in mid-space. "How—how are you?"

"Fine. You?"

"Busy." *Come on, Ella. You wanted to talk, so talk!* "Real busy with the weather and snow and…" *Oh, God.*

"What's up, Ella? I know it's not the weather."

Yes, it is! Why can't we talk about the weather? We should be able to talk about anything! "I want things back to the way they were between us," she blurted.

A sigh whispered through the line. "You can't bring back the past, El. You know that. It's best to leave things alone."

"Don't you miss us?" Now that they were speaking, Ella was determined to get to the bottom of this *thing* separating them. "I miss you, dammit. C'mon, Anna, talk to me. Why are you avoiding us?"

"Us? As in you and the boys over there, and me over here?"

Ella swallowed a swell of ire. "I can't believe you just said that. Don't you get that we love you? We *all* miss you. You and I used to be so close, we shared everything.

I miss that. I want to know what's going on in your life. I want to share what's going on in mine, that I'm—" Before she spewed regretful words, Ella shut up.

"What's going on with you?" Her sister's voice softened.

"Nothing. It doesn't matter." *I think I'm falling for a guy who's on the wrong side of the fence. And I want to sleep with him, but he's had women—and I've never done it.*

Humiliation washed through her. How could she explain *that* to her sister? Here she was almost thirty *and a doctor*, and a man hadn't touched her in that way, not once. The idea of spilling her guts about J.D. brought on an unexpected shyness.

"I can't talk about it," she said, heart heavy.

"Does it concern a man?"

Oh, yes. Anna knew her well. "I—I don't want to talk about it," she repeated.

"All right. Sure." Her sister's voice cooled.

"Don't get in a huff. It's hard for me to explain because…." *I feel abandoned by you.* "I don't know if you'll be here all the time."

"Emotionally, you mean?"

"Yes."

Pause. "Maybe we should try and rebuild."

"Can we?" Ella asked.

"Maybe with small steps."

She closed her eyes, took a sustaining breath. "Anna, I've never…" *Slept with a man.*

"Never what? Felt this way about a guy?"

"No."

"Is he a local? Someone I would know?"

"He grew up here, but he lives and works in New York now. For some health-care company."

A weighty quiet descended through the line. "Anna?"

"What company?"

"Northeastern HealthCare. He— The man in question is collecting all kinds of data about Walnut River General."

"I see."

"Peter thinks they're trying to take over the hospital. Sometimes I believe him and sometimes I don't know what to think. Personally, I just want to do my job and forget all this gibberish."

"Then that's what you do."

"What if Peter's right, though? What if this man's trying to manipulate us for his corporation?"

"I can't answer that, Ella. I'm not there. Look, it's late and I have an early meeting in the morning."

"Sure," she said, taken back by Anna's abruptness.

"Let's keep in touch."

"OK. 'Night, Anna."

"Goodbye."

The line disconnected. Ella stared at the photograph. Goodbye.

As if she were a stranger.

If Anna had said *don't count on me* she couldn't be more clear. Ella sighed. Why had she expected more? Because tonight she'd tried to reach out, tried to mend the hole in the bridge of time. Except Anna hadn't followed. The moment Ella mentioned Peter and the hospital her sister withdrew.

Heart sore, Ella shut off the lamp. She was no closer to connecting with Anna than she was at figuring out J.D.

Peter met her in the hallway as she headed for the O.R. the next morning to repair a forty-year-old man's fractured tibia.

"'Morning, El," her brother said, falling in step. "Can you meet Simone, Bethany and me in the cafeteria at eleven? I'm buying. Though you might not like what's on the menu."

Peter's dark eyes were serious. He wasn't talking food lists.

"What's up?" But she knew before he said the name.

"J. D. Sumner. See you when you're done." On a quick heel, her brother turned and strode back the way they had come, white lab coat fanning behind his long legs.

Ninety minutes later, with the patient in recovery, Ella headed for the change room to tug on a black skirt, pink blouse and lab coat for her afternoon appointments—and the cafeteria meeting.

Heads bent together, Peter and Bethany sat at a corner table.

Thank God for small favors, Ella thought. *About time my big brother found a mate.*

He was forty, his youth flying into the wind. *Like mine.*

The thought pricked. They were here to talk about J.D. and she'd guarantee it wasn't because he haunted her dreams.

She pulled out the chair across from Peter. "Hey, lovebirds."

Bethany smiled into his eyes. "Are we lovebirds?"

"You bet," he affirmed. Had they been alone, Ella believed her brother would have kissed the beautiful redhead. Instead, he straightened and glanced at Ella. "How was the surgery?"

"Good. Patient has a strong left leg again."

Dressed in nurses' scrubs, Simone Garner squeezed in beside Ella. "Did everyone eat already?"

Ten minutes later, salads, sandwiches and bowls of minestrone soup decked the table. Peter said, "You three are the only people I can discuss this with."

This. Ella had no doubt he meant NHC. His gaze on Ella, Peter continued. "For the record, J. D. Sumner is no longer your patient. I checked. Apparently, he's had his files transferred to Springfield and is seeing a doctor there. Do you know why?"

"He…um… Look, it's personal." And it was. Her private life did not belong to her family.

"What is said here, stays here," Peter stated.

Ella darted a look at the other two women. "All right," she began cautiously. "He asked me out, but because he is—*was*—my patient, I wouldn't go."

Peter's eyes were steady. "And did you? Once he transferred?"

Ella sat back in her chair. "Okay, is this an inquisition on my character, Peter? Because if it is, I'm out of here."

He shook his head. "I'm just trying to see where you stand before we go further."

"Where *I* stand? I hope you're not insinuating something nasty because if you are, Peter, you and I need to have a private chat."

"Hear, hear," Bethany said. Her expression held empathy for Ella and reproof for Peter.

He stared at his plate. "Okay, I screwed up. Sorry."

Bethany set a hand on his arm. "Whether or not she's dating J.D. isn't our concern, Peter." She glanced across the table. "I'm sure Ella will be on our side about this."

This, again. Her hands cold in her lap, Ella said, "The last thing I want is for our hospital to be put on a chopping block."

Peter nodded grimly. "We know NHC has done similar machinations with other small medical centers throughout New England. NHC comes in subtly and before you know it, the hospital becomes part of the corporation."

Simone shifted in her chair. "A patient who moved here last year said it happened to the hospital in her hometown. Tenure staff were replaced with new doctors and nurses."

"That," Peter said adamantly, "isn't going to happen at Walnut River General."

"What about the fraud claims?" Bethany asked.

"Exactly," Peter intoned. "We need to find out if these claims are coming out of the woodwork to make WRG look inefficient."

Ella set down her salad fork. Both Peter and West MacGregor had implied that J.D. was involved in the fraud claims. Still, she could not picture him as a deliberately malicious man.

"What are you saying, Peter?" she asked, holding his gaze. "That Mr. Sumner is the root of the problem?"

Her brother stabbed a shred of lettuce. "I don't know. But I do know we could lose our hospital if we sit on our hands."

"What do you propose?"

For a long minute no one said a word. Their plates and bowls sat half empty, untouched.

Simone offered, "We could go to the media."

"The media?" Bethany blinked. "They'd have a free-for-all with this kind of information."

"Not if we play it right." Peter leaned forward. "Ella, you help Rev. Blackwell with the homeless on Sundays. What if we get the *Courier* to write a story about that? Who knows, maybe we can get patients and families to rally behind the hospital in other ways. It would give us a fighting chance, at least."

She winced. "I don't like the idea of using people, Peter. And neither would Oliver Blackwell."

"Will you feel the same when your level of care is diluted due to a bunch of rotating surgeons selected by NHC?"

Please, no, she thought. But wasn't it what J.D. had alluded to, if NHC took over? More medical staff, more equipment? Was that why he'd asked if she would one day work in a larger hospital where all types of opportunities were available?

Gut instinct said J.D. wouldn't deceive her. They had shared bits of their histories, they had laughed. *Kissed.* He wouldn't use her.

Stubbornly, she pushed back the possibility, and her chair. "I have to get to work."

"Think about our proposition, Ella," Peter said. "We have to fight this somehow."

"I know." Stomach in a clench, she hurried from the cafeteria.

Chapter Eleven

Growing up, J.D. had sauntered down Lexington Avenue a thousand times, knew every store, every shop. Over the years some had disappeared, changed owners, changed stock; others had facelifts; still others retained the identifying marks of bygone years.

One was Prudy's Menu.

Around five on Thursday afternoon, he parked the rental at the New England Ranch Market and walked to the shop he had visited as a kid, where Prudy once baked her famous cookies and squares.

Swept clean of snow, the sidewalks were alive with people hurrying home to family and loved ones. The notion stuck like a wad of tissue in his gut. When had he last hurried home to someone at the end of the day? Not since he'd been a kid in grade school, hoping for a simple *How was your day, boy?* from his old man.

So why walk the street to the shop where Prudy worked?

Why this urge to connect with his past?

Hadn't he done that when he knocked on Pops' door? Saw Prudy and her grandkid? Saw his old bedroom?

J.D.'s chest constricted. In a skewed way, his old man loved him. Had always loved him—if those memories resurrected in his old bedroom meant anything—like the time Jared took him to the bake shop and bought a chocolate chip cookie four inches in diameter.

Jerking to a stop, J.D. stared at the yellow script announcing Prudy's Menu above the old wooden door. How had he forgotten?

He'd been eight, helping Jared in the gardens of an upscale residence on the north side of town. On the way home, with dirt on their clothes, the old man had stopped at Prudy's, bought him the cookie. *Y' done good today, boy.* And Pops handed him the treat.

Sparse and rare, the old man's compliments were long-lost treasures buried but preserved forever.

Trouble was, as a mutinous teenager he'd piled a load of loneliness on top of those treasures, sinking them so deep he'd forgotten each word—and the emotions attached to them.

Hell. If ever there was a head case, here he stood.

Ella should find him fascinating as a partner. *Partner?* Where the hell had that come from?

But he knew. From the moment he'd tumbled down those hospital steps, the journey into his past had been a strong arm directing him to things as they *were*, rather than the dark illusions he'd conjured for eighteen years.

Yes, he was successful, ambitious and, at times, insensitive. But he was also...*lonely*. He shook his head to dislodge the emotion burning deep inside. Partner. The word hung in the winter air, mellow as a puff of warm smoke, entreating, enticing, evolving.

Partner...friend...mate...lover...

On a soft curse, he pushed through Prudy's door. The bell above tinkled pleasantly, a reminder two decades old.

Standing on the threshold, J.D. took in the alterations: green bistro tables along the front windows; a raised platform with its railing covered in live vines; a mural of the Berkshire Mountains.

At the soda counter on the right stood Prudy's daughter, the girl he'd gone to school with.

"Hey, Belle," he said, walking over. "Long time no see."

She gave him a sharp look. "J.D.? Hey! Heard you were in town. Your dad's over the moon you're home."

"Yeah." Suddenly uncomfortable, he checked the menu with its fancy script on the wall chalkboard behind the counter. "Wouldn't mind a turkey club."

"Sure. Fries or salad?"

"Both. And I'll take a cinnamon roll as well." He dug out his wallet, laid the bills on the counter. "Keep the change."

"Well, thanks, J.D.," Belle said, punching the order into a computerized till, another update. Over her shoulder she called to the open kitchen door, "Fergus, order in." To J.D. she said, "My beloved." And she smiled. Not husband, *beloved.* "Fergus," she yelled again. "Come out here for a sec. Want you to meet someone."

A man in a long white apron stepped from the kitchen. "You bellowed, darlin'?" he inquired, a twitch to his lips.

"This here's J.D. Used to live next door to us. Jared's son."

Fergus offered a hand, a grin. "So. You're the elusive son. Wouldn't've known Jared had a kid but for Belle and Prudy."

"Yeah." J.D. shrugged. "I don't get back much."

"Well, hopefully that'll change. Hey, if you ever want to do some fishing, let me know. Got a cabin along the Hoosic, if you like rainbow trout."

"Thanks." J.D. swallowed hard. Small-town gene-rosity. All the years he had lived in New York, not a single friend or colleague doled out friendship as Fergus did, a man who took him in simply because he knew Belle and Prudy and Pops. "I'll keep it in mind."

"Looking forward to it. Club to go or stay?"

"To go."

"Coming right up."

"J.D.?"

Her soft, feminine voice had him snapping around.

"Ella. Where…?" And then, beyond her shoulder he noticed the leather sofa, cushy chairs, the gas fireplace on the raised platform. And the blond man sitting on the couch, watching them.

"I'm doing an interview for the *Walnut River Courier.*"

"Oh?" he said, noticing the way her dark hair swung

loose above the collar of her green sweater. A sweater molding breasts that enticed a man's hands to… He glared in the direction of the couch. "On what?"

"The hospital and its community." Not catching the nip of jealousy in his voice, she smiled. "How a number of our staff works with the less fortunate."

Once more she surprised him. He glanced at the young reporter whose notes were spread across the coffee table. "Does that include you?" J.D. asked refocusing on her.

"I work with the church's soup kitchen every Sunday if I'm not on call. Several of my patients are Reverend Blackwell's customers. I like to make sure they're healing properly."

"As in a pro bono assurance?"

"Yes."

He was more than intrigued. "Where else do you volunteer?"

"Wherever I can. I may be an orthopedic surgeon, J.D., but I'm a doctor first. Patients can't always make it in to my office."

"You make house calls?"

"Sometimes."

His mouth tugged into a smile. "The way you give patients a ride home?" The way she'd offered to shuttle him back to the inn when he could have taken a taxi.

"It's part of who I am, part of what our hospital is about. Peter does the same, as do other doctors and nurses. WRG is a community-based hospital, which means we service the people of our town not just with our professional skills, but also with empathy." She raised a shapely brow. "But for a man hoping to change those standards into drive-through services, it's probably difficult to understand."

He couldn't help the twinge of guilt—then anger. "Who told you that? As I've mentioned before, NHC would like nothing more than to upgrade Walnut River General. Which includes your unit, Ella. Either way, you'll benefit."

She smiled sadly. "Multimillion-dollar companies like NHC don't upgrade out of the goodness of their hearts. There's always an ulterior motive, and those motives are buyouts."

"Would that be so awful?" he asked quietly when he noticed the reporter leaning forward, trying to catch their conversation. "The hospital would have only good things to gain." At least that's what he hoped. For her sake.

"And everything to lose. Look, I need to finish this interview."

He caught her arm before she walked away. "Can we talk later?"

"I'm going home after this. I haven't eaten, nor has Molly."

"I'll bring some Chinese." When she would've protested he set a finger against her soft mouth. "We never did get the chance to eat with chopsticks."

Belle set a brown paper sack on the counter. "I'll see you at your house in an hour," he told Ella as he grabbed his meal.

"You plan to eat a sandwich *and* takeout? You must be famished." She laughed.

Oh, he was famished, all right. For her. So much so he ached with the prospect of nibbling on her delicious lips…and other parts. "I'll see you soon." A nod to Belle, he left the shop.

And smiled all the way back to the inn.

True to his word, J.D. rang her front doorbell an hour later. After he'd left the deli, she had wanted nothing more than to end the interview with Phil and rush home. The reporter had given her odd looks the moment J.D. walked from the shop. The one question she had granted him was, "Is that the NHC rep?" to which she had replied, "Yes, and that's as far as we'll go with that topic." She wasn't sure whom she wanted to protect: J.D. or WRG.

She hoped Peter would like the interview. She'd explained the hospital's volunteer program embracing the methods of care and skill the doctors used to make the process of healing as gentle and easy as possible for their patients.

She'd talked about giving back massages to long-term bedridden patients and rubbing lotions into chapped skin and sores. She talked about medical staff—including her—waiting at a bedside to ensure patients took their meds. She mentioned how, if no one was available, doctors changed sweat-soaked gowns and linens and fluffed pillows—all for the comfort of the patient.

She had talked until she was drained.

And then J.D., in that dangerously elegant long black coat, walked into the shop and her heart had flown against her ribs.

And it still beat like a toy drum as she hurried to the front door.

Upon arriving home, she had debated whether to slip into something sexier…a dress, perhaps.

In the end, she'd forfeited sex appeal for what he saw at Prudy's Menu: green knit top, chocolate cords. Although she did reapply her makeup and run a brush through her hair.

He stood on the stoop holding a cardboard box from Ling Hu's in one hand and a potted hot-pink orchid in the other. A bottle of wine poked from under his arm.

A few snowflakes clung to the black wool across his big shoulders and winked in the red-brown depths of his hair. It had begun to snow again.

"We eating in the doorway, Doc?" he asked, levity gleaming between his black lashes.

"Sorry. Come in." As she stepped aside, J.D. entered her cramped foyer. The door was barely closed when he set his gifts on the tiny table opposite the coat closet, turned and took her face between his hands.

"I've been waiting for days." And then he kissed her.

At first a touch of lips, then he sank in to stay.

The kiss was mobile and wet and so erotic, Ella caught his wrists simply to hang on. With a burst of clarity she thought, *This is how it'll be in bed with him.*

Somewhere in the back of her mind, she became aware of his hands, running over her shoulders, down the slope of her spine to her hips. He walked her backward three steps, until she was flat against the door and his hands were on her face again, in her hair and he maneuvered her mouth in a race of need.

"Ella," he groaned, his hands everywhere, tripping everywhere. "You drive me crazy. *Crazy.*"

"Same," she whispered. Quivering, her nerves sensitized to the point of pain, she pushed at the lapels of his coat. She had to feel him, had to free him of that barrier keeping her fingers and palms from the warmth of his flesh.

Lips joined, he offered aid, shrugging from the wool, tossing it onto the pony-wall dividing the entrance and her living room. Then, he boosted her to that pony-wall and he set his lips to the flesh over her collarbones and sucked gently.

"You shouldn't have lifted me," she said. "Your knee—"

"To hell with my knee," he muttered between kisses. "Where's your bedroom?"

Just like that, she froze—and understood he sensed something had gone off-center.

"Ella, what is it?"

She was still wrapped around his waist, around his neck, where she hid her face. Oh, she wanted him. Her body cried with it. Twenty steps and they would be in her bedroom. Twenty seconds and he'd be inside her.

A first for her. But not, she knew, for him.

What would he think of her, an almost-thirty doctor and still as naive as she was at thirteen?

Weird, that's what he'd think. Ella, the doctor who's stood witness to countless naked bodies, but never had a man in her bed.

The more she thought of it, the more certain she became that he would wonder and question her failure at the male-female connection, question her inability to attract a man before this moment.

Worse, what if he saw her behavior as a ruse to keep him from reporting whatever information he was gathering to NHC? After all, he had seen her with a newsman this afternoon.

J.D. eased her face from the crook of his neck. "Honey, what's wrong?" Worry darted over his features.

She lowered her gaze to the collar of his rust-colored shirt. "We need to slow down, J.D." Slipping from his waist, she said, "I'm not ready for this. I'm sorry."

They remained at the pony-wall, his groin against her stomach where she felt the rise in him, the solidity, and she heaved a sigh. She had failed with a man once more.

Maybe she should hire an escort and just…get the deed done. That way men like J.D. wouldn't think her an intimacy oddball.

A frigid oddball.

Gently, he lifted her chin, his eyes warm and a little amused. "Why don't we eat that takeout before it gets cold? Nothing worse than chilly chow mein." He kissed her nose, helped her to the floor, and stepped away to collect his coat from where it had slid to the hardwood.

They set up in her kitchen. Molly, on the scent of sweet-and-sour chicken, twined around Ella's legs with disgruntled meows.

"You've already had your dinner," Ella told the little cat. "Be content. It's not nice to be greedy."

Chuckling, J.D. popped the wine. "At least she asks. Colleague of mine has a cat that snitches scraps from the table. He can't seem to train it to stop. So…I don't eat at his house anymore." He shot Ella a look. "Don't get me wrong. I like animals. A lot. But I'm not into sharing my placemat with them."

"Table manners are a learned art for all species." She set his beautiful orchid on the table. "I meant to thank you for this, by the way. I wasn't being neglectful."

He shrugged. "We were a little busy at the time."

Ella ducked her head. "I've never been that distracted before."

Holding two glasses of chardonnay, he came up behind her, laid his mouth against her neck. "The thought turns me on. You, distracted because of me."

"Exhibiting your ego again, Mr. Sumner?" But a thrill toured her spine.

He set the glasses on the table, caught her lips with his. "No ego, sweetheart. Just in lust with you, is all."

In lust. Two words, and he'd leveled her again. "J.D."

"The way you say my name…" He cupped her cheek. "Makes me want to take you right here, right now. All night."

She thought he would kiss her again, but no, he gave her a half smile instead and touched his thumb to her chin, then removed the waxy boxes from the sack, opened their lids, eliciting the pungent scent of takeout.

Although her insides quivered, Ella drew a pair of blue plates from a cupboard. "Our own blue-plate special," she said, her heart bumping hard at the sight of him at her table.

Truth was, no man had sat at this table, not even Peter.

J.D. was the first. And if she was to admit another truth, J.D. was the first in many aspects of her life. The first to woo her with a simple look. The first she dreamed about at night. The first she pictured touching her when she stood in the shower.

The first she imagined making her a woman.

Was love at first sight possible?

She looked over at him, saw how the soft lighting graced his cheeks and jaw and broad shoulders, pitched flames into the richness of his hair—and she fell.

She fell long and hard and down and down, into the vortex of his forest eyes and…

Oh, my God. I'm in love with him.

It wasn't a matter of pondering—Yes? No?—but a matter of reality, of conviction. She sat back stunned.

J.D. paused, chopsticks perched over his plate. "Ella?" A deep crease slashed between his brows.

She blinked. "I'm…You're…Thank you for the food and wine," she stammered, unable to think lucidly. "They're delicious."

"You're welcome. So what's really on your mind?"

"I realized I've been very remiss tonight."

"Are you thinking about how my presence at your kitchen table will affect our relationship at the hospital?"

Cold as rain water. And she was glad for the dousing. She dove right in. "The hospital has nothing to do with my personal life."

He looked around, came back to her. "From what I've seen, your personal life is the hospital. When have you taken a break, Doc? An honest-to-God vacation that lasted more than a weekend? Hell, come to think of it, when have you gone away for a weekend? Seems to me that hospital is eating up your life. Even on your days off you volunteer at soup kitchens and the abused women's shelter."

When her brows jumped, he offered a rueful smile. "I have my sources." He reached across the table, caught her hands. "You're a great doctor, Ella. Brilliant, in fact, and for that my knee will always be grateful, but I'm going to offer you some time away. Come to Vermont with me."

"Vermont?"

"I have a cottage across the state line, about fifteen miles off Highway 7 in Bennington County. Place is a little rustic, but it's quiet, with no phone except my cell, which I turn off. And the only visitors are squirrels, deer, birds and a bear or two. What do you say?"

She pulled her hands from his, picked up her chopsticks. "I don't know…"

"Tomorrow is Valentine's Day. Are you doing anything special?"

"I'm working a shift for another doctor who needs some time…" *Away with his wife.*

Time away. Exactly what J.D. inferred.

She toyed with a spring roll on her plate. He was right. She didn't take time off. Because she loved her job.

Wrong, Ella. It's because you have no significant other. That's why you make the hospital your home. And maybe that was what Tyler had known four years ago. *Except I never loved Tyler.*

J.D. sat back in his chair, shook his head. "Working

an extra shift. Doc, what good will you be to your patients if you're worn out with exhaustion?"

"I'm not exhausted. I sleep well every night."

"Eight hours?"

"Enough to do my job perfectly."

"I didn't say you couldn't. I'm a walking example. But maybe WRG needs a larger medical base to offset doctors needing a break."

She held his gaze. "One NHC would propose?"

"It's not an evil company, Doc. There is a plus side. However, Henry Weisfield, your hospital administrator, is not one. He's a few months from retirement, which means he's been on golf-course mode for the past two or three years."

Ella leaned forward. "So he's expendable in your view?"

"Considering he doesn't have a ten-year capital-expenditure plan, yes. And does he care? No, because he's leaving. With all due respect, those are not good prospects. Therefore, I hope your board comes up with a damn good administrator to replace him. At least one who'll make sure doctors like you get some downtime by increasing support staff to augment the rising number of patients. As you know, this town has a large population of seniors—my dad included. WRG won't be able to handle the eventual overload if it's not prepared."

Ella rested her arms along the edge of the table. "I'd heard Henry was on your side."

J.D. shrugged. "One day he is, the next not. He agrees with whomever he's spoken with last."

"Doesn't want to rock the boat during his last couple

of months on the job," she murmured. What they needed was someone who could take on NHC, someone with medical and hospital knowledge and expertise in the boardroom. Most of all, they needed the applicant to understand the workings of *their* hospital.

Thankful she had done the story with the *Walnut River Courier*, Ella wondered how J.D. might view the article that touted the hospital's legacy left by her father. Possibly, the man sitting across from her would not agree with James Wilder's "old-fashioned" methods of medical practices, those she had described and explained to the eager reporter. There was also the chance J.D. would regard the story as a means of playing public sympathy to thwart NHC's plans.

Either way, she wouldn't win the argument.

"Maybe," she quipped, "you should apply for the job."

He studied her for a long moment. "Maybe I should."

Her heart kicked. Mercy, had she lost it, suggesting such a thing? If J.D. applied and courted the board into thinking he was the man they needed, he would turn the entire operation over to NHC without a second's thought. He had no vested interest in maintaining the standards set by her father. Yes, his allegiance was to NHC, but… Her breath caught. What if her article placed a splinter of doubt in his mind about NHC's initiative? Dare she hope her words might make a difference?

The more she thought about the situation, the more disillusioned she became. She was in love with a man who could and likely would pigeonhole her hospital into something she would end up hating. She knew it as sure as she was sitting at her table this minute, bumping toes with J.D.

They finished the meal in silence. Done, he helped clear away the dishes. "I'll do them later," she said, heading for the front entrance and his coat.

He chuckled. "In a hurry to get rid of me, Doc?"

"No, just tired." Which was true. She needed a month of sleep.

His eyes turned serious. "Think about that trip to Vermont. It's only forty-five minutes away."

It did sound delicious. And to be with J.D. an entire weekend…

Emotion lodged in her throat and her blood ran thick. After such a weekend, she would not come home a maid.

In a bold move, she wrapped her arms around his neck, and tucked her face into the vee of his shirt where the scent of his skin made her fall harder. Confusion riddled her mind as tears burned behind her eyes. She knew it was wrong to want him, but impossible to stop. Sensing her mental turmoil, he hugged her close.

"It'll all work out, El," he whispered against her hair.

Would it? And if not, where would it leave them? Hating each other? Wishing they'd never met?

She knew exactly where it would leave *her*. With a second bungled relationship.

This time, she initiated the kiss, tugging down his head, nipping his lip, his chin, mating with his tongue. Devouring.

Of all the people she had to fall for, she hadn't predicted him.

She hadn't predicted losing her heart.

Chapter Twelve

J.D. lounged in his room at the inn looking for a movie channel, when his cell rang. After returning from Ella's cozy home he hadn't been able to settle into sleep.

The clock radio on the nightstand indicated it was past eleven. An hour since he'd kissed off her lips—no, *she'd* kissed off *his* lips—at her door and he'd reluctantly left the warmth of her arms to step into another biting winter night.

Argh. He had not wanted to leave her house. He had not wanted to walk away from the peace and quiet and restfulness he felt in her home, in her presence. He'd talked about his cabin offering those amenities, but her home, her little brick-and-mortar Cape Cod with its grand, snow-laden weeping birch in the front yard, its three-foot stone wall bordering the sidewalk…

When had he felt so at home in a dwelling? His dad's house across the back alley, the apartments and condos where he'd lived in the ensuing years—none had the same effect.

He'd always believed his Vermont cabin was the place to restore his mind. Now he realized structure had nothing to do with contentment. It was the people inside.

Reaching across the sheets to the nightstand, he snatched up the cell before checking caller ID, hoping for her voice. "Hello?"

"Hey, J.D. It's Marty Hoskins."

His cottage caretaker. "Marty," he said surprised. "What's up?"

The old man got right to the point. "All this snow we been havin'? Dumped a pile on the porch roof of the cottage, caved in the west end. First saw it when I took a run by this evenin'."

"Any damage to the building?"

"None that I could see. Porch roof will need some fixin', but nuthin' that can't be done in a day or two."

"Thanks, buddy. Listen, I plan on coming Friday. Could it be repaired by then?"

"Oh, hell, yeah. Like I said, ain't nuthin' major. You want the old lady to get in some groceries?"

"If Miss Agnes wouldn't mind." J.D. smiled, knowing respect and good manners plus a nice check in the mail would get the old pair to do almost anything for him. He'd lucked out with the Hoskins living five minutes down the wooded country road.

"Nah," Marty said, "she'd be tickled. An' she'll clean

out the perishables when you leave, give the fridge a scrub-down."

"Thanks, appreciate it. I'll drop by with the check on the way home around five on Sunday."

"That'd be good, J.D. Me'n the old lady'll be glad to see ya."

J.D.'s mouth tweaked as he flipped the phone shut. The cottage would be warm, the roads plowed and the fridge stocked when he took Ella there in a few days. And he was taking her. Somehow he had to convince her to take the trip with him, *to take a chance* on him.

He scrubbed a hand down his face. Take a chance on him? *Jeez.* He was here to do a job, then it was back to New York.

Except you gave her a different impression when you mentioned long-distance relationships. Admit it, J.D. She's not like other women. You've known that from the start. She's done something to you no one has before. She's caught your heart.

Agitated by his thoughts, he clicked off the TV. He needed to *do* something, go for a run. A long, hard run. Which, of course, was out of the question considering the tenderness he still felt in his knee. Besides, she'd have his hide tacked to a wall if he strained the healing process too soon by loping six to ten miles around Walnut River.

Snatching his scuffed-leather bomber from the closet, he headed out of the inn. He'd take the rental and go for a drive, maybe grab a coffee at some hole-in-the-wall diner.

Forty minutes later, after circling downtown three times, sans coffee, he drove down Cedar Avenue, past her house where—yes, dammit—he had wanted to go from the get-go.

Her front windows were dark, so he took the corner and came up the rear alley. No lights anywhere. She had gone to bed.

Where he should go as well. But he couldn't. Not just yet.

He gazed through the silhouetted trees and wondered what it was about her that had him in this state, the one in which he was practically stalking a woman?

Irritated, he tapped restless fingers on the steering wheel.

Rule was, he took women out, had a pleasant time, took them to bed. He never gazed moonstruck at their windows. And he sure as hell didn't wish for a night of snuggling or for kisses at dawn.

Over the years he'd had two real relationships, if seeing the same woman for three months was real.

In either case, the urge to stay in her bed until morning, to—God help him—*settle down* had never entered the picture.

But, looking at Ella's warm little house...

Crazy visions formed.

Him sitting at her kitchen table, eating a plate of eggs and drinking coffee while they went over their daily sche-dules...watching TV with her cuddled in his arms on the sofa...him grilling steaks in the backyard...his dad walking over to join them, teasing their little girl with her dark eyes and chocolate hair—

"Jesus, man," J.D. muttered when an icy rinse of adrenaline crossed his skin. "You. Have. Lost. It."

Booting the gas, he drove out of the alley, sped back to the inn, hurried into the privacy of his room.

Where for the remainder of the night images of Ella zipped in and out of his dreams.

At seven-ten the next morning he sat at one of the tables in the inn's country kitchen. Greta, the female half of the proprietors, baked her pies at five and the scent of apple and cinnamon permeated the warmth of the room.

"How are you this a.m., J.D.?" she inquired, as a warning for him to move the copy of the morning's *Walnut River Courier* so she could set down his order of poached eggs and bacon.

"Very well, thanks, Greta." He placed the paper on an adjacent chair. "I'll need to double my workout when I get back to New York after all this food." He tossed her a charming grin and picked up his coffee. "No offense."

Pleased with his praise, she laughed. "None taken. I like my customers enjoying my kitchen." She filled his coffee cup. "You see this morning's article about the hospital?"

"Not yet." Though he'd caught the headline.

"Well, then. I'll leave you to read it while I run uptown to get a couple trays of muffins from Prudy's." She eyed him a moment. "I hope you'll come back and visit us often, J.D. But more than that, I hope you like our hospital."

He glanced up. "What makes you think I don't?"

She offered a small smile. "Your eggs are getting cold."

Small towns, he thought. *Your business is everyone's business.*

He reopened the paper. On page three Ella and Peter,

in blue scrubs and lab coats, stood in front of Walnut
River General's E.R.

*Our Hospital Treats Patients With Old-fashioned
Kindness* marched across the top in inch-high lettering.
The quote was one Ella had given. Biting into a strip of
bacon, he began to read.

> Walnut River General is a hospital with history—
> and a profound legacy. Established in the fifties, it
> has had growing pains like any institution, but one
> constant over the decades is its standard of compas-
> sionate, old-fashioned patient care.
> 'At Walnut River General patients are not numbers,'
> explains Dr. Ella Wilder, the hospital's newest
> orthopedic surgeon and the youngest daughter of
> the late Dr. James Wilder, whose legacy of treat-
> ment extended beyond the city limits. 'Patients here
> are treated with compassion and decency. They
> aren't ushered in like cattle and sent home with a
> bottle of pills that may or may not work. Yes,
> Walnut River has a process we take pride in. It's a
> process that understands human suffering.'

Fascinated, J.D. read the three columns. Both Ella and
Peter spoke of their father's beliefs, the policies and guide-
lines and standards James Wilder had instilled over four
decades of doctoring and, more recently, as chief of staff.

According to Ella, the reporter wrote, James Wilder
was sometimes considered archaic in his methods by
younger, ambitious medical staff. So she asked:

'If *you* were the patient, how would you choose to
be treated, as a procedure or a person? What kind
of bedside manner would you want your doctors
and nurses to display: abrupt, hurried and indifferent, or friendly, kind and interested?'

Without thinking, J.D. checked off the latter. He'd
been the receiving end of that *old-fashioned* doctoring
and it had comforted him more than he wanted to admit.

During the past ten days, he'd wandered through the
hospital talking to staff who gave him a jaundiced eye
because he was the *enemy*. Oh, yes, he'd heard the grum-
blings in the cafeteria, the solarium, the corridors and
around the nurses' stations—when people weren't always
aware he stood a few feet away.

Rumors flew concerning fraud investigations incited
by him in order to manipulate the hospital to bow to
NHC whims, that his claim of gathering information for
NHC was a ploy to dig its company claws into the tender
neck of the small hospital. And in a sense they were right.
But damn it…

He hated the way staff looked at him when he walked
by. He hated how he felt when Frank Sorenson, his boss,
sent BlackBerry messages with underlying currents: *Do
what you have to. Document everything.*

J.D. couldn't deny the promotion, and its substantial
financial bonus that had initially spurred him to take on
schmoozing WRG's directors and medical echelon. But
after seven years of working as Sorenson's right hand,
he'd hit a wall of stagnation. Then, a month ago, his boss

offered the carrot, the means to get another foothold on the mountain of success: *Get this deal in the bag and the next promotion is yours.* Chief Executive. One rung under Sorenson.

J.D. had always liked his boss, but in the past he'd begun to question the man's ethics, his loyalty. Incidents had cropped up that bothered J.D. The worst was the laying off of Sorenson's secretary after New Year's. Eighteen years the woman had worked for Frank before the company decided her skills were no longer competent.

NHC had succinctly stripped the woman of a full pension at twenty years in lieu of a young graduate starting at a dirt-level wage.

The process stunk in J.D.'s opinion and, for the first time since joining the corporation, he'd questioned his own morals and ethics.

Ella's words in the *Courier* about legacies and old-time philosophies gripped J.D. around the heart.

The methods she listed were those Pops had disclosed the other day. They were the same methods J.D. witnessed while under Ella's care. Even Greta implied there was more to WRG than the outsider would ever see.

Outsiders like NHC. Like him.

Methods such as asking how a patient felt and what s/he worried about at home made sense to J.D.

If the mind and spirit are in sync, the body has a better chance at healing, Ella had been quoted as saying.

Further along in the article, she said:

'Comb their hair if they can't do it. Shave a man's face if he's unable. Connect with your patient.

Put your heart into your work. People think doctors have god complexes, and some do. But at Walnut River General these simple tasks keep us grounded.'

He couldn't agree more.

Leaving the paper and his half-eaten breakfast, he returned to his room to make a few calls. The last was to his father. J.D. had a few things he wanted to discuss with the old man.

"Ella, wait up a second."

Her brother's voice had her pausing at the doors to the stairwell. "Morning, Peter," she greeted. "Can you walk with me? I'm starting my rounds and still need to stop off at my locker."

"Have you seen the paper yet?" he asked as they started for the change room. "The article's great, by the way. Wish Dad could be here to read it. It does him honor."

She glanced his way. "It didn't sound too biased?"

"You said it honestly. 'Our hospital has heart.'" Smiling, he held the door open. "Bethany wants to frame the article and put it in the cafeteria where everyone can read it."

"Bethany's a sweetie."

Peter's mouth bowed. "She is."

Ella chuckled. "You are so gone over her I'm amazed you're not floating up and down these hallways. By the way, are you taking her anywhere special tonight?" It was, after all, Valentine's Day.

He grinned and Ella felt a twinge of envy. What would

it be like to have someone waiting to spend Valentine's with *her*? Would she ever know?

Okay, she had fallen in love with J.D., but she was also a realist. They would never be a couple and she'd never walk around with the ga-ga expression her brother got around Bethany.

"Earth calling Peter," she said, shoving into the locker rooms. "You wanted to talk to me?"

He blinked. "Right." Clearing his throat, he pushed his hands into the pockets of his lab coat and followed Ella to her locker. Thankfully the room stood empty.

"I want you to call Anna because you girls were always close," Peter began. "Tell her what's going on here with J. D. Sumner."

Fingers calm but cold, Ella twirled the lock's combination. The door sprang open. "And what's that?"

Peter sat on a change bench, elbows on knees. "You know when you're trying to make a logical assessment of a patient's condition, trying to pin the problem, and no matter how hard you try you know it's not going to be good? That's what I'm getting from Sumner." He looked up at Ella. "I don't like that he keeps prowling the hospital corridors. Or that he has Westfield's endorsement to do so. It's not in our best interest."

Time. She needed time to respond.

But when she tugged on the lab coat, clipped on her ID, retrieved her pager, closed her locker, she still had no answer, except to ask, "You think Anna can do something?" *Against J.D.?*

"Our sister has an excellent head for business. She'd

know how to handle Mr. Sumner." Peter rose. "We received another fraud claim. Where they're coming from is anyone's guess, but Bethany is wondering if it doesn't have something to do with NHC. It's only a matter of time before the state attorney general sends an investigator."

Ella stared at her brother. "You think J.D.'s at fault."

"I don't know." His eyes held hers. "Are you still seeing him?"

"Would it make a difference?"

He was silent, then said softly, "Watch out, Ella. People are taking a dim view of Mr. Sumner. You dating him might appear like you're fraternizing with the enemy."

"Is that what *you* think, Peter?"

"It's not what I think that's at stake here."

"I think it is." Pushing past him, she headed for the exit. "I'm late for my rounds."

"Talk to Anna, okay?" he called.

"I'll think about it." At the door, she graced him with a haughty look. "And Peter? Unless you have evidence placing J.D. in the driver's seat of those allegations, we are not having this conversation again."

J.D. frowned at the message on his BlackBerry. He'd been maneuvering through some of the physiotherapy exercises in his room when the cell phone beeped, indicating a text message.

Frank Sorenson wanted him to call ASAP. Frank seldom did phone conversations. He was an e-mail man.

J.D. hit three to speed dial his boss's office.

"The man I wanted to talk to," the senior executive boomed, as if he hadn't just texted two minutes ago. "How's your data compilation going?"

"I'll be submitting my report Monday, sir," J.D. said.

"Good, good. The quicker, the better. Now, we've got another project for you. Can you give us some info on James Wilder?"

J.D. hesitated. What did Sorenson want with Ella's father? "Only that he was a fine doctor and an honorable man."

Sorenson scoffed. "No man's an island, J.D. We all know that. Dig up some dirt on him. Depending on the caliber of info, it could be a couple grand for you, plus a couple of extra letters after your name."

Forcibly, J.D. kept his muscles relaxed. "What's the plan, sir?"

"Company echelon wants that hospital. We just bought the Connecticut and Vermont ventures this week, and we want Walnut River General to make the trio complete for this year's budget."

J.D. was familiar with the two rural hospitals NHC had promised to upgrade last summer. At the time, he'd thought the company had decided to bypass the takeovers of those medical centers. Instead, the corporation-take-all policy he'd believed advantageous for Walnut River General on the night he spoke to the board—and crashed on the steps—continued on.

Suddenly, NHC looked like a voracious shark, eating everything and anything in its sight. He imagined Ella's face, the look in her eyes when she discovered how they wanted him to flatten the reputation of her late father—her hero.

"Why bother with James Wilder?" he asked mildly. As if his stomach wasn't twisting like a tornado.

Sorenson snickered. "He was the founder. Nothing like discrediting the founder. We've read the article in the *Walnut River Courier*, and the Wilders' attempt to appear wonderful, but we're also aware of the rumors floating around that hospital."

J.D. felt sick. "Who started those rumors? Our company?"

"Does it matter? They're out there and we want to capitalize on them, make the community think we'll be their saviors. Dig out James Wilder and his son is sure to follow." Another chuckle. "Like father, like son. Hell, make it a triple crown and toss in the daughter, too. Cover those bases and we're laughing all the way to—"

Lowering the phone, J.D. hauled in a breath. Sorenson wanted him to hurt Ella? The balloon of anger in his chest exploded into rage. *No way!*

"Frank," he said, bouncing a fist on his thigh. "Disgracing the family—its wrong." *Disgusting*. "Their whole lifestyle is medicine and helping the ill and injured. The people, the townsfolk know that."

"Give your head a shake, man. Remember the rumors? We don't want a public outcry. We want to be the good guys, the helping hand. You know how it goes."

Bastard. J.D. nearly threw the phone against the wall. "I do know how it goes, Frank, but you'll have to count me out."

"What did you say?"

"I said count me out."

"Are you saying—"

"Exactly."

There was a beat of silence. "You don't do this, J.D., you'll be writing your walking papers."

"Consider them written." He hung up the phone.

His stomach settled for the first time in almost a month.

At 5:45 p.m. that afternoon, she closed the door to her office, sank into her chair and shut her eyes.

Peter's conversation had nagged her all day—through her rounds, a three-and-a-half hour surgery, lunch with Molly, and a number of afternoon appointments.

She understood her brother's concern. It was why she'd done the article for the *Courier*. As much as Peter, she wanted their patients and families, as well as the town, to look upon Walnut River General as a committed, trustworthy, stable hospital.

And if Anna could help achieve that goal…

She dialed her sister's home number; heard it ring seven times before Anna's recorded voice cut in: *You've reached me. Speak your piece.* Which was so Anna. No frills.

"Hey, sis," Ella began after the beep. "Give me a call tonight, will you? I really need to talk about—"

"Ella," a breathless Anna greeted. "I heard the phone while I had the key in the door."

"Ah, heck. Sorry. I'll call back when you've wound down."

"No, no. Now's fine." A grunt and a soft thud drifted

across the line. "I just picked up some groceries for dinner. Nothing urgent. We can talk while I put the stuff in the fridge."

Rubbing her temple, Ella took a breath. "Okay. Here's the deal. Trouble is brewing at the hospital, and Peter thought you might be able to help us figure out what to do."

"What kind of trouble?"

"Allegations that we're not doing…a good enough job." She did not want to get into the details, especially Peter's accusation that J.D. might be involved. "The claims are escalating and we have no—"

"Before you go further," Anna interrupted. "I can't help you with that."

"Why not? You have business experience. You know the ins and outs of how corporations like NHC work. We need to know how to fight them, Anna. We need some advice and we don't know anyone who is more adept to—"

"Stop right there. I cannot help you. Get your board of directors to give you advice. Or the hospital administrator. I'm not employed by Walnut River General. I don't know the details, nor do I want to know them."

"This is Dad's hospital," Ella exclaimed. "WRG was his life. It's where you were born, Anna." And where she had gained a family—a family who loved her whether or not she believe it.

"I know whose hospital it is," her sister said quietly.

"Then help," Ella begged.

"I can't."

"Right," she bit out. "I'll pass on your enthusiasm to Peter."

"I'm sorry, El."

"Yeah. So am I."

"Don't be mad. It's truly nothing personal. It's just…"

"Sure. I understand. Nothing personal." She hung up.

Covering her face, Ella fought the sting of tears. *Oh, Anna. What's happened to you, to us? I don't understand it. Not at all.*

When her heart calmed, she prepared to go home. There she'd take a long, luxurious bath, then read a good book in bed. One day, maybe, she'd spend Valentine's night with someone special.

But not J.D. And not tonight.

Tonight she would return her dreams to that sheltered spot in her heart. And secure the lid.

Chapter Thirteen

J.D. knocked on his childhood home for the second time in a week.

"Son," Pops said, pulling open the door. "Thought you'd gone back to New Yawk."

"No, Pops, I didn't." He toed off his boots, walked through to the kitchen, breathed relief when he saw that his father was alone this morning. "I need to talk to you."

Jared limped after him. "Want some coffee?"

"No thanks. Pops, listen. I've been thinking of staying." He shot a glance at the old man. "What would you say to that?"

Jaw slack, Jared stared at him. "You wanna move back to Walnut River?"

"I was thinking of it."

The old man's eyes sharpened. "You planning on quittin' your job, then?"

"I don't know." *This is the first time I'm questioning the direction of my life.*

"Ah, I get it. You want me to tell you whether it's the right thing to do, that it?" Jared asked. As if he'd climbed into J.D.'s head and saw all his Johnny-come-lately confusion.

"Yeah, Pops. I suppose I am."

"Huh." The old man walked around the counter rubbing a hand over his scalp. He turned to J.D. "Can't, boy. Those choices you make yourself." From the fridge, he hauled a jug of water, drank deeply.

Frustrated, J.D. began to pace. Why had he thought he could discuss life decisions with his dad? Suddenly antsy to leave, he spun around and stared out the window at *her* house.

That's the problem, he thought.

He wanted more than a long-distance relationship. He wanted an everyday one. He wanted to eat at her table, watch *Lost* with her, brush his teeth in her sink. He wanted common everyday events. With her, only her.

His dad hobbled to the counter, set down the jug. "New Yawk must be good for the gab," he said. "Ya talked more in the past week than you ever did growin' up."

"I learned from the best." Regret burned J.D.'s throat.

"Ain't proud of that," the old man said slowly. "Shoulda done better by you. A father does for his son."

J.D. frowned. "You did, Pops." He walked over to the fridge, took down a framed picture of himself in a blue softball uniform. "You hit fly balls for me that summer."

He'd been nine in the photo. Pops had taken it in the backyard because the coach, an absentminded drunk, had forgotten to give J.D. the date for the team photo.

Brushing the dust from the glass, he smiled. "You may not have taught me much about talking, but you taught me how to play first base." He returned the photo to its place of honor on the fridge, thought of the paraphernalia in his bedroom. "And a whole lot of other things. Seems I've been lugging around a barrel of woe-is-me when it comes to you. Did you know I used to pray for you to change, pray you'd be like Prudy's husband next door? He did things like picnics and summer vacations to the New Hampshire coast with his family."

"Prudy's husband used to hit her. Bad."

J.D. stared at his dad. "Jesus," he said quietly.

Jared lowered himself carefully onto a chair; shook his head. "Don't know why I said that. It's her private business."

"It stays in this room, Pops. You got my word."

The old man nodded. "You always were loyal to a fault." An impish gleam entered his eyes. "Except for the prayin'."

"I was stupid back then," J.D. conceded.

"You was a kid, son. Can't fault you for not seein' the whole picture. Lotsa times I didn't see the global picture, an' me a grown man." His shoulders lifted on a sigh. "Know why I put the fear of God into you 'bout hospitals? 'Cause my old man died in one. Your mother's parents died in another. She died there. Hospitals scared the hell outta me. Tainted my view about medicine."

J.D. shifted uncomfortably. "Dad, you don't need to explain."

"Yeah, I do. What I come to realize finally, wasn't the hospital causin' my people to die, but their conditions. Cancer, a car crash, liver disease." He paused. "An embolism."

Which strike like lightning, J.D. thought. "I always figured you blamed me for her death."

His dad's eyes filled with sorrow. "Ah, son. Not once. Not *once*. But I will say this. My attitude changed when you was five an' went a tad deaf with that ear infection. Didn't know that, did ya?" he asked when J.D. blinked. "Temperature shootin' over a hun'red. I damn near went crazy debatin' whether to take you in or not. Called Prudy next door. She wasn't a nurse, but she had four kids. Told me to get my ass down to the hospital *now*."

An edge of J.D.'s mouth curved. "Long story short, I'm here."

"Yeah," Jared said, returning the smile. "You are. Hospital pretty much saved your hearing." He rubbed his hip, nodded. "Truth is, son, I'd be one glad SOB if you lived in Walnut River again. But I'm leavin' that choice to you. All I ever wanted was for you to be healthy an' happy."

What every decent, loving parent wished for their kid.

J.D. looked away, took a hard breath. Pops loved him. It didn't get much more right than that.

After a long Friday at the hospital, Ella entered her kitchen, tossed her coat over the back of a chair and rolled her aching shoulders. With no break since Wednesday the previous week, she was ready to laze around the house in her slippers and pajamas for the next forty-eight hours drinking peppermint tea and snacking on dark, divine chocolate.

When the doorbell rang, she told Molly, "This better be a surprise limo to take me to a weekend spa or there's going to be some serious door slamming."

It was J.D. With a sunburst of Gerbera daisies.

Yellow, gold, orange, crimson, white, violet. Where had he obtained summer in the middle of winter?

And…were those MarieBelle chocolates?

"This," she said through a laugh, "is *so* much better than a spa."

"This," he replied, "is the beginning of a great Valentine's weekend." He leaned forward, touched his mouth to hers. "Ready to go away with me?" he whispered, hovering.

On a groan, she latched her arms around his neck, pulled him into the house, kicked the door shut and let herself fall into his taste.

The fact he held the bouquet and the chocolates and couldn't put his arms around her drove her wild. She was in control. Of her sexuality, of the heat passing between them. She was the pursuer, he the pursued.

"Well," he said when she finished and smiled up at him. "That's the best start to a weekend I've had in a helluva long time. Come to think of it, I don't ever remember that kind of wow factor."

Laughing, Ella eased her arms from around his neck. "Maybe it's time for a lot of firsts." *Especially in bed.* She wondered what he would think when the time came.

Not wanting to dwell on his reaction—or hers—she

took the bouquet and carried it into the kitchen to run the tap, fill a vase. "These are incredible. Thank you."

He set the chocolates on the counter. "They reminded me of you. Bright and quietly elegant. God, I can't believe I said that." He rubbed his nose. "Next I'll be spouting angsty poetry."

She set the vase in the middle of the table. "I love angsty poetry. Used to write reams of it a hundred years ago."

"Yeah?" Grinning, he caught her hands. "I figured you'd be recording biology stats and sketching frog entrails, not drawing hearts and writing love poems."

She lifted an eyebrow. "Why? Because I was the nerd who wore braces and glasses and had two left feet?"

He chuckled. "Ah. The duckling that grew into a swan. Doc, you do intrigue the hell out of me."

"Good." She disengaged from his hold and headed for her bedroom closet. "Let's go to Vermont where you can get intrigued some more."

"You mean where I can get you naked," he called after her.

"We'll see." She winked back at him, then shut the door to change from her work clothes into a pair of jeans and her favorite soft-knit sweater—the hue of a Valentine heart.

Apropos, she thought, checking the full-length mirror on the back of her door where her image showed a woman with respectable breasts and hips, and the sweater tinted her cheeks and lips rosy.

She pulled the clip from her hair, shook her head. At the result, she felt a spike of lust so sharp she almost groaned. Within hours, he would see her hair tousled this way, her face flushed, her breasts and stomach and legs and *everything*…naked.

And then he'd come to her, touch her, kiss her…and be her first.

He would make this her first Valentine night. What would he think? What would he say? Would he be happy, amazed, thrilled?

She'd heard that men got an incredible high when a woman was a virgin. When they could chart the map, so to speak, of unexplored regions, be the *very first one*.

Whether those stats were true for all men, Ella didn't know. Nor did she know how J.D. would react. Heck, she had no inkling how *she* would react. Maybe, after all was said and done, she'd do the Highland fling around his bed. Maybe she would laugh—or cry.

And if she did cry…

Let it be with happiness, not regret.

A million migrating bees in her stomach, she picked up her tote of necessities and flung open the door.

Vermont, she thought, *here we come. Virginity, here you go.*

They headed out of town with J.D. behind the wheel of her Yaris. After ten hours of work, fatigue lay in her bones and all she wanted was to relax.

She tried not to think of what lay ahead—in the bed of a Vermont cabin.

She couldn't stop the nerves, couldn't stop imagining his hands, those big hands dusted with dark auburn hair and easy on the steering wheel, traveling with that same ease over the itinerary of her body.

As the outskirts of Walnut River approached, she attempted to think of more mundane topics. Like her telephone conversation twenty minutes ago with Prudy about Molly's care. Hearing of Ella's trip, her neighbor had said it all. "It's long overdue, dear girl."

Long overdue. Prudy had no idea how those two words fluttered along Ella's nerves. *Truth is,* she mused, staring at the wispy snowflakes drifting into the car's headlights, *it's a decade overdue.*

J.D. glanced across the console. "If you need to catch a few z's, go ahead."

"Why, do I look that haggard?" she teased.

"You look gorgeous. That sweater is going to be my downfall. But you sighed, and when people sigh they're usually tired."

"I am a little," she admitted, though she was too restless to shut her eyes. "Nothing a cabin in the woods won't cure."

He chuckled, reached for her hand and kissed her knuckles. "I'm glad to offer it. You work too hard."

"It's my life," she said simply.

He held her hand on his thigh and she felt the power of its muscle beneath her palm. "I won't argue that," he said. "But even life likes a break now and again. It's called play."

Her lips curved. "Is that what we'll be doing? Playing?"

"Among other things."

"And where will we be playing?"

"Wherever you want. There are ten acres of mountain woods outside the cabin and eight hundred square feet of floor space inside. The playing field is yours for the choosing."

She leaned her head against the seat. "Sounds lovely."

He switched on the CD player; Sarah McLachlan crooned about remembering and not letting let life pass her by. Slow and sweet the song curled around Ella's heart. Years down the road, would J.D.'s memories of her be the same as hers of him?

Doesn't matter. Having sex with someone doesn't make him yours. It's just sex.

Except for one small difference…she was in love with the man.

And if he knew, he'd run for the hills. The whims and wiles of sex might not be her forte, but she wasn't so innocent as to think he'd appreciate changing a virgin to a nonvirgin, then having her declare them soul mates.

As they drove through the snowy night toward Vermont, her analytical mind tried to reason away her jitters. She was a woman, with a woman's needs and wants. Was that so awful?

You should've left your heart at home, Ella.

Her inner struggle followed her into a troubled sleep.

"Ella."

She felt something warm against her cheek—a hand— and pulled herself from the dream of J.D. telling her how to remove a fragment of leg bone in the O.R.

"We're here, honey. Wake up."

Blinking, she sat up…and stared at the cottage ahead with its porch light a warm salutation in the dark. The snow had stopped and they were parked in a plowed spot to the right of a roadway circle fronting the structure.

Ohhh, she thought studying the cottage. *How very perfect.*

"Come on," J.D. whispered, letting his fingers linger on her cheek. "Let's go inside and see what Marty's stocked in the fridge."

They climbed from the vehicle, J.D. taking her tote and his carry-on from the rear seat.

Hands in her coat pockets, Ella gazed at the night sky with its trillion stars and white disc of moon whose pale light brushed the ragged outline of the woods.

"It's…beautiful," she said. "And so quiet. It's been a long time since I've heard this kind of quiet." Again, she took in the sky. "Maybe never."

"It's more noisy in the summer. Bullfrogs won't quit mating."

Mating. A flush seared her cheeks as she surveyed her surroundings. She had come here to mate.

And she'd picked J.D. to be the one.

She came around the car, took his hand. "Let's go inside."

The cabin was exactly as he'd said: rustic, rough and quaint. The logs were weathered gray. Rag rugs covered the main portions of the hardwood floor. To the right was a kitchen of sorts—stove, fridge, counter, a few cupboards. In a left corner, a cushiony sofa, recliner and wooden rocker huddled around a stone fireplace.

Carrying her tote, boot heels thudding against the

wood, J.D. headed for a stairway in the rear. "Bathroom is behind the stairs. Bedroom's up in the loft. I'll take the couch."

He was taking the couch? He didn't want to sleep with her?

Ella hurried after him up the stairs. At the top, she stopped as he set her tote beside a king-sized bed decked in an Amish quilt. "You're sleeping down...down there?"

He turned. "I didn't bring you here to seduce you, Ella."

"You didn't?" She swallowed the surge of disappointment.

He walked to her slowly, lifted a hand to her hair, let it sift through his fingers. "Unless you want me to." His eyes seized hers.

"I do. More than anything." God, yes, more than *anything*. She would take one, two nights with him over no nights at all. Because soon he would be gone and soon this sizzle, this electricity between them would be eradicated under the stamp of work and reality.

His hand settled on her shoulder, his thumb stroking the lobe of her ear. "I want that, too. More than anything."

"Then what are we waiting for?"

"Aren't you hungry?"

"A little," she confessed. "But it can wait."

"We can eat first—"

She slipped her arms around his neck. "J.D., I've waited a long time for this."

"You have?" he asked with a little-boy grin while he traced her bottom lip with the possession of a man.

"More than you know." She stared at his chest, took

a breath. "But…" How to say *I'm a virgin*? "We need to go slow."

His grin was lazy. "Honey, I can do slow. Real slow. So slow you'll be weeping."

"J.D…. I'm…" *Oh, damn.* Now the time had come, she'd lost her ability to speak, to think, to act. Her throat tightened. Her eyes gripped his. Seconds passed. And passed. She fell into his soul.

"Ella," he whispered, trailing his finger along her jaw, down the line of her neck. "You are so fine, so very fine. And I think I've…"

"Yes?" A mere breath.

Dark and enigmatic, his eyes pleaded for her to understand.

"J.D., touch me. Please."

He leaned down, brushed his mouth on hers, dispersing miniscule embers along the way. "I need to tell you something," he said, lifting an inch from her eager mouth. "You…You are the first woman I've…cared for this way."

"In what way?" she tried to tease, though her heart tumbled.

"With serious intentions." His words trembled against her mouth; his fingers shook on her skin. "Ella, I've never felt like this."

And suddenly her nerves fled. "Me neither. And," she tried to joke, tried to giggle, "I've never done this before."

His eyes tugged her in, deeper and deeper still. Right where she wanted to be. "No?" he asked softly.

"I've never had sex." She couldn't look away from

those green, green eyes. "I'm a virgin, J.D. Isn't that the height of jokes? Me a physician, knowing the human body like my own hand, yet I'm a neophyte when it comes to knowing what it's like to have…have a man's…" She huffed a laugh. "I want you to be my first."

He set a finger against her lips, then cupped her face. "Let me tell you something, Ella Wilder. I've never been so honored. Never."

She was going to cry. He wasn't running. He wasn't angry or upset or making jokes. Instead, he engraved his words onto her heart, so that sixty years from now she would remember this instant.

"Kiss me, J.D.," she whispered. "Make me a woman."

Laughing, he swung her up in his arms. "Ah, sweet-heart," he said, carrying her the ten feet to his lake-sized bed. "Before the night's done, you'll be more than a woman. You'll be mine."

Forever, she thought.

J.D. gently laid Ella on the old Amish quilt, raining kisses across the soft, delicate contours of her face. *Ella. Sweet Ella.*

His own joy stunned him. Not because she offered such a sacred part of herself—which in itself was beyond description—but because she was the woman he'd fallen for like a brick from a high rise. She shattered him with her touch, her look, her words.

He wanted this night to be right, incredibly right. Because she had waited a lifetime.

She had waited for *him*.

The notion set his hands trembling as he worked off their coats and boots, as he touched her face, brow, lips.

"Ella," his voice rasped. "You dazzle me."

She drew a finger around his mouth. "J.D., just kiss me."

He did. Kissed her and kissed her until they were rolling across the bed, until his flesh sang with the heat of her.

His hands found her skin beneath the sweater, traveled up, up to the curve of her breasts. He wondered if a man had touched her there. And then he wondered no more, because if he did he'd put a fist through a wall.

No man will ever touch you here, except me. The thought burned his mind. He needed to see her, all of her.

"Ella. I'm going to take off your clothes." His lungs labored to stay calm, his hands to relax. "We'll go slow, honey."

Her eyes were the sky at dusk. Full of mystery and secrets. "Do I get to take off yours?" she asked, and her innocence drove him wild.

He wanted to yell and laugh and jump on couches.

"Yes, and as fast or slow as you'd like. Except," he grinned down at her, "if you go too slow in certain areas, we may run into a little…problem."

Coyness adorned her mouth and suddenly she was Eve and Venus and Aphrodite and every woman since the dawn of time. "Then that's what I'll do," she said. "Go slow. I want you crazy for me."

He couldn't halt his shout of laughter or the streak of heat in his penis. "Babe, you've got me there already." Rolling with her, he brought her above him. "Sit up a little," he whispered, tugging her sweater upward. "Lift your arms."

Gently, slowly, he brought the garment over her head and drank in the sight of her. Breasts shaped to fit his hands.

"Ah, gorgeous," he said, rising to set his mouth over blue lace.

"*J.D.*" Her hands were in his hair, her lips against his scalp.

Lifting his head, he danced his tongue into her mouth. His fingers unlatched her bra, tossed it across the room. Two seconds later he'd shucked his own sweater, threw it in the same direction.

Warm skin to warm skin.

A nip in the crook of her neck, a nibble on her shoulder.

Her scent wrote a medley of music on his soul.

She was purity and carnality and he was drowning in all that was her.

"Ella," he murmured. Only her name. He could not say more, could not get his throat to expel what filled his heart.

He held her face between his hands, looked into her eyes; tried to say *You're the first.*

She ran a hand through his hair. "It's okay, J.D. I'm not afraid."

But I am, he thought. *I'm so damned afraid of what I feel for you, afraid that I might hurt you in the end.*

"Undress me," she whispered. "Please, J.D." Her eyes said she was done with the preliminaries. "I want you."

It was all he needed. "Hang on." He dragged them off the bed to stand on the multicolored mat.

Working off their clothes they bumped heads and hands. Promises to go slow evaporated. And when they were naked, he took her hands, kissed her knuckles—and looked. From the crown of her hair to the tips of her toes, his gaze meandered.

Her cheeks were flushed, her lips swollen from his kisses.

He winced inwardly at the slight beard burn on her chin and neck, on her breasts.

I've put my mark on her, he thought, wishing for a nonabrasive method, knowing what they were about to do would hurt her again.

"I'm going to make love to you now," he told her.

"Thank goodness." Mischief flickered across her mouth. "I thought you might change your mind, you were taking so long."

"I want the first time to be special for you." How to say the words: *I've never wanted a woman this much? I've never needed a woman this much? I've never loved....*

"It will be." She kissed his mouth, a feather's stroke. "Because you'll be right there with me."

Mercy. She could reduce him to a mass of nerves with just a phrase. He sat her on the bed. "I'm going to kiss you first," he said. "Everywhere."

Grabbing a pillow from the bed, he knelt on the rug.

"J.D., no." She clutched his arms, trying to raise him. "Your poor knee—"

"My knee is great. You have a healer's touch."

"But, it's only been two weeks. You'll aggravate it."

"Not for thirty seconds." And then he worked his

mouth down her body—breasts, belly, across her thighs. For all her bravado minutes ago, he sensed shyness when she kept her knees tight. Gently, he parted them. "Open for me, sweetheart."

"J.D. This isn't—"

"It's okay," he said. "Just relax, let yourself float." Cupping her buttocks he brought her to his mouth.

"*J.D.* you're—"

And then her sounds were incoherent.

Later, he kissed his way back to her mouth. Her eyes were glazed. He smiled. "It's time, El."

"That was…J.D., I didn't know it could feel so *good*."

"I know. It gets even better." Reaching for his jeans, he dug the condoms from a hip pocket.

"Let me," she said, tearing a packet open. "Wow." She stared down at him. "You're—*amazing*." Shyness had prevented her from looking before, from touching. And it made him stiff as stone.

"Hurry, babe. Or I won't make it if you keep staring that way."

Quickly, she sheathed him. "Next time, I'm touching for a long time. And kissing."

He released a guttural groan. "Be my guest." And then he pulled her down, shifted her so she was beneath him.

"Wrap your legs around my waist, Ella," he whispered, sweeping her hands above her head. "It'll hurt a bit, but only once."

"I am a doctor, J.D. I know."

But she hadn't experienced it, hadn't felt the sting. And it scared the hell out of him. Because as much as he knew about climbing between the sheets with women, this was a first.

"I'll go easy as I can," he said, misery ruling his smile.

"I trust you."

Trust. Sweat struck his skin. Could she trust him? With this, yes. With her heart...?

He hoped.

"Try to relax, honey." Kissing her, he edged against her. His lips slipped across her mouth, cheeks, eyes.

And then he pressed. Sweat pebbled on his skin. His arms quivered to keep his weight light, the pressure gentle.

Abruptly, before he could decide his next move, she took command of his hips, towing him in with her legs until he felt her give, break. He heard her expel a breath and knew it was done.

Perspiration tickled his temples. Motionless, he let her body accept his, let her adjust to his strength, his size.

"Ella." His voice was sandpaper. His heart hurt with her discomfort. Words eluded him. All that was left was a sensation so powerful it swallowed him whole.

And then along her lips, came the sigh of his name. "Thank you," she whispered, stroking the hair from his brow and he saw tears leak from her eyes and drip to the pillow.

"I hurt you," he said, destroyed.

"No, J.D. You were wonderful. Gentle and tender and...I'll never forget this moment. Never, do you hear?"

He rested his forehead against her damp one, closed his eyes. *This moment.* When his body, his soul, brimmed with an emotion so unfamiliar it snagged his breath. An emotion very close to love.

No, not close. *There*. Right there in his heart.

Big and bold and true.

Kissing her mouth with utmost care, he let the physical govern, and take them to where he found release. To that *next time* when he could promise her pleasure and bliss and satisfaction and he could love her—the way a man did when he loved a woman.

Chapter Fourteen

Lying in J.D.'s arms, with the stars and the moon illuminating the cabin's window, Ella listened to his strong, steady heartbeat against her ear. Under her palm, his chest rose and fell in slumber.

He'd been so selfless and considerate this first time. She'd cried with the intensity of her feelings. He'd made it special for her. But then, *he* was special. He had read her reticence and coaxed her through it with kindness.

He was not a brash man, not flamboyant. He had a side she was just beginning to understand.

And she wanted him again.

In her mind, she compared her body with his. The softness of her calf as it lay over his bony shin. The crisp hair along that line of leg and across the expanse of his chest. The muscles in arms that held her tight to his side.

The quilt covered them, but she wanted to see him below. She wanted to explore him *there*, to know him *there*. Previously, the dark had hinted at potency, dimension, contour.

She wanted reality.

Slowly, her hand crept downward, over the plane of his abs, the dip of his navel, and—*oh, my*.

He was ready again. Very ready.

"Hunting for treasure, babe?"

Her head snapped up at the sound of his deep voice. Amused eyes looked down at her.

"I…wanted to…" *Do it again. Do you again.*

The moonlight showed the arc of one dark brow.

"I want the covers off," she said brazenly.

A lazy smile. "To have a good long look?"

Relaxing, she grinned. "Absolutely."

"Well, then." He kicked down the quilt until they were both exposed and he lay beside her, Adonis in moonbeams. "Look your fill, honey. And whatever else you wish."

She wrapped her fingers around him—and bent her head.

"Aghhh…Ella…" One big hand dove under the hair at her nape, shaping her skull; the other fisted in the bedsheet. "Not fair," he hissed.

"You want me to stop?"

"No! *Yes!*" He hauled her onto the length of his body, grabbed the packet off the night table. Seconds later, he lifted his hips into the cradle of hers. "Hang on, honey. This is going to be one helluva ride."

"Finally," she said, the cells in her body crying out for him. "Make love to me, J.D. All night."

He did.

Huddled in his sweatshirt, she sat beside him on one of the two bar stools at the small kitchen island, savoring the strong Brazilian coffee he had brewed and the veggie omelet she'd prepared.

Decadent. That's how she felt this morning *after*.

As promised, J.D. had loved her until they'd fallen into an exhausted sleep around four. At ten they'd wakened with winter sunshine gilding the room.

"Do you come here often in the winter?" she asked.

His hair was deliciously rumpled, his chest bare. She saw the marks her nails had etched, marks she'd kissed in their shower together forty minutes ago.

He shook his head. "I use the cabin for fishing mostly. Moose Creek up the road has some great rainbow trout." A quick, smug smile. "Caught an eight-pounder last fall. Gave it to my caretakers."

"The people who stocked the fridge and fixed your porch roof?"

When he'd mentioned the snow damage while they cooked breakfast, she went onto the porch in her boots to examine the repairs.

J.D. had stormed outside, yelling, "What the hell are you doing, Ella? Don't you know you'll catch pneumonia walking around in nothing when it's ten-degree weather?"

"Nothing" meant his sweatshirt. And her boots.

He'd dragged her back into the warm cabin, stripped

off the shirt the instant they were on the welcome mat, and made love to her against the door. She'd broken apart in his arms.

Sipping her coffee, she saw him glance back at that same door, remembering. "Yeah," he said. "The Hoskins keep an eye on the place. Agnes likes to bake, so when she knows I'm coming she always has a basket of treats sitting on the coffee table."

Around the handle of the current basket a red bow with tiny white hearts had been knotted. A Valentine gift. The thought of other women, other treat baskets, *other gifts*, stung her cheeks like a slap.

With her steady-scalpel hands, she spread jelly on her toast. "Do you usually bring women here?" she asked casually.

Long moments ticked by. He lifted his coffee, but didn't drink. "Worried you're one in a long line?" In his voice lay an edge of annoyance.

"Who you bring here, J.D., is your business."

"Yes, it is. But for the record—*and* to set your mind at ease—no, I don't bring women here. You're the first." He popped a bite of omelet into his mouth, chewed and swallowed. "And to further the record, I don't plan on bringing another. You'll be the last."

"That sounds ominous." She didn't like the direction of the conversation. Why had she even asked?

Because after all they'd done in the bedroom, she had insecurities about herself.

And then he took the fork out of her hand, laid it along

her plate. "Ella." He rotated the stool so that she faced him, knees between his thighs. "Look at me."

She lifted her gaze, clung.

"Do you honestly think I could have another woman in that bed after last night?" His hands drifted to her bare thighs. "Hmm?"

Her breath stopped. His fingers had inched upward. He leaned forward to nip at her mouth. "Answer me, Doc."

"I was…hoping not." Was that her voice, that hoarse whisper?

"Don't hope." His tongue tangoed along hers, while under the hem of the shirt his thumbs danced their own tango. "Just know."

Needing some fresh air, they drove to a hamlet nestled in a small valley of Vermont's Taconic Mountains where they strolled the streets, peeked in quaint boutiques and antique shops, had lunch at a mom-and-pop diner and drank steaming cappuccinos in a Victorian coffee house—and Ella understood the reason J.D. had bought his cabin in the woods. The ambiance, the leisurely way of the people cloaked her in a charming trance she wished could go on forever…. And then, before heading home, he steered her to one last shop.

"Hey, Ingrid," he said to the grandmotherly lady sitting with knitting on her knees. "Got that pendant?"

"Sure do." The old gal climbed to her feet, went to the counter, reached down to a shelf. "Can't believe you re-membered it." She smiled at Ella. "He called this morning, asked if I still had a necklace that caught his eye last October."

J.D. winked. "Couldn't believe she hadn't sold it."

Ingrid's eyes went soft as she handed over the velvet box. "Sometimes things just need the right owner."

Ella gasped when he lifted the lid. "Oh, J.D...." The tiniest star, moon and sun hung on a gold filigree chain.

"Thought you'd like it. Turn," he instructed, before his fingers brushed her nape and he hooked the necklace.

Facing him, she touched the delicate charms where they lay above the scoop of her sweater. "Thank you," she whispered.

He bent to touch his lips to hers. "You are my solar system."

The action, the words snagged her heart so hard she couldn't think or speak. She knew then she'd fallen into that rare, forever-love described in books.

Behind the counter, Ingrid sighed dreamily. "Yessiree. The right owner."

Ella waited as J.D. settled the purchase, then slipped her hand in his as they left the shop and walked to the car. Still, she couldn't speak. Last night she believed he'd given her a forever moment, and he had, but back in that shop… He had uncovered his heart.

Dusk was sliding down the mountains and snowflakes floated from the sky by the time he pulled in front of the cabin and shut off the engine. "J.D.," she murmured, looping her arms around his neck. "I'll cherish your gift always."

And then she kissed him…until the confines of the car frustrated both, and she climbed over the console into his lap as he shot the seat back into a reclining position, and her long woolen skirt was hoisted, his jeans opened, and flesh met flesh…until the windows fogged over.

The coupling left them both panting. He pushed back the hair from her eyes and framed her face to hold her in place. "I've never given a gift to a woman." His voice was like the night, deep and still. "Pops never had a woman to the house. Except for Prudy the neighbor lady, I didn't have a clue how to act around them when I was growing up. I think when he lost my mother, he went into a shell. When I was a kid he told me he wouldn't marry again because he didn't want to chance losing another wife in a hospital."

"No wonder you were apprehensive during your stay in ours."

He chuckled. "You got that, did you?"

"I did."

A soft kiss touched her nose. "You're a talented surgeon, Ella. You've made me see things I've been blind to."

"Not blind, just a little skewed perhaps."

"Perhaps." He curved her hair behind her ears. "My mother's dying tainted my perception of the medical system. She's why I joined NHC, why I went looking for answers."

"And did you find them?"

"Sort of. Actually, I found I don't need answers. I just need to understand." He gazed into her face. "Most of my life I've carried a big chunk of antipathy. And I'm not laying blame because at a certain age a person is liable for the choices he's made. But then you came along with your big dark eyes, your insatiable need to help. You took the bitterness away, healed it."

"You healed yourself, J.D." She traced his lips with her finger. "I'm not nearly as strong as you think. Did you know I'm seeing a psychologist? That every minute I'm at the hospital I work to gain back a piece of my confidence?"

In the quiet solitude of the car, and hugged by his body, she felt safe and intimate with her secret.

"Two years ago while I was still an intern, I operated on a five-year-old boy who had broken an ankle falling off a pony. The surgery was straightforward, no complications. Except I hadn't realized one of the nurses had gone on an all-night drinking binge and—" a shaky sigh escaped "—she didn't sterilize the instruments properly. The child almost died of blood poisoning. I nearly quit my residency over the whole thing, and to this day I can't look at an instrument tray and not see the parents' expressions, or Joey's white little face."

She swiped at the tears that persisted to wet her cheeks even after twenty-six months.

"Aw, baby…" J.D. stroked her hair, rubbed her shoulder. "I'm so sorry you had to go through that."

"He was so little, J.D."

"I know."

"Now you'll really hate hospitals."

He cupped her face. "Things happen, honey. In every job. I've come to realize that. You are an exceptional surgeon. Trust me on this, okay?"

Trust me. Yes, telling him had been a boulder rolling off her chest. She pressed her face into the warmth of his neck where the scent of him conveyed a comfort she could not explain.

"I've never told anyone," she whispered and felt him kiss her hair and wrap her tighter against his chest. She thought she heard the words, those prized words: *I love you.* Or had it been *Let me love you...?* She wasn't sure.

He kissed away her tears, kissed her—until they both shook for another reason.

She stood at the front door waiting for J.D. to check the cabin one last time, turning down the heat, closing the fireplace flue, and a pang of yearning went through Ella.

For the past two days they had lived in seclusion, made love everywhere. In the shower, against the door, on the kitchen stool, in front of the fireplace. And the past two nights in the loft—

Don't think, she told herself. *Don't think of never coming back.*

Truth was, since waking this morning her heart had hurt with the knowledge that today they'd leave this cozy idyllic home away from home. If she were any other person, she could live comfortably here for the rest of her life. With J.D.

But she was a doctor, he a businessman.

And they had other lives.

He strode toward her. Was he feeling the same bitter-sweet loss?

"We'll be back, El," he said, shouldering her tote. He leaned in, kissed her lightly. "I promise."

His declaration didn't detract from her sense of *never again*. She gave him a smile, went out the door.

Outside, a light wind swept snow off the porch roof, creating a cascade of glittering fairy dust across the steps, where they would leave their footprints, walking away.

Night had fallen when they hit the main highway back to Massachusetts. Ella leaned back in the seat and sighed. Tomorrow she'd be in the O.R. The thought sent a trill of excitement through her stomach. The hospital was her life and, she had to admit, more real than a weekend in Vermont.

But Vermont could be your life, too.

That depended on J.D.

She straightened. *Depended on J.D.?*

Was she that emotionally deprived she couldn't choose to have a good time without the man at her side?

Except J.D. was the one she wanted there.

His deep voice broke through her rumination. "I heard your brother's having the library rechristened in honor of your father."

The dashboard limned his cheeks, his strong jaw and the curve of that mouth—which had kissed her everywhere, which had made her cry his name over and over.

"Yes, at the end of the month," she said. "My father worked his entire life to make the hospital the kind of place where care comes first for the patients. He deserves the honor."

"He does," J.D. agreed. "It's too bad it wasn't done before he died."

"I know. But no one expected him to have a…" *Heart attack*. She could barely say the words nearly two months later. She pushed back a cuticle. "He'd been such a force for years. I miss him. A lot. He was my hero."

"Wish I could have known him."

She gusted a small laugh. "He would've been very hard on you."

"Why's that?"

"He was very protective of his family."

"And I wouldn't have measured up."

"Only because you are a man interested in his daughter."

J.D. shot her a look. "Good." He focused back on the road. In the headlights snowflakes spiraled toward them. "I like a man who looks out for his family."

"After the library dedication, Peter's hosting a cocktail party at his house for friends and family. Would you like to come with me?"

"Will Peter be okay having an NHC man in his home?"

"If he doesn't then I won't go."

"Ella, I'm honored, but you should be there, regardless. It's for your father."

"I want you there," she said stubbornly. "Peter will just have to accept that."

J.D. took her hand, held it on his thigh. "I'll be leaving soon, El. Tomorrow, actually. But I'll be back for the party."

Gooseflesh ran over her arms. "I see," she said slowly, thankful the dark hid her pinched lips. "Then this was the end?"

"End?" The word held a frown. "Not on your life. I may be going back to New York, but you and I will have—"

"How, J.D.?" she interrupted unhappily. "I come to your house one weekend, you come to mine the next? With the main item on the agenda concerning a bed?"

"Is that what you think we had? Just sex?"

She shook her head. "Weekend relationships won't leave a whole lot of time for much else." And just like that she felt something go out of the wonder of the last two days. He hadn't meant to be with her. Not in the way that it counted.

What do you expect? a voice grumbled. *He has a job to do.*

A job for NHC.

How could she forget? Vermont had put a rose-colored glint on the world, including her hopes.

Well, it was time to get back to reality. She tugged her purse into her lap and dug out her pager. There were three messages, one from the hospital and two from Rev. Blackwell. She frowned. The preacher never contacted her. Booting her cell phone, she sighed.

"Something wrong?" J.D. asked.

"Not sure." She clicked onto her voice mail. Blackwell's was the only call. Would she call Mrs. Parker? The old gal was having trouble with her hips and couldn't get out of bed. Her granddaughter was worried the woman had taken a fall she wasn't eager to disclose.

Ella shut the phone. "Can you stop at a house on Maple Street when we get back to town? I need to check on a patient."

"House calls on your days off?"

"It's who I am, J.D."

Again he took her hand, this time bringing her finger-tips to his lips. The warmth of his breath, his touch, lique-fied her insides. "I wouldn't have you any other way, Doc."

As long as she fit into those eight days a month, give or take her On Call weekend.

Biting her cheek, she turned her face to the darkened side window and listened to the hum of snow tires on the frozen pavement.

Leaving physiotherapy on the main floor, J.D. clutched the two pages of exercises Ashley had outlined for the next month and headed down the corridor for the bank of eleva-tors that would take him up to the medical offices and Ella.

It was almost noon and he wanted to catch her before she left on her lunch break and before he left for New York.

From another hallway, Peter Wilder swung into step with J.D. "Got a minute?" the chief of staff asked. "I'd like to talk to you in my office." He nodded to the elevator bank. "Fourth floor."

"I'm heading up there anyway," J.D. said.

Peter eyed him as they waited for the car. "To see my sister?"

"I'm going back to New York in a few minutes. Just wanted to say goodbye."

The doors opened and they stepped in. "Heard you two went to Vermont over the weekend."

J.D. breathed slowly. "We went to a cabin I own." He looked straight at Peter. "To relax." He waited a moment. "Not that it's any of your business, Dr. Wilder, but I care about your sister. A lot."

"As much as you care about this hospital, I'll bet."

J.D. shook his head. "Guess I deserve that. Considering what NHC is after."

"Ah." Peter crossed his arms. "The truth comes out. Does Ella know?"

They reached the fourth floor. "Why don't we discuss it in your office?" J.D. said smoothly.

Ten seconds later, both men were enclosed in Peter's narrow office which was congested with an overflowing bookshelf and desk, and featured a view of the parking lot.

"Let's get to the heart of the matter, Mr. Sumner," Peter began as he sat behind his desk and J.D. chose a guest chair. "I'm not a fan of you or of NHC. I don't know what the hell you've been up to, wandering these corridors for the past couple weeks, nor do I care. But if you think I'm going to believe the bull you've been feeding Henry Weisfield about NHC possibly donating funds to a specialized unit, you're wrong." Clasping his hands on a pile of files, he leaned forward. "I think you've been here to get information to take back to your employer. Information they can twist and turn against us. Know why I think that?"

"I do." J.D. watched the other man sit back in astonishment. "I came here under the auspices that we—NHC—would encourage your hospital to integrate into our network of regional hospitals. In the past NHC has bought out other smaller hospitals—with their consent," he stipulated. "But during my stay at Walnut River General, I came to understand its uniqueness, and its place within the community." He paused to let that sink in. "What I didn't know—until four days ago—was that NHC isn't on the same page as I am, isn't committed to the same things."

"In other words," Peter muttered, "they break promises."

J.D. shrugged. He would not, could not, surmise what actually happened or tell Peter his assumptions.

The chief of staff studied him for a moment. "You're not new to the company, are you?"

"Correct. I've worked for them for seven years. Worked my ass off and climbed the corporate ladder. This was my first assignment as an executive. I was thrilled to get it."

"I just bet."

J.D. ignored the jibe. "However, when they began asking for information I couldn't obtain legitimately…" He sighed. "Anyway, I made it known I wasn't in favor, that I wanted out. They gave me an ultimatum. I had a job to do and if I wasn't prepared to do it the way they wanted, they'd find someone else."

Peter's eyes narrowed. "They fired you?"

"No," J.D. said. "I've decided to resign."

"That's pretty drastic, isn't it?"

J.D. rubbed his temple. "Probably. But this wasn't the only incident. There've been others over the years that have bothered me, things I don't want to get into, but suffice it to say, I didn't like what I was seeing or hearing."

"Ah. You grew a conscience."

"I've always had a conscience, Dr. Wilder," J.D. shot back.

A contrite expression crossed the man's face. "Sorry. That wasn't fair." His eyes softened. "Ella know?"

"I haven't told her."

"Will you?"

"Not until the ink's dry. I'm going back today for some face time with my boss before I hand him my papers." He looked hard at Peter. "Can you keep this confidential for now?"

The man across the desk dipped his chin. "Done." He steepled his hands, tapped his lips. "Any future plans?"

J.D. shrugged. "Might do a little fishing in Vermont till I figure out my life." And told Ella he loved her, that whatever goals he aspired to would never hit the mark without her.

Peter's eyes were somber. "Would you be willing to offer some tips as to how we get NHC's monkey off our backs?"

For the first time since his alarm went off this morning, the tension in J.D. dissolved. "Are you asking for my help?"

"I suppose I am." Peter nodded. "Off the record, of course."

"Of course. However, I won't malign the company."

"I'm not into smear campaigns, J.D."

J.D. No longer foe, yet not ally, but perhaps the initiation of a cautious friendship. "Got a pen and a piece of paper?"

He had to wait until she was between patients before the nurse—Beryl—slanted him a leery look and led him down the short hallway to Ella's office.

On par with her brother's, the room was small but held a touch of home. One wall hosted several watercolors of mountains, sunsets and flowers; on another she'd hung three sketches of Molly. Her desk was full, but organized; in a corner of the window a pair of sun-catchers dangled—a hummingbird and a cottage garden.

Ella sat behind her desk, her slim hand jotting notes in a file.

"Your visitor's here, Dr. Wilder," the nurse said.

"Send him in." She hadn't yet looked up.

Slipping his hands into his trouser pockets as the door closed behind him, J.D. looked down at the woman he needed in his life.

Today her hair was in a stubby ponytail. A black-banded watch peeked from the sleeve of her lab coat. He'd bet the pink Nikes were on her feet matching the ever-present pink stethoscope around her neck, its bell tucked into the coat's breast pocket. His gaze drifted to the strip of blue blouse with its V of pale skin he'd already tasted a hundred times, where his pendant hung.

God almighty. Not once in all his years had he thought he'd be standing in a dinky hospital office at thirty-six years old, humbled.

But that's what he was, pure and simple. Humbled.

By her.

Because all along, she had believed in him. Deep down in her core, she had believed in him. Believed he was a sincere and forthright person. Yes, in the beginning she'd had her doubts.

She'd questioned him, hesitated over his reasons,

argued about his intentions. But when the chips scattered to the wind, she'd been the one left standing with her hand out in welcome, in friendship and more. So much more.

That first night—*that first time*—in the cabin's bed had been proof.

First she'd offered her trust, then she'd offered her belief *in him* when she disclosed the secret of her fragile confidence as a doctor.

And so he stood watching her, a thousand thoughts traversing his mind. "Ella," he said, his voice gravel.

Her head jerked up. "J.D.," she exclaimed, glanced at the closed door. "I hadn't realized Beryl had shown you in."

Brushing at her bangs in a gesture he recognized as solely her, she came around the desk and, as natural as a homing pigeon, stepped into his arms.

He set his face to the crown of her hair. "God, you feel good. I've missed you."

Around a chuckle, she said, "Me, too. It's been twenty hours since—"

"You kissed me blind at your door?"

After their return from Vermont last night, he'd dropped her off at her home on Cedar Avenue before she sent him back to the inn.

He had stood quaking in his boots, believing she was breaking it off, because confusion rode his brain and he hadn't figured out exactly where his life would go, only that he wanted it with her.

They both needed a good night's sleep, she'd told him. Then she had cupped his cheeks and kissed him, hard and long—as if she needed to stamp him into her memories.

If she only knew…

A twitch began along his lips. "That a blush I see?"

Her hazelnut eyes were luminous. "Amazing, isn't it?" She tripped a finger along his jaw. "After everything we've done?"

He kissed her nose. "It's what I love about you, those blushes. Never stop."

A nickel's worth of seconds passed. Her eyes held his. "You've come to say goodbye."

"Not goodbye. I'll be back next week for the party."

He couldn't tell her yet he'd rebooked the inn for the night, and would be returning to Vermont to decide on his career and life's direction. That his goals had quieted.

Once he had everything shipshape, in order, planned out…*then* he'd tell her, come for her. And hope like hell she'd have him.

Slipping his hands into his pockets, he retreated a step. "Soon," he said, meaning it in the most literal sense.

She caught her elbows. Her smile trembled. "Keep safe."

"You, too." A last look, and then he opened the door and left her standing alone in her office.

Chapter Fifteen

Ella stared at the door J.D. had closed without a sound. If she were a teenager, she'd run after him.

But she was fifteen years too late for those elements of drama. Plus, drama had never been her calling. And in high school, she'd been too engrossed in looking at a piece of frog bowel under the microscope to bother fretting over a boy.

So, why are you now?

Because seeing J.D. again, knowing they were done stung her heart with a pain she hadn't thought existed. Of course he said he'd be here for the renaming of the library and they'd see each other again. But this *thing* between them? Done, finished. *Concluded here.*

And that desperate kiss last night? Done solely

because she hated grudges and icy walls between her and the people she loved.

The way it was between her and Anna.

So she told herself.

Right, Ella. Keep the friendship channel open. Easy, accessible and noncommittal.

Exactly what she needed—and he wanted.

Blinking back the burn in her eyes, she turned to check the schedule on her desk. Time for her next patient.

The next nine days were crazy. She had five major surgeries slotted, plus a weekend's rotation. Afraid she'd think too much about J.D. and the reasons he hadn't contacted her in a week-and-a-half, she returned to the hospital the following Wednesday—her day off—and fell into bed that night, exhausted. She'd been going flat-out from five each morning until nine each night.

She would not think of J.D.

She thought of him every spare second.

Thursday morning, the day of the hospital's library event and Peter's cocktail party, dawned bright and cold. She awoke as she had for the past three weeks with J.D. in the ebb of her dreams. She arrived at the hospital at five, did her rounds and was in her office at eight-fifty when her pager went off.

Simone Garner needed Ella down in the E.R. Ambulances had brought in two patients, an adult woman and a child. Both had been in a car crash five miles north of town on the same highway Ella and J.D. had traveled eleven days ago.

"The mother, Courtney Albright, is stable," Simone told Ella when she halted momentarily at the triage station to assess the information the paramedics recorded on the victims.

Ella's head came around. "Courtney from the gift shop?" Everyone in the building knew the single mother who managed the shop on the main floor.

"The same." Simone spoke in her practical no-nonsense voice. "It's not good, Ella. The car was small. Took the fire department an hour to get them out. We've got the child stabilized, though she took the brunt of the injuries."

Ella flipped open the chart. "X-rays?"

"Lab is sending them. But there's also…. Courtney is going a little crazy. The child's facial damage is quite severe. Possible broken cheek and jaw, nose and left wrist. Also a torn ear and one eye has a deep gouge at the corner."

"Poor little thing. Courtney?"

"Could have a mild concussion, and she's unable to move her left wrist. Very painful and twice the normal size."

"Likely a fracture. If it's swollen we'll have to wait to cast it. Where's Peter?"

"Trying to calm Courtney."

Ella glanced toward the E.R. "Which one?"

"Seven."

Chart in hand she headed for the room. Her brother stood talking to a young blond woman holding the hand of a tiny child under a lightweight blue blanket. Janie.

Nodding to Ella, Peter stepped aside. "Courtney," he said, "I've called Dr. Wilder in to assess your wrist and Janie's injuries. She'll know exactly what to do."

Ella understood he was trying to lessen the worry in the mother's eyes. With a smile she didn't feel, she went to the opposite side and looked down at the child. Thank God for medicine. Though her face was bloody, distended and bruised, the little girl was almost asleep with the medication dripping into her tiny veins from the IV pole.

"Hi, Janie," she said softly. "I'm Dr. Wilder. But if it's easier to remember, you can call me Dr. Ella." She'd found that a first name often put children more at ease.

Simone strode into the room. "Just in." She slapped the X-rays onto the viewers. Peter and Ella quickly surveyed the negatives.

"Janie." She returned to the bedside. "You've broken a little bone in your wrist, so once the swelling goes down I'll put a cast on it, okay? Let me guess your favorite color…pink?"

The child's battered lips tried to smile.

"Mine, too," Ella said, checking each tiny finger, the forearm and elbow where skin had been scraped. "One pink cast coming up. Now, I'm going to talk to Mommy and Dr. Peter for a minute, okay? We'll be right outside the door. Mom can hear if you call. You going to be a brave girl for her?"

"Mmm." The child's eyes blinked slowly.

"See you in a bit," Ella whispered.

In the corridor, Courtney turned on Ella. "What about her face? I don't want her face made worse than it is." Shaky fingers rubbed her forehead. "It was my fault, you know. I should have waited until tonight and gone after school instead of before. But they told us she was going to get an award as February's student and I wanted to celebrate before I went to work so she'd have something for Show and Tell this morning. God, why couldn't I have waited till tonight?"

Peter set a hand on the woman's shoulder. "Courtney, Janie will get the best possible care. We'll order several more scans and tests before we proceed. Right now, I need you in a bed. You could have a mild concussion."

"I can't leave her. I *won't* leave her." Full of despair and panic, her gaze darted between Peter and Ella. "I'll just have to wait." She drew in a hard breath. "This is awful. *Awful.*" She glanced down the hallway. "I've been hearing things about the hospital and…and this corporation that wants to buy it, and—and—what if they close the gift shop? Oh, God." She pressed her fingertips against her eyes. "Who'll fix my baby's face? Her cheek is fractured, isn't it? That one X-ray…"

"Courtney, we—" Ella began.

"I can't afford a plastic surgeon. I just can't." Tears wet her cheeks as she looked at Ella. "Please… Tell me what to do."

"First off, let's concentrate on getting you fixed up so you can be there for Janie. Peter and I will decide who is best for your daughter's reconstructive surgery." She offered an encouraging smile. "She'll be in the best hands. Trust us on that. And we'll sort out the expenses as we go. Okay?"

Courtney glanced over her shoulder where Janie slept on the other side of the doorway. "I just want my baby to be normal again."

"She will be."

"She's all I have."

"I know." Ella's heart ached for the young mother. "We're going to take care of her. But she needs rest and to stay calm until the swelling goes down. Most of all, she needs her mom to stay calm."

Courtney sniffed, swiped her good wrist under her nose. "Okay. I can do that for her."

Gently, Ella touched the woman's shoulder. "Peter and I will be back in a little while."

They watched Courtney slip into the room again before they headed for the nurses' station. Ella said, "I want to call David." Their brother had a star-studded practice that put youth back into the faces of celebrities.

"He's in New York at a symposium."

"I know. Which means he's nice and close. No excuse. I want him to look at the girl, Peter. Maybe take on the case."

"And how is he going to do that, Ella? Have you forgotten he has a practice and patients in L.A.?"

"Who can afford to wait. Janie Albright can't. Besides, Courtney's worked in that gift shop on the main floor since she was twenty. She's been a part of this hospital for eight years. Always treated the staff and visitors with a smile. Even sends gifts to patients who have no visitors or family. Don't know how she finds out, but she does." Ella sighed. "I think we owe her one."

Peter nodded. "Can't argue that. All right. Give Dave a call." He started away. "And tell him since he'll be in town anyway, I'll expect him at the party tonight. Might as well do two birds with one stone."

Ella grinned. "I'll tell him he can stay with me tonight."

Peter's eyebrows rose. "Won't that be a little cramped? I thought J.D. was coming to the party."

Hearing his name, she felt her heart kick. "Even if he is, what makes you think he'd be staying at my house?"

Peter grinned. "Uh-oh. Trouble in paradise already?"

"Don't you wish."

"Actually, what I wish is for you to be happy, El."

"Who said I'm not happy?"

Peter simply looked at her. "You've been wandering around this place like the Tin Man from Oz."

"I've been crazy busy."

He chucked her under the chin. "Tell it to someone who doesn't know you. Get back to me on David."

Ella watched Peter walk away. Had her heavy heart been so visible? Nine days J.D. had been gone and she hadn't received a phone call or an e-mail. Nada. It was as if he'd never touched her.

Except he had. He'd done more than touch her life; he'd been in it completely—*in her*—for two nights and two days.

And then he had done what she had hoped, had prayed, he would not do. He'd walked away and not looked back.

He hadn't called to let her know he wasn't coming. With a smile that ached with every hour, she'd watched and waited through the rechristening ceremony at the hospital, through dinner with Peter, Bethany and David, and now at Peter's cocktail party.

J.D. had stood her up.

Should she be surprised? He'd made it clear he hadn't wanted a real relationship with her. What made her think his promise to show up for a party—to which he would need to fly—would have him back in her arms?

He'd gotten what he wanted.

With a bonus.

What a fool she'd been. Her virginity and her vulnerability. All in a single weekend. *Dumb, dumb, dumb, Ella.*

"So, sis, are you enjoying doctoring as much as you hoped?"

David came beside her as she stood, wine in hand, staring out the living room window where snow dusted the street lamps' luminosity.

"Loving every second. Hmm, don't you look handsome tonight?" Her gaze zoomed over his tailored charcoal suit, the crisp white shirt.

He chortled. "You know, if you weren't my sister I'd think you were hitting on me."

"And it's nice to know your ego hasn't diminished. Have you decided to take the Albright case?"

He sipped his beer. Her brothers had always preferred beer to wine. "It's…complicated."

"I'm sure it is," she said, thinking of the girl's face. "Well, I know you'll make the right decision, one way or the other. How was Courtney when you did your consult?"

"Won't leave the girl's side. Which is understandable." He gave Ella a sideways look. "Does she have a problem with doctors or men in general?"

"Not that I know of. Why?"

"Just some comments she made." He lifted his beer, sipped. "Thinks I'm some hotshot, golf-playing face-lifter in lala land."

Ella laughed. "Can you blame her? You're a handsome man—even for a brother. And you doctor the rich and fabulous."

He grunted. "Don't know if I should be pleased or not by that."

"Oh, you'll sleep tonight, trust me." She grinned. "Incidentally, you're staying at my house, right?"

"Nope." He flicked at her hair. "Just to evade your scorn, li'l sis, I've booked into the Walnut River Inn."

The place J.D. had lived for almost a month. Before he vanished from her life. She shook off her melancholy. *Don't be a whine, Ella. Get on with life.*

And that's when she saw him. He'd come into the foyer, long black trench to his boots. His eyes caught hers, held. "Excuse me," she said to her brother.

Wending her way through the crowded living room toward him, her heart skipped.

"Hey," she said, unable to hold back her smile.

"God, you look good enough to eat," he murmured, leaning forward a few inches as if to inhale her scent. "That little number…Jeez, Ella. Do you have any idea what that shade of gold does to your eyes and skin?"

She gave him a coy smile. "Possibly." The dress she'd bought with him in mind—and those Gerbera daisies he'd given her for Valentine's Day.

He groaned softly. "Listen, honey. Sorry I'm late. Flight was delayed because of deicing."

Yet David's plane had no problem with ice. Had the weather changed within hours in New York?

Shoving her mental debate aside, she stepped up and gave him a hug. "I'm glad you're here," she said, motioning for him to hang his coat in the closet.

A few minutes later she led him into the crowd, introducing him around to those who hadn't met him before, including David. Peter and Bethany caught up to them there.

"J.D.," her eldest brother said, offering a hand, surprising Ella with the gesture and the friendly smile. "Good to see you made it."

Ella's shoulders relaxed. He had come, he held her hand, he looked at her with those intimate eyes.

An hour passed. To J.D., she said, "I need water. Want some?"

He held up his beer, grinned. "Still working on this."

She squeezed his hand, then headed for the kitchen. There, dozens of people munched on finger food arranged on counters, and chatted in pairs or small groups.

What is it about kitchens? she mused weaving her way to the fridge. No matter how many parties her parents had hosted, guests always gravitated to the kitchen, the hub of the home. Peter's house, with its dark wooden cupboards, offered the same warmth which Ella surmised was part of Bethany's touch.

Plucking a bottle from the shelf, she moved near the dining room entrance. At least sixty people milled throughout the house.

She recognized many. Physiotherapist Ashley chatted

with nurses June and Lindsey. Medic Mike O'Rourke stood in deep conversation with Simone Garner. At the large butcher-block island, Henry Weisfield loaded chicken wings on a paper plate. Among the guests, a waiter wielded trays of champagne and hors d'oeuvres. And then J.D. wandered into view, his tall frame placing him above most people, his chestnut hair igniting under the lights.

Two seconds later his eyes locked on her. He'd come seeking. She felt it in her bones. God, but she wished they were alone, that she could simply walk over, slip her arms over those sturdy shoulders and hold on forever.

Except for those few words at the door, they hadn't a chance to speak alone. She wanted to ask him a million questions, dole out a million kisses. She was sick with want and need and desire for him.

Somewhere music played, and she caught lyrical snatches about stories and rules being broken and she recognized Brandi Carlile, an artist she'd recently come to favor. The song burrowed into her heart while J.D. kept her immobile with a slow, secret smile, and she thought, *It's more intimate than a touch.*

Suddenly, a woman's words intruded. "…almost lost her medical license over it…" The speaker stood behind Ella, several feet inside the dining room.

"Really?" a man queried softly. "In Boston?"

"Yeah…dirty scalpel or something…should've checked…"

"…the little kid?"

"Lived, thank God."

More murmurs. The man said, "Heard she's a great doctor...."

"Yeah. Father was..."

A few feet in front of Ella a group laughed, drowning the name, but she didn't need confirmation as to who held their interest.

Riveted where she stood, she let pain spin through her chest. *J.D.*, she thought, watching him cant his ear toward Henry Weisfield, who snagged his attention.

Why?

She had told only two people about those terrifying days following that Boston surgery. Her counselor and him. She'd talked her fool head off, *to him*. About the scrub nurse, about the days she'd waited, her insides churning, as the child's life wavered on the life-and-death fence. About her fragile confidence and the strides she had gained.

Easing away from the refrigerator, she turned enough to catch sight of the couple alone in the dining room. The man had his back to her, but the woman faced the kitchen. Ella recognized her as the young pediatric nurse she'd briefed three weeks ago about a six-year-old boy with a shattered elbow following an ice-skating tumble.

Why had the nurse been invited to the party? Clamping a vice on what could be nothing less than J.D.'s betrayal, she turned and walked into the dining room.

"Hello, Clarice," she said, watching the woman's mouth drop. "Having fun?"

"Y-yes. Thank you."

Ella smiled at the man, whom she recognized but couldn't place, likely Clarice's date.

Gossip, Ella knew, fed through the hospital corridors like grassfire. She said, "I overheard what you were telling your friend about an intern. For the record, Clarice, your information is completely incorrect. So. If I hear of it *anywhere* again, I will personally see that neither of you ever work in another medical facility." With a smile that hurt her cheeks, she left them to find J.D.

What the hell happened? he wondered.

Standing by the glass doors leading out to a vast back deck, J.D. waited as Ella pushed through the crowded kitchen.

"What's wrong?" he asked, the instant she grabbed his hand and began pulling him through the house.

Not a word and, except for those dark eyes flaying his hide when he asked, not even a look.

"Ella. What is it?"

She yanked her coat from the entrance closet. "We need to talk. Privately."

"O-kay." He was all for private. He'd wanted it for the past ninety minutes.

"Hey, you two." Peter strolled into the foyer, smile on his face. "Leaving so soon?"

She flung open the door. "I need some air."

"We'll be right back," J.D. said with a wink to ward off any red flags.

"Ahh." Peter chuckled. "Gotcha."

Outside on the front porch, the crisp February air streamed into J.D.'s lungs. "El—"

She wheeled on him. "Why did you take me to

Vermont, J.D.? Was it to lull me into submission, to—to find out a few dirty little secrets so you could use them to make Walnut River look like a bungling hospital staffed with inept doctors? All those rumors floating around about overbilling and the state medical examiner's office sending letters about fraud—was that you?"

He stared at her. "What the hell are you talking about?"

"Why haven't you called since you went back to New York?"

"Is that what this is about?"

"Not at all. Because I know why you didn't call. You didn't have the guts. But what really galls me is that you had the audacity to show up here tonight with that Mr. Innocent look on your face."

"Jeez, Ella." A frustrated hand drove through his hair. "Would you make sense, please?"

She stalked across the porch, its soft amber lamp outlining the delicate line of her brow and cheek. In the vee of her blouse, her pulse beat like tiny bellows, making the pendant he'd given her quiver.

"I had a conversation with a nurse two minutes ago," she hissed and he saw the angry sheen in her eyes. "*After* I overheard her talk about an intern operating with unclean tools that almost cost a child his life."

Stunned, J.D. blinked. "Did she mention names?"

Ella snorted. "She didn't have to. I heard enough to know *who* she was gossiping about. Do you know I've never told a single soul about that mistake? Not Peter, not even my father before he died. The only person who knew was my counselor in Springfield."

And him.

J.D. rocked back on his heels. "Ella, every conversation we had has stayed in here." He thumped his chest. "And here." He tapped his head. "My private life is not open for public forum."

"But mine is, that it?"

He shook his head. "Don't you get it? Yours became part of mine the moment you were my doctor in that E.R."

She stepped back, tears clouding her eyes. "Have a nice life at the top of that ambitious ladder, J.D." She spun away to hurry down the porch stairs.

"Ella!" He strode across the deck as quick as his knee would allow, but she was on the run to her car and within seconds disappeared around the hedge bordering Peter's front yard. *Dammit.* This was not how he pictured an end to the evening.

All day, he'd been impatient to return to Walnut River, to tell her his news. Hoping, praying she would accept his offer.

Down the street a car gunned and roared away.

Okay. If she needed time to cool down, he'd stay out of the way for a day or two. But he wouldn't wait forever. If she didn't come to him, he'd go after her.

One thing she would discover about him. He wasn't a guy easily swayed when things got edgy. Fact was, he thrived on edgy.

Oh, yeah. Anger smoldered in his chest.

Three strides and he pushed back through Peter's front door. Someone was smearing Ella's name and he was going to find that individual if it took all night.

Chapter Sixteen

One hand on the steering wheel, Ella swiped the tears wetting her cheeks. Such a idiot she'd been. Such a *stupid* idiot.

Instead of running, she should have forced him to leave. But no. Embarrassment had her stumbling like a drunk down the sidewalk to her car. She might have held it together, too, had she not spotted Simone Garner and Mike O'Rourke in a lip-lock across the street beside his vehicle.

God. That had been her with J.D. eleven days ago.

She had wanted to yell at Simone, *Don't let that kiss fool you! It doesn't mean a damn thing!* Instead, she'd jumped into her car and raced off like Danica Patrick at the Indy.

Swinging into her alley, Ella sought the little garage

beyond the headlights. Several minutes later, the warmth of her house wrapped her in a welcome cocoon.

"Hey, sweets," she said, bending to pick up Molly weaving between her ankles. "Want some cuddles?"

By the time Ella donned her pajamas and crawled under the covers, it was nine o'clock. The earliest she had gone to bed in years. Well, she would catch up on some of her reading.

She was midway through an article about shoulder arthroplasty in *The Journal of the American Medical Association* when her phone rang. Caller ID indicated Peter.

"Where'd you disappear tonight, El?" her brother asked.

"Sorry, Peter. I'm just tired."

"Nothing else going on?"

"Nothing that won't rectify itself."

A beat of silence. "Wish you could have stayed. After everybody left Dave, Beth and I had a great catch-up session. We missed you. And J.D.," he added.

"What is it with you and this *J.D.* stuff?" she scoffed. "Like you're friends all of a sudden." She sounded twelve, but she was past caring. "Anyway, he's gone back to New York."

Another pause. "Actually, he's staying at the Walnut River Inn with David. You guys have a spat, honey?"

Both her brothers always had been able to key into her emotional nuances. Not that she didn't appreciate their concern, but sometimes she wished they would simply butt out. "I don't want to talk about it."

"All right. But if you need any—"

"Fine," she blurted, her emotions surging like Mount

Saint Helen's. "You want to know? Here it is—you were right. I was a fool to get involved with him. The man's not to be trusted."

"Oh?"

"He broke a confidence," she cried, the hurt cutting her in two. "Something that happened to—to me a while back."

"Would this something concern Clarice Yves?"

Omigod. The woman had told the world. "What about her?" Ella snapped.

"J.D. and I had a chat with her tonight."

Ella's jaw dropped. "You what?"

"It's okay, El. We got it straightened out."

"What do you know?" she asked, suddenly drained.

"Not much. J.D. wouldn't say exactly, only that she was spreading unfounded gossip. He alerted me. We took her into my study and had a chat. Apparently, a friend of her mother's is a scrub nurse who worked with you in Boston."

"So, you know it all, then."

"Not the details. Seems the woman showed up today, unannounced, and wanted lunch with Clarice in the cafeteria."

"Convenient," Ella mocked.

"According to Clarice, the woman is bitter because she was fired. However, J.D. set the record straight about who was at fault in that O.R. when you were interning. Clarice will apologize to you first thing in the morning."

Ella sighed. "Yeah, well, the damage is done." *In more ways than one.*

"If you're worried about the guy she told, he's her boyfriend, a cop in North Adams. He worked the Albright crash."

Several moments passed. Ella took in what Peter had said, imagining the scene in his study. J.D. had gone back into the crowded house and sought out Clarice—and saved Ella's name. And what had she done? Called him a traitor and a liar.

"God, I've made such a mess of things."

"J.D.'s all right. So I'm beginning to discover."

"Make that two of us," she lamented, feeling sick.

"Oh, I hear you. I had my doubts at first. But when he told me he was resigning from NHC, I knew I'd pegged him wrong—"

"He *quit* NHC?"

"You didn't know? Oh, hell," Peter muttered.

"When?"

"You need to talk to him, Ella."

"When?"

"When he returned to New York. He told me the morning he left. We had a little, um, meeting before he went to see you. Apparently, he's been tying up loose ends this past week, even put his condo up for sale. He plans to move back here."

She was speechless. J.D. was moving to Walnut River?

"Did he tell you why he resigned?"

"Only that he didn't like the way things were going with NHC."

Why hadn't he said something to *her*, given one tiny hint of his decision? Why had he left her guessing, wondering, waiting? And why hadn't he called her from New York? Why, why, *why*?

She couldn't stop the hurt that he'd shared such life-altering information with her brother but not her. Not even a clue last night.

And she'd spent almost two hours with him, smiling, chatting, listening, holding his hand. Breathing his scent. *Dying to kiss him.*

"You know," Peter interrupted the train wreck in her mind. "With Henry resigning as hospital administrator in a couple months, J.D. should consider applying. I think he'd be a damn fine replacement. You should put the bug in his ear."

"Yeah," she said, sapped of feeling. "Sure." *When I see him. If I see him.* "Good night, Peter."

"You going to be okay, El?"

"I'm fine." *Hunky-dory.* "See you in the morning."

Evidently he didn't want to let her go yet. He said, "The ceremony this afternoon was nice, don't you think?"

"Dad would've been proud."

"Yeah," he said. "He would've been. The James Wilder Library has a nice ring to it."

"He loved research and the hospital," Ella put in.

"Having your *Courier* article framed and hanging by the door was a great idea."

"Give Bethany a kiss for that. It was her idea."

"I will. 'Night, El."

After setting the receiver back, she sank into the pillows, a warm glow in her heart. The library had been upgraded with five hundred new books—and an honored name.

She couldn't wait to tell J.D.

That fast the warmth vanished, and a shiver took its place.

She had walked away from J.D., had shattered that special something between them with her distrust, her accusations.

"Oh, Molly," she murmured to the cat purring against her side. "What have I done?"

She rose at dawn, eager for new beginnings, for righting wrongs. All night she'd wrestled with worry that she would be too late, that he would be gone and her chance gone with it.

En route to the hospital, she planned to stop at the inn, rouse him from bed, argue if need be. Whatever it took, she had to convince him they could get through this. Failing that, she intended to strip off her clothes and seduce him.

She had to make him understand, make him see her error, beg forgiveness and a second chance.

At 5:35 a.m., bundled in her knee-length woolen coat, she picked up her briefcase and purse and stepped out onto her back porch.

Night still enveloped the world. Across the alley she saw that old Jared was up earlier than usual and had turned on the light above his back stoop, revealing a trillion snowflakes eddying out of the dark. A car—she was sure it was a taxi—drove slowly down the alley.

Suddenly a figure walked through the gate next to her garage and headed across her backyard toward the house.

Apprehension rushed through her veins. She hadn't

turned on her own porch light, but it wasn't difficult to see by the broad shoulders, the height, that it was a man.

Her fingers tightened on the briefcase. If he meant her harm, she would not go down without a dirty fight.

He approached steadily and suddenly there was something familiar about his shape and coat, that long, black boot-length coat.

"J.D.?" she whispered, one gloved hand reaching for support of the porch pillar.

He stopped a half-dozen paces from the bottom stair. "I was hoping you hadn't left." The deep tone of his voice sang in her heart.

"I was coming to see you," she said. "To the Inn."

"I'm no longer there. Checked out fifteen minutes ago."

A smile tugged her lips. "What are you doing here?"

"Don't you know?"

He hadn't moved, hadn't stepped forward. But hope soared anyway. And then she saw it, the suitcase. "You're leaving again."

"I'm leaving," he acknowledged.

Something in her died. He hadn't come to reunite, or to let her patch the problem she'd created. He was—

"Leaving New York," he said as if tuning into her despair.

Confused, she blinked. Then the words righted. "You *are*?"

He set the suitcase in the snow, came the last distance of the snowbound path. Slowly, he climbed the stairs, halting on the step below. Her gaze leveled with that resolute and stubbled chin.

Snowflakes dappled his hair, his big shoulders, clung

to his eyelashes. "Dad's coming along to help with the personal stuff. I wanted to come here first. I've sold my condo, Ella. Quit NHC."

"I know," she whispered. "Peter told me last night. He told me…. Oh, J.D. Can you ever forgive me?" *Please touch me. Please hold me.* Her eyes smarted.

"Nothing to forgive, honey." And then he brushed away the tear that spilled to her cheek. "I should've told you right off about my decisions, but I wanted it to be done with, to come back here free and clear of anything unsavory."

"And then I made a mess of it condemning you with—"

"Shh." He touched her lips gently with a finger. "That's done and over. We all take a left turn now and again." Smiling, he set his forehead to hers, caught her hands in his. "I want to start again, Ella."

"Me, too. Where will you live?"

He raised his head. "Well," he said with a wry grin. "Considering Dad brews the best damned espresso north of New York and creates a clam chowder that would make Bostonians cry, and considering those are my two favorite food groups, I don't think I have a choice here."

She laughed. "Your stomach's chosen well."

"So has my heart," he said, the grin slipping. "I love you, Ella. I've never said that to a woman, nor do I intend to say it to another. You fill me to overflowing. I want to make a family with you—if you'll take a chance on a briefly unemployed business geek."

Laughing through a mist of tears, Ella wrapped her arms around his neck. "Yes," she said, crazy for his scent, the one mixed with snow and the day's beginnings and wonder. "Every chance. I love you, J.D. I thought I'd lost you and I didn't know how to get you back. Oh, God." She began to cry in earnest.

"Ah, babe. You had me from the get-go. All you did was look into my eyes with that ophthalmoscope and I was a goner."

She cupped his cheeks. "There's an administrator's job coming open in two months…"

"I know. Peter got me an application."

"We Wilders know a good man when we see one."

"And what do you see?" he whispered.

"The man I want to sleep beside for the next fifty years."

"Only fifty?"

"Okay, sixty."

"Make it seventy and it's a done deal."

She smiled into his summer eyes where their future lay and then he kissed her. And it was long and wonderful and warm and told her of his heart and, when he lifted his head, she nodded to the suitcase in the snow. "Why don't you bring that inside for a minute?"

His grin was powerful. "Think I will."

He kissed her again, and the snow fell in hushed beauty around them.

* * * * *

PAGING DR DADDY

BY
TERESA SOUTHWICK

Teresa Southwick lives with her husband in Las Vegas, the city that reinvents itself every day. An avid fan of romance novels, she is delighted to be living out her dream of writing for Mills & Boon®.

To Robert Magnus Johnson, who took time out from "the law stuff" to answer my questions about the Servicemen's Group Life Insurance.
And you thought I was joking about dedicating this book to you. Thanks for your help, Bob.

Chapter One

She would beg, borrow, lie, cheat or steal for her child.

Courtney Albright knew what she had to do was one notch down from all of the above, but for her it was worse in some ways. She needed a favor from a man she had no reason to trust. Dr. David Wilder, genius plastic surgeon, lousy family guy. She supposed it made sense that a man empty and hollow enough to ignore and neglect the people who loved him would dedicate himself to enhancing outer beauty.

The problem was she'd just had an accident with her daughter in the car. Janie's face was broken and the doctors here in Walnut River were saying they didn't have the specialized skills she needed. David Wilder did and he'd agreed to a consult. It was a favor and Courtney didn't trust favors. Especially from men.

But her little girl was lying in a hospital bed with half her face covered in gauze bandages and fallout from a favor was a small price to pay for her little girl's health. So where was he? What was taking so long? Maybe he wouldn't show up.

With every ounce of willpower she possessed, Courtney held back the sob that pushed up from deep inside and lodged in her throat. Tears wouldn't help—they never had and never would. Especially not now. To get through this crisis, her six-year-old needed strength, not a mother who ran away. Hysterics would be like running away, and she couldn't give in to that. Her own mother had just taken off without a word. Courtney had had her father, such as he was. But Janie's father was dead. Janie only had *her* and she'd do her best not to let her baby down.

At least not again.

The accident was bad enough. And if she could, she would trade places with Janie in a heartbeat. Courtney had a bump on the head and a broken wrist, but that was nothing compared to what her little girl was suffering. Courtney had refused to let them admit her as a patient. She'd insisted they let her be with Janie. Hospitals were scary. She worked here, but not in patient care.

"Mrs. Albright?"

At the sound of the deep voice, Courtney glanced over her shoulder. It was him—David Wilder. He was really here and, if possible, more handsome than the one and only time she'd seen him. She shuddered with relief although it shamed her. She hated needing something from him or anyone else. But she'd have hated it more if he'd blown her off.

"You're here. I didn't think you'd…" She pressed her lips together, cutting off what she'd been about to say. "Thank you for coming, Dr. Wilder."

"You know me?" he asked.

"I saw you at your father's funeral."

James Wilder had died of a heart attack not quite two months ago and Courtney still missed him. He was the only man she'd ever known who had been kind to others without expecting anything in return.

"There were a lot of people there." David frowned as if he was thinking back.

He was a famous Beverly Hills plastic surgeon to the stars so there had been a lot of talk about him that day. About him in the tabloids, linked to A-list movie actresses. About him featured on TV gossip shows in regard to cosmetic procedures on models. Him dating a bevy of beautiful, high-profile women for about a minute until he moved on.

The Dr. David Wilder could be in the movies himself. Dark hair meticulously mussed, vivid blue eyes. Square jaw with some serious scruff which was how the "in" celebrity males accessorized these days, though he wore it better than most. A battered leather jacket fitted his broad shoulders and gave him a bad-boy-biker look along with worn jeans that hugged his lean hips and muscular thighs. He looked like the guy next door—the good-looking guy next door.

Even if he didn't live on the other side of the country, their paths would never cross because they didn't travel in the same social circles. He had no reason to remember the unremarkable nobody who ran the hospital gift shop. She'd lived in Walnut River for over six years and had never laid eyes on him until his father's funeral.

"I wouldn't expect you to remember me," she said.

"Then you'd be wrong, Mrs. Albright. About remembering you, I mean."

His smile was friendly and attractive and she felt it go straight through her even as she wanted to ask how that bedside manner was working for him. But she had to give him points for showing up.

"Thank you for coming," she said again.

"You sound surprised." The smile disappeared.

"Ella said you were at the airport in New York on your way back to California. I just— I was afraid— Walnut River is so far out of your way that I wasn't sure you'd come."

Boy, was she wrong. But it didn't make sense in her frame of reference. On the spur of the moment a successful, busy plastic surgeon came all this way to see a patient he didn't know? And so fast. Although it felt like a lifetime, the accident was only a few hours ago.

"As it happens, I was in New York for a plastics symposium when my sister called. I came as quickly as I could."

"Out of character for you—" She couldn't believe she'd said that out loud. The words popped out of her mouth before she could stop them. It had been the worst few hours of her life and she was taking it out on him. "Scratch that. How incredibly ungrateful that sounds. I apologize. I'm not at my best right now."

"Forget it," he said, but shadows crept into his eyes. "I understand you work here at the hospital but can't—" He stopped and didn't say whatever it was he'd been about to, but something suspiciously like pity crept into his eyes. "Walnut River isn't that far out of my way and Ella said your daughter's facial injuries are pretty serious."

Tears welled in her eyes again and she turned away, embarrassed by the show of weakness. When he put a comforting hand on her shoulder, the urge to give in to her fear and grief swamped her. With an effort, she pulled herself together and faced him again. She might be the nobody who ran the gift shop but if that connection was what got him here it was one more reason to be grateful for it.

She looked at the half of her daughter's face that she could see and noted the pale skin on Janie's normally healthy pink cheek. "She's been sleeping off and on since the accident."

"That's a combination of shock and medication to keep her comfortable," he explained.

"They told me."

The staff had done an excellent job of keeping her informed. They were her friends as well as coworkers and if not for them, she wasn't sure this wouldn't have broken her.

He walked around to the other side of the bed and very gently pulled away the strips of paper tape loosely holding the gauze over Janie's cheek and ear. "I just got here and wanted to introduce myself and have a quick look at the patient—"

"Janie," she said. "My daughter's name is Jane Josephine Albright. Everyone calls her Janie."

"Janie." He met her gaze, then looked down and continued his examination. "She's a beautiful child."

"Yes, she is—" Courtney stopped, choked up because she wanted to say *was*.

She'd known it was bad or he wouldn't be here.

Courtney remembered very little about the accident and nothing about the helicopter flight that airlifted her and Janie to Walnut River General Hospital. She'd come around and remembered being X-rayed and having her wrist immobilized. The E.R. doctor had ordered CT scans for Janie, then they'd cleaned her up, covered her face and called in a specialist.

No one had pushed Courtney to look and she didn't really want to see. If that made her a coward, so be it. But she didn't think she could bear it, knowing what she'd done to her own child. If she could have her choice of days to do over, today would be at the top of a very long list.

She'd been taking Janie out to an early breakfast before work and school. It was a rare treat because she couldn't afford meals out but Janie had been named student of the month and they'd planned to celebrate. Courtney's gut had told her it wasn't a good idea. The weather was bad. What was that saying? March came in like a lion, out like a lamb? It was true. And she'd worried about the roads being safe.

She should have listened to her gut. She could try and pin this on Mother Nature or God, but the fact was, there was no one else to blame for a single-car rollover accident.

She knew part of her was always trying to make up for the

fact that Janie didn't have a dad. It didn't matter that if he'd
lived, Joe wouldn't have been a very good parent. All Janie
knew was that her father was gone forever.

Courtney was the mom and trying so very hard to be a
good one. Trying *not* to be like her own mother. A powerful
wave of guilt washed over her. Her mother had walked out,
which was unforgivable, but Courtney had never ended up in
a hospital intensive care unit. So which one of them was the
worst mother ever? Janie *was* a beautiful child, but she might
be scarred for life—and it was all Courtney's fault.

The doctor replaced the gauze and brushed Janie's blond
hair off her forehead in a surprising and unexpectedly tender
gesture. He met her gaze. "I'm going to look at her chart."

"Is she going to be all right?"

"Her condition is serious, but her injuries aren't life-threat-
ening."

"They already told me that. I want to know if her face is
going to be all right."

"I need to evaluate all her test results."

"What aren't you telling me, Dr. Wilder?"

"Please call me David."

She'd call him the devil himself if it would help Janie.
She'd call him anything he wanted if he would simply tell her
the truth. "David, what are you keeping from me?"

He glanced at Janie and sympathy slid into his vivid blue
eyes. "The injuries to her cheek, eye and nose are severe, but
I can only see the soft tissue. I need information about
muscles, nerves and bone involvement before I can evaluate
the extent of the damage. Until I see everything, I can't tell
you what kind of outcome you can expect."

"Okay." That made sense. If the little patient in the big bed
were anyone other than her child, she'd have realized that
without him telling her. It's true what they said about losing objectivity when it concerned someone you loved. "But when you

have answers, I want you to tell me everything. The whole truth."

"You have my word, Mrs. Albright."

"Call me Courtney."

He nodded, then walked out. She felt inexplicably alone, which was weird since she hadn't expected him actually to show up at all. Why would he go out of his way? Unless there was something in it for him. She was probably the most ungrateful woman on the planet for thinking such thoughts. But not listening to her gut had cost her in the past and she'd paid a high price today for another lesson.

She didn't have to like the situation, but in her circumstances she had very little choice but to go along with it. The old children's rhyme Humpty Dumpty kept going through her mind.

All the king's horses and all the king's men couldn't put Humpty Dumpty back together again—but none of them were a mom.

David would rather be anywhere but Walnut River, and the feeling wasn't about the CT films he was studying on the viewer. Although it would require a great deal of work, he could repair Janie Albright's face and she would grow up to be as beautiful as her mother. Courtney.

He hadn't known her name until today, but he remembered seeing her the day they'd buried his father. She'd been the single bright spot in his dark void of what-ifs and self-reproach. With her blond hair blowing in the frigid wind, she'd been like a beacon in the sea of pitch black. Her warm brown eyes had been full of sympathy and sadness and he had wondered why she looked that way.

What was her relationship with his father? Why did she mourn so deeply for the man David had disappointed so many years before? More than once since that day he'd recalled her all-American beauty that included a matching set of dimples. His patients who were searching for physical perfection would pay a lot of money to duplicate her looks.

From what Ella had said, Courtney didn't have a lot of money. That meant she needed him. And that made him wary. It wouldn't have if he hadn't been instantly and intensely attracted. But he'd learned a long time ago that intense feelings for a beautiful woman could make a man do stupid things. Life-altering things.

Still, she wasn't the reason he didn't want to be here. That was all about a past filled with mistakes and regrets. It was all about the things he'd done wrong and could never make right. His father was dead and he could never get back time with him or the relationship he'd lost.

At the airport when he'd talked to Ella, his initial reaction had been to plead schedule conflicts that prevented him from coming here. The truth was, he wasn't due back in his Beverly Hills office for several days. The other doctors in the practice would pick up the slack for him. When he'd intended to say no, the word *yes* came out of his mouth. Before she'd hung up, Ella said since he'd be in town Peter would be expecting him at a cocktail party following the rededication of the hospital library in honor of their father. And so it began…

But there was a pressing problem. How was he going to tell a worried young mother that her daughter's damaged face needed extensive work if she was ever going to look normal again?

David pulled Janie's films from the viewer and clicked off the light. After looking through the chart, he walked down the hall and into ICU where he saw Courtney holding her daughter's hand. The little girl was awake and when she saw him, she tensed.

"Mommy—"

Courtney glanced over her shoulder. Like mother, like daughter. She tensed, too. But he had a feeling her fear wasn't all about what he had to tell her. On some level it was personal. Instinctive. He wasn't sure how he knew that, but he'd bet his favorite stethoscope it was true.

Her arm immobilized in a dark-blue sling, she looked back at her daughter. "Sweetie, this is Dr. Wilder. He's come a long way to look at you and tell us what to do to make you better."

David walked over to the bed and smiled down at his patient. "Hi, beautiful."

Janie studied him with her one good eye. It was blue. "Hi."

Underneath the bandage he knew her shattered cheekbone was dragging down her other eye and there was damage to the eyelid. The long gash on her chin and the injury to her ear were the least of the problems and the easiest to fix. There was a six-hour post-trauma window during which repair work could be done without debriding in surgery to avoid infection. It was simplest for the patient and the clock was ticking.

"If I take your mom away for a few minutes will you be all right?" he asked her.

She glanced apprehensively at her mother, then back at him and her mouth trembled. "Why does Mommy have to go with you? Are you gonna fix the bump on her head?"

David knew the injury didn't need his intervention and would heal nicely on its own. Courtney's face would be as flawless as the first time he'd seen her. The fact that she'd refused anything besides basic medical attention in order to remain at her daughter's side showed selflessness and character and a beauty on the inside where it counted most.

He smiled at Janie. "Your mom will be fine without my help. But I need to talk to her for just a couple of minutes."

"'Bout me?"

"Yes," he answered.

"'Bout my face?" Janie asked, a tear sliding down her good cheek. "Mommy said my arm is broken. Is my face broken too?"

Something shifted and stretched in his chest and the feeling made him acutely uncomfortable. A doctor wasn't supposed to become personally involved with a patient, but some had a way of sneaking through his defenses. Janie Albright could easily be one of them.

"Did your mom tell you that Dr. Ella fixed your arm and that's why it's in a cast?" When she nodded, he said, "It's going to be good as new." He chose his words carefully. "There are doctors who can make your face good as new."

"Really?" Courtney asked, hope chasing the wariness from her eyes.

"Really." He looked at the little girl. "And I need to tell your mom all about that, but it's pretty boring. Is it okay with you if we go over there?" he asked, pointing to a spot just inside the door. "You can still see her and we'll be right here if you need anything. How would that be?"

"Okay, I guess," Janie said uncertainly.

"Do you hurt anywhere?" he asked.

"A little." She glanced at the cast on her wrist. "My arm."

"They gave her something for pain a few minutes ago," Courtney told him.

He nodded. "Give it a few minutes, kiddo. You'll feel better. I promise."

"Okay," Janie said.

David moved away from the bed and Courtney followed, cradling her injured arm.

"You promised to tell me like it is," she reminded him, as if she didn't believe he would keep his word.

"And I have every intention of doing that."

She nodded and winced at the movement. "Okay. How bad is her face? Will she really be all right?"

"Yes," he said firmly. "Before I get specific you need to know that she will look normal again."

"Thank God," she said, breathing a sigh of relief.

"But it's going to take work."

Instantly, worry snapped back into place. "Please, explain."

"The damage needs to be repaired in two phases. There's a long deep gash in her chin and her ear needs repair. Also a nick near her eye. With facial trauma we like to suture the damage within six hours of the initial injury or the repairs need to be done in surgery."

Courtney glanced at the clock. "Then there's still time."

"Yes," he agreed. "The second part comes later. Her cheekbone is shattered and the right side of her face needs to be realigned."

Her mouth trembled, and she caught her top lip between her teeth, composing herself as if by sheer force of will. "Go on."

"Instead of trying to piece together the bone fragments, it's my opinion that she'll have a better outcome with an implant."

Courtney considered that for a moment. "She's only six. She's still growing. Will she need more surgery in the future?"

"Possibly. But let's take it one step at a time. And the first step is repairing the superficial damage. Since I'm here, I'll take care of that."

"I don't mean to sound mercenary, especially with my daughter's welfare in question," she said. Her chin lifted a notch as if fierce pride was in major conflict with her survival instincts. "And I'm grateful that you were able to examine her, but it would be best for Janie to have a doctor who's covered under my insurance plan here at work."

"They can do it," he agreed. "But without a specialist's training, the results won't be as favorable. If you want the best possible outcome for Janie, a plastics guy is the way to go. My brother has extended me temporary privileges here at Walnut River General."

"Does that mean my health insurance would cover your services?"

"No." But he was here and this child needed his help now. "But I'm the best man for the job, and there won't be a charge."

She stiffened. "Charity?"

"Your independent streak is showing. I just want to help Janie."

A range of expressions crossed her face, all the way from wariness to resignation. She sighed and said, "Thank you."

"Don't mention it."

She looked fragile, vulnerable and more worried and desperate with every word that came out of his mouth. "How long until phase two?" She took a deep breath. "The implant?"

"After the swelling goes down. My best guess is about three to four weeks."

"Tell me it's not more complicated than phase one," she said.

He met her gaze head-on. "She's going to need surgery."

"That's complicated."

"And someone who specializes in reconstructive surgery," he confirmed.

"Okay. Three to four weeks." She nodded and glanced at her daughter, clearly trying to process the information as rationally as possible. "Then I'll have time to check out my health-care coverage."

David knew for a fact that there wasn't a doctor in Walnut River who could do the procedure. "I'd be happy to recommend someone good who's as close to Walnut River as possible."

"So there could be more out-of-pocket expenses," she said absently, almost as if she were thinking out loud.

"It's possible." Ella had told him she was a single mother. That probably meant divorced. He wished he could be indifferent to the fact that she was unattached but there was a part of him that couldn't seem to work up a proper level of regret. Still, divorced parents came together for their children. "Surely Janie's father will help—"

"Hardly." Unexpected bitterness filled Courtney's gaze. "Her father was a soldier."

Too late now to wish he'd paid more attention when his sister had told him about a single mom who had big trouble. "Was?"

"He died in Iraq. Unfortunately he wasn't as conscientious about military dependent's benefits as he should have been."

"I'm sorry."

About that and so much more. He was an idiot. An idiot who made assumptions. An idiot who felt himself being sucked in by big brown eyes and a pair of dimples that wouldn't quit. Courtney Albright desperately needed his help.

The last time he'd become involved with a desperate woman it had cost him everything.

Chapter Two

Courtney held her little girl's small hand while they both watched David snap on his latex gloves, then inspect the metal tray full of medical tools beside him. She was pretty sure her own eyes were as wide as her daughter's and the fear factor was up there for both of them. If only she was the one facing the procedure. That would have been so much easier than watching Janie go through it. And that wasn't the end of the ordeal. There was still a surgery, but she couldn't deal with that now. One trauma at a time.

David had changed into blue scrubs and it was disconcerting that he looked just as good as he had in his jeans and leather jacket. How stupid was she for even thinking that?

"Okay, beautiful, are you ready?" David asked.

She assumed he meant Janie since he was looking at her. "Do you have any questions, peanut?" Courtney questioned.

"Is it gonna hurt?" Her mouth trembled as she looked at him.

He looked at Janie. "I'm going to give you some medicine so it won't hurt. A small pinch and then nothing."

"Promise?"

"Yes."

"What else is gonna happen?"

"I won't lie to you, Janie." David met her gaze. "I'm going to tell you exactly what's going on."

"No medical doublespeak requiring a translator?" Courtney asked.

"Honesty is always the best policy." He must have seen the skepticism in her eyes because he added, "Especially with children. They always know when something's not right. It's my goal to keep her calm. If she's not prepared for this she's going to get agitated. Agitation is quickly followed by restlessness, then tension and stress. None of that is helpful."

That made sense. "I see your point."

He nodded, then focused on the child. "You're going to feel a little pulling. Do you think you can be very still for me? More still than any other six-year-old girl ever?" When Janie nodded solemnly, he smiled. "Okay. Let's do this."

Courtney squeezed her daughter's fingers while David picked up a swab and dabbed it over the area. He'd already explained that it was a topical anesthetic to take the edge off the injection that would numb her for the procedure. Now was where she did her mom thing. She needed to distract Janie while David worked.

"I think a six-year-old who can be more still than anyone ever deserves a special prize," she said.

"What?" Janie asked, her attention snagged as hoped for.

"It's got to be pretty special. What's the most special thing you can think of?"

"What about ice cream?" David suggested.

"I like vanilla ice cream," Janie said. "Milkshakes are best. But I think a toy would be good, too."

"What toy?" Courtney asked.

"Maybe a doll. With a stroller."

"Okay, Janie. It's time to hold still for me. Then we can get serious about that doll-and-stroller thing."

Janie tensed and whimpered when he did the injections but she barely moved a muscle.

Several moments later he announced, "All finished with that part. And it's the worst. I promise. Now we wait for the medicine to do its work."

"Do I win the prize?" Janie wanted to know.

"Hands down," he agreed.

"Are you finished?"

He shook his head. "I still have a little more to do."

"What?" Janie asked. She glanced at the tray of instruments beside him. "Where's the needle?"

Courtney winced and felt David's gaze on her. "I think everything the doctor is going to use is wrapped up there on the tray."

"Why?"

"To keep them sterile," David explained. "To keep the germs off. Did you ever have a scratch or scrape that got infected?"

The little girl pressed her lips together. "One time. It got really red and hurt. Mommy had to pour this stuff on—"

"Hydrogen peroxide," Courtney said when Janie glanced at her for clarification.

"Then she put on cream and I got a Band-Aid."

"Your mom did just the right thing," David said.

Courtney felt the power of his praise course through her but that made no sense. Why should it make any difference to her whether or not he approved? And yet it did. How irritating was that? The good news was that Janie had been successfully distracted.

"You'll heal faster if these cuts don't get any germs in them," he explained.

"You have to sew up my boo-boo?" she asked.

He thought for a moment. "I have to pull the edges together so it heals neatly."

"Are you gonna use a big needle? Like the one my mommy uses to fix my jeans?"

His face was intensely serious as he answered the question. "I'm not sure what your mom uses for that," he said, "but for what I'm going to do we need everything as small as possible."

"'Cuz I'm small?"

Courtney's throat tightened with emotion. Her child was too small to go through this, she thought. She knew she should say something, but couldn't get anything past the lump in her throat. Some pillar of strength she was.

David's sharp-eyed gaze seemed to pick up on her state of mind. "Janie, even if you were as big as Shrek I would use very tiny stuff."

"How come?"

"Because tiny stuff will make the scar almost invisible."

"So that stuff is magic?"

"In the right hands it is."

Courtney looked at his long, elegant gloved fingers. "Are your hands magic?"

"Yes." He smiled.

His tone wasn't arrogant, just matter-of-fact. There was nothing even remotely sensual or suggestive in his response or the way he looked at her, but Courtney felt that smile dance over her skin and touch her everywhere. She swore she felt tingles and considering her opinion of this man, he wielded some kind of powerful magic.

"You said 'almost' invisible. That means a little bit visible," she said, glancing at Janie.

"It does." He glanced at Janie, too, gauging her reaction. "Believe it or not, there's some good news."

"I could sure use some of that," Courtney answered, and she'd never meant anything more in her entire life.

With a gloved finger, he pointed to the long gash on her chin. "Because this is on the jawline, it will be practically unnoticeable under her chin. Her ear, while exceptionally lovely and delicate, has creases and folds."

"Like Mr. Potato Head?" Janie asked.

David laughed. "You're much prettier than he is. But here's the thing, ears have lots of places to hide the sutures. And so does your eye—a natural fold between your eyelid and brow bone. It's a matter of using what nature gave you for camouflage. All of that makes my job easier."

Courtney was relieved to hear that, but wondered if he took the easy way out in his personal life, too. It was as if he was all about how things appeared on the outside. He'd come home for his mother's funeral, then his father's. But nothing in between. She'd known James Wilder pretty well. For some reason the man had taken an interest in her and Janie and his passing left a big hole in her life. But while his father was still alive, David never came to visit. It wasn't a stretch to conclude that he didn't take after the elder Dr. Wilder who'd cared more about the inside of people than the outside.

"Okay, Janie, I'm going to start. Are you ready to hold still again?"

"You don't need a nurse?" Courtney asked.

He shook his head. "I'm used to working alone, and they're busy."

"Is it okay if I shut my eyes?" Janie said.

"If you want."

Courtney wished she could shut her eyes too, but from where she was sitting in the chair, she couldn't really see much anyway. Just the slow, methodical way his elegant hands moved. The suture material was so fine it was barely visible and he held it with forceps. Between the pain medication she'd received and being physically drained from what she'd been through, Janie actually drifted off while David worked.

He might not be much like his father, but he was really good with her daughter. It seemed natural, something she wouldn't have expected. "Where did you learn to get along with kids?"

His gaze met hers briefly. "I was one once."

So was she. About a million years ago. On second thought, she didn't actually remember being a kid. It seemed as if she'd always been the grown-up, handling one crisis after another when her father was too drunk even to take care of himself.

But if David had taken a course in med school on how to charm children, apparently he'd aced it. The man was putting sutures in Janie's chin and she trusted him enough to fall asleep. The ability to do that didn't mesh with what little Courtney knew about him.

"But you're not a kid now," she said. That was the understatement of the century. He was a man who sprinkled sex appeal like fairy dust wherever he went, if tabloid stories linking him to models and actresses were anything to go by. "And you didn't talk down to her."

"Kids know when you do that. They don't like it."

She actually laughed. "That's true."

Who'd have thought anyone could make her laugh under the circumstances? Maybe he was magic. That thought made her uneasy and when she was uneasy it was time to fall back on defenses.

"So why did you agree to look at Janie?" she asked.

He glanced at her. "Because my sister called."

"But you're not helping your sister. Janie and I are total strangers to you." And from what she gathered, his family wasn't too much more to him. Yet he was here because Ella called. By any definition that was a nice thing. Men who did nice things usually wanted something and she wasn't comfortable with that kind of balance sheet.

"Let's just say this is the least I can do for the widow and daughter of a war hero," he said.

Courtney cringed at his words. It was what everyone thought, and it couldn't be further from the truth. The anger welled up and after a day like today she didn't have the emotional reserves to bite her tongue.

"Joining the army wasn't about truth, justice and the American way for Joe. My husband was a lot of things, but noble wasn't one of them."

David's hands stopped moving and he looked at her. "He gave his life for his country. That seems pretty noble to me."

It would have been if his reasons for joining the military hadn't been about getting away from his wife and baby girl. He'd gone because he wanted liberty, but not for his country. For himself. He wanted freedom from domestic restraints so he could play around with women, any woman who wasn't his wife.

As quickly as the rage reared up, it let her down. She was so tired. Tired of being angry about something she couldn't change. Mostly she was just tired. And sore. It felt as if every muscle ached and her body was the percussion section in a marching band. Her head throbbed, then her wrist pounded. And that was her only excuse for revealing relationship failures to the doctor who'd been nice enough to help Janie.

She met his questioning gaze and sighed. "Is it too late to take that back?"

"Pretty much," he confirmed.

She sighed. "Ordinarily I'm not prone to sharing personal information. Especially with someone I don't know. Someone who went out of his way to do a nice thing. I can only plead probable brain damage after hitting my head. How about we pretend I didn't say anything?"

"Okay."

That was too easy. Or maybe not. He probably didn't want to hear her tragic story any more than she wanted to tell it. When his good deed was done, he'd be out of here. And it couldn't be too soon for her. The man did things to her. He'd surprised her when he was so good with Janie. It surprised her when he'd picked up the slack in the support department when she was feeling about as strong as a fettuccine noodle. She didn't like surprises.

They were never good.

David rolled his disposable gloves off and dropped them on the tray beside him, then studied his work. He'd made the sutures as tiny as humanly possible and knew that the stubborn little chin would heal nicely. When he noted Courtney's pale face he figured it best not to make her study the finished product.

But he couldn't resist saying, "Not bad."

"Humble, aren't you?" Edgy sarcasm laced the words, but he had a feeling that spirit was the only reason she was still on her feet.

He decided to help her out. "Haven't you heard? Arrogance is a prerequisite for doctors."

"I've heard that. But I haven't seen it up close and personal until now."

He vaguely remembered Ella saying Courtney was a hospital employee, but a bad connection while he was in the airport had prevented him hearing in what capacity. Because of that call, he was here instead of on a plane to L.A.

When he looked at Courtney's mouth, his wish that he were on a plane to anywhere took hold. Her lips took up forty-five percent of her face—a slight exaggeration, but if she didn't have the sexiest mouth he'd ever seen, he'd turn in his forceps and start making house calls.

"You *do* work here at the hospital," he clarified.

"I manage the gift shop."

"So you don't work directly with doctors?"

"No."

She met his gaze and didn't look away, but he'd swear her self-respect took a hit. Something in her eyes dimmed, some inner spark that was struggling to burst into flame all but sputtered and went out. He wasn't sure what he'd said, but he wanted to fix it, even though he'd tried fixing things for a woman once and it hadn't gone well.

"You're lucky you don't work with doctors," he said. "There's a whole needing-to-be-right, needing-to-be-worshipped thing that can get pretty annoying."

"With so many doctors in your family, that must be an interesting dynamic."

It probably would be if he'd spent any significant time with them. But he hadn't. Not since his father had told him he couldn't stand the sight of him. David had lashed out, defended actions that really had no defense. But he'd been in love and the woman who'd captured his heart had stolen his soul. It wasn't long before he found out she'd been using his feelings for her to make him a puppet who jumped when she yanked his strings.

He'd lost the person he cared about most because of her and no matter what he did, there didn't seem to be any way to fill up the void.

His thoughts hadn't taken this pathetic a turn for a long time and when he looked at Courtney's full lips, it occurred to him that the sooner he got out of Walnut River the better.

And he would. But right now Janie needed a sterile dressing on her chin. He could have called a nurse to do it, but after the arrogance discussion, he figured it wouldn't hurt to do it himself. Which wasn't a problem. He'd had a lot of practice on his overseas trips. Arrogance had no place in a Nicaraguan jungle or an African desert.

After cutting several strips of paper tape, he unwrapped a nonstick pad and secured it to the little girl's determined chin. It crossed his mind that she'd inherited that from her mother, along with her dimples. At some point he was going to have to break the news to Courtney that her daughter wouldn't ever again have a matched set. So far that detail hadn't come up, most likely because she'd been more worried about the big picture. And for now that was more important.

When he saw Courtney watching him intently, he said, "She's going to be sore for a while. Chewing will probably cause her some discomfort and she may not want to eat, but she has to keep her strength up. Here in the hospital they'll give her soft foods, but when you take her home, she probably won't want a steak for awhile."

"Okay. And, for the record, she doesn't really like steak."

"But you get my drift." He gently smoothed the edges of the tape. "These sutures should be checked in a day or two and will probably need to come out in about a week. For facial trauma, we don't like to leave them in too long."

"Why not?"

"Too long can be worse than not long enough. If soft tissue heals around the suture, it's too hard to remove and can cause pulling. Not what we want."

"Okay."

"In plastics, one of the first things you learn is that the tenderest tissue needs the gentlest touch."

Courtney's battered face was clear evidence that fate hadn't dealt especially gently with her today. But it was the shadows in her eyes that made him wonder about her past, the personal stuff she'd let slip. Patients didn't always tell the truth and doctors learned to read between the lines. It seemed likely that Courtney was bruised and tender on the inside and needed a very soft touch. From someone besides him.

David walked around the bed and looked down at Courtney. "That's all we can do for now. She's resting comfortably. It's time you took care of yourself."

"I'm fine."

"That's a nasty bump on your head."

"That's all it is. Nothing showed up on the CT scan."

"What about your wrist?"

"Dr. Wilder—" She stopped as one corner of her mouth curved up. "Your sister looked at the X-rays and said it might need surgery but she couldn't be sure until the swelling goes down. So I don't have an appointment for the O.R. tonight."

Was that a hint? Not likely if the semi-hostile looks she'd lobbed at him were anything to go by. "And no hot date?"

"Oh, please," she said wryly. "I've sworn off men."

"And you're sharing that only because of that bump on your head?"

"That's my story and I'm sticking to it." She pointed to the nasty-looking contusion. "However bad you think it looks on the outside, it's way worse on the inside."

She meant her body, but he'd been talking about her spirit. Must be something about being back in Walnut River, in the hospital his father had nurtured into the fine facility it was today. Something was turning his thoughts to a dark, introspective place and he didn't much like going there. It was pointless to spend any energy on things he couldn't change. Practical considerations were much less complicated. Like what his sister, Ella, had decided about Courtney.

"I'll ask Ella to give you something for the pain," he suggested.

"No. I'm fine. Over-the-counter pain meds are taking the edge off. Anything stronger will make me sleepy and I need to keep as clear a head as I can. For Janie."

"She's being well cared for. Maybe you should take the doctor's advice and be admitted to the hospital."

"Not even on a bet."

"Why?"

"Because I don't need to take up a bed."

"Why are you fighting it? You have insurance—"

"There's a deductible," she interrupted. "And I'm okay. Besides, I can't take care of Janie from a hospital bed."

"You can't take care of Janie at all if you don't take care of yourself first. If you won't take the doctor's advice, at least go home and get some rest."

"I don't have a car. It's a little banged up, too. And even if I did, Ella said I probably shouldn't drive for a couple of days."

David folded his arms over his chest as he stared down at her. "So you embrace the orders you like and scrap everything else."

"Pretty much."

"I'll take you home," he said, then cursed himself for knuckling to the appeal of a needy woman.

"Thanks, but I can't leave. Janie and I appreciate everything you did, David. Thank you for coming."

That was a dismissal if he'd ever heard one. She was telling him to go, that his work here was done. That she could take it from here. He *should* go, and he planned to…until he made the mistake of looking at her, sitting in a chair and holding her sleeping child's hand. By sheer strength of will she was going to sit here. Probably all night. He stared for several moments at her delicate profile, the strain, the bruises, the pride, the guts and he couldn't just walk out.

One more time. "Courtney, your body has been through a trauma, too. Rest is the best thing—" He stopped when she shot him a look—fiercely female and protective.

"How can I rest when my baby is in the hospital? What if she wakes up and gets scared? What if she needs me? It's my fault she's here in the first place. I have to live with that, but I could never live with myself if I left her here all alone." She shook her head with a vehemence that had to hurt. "I'm not going anywhere. Again, thanks for everything. Good night, David."

He sat down in the chair beside hers and noticed her staring. "What?"

"That's what I'd like to know." Courtney frowned. "What are you doing?"

"Probably the reason Ella wanted you admitted was for observation. To make sure you're okay. Consider yourself observed on an outpatient basis."

"Oh, for Pete's sake. That's silly. You should go. I'm fine. And if I'm not, the nurses are in and out. Help is right here."

"You can't stay here all night. Sooner or later they're going to throw you out."

"I'm willing to risk it."

"Okay." He stretched out his legs and rested his hands on his abdomen. He didn't need to be at Peter's cocktail party for a while. "I'll keep you company."

Courtney looked puzzled. "I don't understand why you're doing this."

That made two of them. "Does it matter?"

"It kind of does in my world." She stared at him. "I haven't known many people who gave to others without having a personal agenda. Your father was one."

"What did he give you?"

"My job in the gift shop for one thing. I needed it badly and somehow he knew that. He sort of took Janie and me under his wing and watched out for us. Never once did he ask for anything in return."

But *he'd* been on the receiving end of his father's dark side. Everybody had one, even James Wilder.

"Hell of a guy," David said.

"That he was. You look a lot like him," Courtney observed.

"Is that a compliment?"

"Maybe. Mostly just stating a fact. But you're very different from him."

"Another fact?"

"Just an observation."

"Based on what?" he asked.

"Based on the fact that your father went out of his way to befriend a stranger."

"And?"

"What makes you think there's an 'and'?"

"Don't ever try to bluff in a poker game, Court. Your feelings are all over your face," he said. He should know. Faces were his bread and butter.

"Okay. Remember you asked. I can't imagine your father going long periods of time without visiting his family."

"Unless they screwed with his moral code," David snapped. She was right. He shouldn't have asked.

"So your father disapproved of something you did?" she guessed.

His father had disapproved of almost everything he did. "Didn't he tell you I was Walnut River's resident bad boy?"

"Really?"

He nodded. "Every time I rode my motorcycle through town people said there goes that Wilder boy, living up to his name again." When he looked over at her she was smiling, which somehow took the sting out of the memories.

"You had a motorcycle?"

"I paid for it myself."

"So you and your father had issues?" she asked.

"My father said I needed my head examined and if I insisted on riding the bike it was only a question of time until it happened."

"Want to talk about the deeper issues?" she asked.

"You want to talk about your husband?" he shot back.

"Not especially."

"Me either," he agreed.

She was quiet for several moments before saying, "It just seems to me that whatever you did must have been pretty bad to cut yourself off from family."

"So you're an expert on family matters?"

"Hardly." She shook her head. "I never had one, which is why it strikes me as so incredibly sad that you'd ignore a perfectly good one."

"Have you ever heard that saying—don't judge someone until you've walked a mile in their shoes?"

"Yes. And I stand by what I said."

"Meaning you don't think much of me."

"Look, I don't mean to be an ungrateful witch. And my opinion is worth exactly what you paid for it—"

"But?"

"I knew your father and the distance between you must have hurt him a lot."

"Distance goes both ways," he shot back, knowing it was lame and childish.

But the anger was gone as quickly as it ignited. Not reaching out was one more transgression in a long list. David had always thought there would be time to make things right. Even if Courtney had a point, which he wasn't saying she did, there was no way to fix it now. His father was dead and any chance of rectifying the past had died with him.

Speaking of death, she was a widow and obviously understood losing someone—even someone she had issues with. But the man had died in service to his country. Either her standards were a tad high or she had just cause. He found himself curious when he didn't want to be interested in anything about Courtney Albright.

What he'd done had violated more than his father's moral code. And he'd done it because he was desperately in love with a woman who needed him. He'd thought they loved enough to do anything for each other. But that woman was only thinking about herself when she used him. He had a hunch Courtney was in desperate need, which made trusting her a no-brainer. But he couldn't resist wanting to help her either. Over time he'd learned how to help without getting emotionally involved, but that was a dangerous slope and already his hold was slipping.

That was why he needed to get on a plane back to L.A. as soon as possible.

Chapter Three

In the bathroom down the hall from the pediatric ICU, Courtney pulled on the blue scrubs the nurses had found for her and tugged the waistband tight. She wouldn't win any fashion awards, but at least they were clean. It felt good to wash the accident off. Then she glanced in the mirror and nearly shrieked.

Her hair was drying naturally and without a blow dryer the effect wasn't pretty. There were bruises on her forehead and the ones on her cheekbone could be an extension of the dark circles under her eyes, a by-product of not sleeping the night before. Catnaps in the chair beside Janie's bed didn't count, but there was no way she would abandon her child. It had taken a lot of persuasion and the threat of physical intervention for the nurses to talk her into leaving long enough to clean up.

As she walked down the hall alone, preparing to deal with whatever came along today, she remembered how good David's company had felt until he'd excused himself for a cocktail party hosted by his brother Peter following the rededication of the hospital library to their father. But that was yesterday. Today was situation normal—her and Janie against the world.

When she walked into her daughter's room, she stopped short. Correction: Janie wasn't alone. David was there, looking far too good in his worn jeans and black body-hugging T-shirt. It made him look every inch the bad boy he'd said he used to be. The leather jacket was draped across the back of the chair she'd slept in last night.

Her heart stuttered, sputtered, then shifted into high gear as a wave of warmth swelled through her and settled in her cheeks. He looked like a movie star and she looked like a really unfortunate "before" picture. Courtney knew it was bad to care about how she looked to him and worse to be so ridiculously happy that he was here. Bad to worse didn't change the fact that both were true.

Her daughter waved and pointed to the biggie-sized cup bearing the logo from Buns 'n' Burgers that he was holding.

"I'm so happy to see you eating something." She walked over to the bed and kissed Janie's forehead then checked out the contents of the cup. All evidence pointed to the fact that it was a vanilla milkshake. "Wow, sweetie, your favorite. Where did you get that?"

"Buns 'n' Burgers," David said.

She slid him a wry look. "Let me rephrase. Buns 'n' Burgers isn't a delivery kind of place. How did it get here? Did one of the nurses bring it?"

Janie shook her head and pointed to David.

He shrugged. "When I called for a progress report, her nurse said she wasn't eating. So I took the liberty—"

"It wasn't necessary for you to go out of your way," she said. "I could have gotten her one here at the hospital."

"Rumor has it that Buns 'n' Burgers is her favorite place. Besides, I wanted to see if the food is as good as I remembered," he explained.

"And?" Courtney asked.

"I've been all over the world and never tasted better."

"And you remembered that vanilla milkshakes are her favorite."

Janie nodded and rubbed her tummy.

Courtney frowned. "Is something wrong? You haven't said anything, kiddo."

"She told me that it feels weird on her chin when she talks. So I suggested she not talk." David folded his arms over his chest, drawing her attention to his wide shoulders and flat abdomen.

As soon as the word *hot* popped into her head, Courtney turned back to her daughter. The little girl pointed to her arm, which was in a sling.

"She wants to know if your wrist hurts," David said.

"I got that." Amused, Courtney looked back at him. "But since when did you learn to interpret sign language from a six-year-old girl?"

"You've heard of a horse whisperer," he said.

"Yes. And you're what? A babe whisperer?" She couldn't resist the zinger or hold back a smile.

"Exactly," he said, not without smugness. "I understand women from six to sixty."

"Word on the street is that you concentrate your powers of persuasion in the twenty-to-thirty range."

"Do you always believe everything you hear?"

"Yeah," she said, nodding. "Pretty much."

Janie tapped David's arm and he lifted the cup closer to her mouth. She made a noisy job of finishing every last drop of her milkshake, then reclined in the bed with a satisfied sigh. She was on the mend, thanks to David. But Courtney hadn't expected to see him again.

She looked up at him. "I thought you'd be on the first plane back to L.A."

"I wanted to check in on Janie. Make sure everything's okay this morning."

And bring her favorite food to coax her to eat. Courtney didn't trust this heroic act and wondered what he was after.

"And?" she asked.

He grinned. "I'm happy to say the stitches look good and there's no sign of infection."

"If every part of my body didn't hurt, I'd be doing the dance of joy," she said.

"Can I have a rain check?" Amusement was another good look for him.

They stared at each other for several moments and the pulse at the base of her throat began to flutter. "So," she said, dragging out the word slightly, "the airport is probably your next stop after you leave here?"

His expression was bemused. "Since I'm here, I thought a short visit would be nice."

"Family before facelifts?" As soon as the words were out, she put her hand over her mouth.

"Shoots and scores," he said, one eyebrow lifting.

"David, I—" She shook her head and felt like the world's biggest jerk. "I'm not sure why you bring out my snarky side—"

"So it's my fault?" His mouth twitched with amusement. "If I were a shrink," he said, "I'd have a field day with how you can't take responsibility for your sarcastic streak."

"I'm pretty tired." She blew out a breath. "In my own defense I have to say that spending the night here doesn't reveal my naturally sweet disposition."

"I'll look forward to seeing it."

There was no good way to interpret the cryptic comment so she refused to think about what he meant. "I was teasing and it came out wrong. Your relationship with your family is none of my business."

"True. But since we both seem to be defending ourselves, let me say that my family understands being busy. Medicine is a demanding mistress and everyone but my sister, Anna, is a doctor."

Courtney noticed the slight frown when he mentioned his sister, which was a different—darker—expression from when he'd talked about his other siblings. She wanted to ask, but until she could regain full function of the filter between her brain and her mouth, she figured it was better not to comment.

The fact was that doctors *were* busy. His father had put in long days here at the hospital until he retired. It's where she'd met him after Janie was born. When her husband had moved them to Walnut River—scratch that. He'd dumped her pregnant and alone in this town, then taken off to join the army. Like everyone else, at first she'd thought him noble and patriotic. It wasn't until later that she'd found out his motives were selfish and shallow. Everything he'd done—and what he hadn't done—had cost her. Everything except leaving her here.

She'd grown to love this place and that had started with James Wilder. She knew his son Peter from working here. And recently Dr. Ella Wilder had returned. But Courtney had never met his other sister.

"I don't know Anna," she said.

"Me either," he answered, so softly she wasn't sure she'd heard right. And his frown deepened.

"Mommy, I'm a little bored."

Janie wasn't too uncomfortable to talk. But that wasn't the only reason Courtney felt tears well in her eyes. A lump of emotion jumped from her chest to push against her throat. "I'm so glad," she whispered.

David looked puzzled. "The dance of joy because she's bored?"

"What happened to the 'babe whisperer'?"

"I guess my radar is down. Care to explain?"

"Normally those words are enough to send a mother over the edge. But in this case they're so incredibly normal. After what she's been through, it's dance-of-joy worthy."

"Ah," he said. "Keep in mind that kids are pretty resilient."

She knew he was warning her to keep a stiff upper lip through what was to come, but she couldn't think about that now. She'd take every victory she could get.

"Do you have many patients who are children?" she asked.

"Some," he said mysteriously. But there was something in his eyes, something he wasn't telling.

"Mommy, what am I going to do?"

"I'll turn on the TV," she suggested.

Janie shook her head. "It's all cartoons or baby shows."

"And you're so grown up," David teased. He walked over to his jacket and pulled something out of the pocket. "How about a game of cards?"

"I don't know how to play," Janie said.

"Then I'll teach you."

"Do I hafta hold 'em?" Janie lifted her right arm and showed off her hot-pink wrist cast.

"No." He pulled over the mobile table, then rested his hip on her bed. "You can put your cards in your lap face up. I won't peek."

"Promise?" Janie said.

He made an *X* over his heart. "Promise."

Courtney's heart would have to be three sizes too small not to be moved by his attention and gentle caring. She watched David patiently explain the rules of Old Maid, Go Fish and solitaire. Although one eye was covered in bandages, Janie's good eye sparkled when she looked at David. Her little girl liked the handsome charmer.

Courtney's feelings were far more complicated. She was

attracted to and wary of this man in equal parts. They said patients fell in love with their doctors, but she wasn't sure that held true for mothers of patients. Fortunately she wouldn't have to test the theory.

He had a glamorous life clear across the country, as far removed from the Walnut River lifestyle as you could get. Courtney was both incredibly grateful for what he'd done and extraordinarily relieved that there wasn't a snowball's chance in hell that he'd be staying to tempt her.

It was dark outside when David peeked into Janie's room much later that day. Courtney was sitting exactly where he'd left her earlier and the oversized blue scrubs were a big clue that she'd been there without a break. Over twenty-four hours had passed since the accident. Had she slept properly? Eaten anything? And since when did patient-care protocols extend to the patient's mother? Was she the reason he kept coming back here to check? Because there was nothing further he could do for Janie.

Correction: nothing until her initial injuries healed. By that time he'd be back at his Beverly Hills office. He remembered the way worry had darkened Courtney's eyes when she realized everything would be more financially complicated because the procedure couldn't be done here. Insurance companies could get squirrelly about paying for medical costs that were considered "cosmetic." But this little girl could be disfigured for the rest of her life if the repair wasn't done. He told himself that's why he couldn't get Courtney out of his mind.

She stood by the hospital bed and stretched her good arm over her head, then rolled her shoulders as if everything were stiff. The baggy scrubs didn't hide the fact that she had curves in all the right places. If anything, that made him want to see for himself. A warm twang in his chest startled him and when she glanced in his direction, he thought the sound had found its way out.

"Hi." Her voice reflected the surprised expression in her eyes.

He raised a hand in greeting. "Hi."

"I didn't expect to see you."

"I came back to see my brother." Only half a lie. Peter had gone for the day, but there was no reason to mention that. "How's Janie?"

"Asleep." She took a quick look, then walked over to him. "She was in some discomfort so they gave her something. On top of that I think she's pretty exhausted."

"Sleep is the best thing for her. Is she eating?"

"A little. They're trying to tempt her with burgers, mac and cheese and chocolate puddings. But she said her favorite thing was the milkshake you brought her. That was very nice of you, by the way."

He shrugged. "I'm glad she enjoyed it. Good to know some things don't change—like the food in your favorite hangout."

"Must have been nice to have a hangout," she said wistfully.

The remark made him curious. "Where did you and your friends spend time?"

"Here and there," she said vaguely. "So, how much longer will you be here?"

"You seem awfully anxious to get rid of me," he accused.

"No." The denial was too quick and the look on her face too much like the proverbial deer caught in headlights. "It's just you're a busy doctor and I figured you needed to get back to your patients."

"Janie is my patient, too."

"And you've done everything you can for now. But you're just passing through and we don't want to keep you from—"

He held up his hand. "If it's not nice, you'll hate yourself for saying something snarky."

Her expression was exaggerated innocence. "I was just going to say that all those rich women desperate to smooth out the worry lines in their foreheads need love too."

David couldn't shake the feeling that this was her way of saying "don't let the door hit you in the backside on your way out." Her sincere gratitude for his help was real, no question about that. So there must be another reason she was anxious to get rid of him. Did she feel the sparks between them too? The more she pushed, the greater his inclination to push back, to dig his heels in and see how she reacted. How perverse was that?

"Have you eaten anything today?" he asked, changing the subject.

She blinked. "What?"

"Have you taken a break from this room and had anything to eat?"

"I'm not your patient, David."

"That doesn't mean I'm not concerned about you."

"Don't be. I've been taking care of my daughter and myself for a very long time."

Since her husband died. But he had the feeling it had started even before that and he wanted to know more.

"Have dinner with me," he said.

She glanced over at the bed where Janie was still sleeping soundly. "I can't leave her."

"Do you have a cell phone?"

"I'm not sure that's relevant, but yes," she said.

"If she needs you they can call. You need some fresh air and non-hospital food."

"I'm fine." But her stomach chose that moment to growl. Loudly. She met his gaze and her expression turned sheepish when she knew he'd heard, too.

"Fine, but hungry."

"In spite of what you heard, I don't have much appetite," she protested.

"Look, you can keep throwing out lame excuses, or just suck it up and let me take you to dinner."

"David, I'll just cut to the chase." She suddenly looked drawn and tired. "You're obviously a caring man but you've let things slip. I'm fairly certain that handsome face of yours hides all kinds of demons. The truth is, I just don't need one more challenge in my life."

"Was that a compliment?" he asked.

"Which part?" she said, her forehead furrowing as she thought.

"The handsome part."

A flush crept into her cheeks, welcome color to chase away the paleness. "Must be post-accident loose-tongue syndrome again."

"Must be." He slid his fingertips into the pockets of his jeans. "Would you say yes to dinner if I promise to leave my demons in the car?"

When one corner of her mouth curved up it was clear she was weakening. "Can it be my treat?"

"Okay, as long as we take my car."

She sent him a wry look. "Since I don't have a car at the moment, I have to ask—is that sarcasm, Doctor?"

"I guess I've been hanging out with you too long. But it has to be said that I've learned from the best."

David found himself back at Buns 'n' Burgers on Lexington Avenue for two reasons—it was close to the hospital and in Courtney's budget. They ordered at the counter, got a number for table delivery and he carried their tray to a secluded corner booth.

She slid in with a tired sigh. "I feel so darn guilty."

"Because?" He sat across from her.

"The fresh air feels so good. What kind of mother am I to be enjoying the world outside Walnut River General while my child is there?"

"She's asleep, Court. She doesn't know you're not there. If she needs you, they'll call. Relax and recharge your batteries."

A teenage boy in a yellow Buns 'n' Burgers shirt and matching hat delivered their cheeseburgers and fries, asked if they needed anything else, then left after an automatic, "Enjoy your meal."

With her good hand, Courtney picked up her burger and wolfed it down as though she hadn't eaten in a month. She chewed the last bite and—he was going to hell for this thought—she looked like a woman satisfied by the best sex of her life.

"Good burger?" he asked. Even if he didn't feel the physical evidence, the inane question would have been positive proof that blood flow from his brain had been diverted to points south.

"I'm fairly sure that was the best hamburger I've ever had." She took her time with the fries. "So, tell me more about growing up in Walnut River—specifically about being 'that Wilder boy.'"

"I thought you wanted me to leave my demons in the car."

"Now that I've been fed and watered, I find myself with the strength and curiosity to pull those demons out and take 'em for a spin." She dipped a fry in ketchup, then popped it in her mouth and chewed thoughtfully. "There's something I don't understand. You seemed to have a great childhood. So where did the demons come from?"

So many demons, so little time. One was a father devoted to his work and any time left over had been lavished on an adopted daughter at the expense of everyone else in the family—including his mother.

"Can we just chalk it up to sowing my wild oats?" he asked.

"No." She grinned. "So out with it—any smoking, drinking and general wickedness?"

"You have quite the imagination," he said.

"You're evading the question," she accused, jabbing the air in his direction with a French fry.

He thought back. "There were the usual lectures about grades and living up to my potential. Curfew violations. Typical rebellion. A couple of run-ins with the cops. After all, I was 'that Wilder boy.'"

"Did you really have a motorcycle?"

"Yeah. No pun intended, but it drove my parents nuts."

"I don't blame them," she said. "What were you thinking?"

"Short answer—I wasn't. Teenage boys aren't notoriously rational. It's more about testosterone."

"Just as teenagers?" she teased.

He shook his head. "Not going there. That's a demon not pertinent to this discussion."

"Why not?"

"Because it's your turn."

"For?"

"Childhood confessions." The shadows in her expression took him by surprise. Suddenly the spark flickered and went out. He was torn between really wanting to know about her and needing to put the smile back on her face. "What is it, Courtney?"

"You don't really want to hear the sad details."

"You're wrong."

"You're leaving."

"I'm here now."

She hesitated for several moments, then said, "My mother skipped out on my dad and me when I was Janie's age. No note. No good-bye. Just one day when I woke up she was gone."

She was so obviously deeply committed to her child and

he had instinctively assumed the fruit didn't fall far from the tree. For some reason, he hadn't expected that. "I don't know what to say."

"You could say it sucked. Because it did. I never saw her again."

"How did your dad take it?"

She laughed but it was the saddest sound he'd ever heard. "I can't say he didn't drink before she walked out. But I can tell you with absolute certainty that he was rarely sober after. Trauma tends to highlight things like that."

"Courtney—"

"Don't." She held up her hand. "I hate hearing clichés and despise being one even more. But in this case it's the God's honest truth. I'm walking, talking, *surviving* proof that what doesn't kill you definitely makes you stronger."

"So you never really got to be a kid."

She looked resigned. "I had my hands full. Dad had trouble keeping a job, which made a roof over our heads an ongoing challenge. When I was old enough I got a job. I was determined to go to college. It was the only way to have a better life."

Good God, he felt like a selfish, shallow jerk. He'd thought he'd had it rough, had given his parents a pile of grief growing up because of it. This woman had become a caretaker to her father when she should have been playing with dolls.

"And did you? Go to college, I mean?" Starting out in college had definitely not been *his* finest hour, but the life lesson was one he'd never forget.

"Yeah. I was doing pretty well, until—" She looked down, and a muscle in her delicate jaw jerked.

"What?"

"I got pregnant with Janie and had to drop out." She met his gaze with the same fiercely defensive look he'd seen when she'd watched over her child. "My only regret is not graduating, but I could never be sorry about having Janie. She's the best thing that's ever happened to me."

Reading between the lines he figured she regretted other things. But what she'd revealed explained something of why she was reluctant to accept help. When you couldn't count on the two people you'd trusted most in the world, leaning on strangers wouldn't come easily.

He reached across the table and took her hand in his own. "You are a remarkable woman, Courtney Albright."

"Not really."

He didn't argue with her because he didn't like what he was feeling. Respect for her was a no-brainer. Against the odds, this woman had made a life for herself, welcomed a child into it, lost her husband and now carried the burden of raising her daughter all alone. Of course he respected her.

What troubled him was the possibility that he felt something more than admiration. Attraction was an A-word too, and it was growing stronger every time he saw her. If he was as smart as everyone told him, he'd get on that plane she'd been trying to get him on. He'd get out of Walnut River before this turned into something that got him into the same kind of trouble he'd found in college.

He'd fallen for a girl and she'd needed his help. When the dust settled, he'd been the one in hot water, and she'd walked away unscathed. Then she'd dumped him. That trouble had cost him more than time, money and his innocence.

That trouble had messed up his life.

Chapter Four

David had been driving his rented BMW around town for hours and not just because the car was sweet. He couldn't remember the last time he'd had so much time on his hands. After the disaster in his first year of college, his father had cut him off financially and every hour of every day every year afterwards had been consumed with classes, study and working to survive. Something he had in common with Courtney. At least his father hadn't been an alcoholic. Work had been James Wilder's obsession of choice.

After school, David had been consumed with keeping himself too busy to think, repaying student loans and building his practice. If he had less testosterone and more common sense, he would be on a plane back to that fabulous life in California.

Why, suddenly, was he resisting it? Why was he still here?

He passed Buns 'n' Burgers and a vision of Courtney's smiling face flashed into his mind. She was a beautiful woman and he had wanted very much to kiss her. After taking her back to the hospital, he'd spent a lot of time thinking about it. Maybe if he kissed the living daylights out of her, he could move on. If he didn't, his weakness for damsels in distress might rear its ugly head and land him in trouble again. It was something else he was thinking too much about since coming home.

That thought made David execute a quick right turn and whip the Beamer into the hospital parking lot located in front of the older structure. The new tower was visible behind it. He got out of the car, locked the doors and walked into the lobby.

His brother, Peter, had his office in the same hospital where their father had once worked. Growing up in this town, David had pushed the envelope and tried to shake things up. For some reason he was glad that very little had changed. Including this building. Maturity was a funny thing.

Not much was different—lobby, gift shop, information desk and signs pointing the way to the different ancillary departments. It smelled of floor polish, antiseptic and the fragility of life. Nostalgia enveloped him as he entered the elevator and proceeded to his brother's office on the fourth floor.

As he walked down the hall, David was bombarded by memories of this place. Very often, to see his father at all, he'd come here. He'd been a "fit in" between patients, rounds, emergencies and paperwork. He was all grown up now and it shouldn't still bother him. But ignoring the knot in the center of his gut and its connection to the past wasn't going to happen. Maybe he wasn't so mature after all.

David walked into the office and looked around the waiting room. Unlike his own professionally decorated offices in Beverly Hills, this one had generic chairs and tables, inexpensive prints on the walls and a TV mounted in the corner. Peter Wilder was older by four years, but that wasn't the only reason they hadn't been close growing up. Each of them reacted to their environment in their own way. His brother had followed in their father's footsteps. David had chosen a wilder path, no pun intended. He wondered if Peter's way was working for him or if he felt a similar emptiness.

When he stepped into Peter's private office, his brother looked up and grinned. "The prodigal son returns."

Shades of his own thoughts. "Hi."

David remembered people saying that the two Wilder boys looked a lot alike, but that's where the resemblance ended. Peter had set a high bar and David had suffered in comparison. More than once his father had asked why he couldn't be more like his older brother. Peter's hair was cut short and combed conservatively. His own was short but styled by running his fingers through it. Peter wore a shirt, tie and slacks under his lab coat unless he was doing his E.R. rotation. David was a jeans kind of guy with an incredibly successful practice. But he couldn't shake the feeling that he was missing something.

"Do you have a minute?" David asked.

"Of course. Glad you stopped by. Have a seat." Peter indicated the two chairs in front of his desk.

"Thanks." David took the one on the left because nine out of ten people would have gone to the right. Old habits died hard. "How've you been?"

"Good. I didn't expect to see you again so soon after Dad's funeral."

"Yeah." The knot in David's chest tightened.

"I wish the visit was under more pleasant circumstances. Thanks for coming by to look in on Janie Albright."

"I was in New York for a conference anyway."

"It was clear when that little girl was brought into the E.R. that her case was more complicated than we could handle. Courtney is part of our hospital community. On top of that, she's a widow struggling to make ends meet."

"I gathered that." And a whole lot more.

"How's Janie?"

"I did the superficial repairs and they're healing nicely. But she'll need another surgery for the more complicated reconstruction."

Peter frowned as he nodded. "From what I understand about her circumstances, that will be tough on Courtney. Besides the medical costs, there's no one on staff here at the hospital who can handle that kind of procedure. It will add expenses that she can't afford."

"I can recommend an expert in plastics as close to Walnut River as possible."

"I'm sure Courtney would appreciate that." Peter thought for a moment. "The hospital might have some programs to assist her financially. I'll check into that." He leaned back in his chair and linked his fingers over his flat abdomen. "So, how does it feel being back here?"

"The truth?"

"I'd expect nothing less."

"Weird," David said, not sure how to put it into words. "Brings back memories of Dad."

"From the expression on your face I gather the memories aren't good ones."

David glanced up. "Some good. Some not so good. Some downright bad."

"You just described life, little brother."

David laughed. "I guess so."

"Do you want to talk about what happened between you and Dad?"

"Not really." What was the point? His father was gone, along with any chance of making things right. The emptiness inside him opened just a little wider. "But I would like to talk about the hospital."

"I'm glad you brought it up."

"Oh?"

Peter leaned forward and folded his hands on his desk. "It's nice having Ella here—on a personal and a professional basis."

David tamped down an odd feeling of third-man-out and reminded himself that he had a pretty great life. "Yeah."

Of all the siblings, only Anna and David had chosen to live elsewhere. The thought of his adopted sister didn't bring back warm memories. In fact, life as he'd known it had changed dramatically when his parents took her in. Again he had the feeling he should be over it, but couldn't quite pull that off.

"Ella's a damn fine surgeon and her specialty is a welcome addition to the staff here at General. We needed someone in orthopedics."

"You're lucky to have her. Although, from what I've seen it's good for her, too. This is a terrific facility."

"I'm very proud of it," Peter said, intensely serious. "So was Dad."

David felt a twinge of regret that his father had been pleased with this hospital—a *building*—and not his own son. For the third time his inner child was acting like a child. Nothing like a trip down memory lane to make a guy feel all grown up, he thought ruefully. It was time to get out of here.

"That's great," he said, standing. "I'm sorry I can't stay longer, but—"

"Peter, I—"

The female voice made David turn and in the doorway stood Bethany Holloway. He remembered meeting the beautiful redhead with big blue eyes at Peter's cocktail party. She was a member of the hospital's Board of Directors.

"I'm sorry, Peter. Didn't mean to bother you. I didn't know David was here. I'll come back—"

"No." Peter stood. "Don't go."

"Are you sure?" When he nodded, she moved closer. "Nice to see you again, David."

"Same here."

Peter came around the desk and slid an arm around her waist as he drew her close and kissed her cheek. "You're not bothering me. Just the opposite. You're a sight for sore eyes."

"Your eyes saw me earlier this morning," she reminded him, a sparkle in her eyes.

David wondered when that morning his brother had seen Bethany, because if he had to guess, he figured they'd been in bed when the looking happened.

"My eyes can never get enough of you," Peter said, smiling down at her.

David knew they were engaged to be married, but even if he hadn't, the love shining on their faces was there for all the world to see. He could compare his career success to Peter's and come out a winner, but he envied his brother's obvious happiness and contentment. Again he suffered by comparison.

"Did I congratulate the two of you at the party?"

"You did. But thanks again. I'm a very lucky man." Peter gazed lovingly at his fiancée for a moment, then asked, "So what's up?"

"Stuff with the hospital," she said vaguely, sending a wary look in David's direction.

"It's okay to talk in front of David. He's just passing through. Besides, I have a feeling whatever it is won't be kept quiet for long."

"What's going on?" David asked.

"The easier question is what's not," Peter said ruefully. "First of all, there's a company—Northeastern HealthCare—that's making noises about taking over the hospital."

"That's bad?" David asked.

"Only if you're concerned that the standard of patient care Dad instituted here at the hospital will suffer. Their bottom line is a dollar sign."

"It's a rhyme," Bethany said. "And not in a good way."

"No kidding." Peter sighed. "So what brought you in here to bother me?"

She gave him a sassy look before saying, "A reporter from the *Walnut River Courier* just called me. He wanted a source on the record to confirm rumors of insurance fraud connected with Walnut River General's billing practices."

"What did you say?" Peter asked.

"I told him you were personally responsible for double-dipping and billing Medicare for procedures never performed."

"Beth—"

She looked at David and burst out laughing. "Did you know your brother can't take a joke?"

"So you never had that sense of humor surgically implanted?" David asked.

"Great." Peter shook his head. "It's not bad enough I have to take it from the woman I love. Now you're piling on?"

"What are brothers for?"

"Helping fend off a hospital takeover for one thing," Peter said grimly.

Before David could respond to that, Bethany said, "There's more to worry about than just the takeover. This reporter thing worries me."

"Why?" Peter asked, frowning.

"I think someone is leaking information to the press. He was citing cases, Peter. Enough of his facts were right to put a doubt in anyone's mind. Enough were wrong to cast a shadow on the integrity of Walnut River General. Either way it's the bad stuff that makes page one. Retraction is an afterthought in the classifieds. Negative publicity could make Northeastern HealthCare's takeover easier to pull off and cost them less money when they do. None of that works in our favor."

"I see your point," Peter said. "What did you tell the reporter?"

"Before I hung up on him I said 'No comment.'"

"Smart girl. Any inadvertent slip just gives them ammunition. It's already going to be an uphill battle to save this hospital. A David-versus-Goliath fight. No pun intended, little brother."

"Good one, Peter."

Bethany sighed as she glanced between the two of them. "Look, I'm sorry to interrupt. You don't see each other very often and I feel badly about raining on the reunion. I'm just going to leave now."

"Don't go on my account," David said. "I was just saying good-bye."

"You can't stay a little longer?" Peter said. "The last time you came home doesn't count. We buried Dad and you had to rush off."

"I know. I wish—"

"I'd like a chance to visit with you, David." Peter's gaze locked with his own. "I really mean that."

David wasn't so much surprised by his brother's sincerity as he was by his own response. Emotion welled up, intensifying the sense of isolation. "I believe you. But—"

"Just think about it, David."

"I will," he said, shaking his brother's hand. "Nice to meet you again, Bethany."

"Same here."

David walked into the hall and wished that Walnut River in general and this place in particular didn't mess with his mind so much. He was a successful plastic surgeon, not the insecure kid who'd disappointed his father. That was ancient history, a blast from the past, and had no bearing on his current life. Peter was a doctor and would understand the demanding workload. But this sudden need to connect was disconcerting and he had no doubt that the honesty Courtney had blamed on her accident was part of the catalyst.

He preferred to believe that her words, not the woman herself, were responsible for all this soul searching.

* * *

For the last couple of days Courtney had been hitching rides to and from the hospital with her friends who worked there. No one made her feel guilty, in fact just the opposite. They'd been eager to help. The guilt was a by-product of her own emotional baggage. But even that paled in comparison to her need to be with her child. She simply couldn't rest unless she could see with her own eyes that Janie was okay. She'd only spent one night in the pediatric ICU, which was a blessing.

Right now her daughter was dozing, so Courtney went downstairs to the hospital's main floor and checked in on the gift shop. No matter what was going on in her life, this was her responsibility. At least she didn't have to impose on someone for a ride to work from Janie's bedside. She made sure operating hours were staffed and checked over inventory. Everyone was pitching in, covering for her, going the extra mile to help her out. It's what she'd come to love most about this town, the hospital and her job.

On her way back upstairs, as she exited the elevator on the third floor and rounded the corner, she practically skidded to a stop. At the nurse's station David Wilder was chatting up Diane Brennan, a tall, beautiful, brunette R.N. He had his back to Courtney and she wished for powers of invisibility to walk by them and not be seen. Partly because she wasn't wearing makeup and her hair made her look like a reject from a make-over show, but also because her worn jeans and sweatshirt made her feel thrift-store poor beside his designer denim and pricey cotton shirt. Mostly, however, because it wasn't good the way her insides pulsed with excitement at the sight of him.

Diane slid him a sultry smile. "I heard the actress from that TV sitcom had her nose done. Do you know anything about it?"

"I'll never tell and there's nothing you can do to make me," he said, his flirtatious tone implying there was much she could do.

Courtney wanted to gag.

"Don't be like that. Inquiring minds want to know. Who have you done work on in Hollywood? Who has boobs by the famous Dr. David Wilder?"

His back to her, David leaned against the counter and folded his arms over his chest. "Nurse Brennan, you know that would be a violation of patient privacy. Besides, a gentleman never tells."

"And you're a gentleman?" Diane smiled up at him.

"Most of the time."

Courtney was glad, or would be really soon, that the two were so caught up in each other that neither noticed her walk by. She was crabby. Her wrist ached and she was so tired. But it was the hit to her heart that took her by surprise. Maybe that was a direct result of sharing burgers and backgrounds. She'd seen a different side to him; his vulnerability had seemed sincere. And that chink had made her feel comfortable enough to reveal some of her own painful past.

How naive could she be? He was standing there taking his sex appeal out for a spin and that was a punch-to-the-gut, catch-her-breath, hit-her-between-the-eyes moment.

A moment that opened her eyes once and for all. And just in time to avoid a full-blown crush on Dr. Delicious, she realized. And, while it had been an extraordinarily kind gesture, a clandestine milkshake for her little girl didn't change who he was. Once a playboy, always a playboy.

Courtney needed to focus her attention on her daughter, who was awake now.

"Hi, Mommy."

"Hi, baby. How do you feel after your nap?"

"Not so sleepy."

Courtney smiled. "Then, as naps go, it was a rousing success."

"I guess." Janie frowned.

"What is it, sweetheart?"

"Dr. David hasn't been to see me today."

"He probably got sidetracked." By a pair of long legs and an impressive bosom, Courtney thought. "You know he doesn't live here in Walnut River."

"He said he used to."

"That's true. But now he lives all the way on the other side of the country. In Los Angeles. Where they make TV shows and movies."

"So he fixes people there?"

"He fixes them all right," Courtney agreed. "On the west coast there's a lot of job security in designer medicine."

"What's that?" Janie asked.

"Nothing, sweetie." She sat beside the bed, rested her sling-braced arm in her lap and took her daughter's small fingers in her other hand. "You just have to be prepared for the fact that David isn't staying. He has to go back home." Janie's frown was troubling. Time to change the subject.

"What do you say, pumpkin? Are you ready to get out of here and go home to sleep in your own bed?"

"Can I?"

"Maybe soon. All the nurses say you're getting better really quick."

"I know. 'Cuz I'm the fastest."

Once Courtney had her at home, she could do some research on the Internet for a doctor to do the facial repairs. David said he'd recommend someone, but counting on that would be foolish. And somehow, she would find a way to pay for it. All she'd ever wanted for Janie was a normal life, the kind of childhood Courtney'd never had. There had been a few setbacks, learning what kind of man she'd married, then losing him overseas. But they'd survived that and they'd get past this.

"Word on the street is that there's a party in this room."

David stood in the doorway looking like temptation for the taking. "I can't believe no one invited me."

Courtney's heart bounced into her throat and her breath caught, but she managed to say, "Hi, David."

Janie giggled. "I'm not having a party."

He moved forward and stood by the bed. "I bet you're ready to have some fun."

"I think the Albright girls are going to need a little more recuperation time before we party."

"Dr. David, are you having a going-away party?" Janie asked him.

David looked at her. "Is it genetic? This thing the Albright girls have about getting rid of me?"

Her old friend Guilt nudged her. "Of course not. But you're only in town for a visit. By definition that means not permanent. So, sometime soon you're going back to your real life."

He folded his arms over his chest. "Correct me if I'm wrong, but every day, no matter where I am, is actually my real life."

"I meant back to your practice," Courtney amended, ignoring the way her pulse was jumping simply because he stood there and smelled so good.

"What's designer medicine?" Janie interrupted.

"Where did you hear that?" David didn't raise his voice, but there was a definite edge to it.

"Mommy said you have a job in security for designer medicine. What does that mean?"

Courtney had thought she'd successfully distracted Janie from her slip of the tongue, but no such luck. She wanted to crawl into a hole, curl up and come out when the coast was clear and David was clear on the other coast.

He looked at her. "Do you want to take a stab at explaining that?"

"I think not."

"There's a lot more to what I do than Botox and augmentation."

"I know that." She couldn't shake the crabby mood and knew it had something to do with witnessing him playing Dr. Don Juan at the nurses' station. One more in a growing list of reasons she would be better off when he was gone. "And I've thanked you numerous times for everything you've done for Janie."

"But I'm not all better yet, Mommy."

"I know, baby." Courtney still hadn't been able to force herself to look at her daughter's shattered cheek. Living with the guilt of what she'd done was hard enough without seeing the damage right in front of her. She brushed silky blond hair from the little girl's forehead. "But you'll be good as new before you know it."

"How?"

"What do you mean?"

A tear trickled out of Janie's good eye and her lips quivered. "Who's going to take care of me after Dr. David leaves?"

Please, please don't do this to me, Courtney thought. She could stand anything except this. How could she reassure this child when she had no idea what she was going to do? Tears burned the backs of her own eyes.

"Don't cry, sweetie. Don't worry. I promise you'll be fine. I'll find a doctor for you—"

"No, you won't," David interrupted

Courtney stared at him. "Excuse me?"

"I'm going to be your doctor," he said to Janie.

"You can't," Courtney answered.

"Oh?"

"I mean—how? You'll be on the other side of the country. Won't it be too inconvenient for you to take charge of her case?"

"I've been thinking," he said.

"There's a dangerous prospect."

"Be nice, Courtney."

"Sorry." She rubbed her nose. "It sounded better in my head. You were saying?"

"I've been working nonstop for a long time. I can't remember the last vacation I had."

"Walnut River isn't exactly the vacation capital of the planet."

"That's why it's perfect. Nothing to do but relax."

"What about your practice?"

"I'm not the only doctor. There are three other specialists and they'll pick up the slack."

"David, this is crazy—"

He held up his index finger. "Calling me names is not an especially good example to set," he commented, angling his head slightly toward the little girl in the hospital bed. "Do you have an objection to me being Janie's doctor?"

"Of course not. You're wonderful with her."

"So you trust me?"

"Medically speaking?"

"Yes."

"Of course I trust you." Personally, not so much.

He looked at Janie. "Would you be disappointed if I wasn't your doctor?"

"Yes," she said emphatically.

"Then, it's settled. I'm not going anywhere for a month."

"Yay!"

"Thank you, David." Courtney smiled at him and squeezed Janie's fingers.

As far as good news/bad news scenarios went, this was a classic. The worry of who would fix her daughter's face was no longer an issue. But Joe Albright had taught her that deeds come with a price. She had to conclude that David had an agenda.

All she could do was hope that whatever he wanted wasn't more than she could afford to pay.

Chapter Five

Smart men learned from their mistakes, and David considered himself a pretty smart man. Until now.

The next day he was still trying to figure out what he'd been thinking to volunteer his services. Courtney Albright was his personal train-wreck-in-waiting and ever since meeting her he couldn't seem to jump the track. Apparently he'd dumbed down since returning to Walnut River. What else would explain his offering to be Janie's doctor? He didn't owe them anything just because of his father's friendship. But when Janie had cried and Courtney had struggled not to, he couldn't hold back the words.

At midmorning he left his first-floor guest room at the Walnut River Inn. With its four-poster cherrywood bed, wallpaper in mauve with steel-blue flowers and stripes and a cream-colored porcelain sink and shower, the place was a little feminine for his taste. Of the eight guest rooms, it was the most expensive and that gave him great satisfaction because his father had once said he wouldn't amount to anything. He drove away from the picturesque gardens with their sculpted boxwoods and went to the hospital to see his patient. His only patient.

That felt weird.

Fourteen-hour days and as many procedures as he could fit into those hours were the norm. Keeping busy was his life. When he took a break from the routine, he did it in a third world country where he could make a difference to poor people without access to medical intervention. He worked fast to help as many as possible. It also meant there wasn't time to get personally involved with patients or their families. But he was involved now. What else did you call putting your life on hold for a little girl with facial trauma and her pretty mother with sass to spare?

When he arrived at the hospital, he went directly to the pediatric floor. He walked into Janie's room and was surprised not to see Courtney there. That was different. He hadn't realized he'd been looking forward to seeing her until he didn't.

"Hey, beautiful." He smiled at Janie. "How are you feeling today?"

She lifted her arm with its hot-pink cast. "It hardly hurts at all. Dr. Ella said that's good."

"She's right."

Janie nodded. "And my chin itches. Where you fixed it. But I'm not scratchin'."

"Good girl." In his opinion she was ready to leave the hospital, but he wanted to talk to her mother about that first. "Where's your mom?"

"The nurse came in and told her to go to the cafeteria and eat."

He wondered if she'd put up a fight with someone besides him. "Okay. You sit tight. I'm going to talk to her."

The cafeteria was in the hospital's basement and he took the elevator down. When the doors opened, he walked the short distance. Even if the route hadn't been familiar, the smell of food would have led him in the right direction.

He'd seen his share of hospital dining areas and knew they were pretty much all the same. But when he rounded the corner and walked in, he was swamped by déjà vu. The open room had the requisite tables and chairs, steam tables and salad bar. A sign featured the day's entrees.

Not much had changed from when he was a kid having lunch with his father. It was like every other cafeteria except that along with bad food and generic decoration, this one served up memories.

He felt a whack in the center of his chest that didn't ease until he spotted a familiar blonde sitting by herself. Since it was too early for lunch, the room was nearly empty. He watched her as he moved closer and the dark circles beneath her eyes tugged at him.

"Mind if I join you?" he asked, stopping beside her.

"Of course not. Good morning. How are you?"

"Great. And you?" She looked tired. He didn't like that he'd noticed, partly because he wanted to fix it. Mostly it was because he shouldn't notice at all. He never got this close.

"I'm fine, thanks."

He pulled out the chair across from her and sat. "Janie told me the nurse ordered you to eat something." Looking at her barely touched ham sandwich, he added, "Looks like following orders isn't your thing."

"I'm not very hungry." She took a sip from her coffee cup.

He glanced around, trying to decide if the walls had always been that color of green. "When I was a kid, I used to think the food here was the best."

"So your folks kept you on a diet of bread and water?" she teased.

"No. When I was in trouble, my punishment was losing the privilege of lunch with my dad."

"Ah." She nodded knowingly. "It was the company, not the cuisine."

"Something like that."

"Were you a naughty little boy who was disciplined often?"

"I followed Peter the Perfect and my mother wasn't ready for me," he said. His mother had died of cancer five years ago, but David had never felt he'd lived up to her expectations any more than he had his father's. He couldn't remember her being anything but moody and depressed. Whether it was the truth or not, he had the sense that she blamed him for his father not being around. "Having lunch here was the best way to spend time with my father. He was at the hospital more than home."

"I got that feeling," she said almost reverently. "I used to see him here a lot. In fact, I still half-expect him to walk in and join me for a cup of coffee."

"That must mean you work a lot. Where's Janie when you're here?"

"Day care after school. Summers and holidays are more complicated, but I have a good support system to pick up the slack." She looked pensive for a moment, then said, "I wish—"

"What?"

"Nothing."

He studied her for a moment and thought he saw regret in her expressive brown eyes. If anyone should recognize the emotion, it was him. He had regrets to spare. "For what it's worth, now that I'm a doctor, I understand that my father needed to be here for his job."

Defensiveness slid into her expression. "Managing the hospital gift shop isn't in the same league with saving lives, but it's a service that patients and visitors both appreciate. We're all on the same team in terms of patient satisfaction and well-being. When someone has no visitors, I make sure to send flowers, or a stuffed animal or a balloon bouquet. Something to let them know they're not alone."

Her tone was normal, conversational, but he felt the slight edge. He remembered it from when she'd first told him she didn't work with patients, as if her job wasn't as important. He'd never meant to diminish her in any way and the yearning to touch her was overwhelming.

He reached over and took the fingers of her good hand into his own. "State of mind is an important part of the healing process. The patients are lucky to have you."

Her guarded gaze slid from his to their joined hands, but she didn't pull away. "So, you were looking for me?" His expression must have been blank because she added, "You said Janie told you where to find me."

"Right." With an effort, he dragged his gaze away from her mouth and the overwhelming desire to kiss her. "I'm discharging Janie from the hospital."

"She can go home?" Her expression was both pleased and fearful. "Is she ready?"

He nodded. "For now everything medically necessary has been done. She's on the mend and home is the best place to build up her strength. It's familiar and comfortable. Normal."

"There's no place like home?" she said wryly.

"Exactly."

"What about the other doctors who looked after her?"

"I'm the point man on her case. Ella signed off on her release so the final decision is up to me."

And why he'd offered to take over her case was as big a mystery now as it had been when the words came out of his mouth yesterday. He remembered Ella telling him the night of Peter's cocktail party that he'd do the right thing where Janie was concerned. But was it right for him? Every time he saw the little girl, she got to him just a little more. And her mother…

Courtney had accused him of having demons, but that was the pot calling the kettle black. Otherwise she wouldn't use crabbiness the way a crab uses its protective shell. On top of that, she was under a lot of stress—worried about her child's future and how to pay for the best medical care that would ensure a bright one. The more she'd pushed him away, the more he'd wanted to help.

Smart man, stupid choices.

Courtney blew out a long breath. "Wow. Okay. I—" She ran her fingers through her silky blond hair.

"What's wrong?"

"Nothing. This is great news. I just have a million things going through my mind."

"Like?"

"I don't want to bother you with it."

"If I didn't want to know, I wouldn't have asked," he said.

"I have to speak with someone in patient services about arranging transportation home." She held up the blue sling cradling her injured arm. "Even if I could drive, I don't have a car. Good thing Walnut River General provides the assistance."

She was trying to push him away again. And again he dug his heels in. "I'll drive you home."

"You've already done so much for us, I don't want to take advantage." She shook her head. "I can't ask you to chauffeur us."

"You didn't ask. I volunteered."

"Surely you have better things to do."

"Not really. I'm on vacation."

"Wouldn't you rather take a cruise?" she asked.

"I get seasick. It's not pretty."

Her gaze narrowed skeptically. "Have you ever been on a cruise?"

"Okay. No. But I earned this time off and I should get to decide how to spend it."

"Don't you want to do something more exotic than drive us home?"

She was giving him an out and a voice inside was warning him to take it. But, as David stared into Courtney's big brown eyes, he couldn't think of a single thing he'd rather do.

After the discharge paperwork was completed, they were finally on their way home. Courtney wasn't sure whether to be relieved. Winter had robbed the trees of their leaves and the branches stood out like dark sticks against the gloomy gray sky. She lived in a "mature" section of Walnut River, where average working-class people owned homes. Big maples, sycamores and elm trees lined the streets and she thought it charming and quaint.

"Turn right on Maple. It's the fourth house," Courtney directed David, very glad the ride was almost over. She wasn't sure how much longer she could smell his amazing cologne and stare at his gorgeous profile and not embarrass herself somehow. Her hormones were jumping like toddlers on sugar overload.

He pulled up to the curb in front of an older three-story house in which each floor had been converted to a separate apartment.

"I know this area," he said, turning off the ignition. "Riverdale."

She was surprised. "Really?"

"My grandmother had a house nearby and now my sister, Ella, lives in it. It's a little Cape Cod over on Cedar."

Must be nice to have family who'd give you a head start on life, Courtney thought. She didn't feel sorry for herself any more. It was unproductive and a waste of energy. So this slip could only be blamed on a stressful couple of days.

"You must have some wonderful memories of growing up here," she said.

He looked around and frowned. "Not all wonderful, but definitely memories."

That made her curious. "It's a great neighborhood. I rent the top-floor apartment."

"Because it's the best?" he asked.

"Nope. The cheapest," she answered honestly.

He got out and came around to her side of the car, then opened her door. He held out his hand to help her and she put her fingers into his. The warmth and strength burrowed inside her, lighting up a bleak and desolate place. Strength and support were two things she'd learned never to expect from a man. Either she was doomed to disappointment or there was a price to pay. It wasn't self-pity or pessimism, more an educated guess based on experience.

Standing on the sidewalk, David glanced over his shoulder and looked up to the top floor of the tall structure. He met her gaze. "That's a lot of stairs."

"It's how I keep my girlish figure," she said.

One eyebrow rose as he checked her out from the top of her head to the tips of her sneakers. "I mean this in the very best possible way—it's definitely working. People in L.A. spend a small fortune on Pilates and yoga when all they need is stairs."

The compliment and approval in his eyes did dangerous things to her insides and she figured it was time to run for cover. "I'd better get Janie upstairs." Checking the rear seat, she saw that the child had fallen asleep. "I should have known. She was too quiet back there. I guess I'll have to wake her."

"Don't," he said. "I'll carry her up."

"It's three flights of stairs," she reminded him.

He tilted his head. "Are you challenging my manhood?"

Her gaze slid to the center of his chest and the navy sweater that covered it. Over his collared shirt and jeans it was a decidedly preppy look that worked for her as well as his bad-boy-biker one. But which was the real David Wilder?

By any standard he was a incredibly masculine and exceptionally handsome man. Any challenge to his manhood was an exercise in futility.

"Heaven forbid I would insult you. It's just that this is above and beyond the call of volunteer duty."

"I'm also her doctor. And I prescribed rest."

Courtney studied him. She got the feeling that he would meet her stubborn and raise her an obstinate or two. The thing was, she really didn't want to wake Janie. "I sense this is a battle I'm going to lose."

He grinned. "Smart girl."

He quietly opened the back passenger door and undid Janie's seatbelt before gently lifting her into his arms. The sight of him holding her child made Courtney's chest hurt and tears sting the backs of her eyes. It showed her what Janie was missing out on. It didn't matter that her own father, the one man who should have loved her the most, would never have been there for her even if he'd lived. Courtney's heart broke because she couldn't give Janie that most important thing— a father's love and support.

She couldn't stand for David to see her weakness and reached into the backseat to pull out the plastic bag that the nurses had put Janie's things into. Then she took the lead, unlocking the outside door to the building. She started up the stairs and stopped on the first landing.

"Are you okay?" she asked.

"Fine."

They took the second set of stairs and she glanced back. "Still okay?"

"Yes."

When they got to the top floor, she unlocked her door and opened it. "Home sweet home," she whispered.

He walked inside and looked around. "Very nice," he answered quietly. "Where's Janie's room?"

She motioned for him to follow, then she walked through the small living room, turning on lights to chase away the gloom. "It's the first doorway on the left."

She went in ahead of him and pulled down Janie's rosebud comforter and the pink blanket and sheet. David settled her on the mattress, then gently pulled the bedclothes over her and brushed silken strands of hair off the child's cheek. Along with the curtains and accessories, almost everything in this room was a shade of pink. In this environment a lot of men would look out of place, but not David. If anything, he looked bigger, broader, more rugged—more manly. And somehow that added balance.

They walked back to the living room and he met her gaze. "I thought my room at the inn was girly, but it has to be said that your daughter is definitely in a pink zone."

"Her favorite color," she said, shrugging.

He studied the room. "And yours is green."

"And gold and brown." Earth tones. She followed his gaze. "I painted and I picked out that fabric to recover the sofa. And I made the throw pillows." She pointed to the chocolate-brown trim. "They match the accent wall."

He glanced around and didn't look shocked or appalled. Maybe surprised in a good way. "You recovered the sofa?"

"Someone threw it away and I could still see possibilities." Plus she'd needed to furnish this place on very little money. "I also found the coffee and end tables and refinished them."

"It's charming."

"Is that your way of saying you hate it without saying you hate it?"

He looked serious. "That's my way of saying this is a

beautiful and inviting room. You're a very talented decorator."

"Thank you." She chose to believe he meant that. "What's your place like? I mean in L.A."

He frowned as he glanced around again. "Condo. Lots of space. Chrome and glass."

Sounded cold to her. As if there'd been any doubt, it proved they were oil and water, fire and ice—all things that don't mix. Normally she'd have let it pass, but he'd insinuated himself into her world and she wanted to know more about him.

"So tell me why a famous Beverly Hills doctor like yourself would make a long-distance house call?"

"Believe it or not I care about people."

Courtney felt an unpleasant twinge in her chest when she remembered him flirting with the tall, pretty nurse at the hospital. "Women-type people?" she asked before she could stop the words.

"*All* types of people. As I said before, plastics isn't just about big boobs and nose jobs."

She remembered the defensive look on his face when Janie had mentioned designer medicine. Now she was curious. "So tell me what plastics *is* about."

"It's about helping people feel better about themselves. I do procedures on men as well as women because the way someone looks on the outside can effect positive changes on the inside."

"How so?"

"Looking the best you can builds self-esteem and confidence. It's especially true when someone has catastrophic facial trauma."

"Like Janie—"

"Yes." He put a finger beneath her chin and nudged it up. "I've seen worse injuries than Janie has. This is the absolute, honest truth, Courtney. I promise that I will make your daughter's face whole—"

When he stopped, Courtney got a bad feeling. "What is it?"

"Her dimples," he said.

"What about them?"

"After the surgery, she won't have a matching set."

Courtney touched her own cheek. From the time Janie was a baby, she'd always told her she had dimples just like Mommy's. It was part of their identity and it was her fault Janie's would be altered.

"You can't fix it?" she whispered.

He blew out a long breath. "No. We're trying to perfect the technique, but haven't been successful so far. But I promise, no one who didn't know her before will notice anything except that she has a dimple on one cheek."

That was good. People wouldn't stare at her child out in public. It was a change, nothing more, she told herself. She swallowed hard and nodded. "Thank you, David. For everything."

"You don't have to thank me. I told you, I care about people."

"I believe you. Until now—with Janie—I don't think I truly understood what you do. Is it too late to take back every snarky remark?"

"I'll have to think about that," he said.

"While you're thinking, keep in mind that I didn't mean to sound ungrateful." What she'd meant to do was keep a distance between them. Here, in her little place, it was a bad time to realize she was failing miserably. "I think the strain of everything is getting to me."

"Define *everything*."

"Finances, for one." She moved over to the sofa and sat down. "My budget is stretched to the breaking point under the best of circumstances and this gives a whole new meaning to *breaking point*."

"I understand."

"If you hadn't so generously offered your services, I hon-

estly don't know what I'd have done. But that's just one of
my problems. My car is in pretty bad shape, if not completely totaled. They're going to let me know. I've already
missed several days of work which I can't afford."

"Peter might be able to help you out."

When he sat beside her she felt the warmth of his body
even though he wasn't touching her. She shivered and it had
nothing to do with the cold outside and everything to do with
the man inside.

"Maybe he could do something," she said thoughtfully.
"As the acting Chief of Staff."

"So why do you still look so worried?"

"There's a rumor that the hospital is going to be taken over
by a corporation."

"Peter told me." He leaned forward and put his elbows on
his knees as he looked at her. "Change isn't always bad."

"No?"

"They could bring in a lot of research dollars and capital for
new equipment and staff. If that were the case, there might be
a plastic surgeon here in Walnut River and you wouldn't need
me."

She didn't want to need him and had a bad feeling that it
was becoming more personal than professional. "It's not just
about health care. With a corporation we'd lose the human
component. Peter wouldn't be able to do anything about my
situation because it's all spreadsheets, computers and the
bottom line. Change is almost always bad."

"Has anyone ever told you you're a glass-is-half-empty
kind of person?"

She had good reason. Life had knocked her around and it
was much easier not to have expectations. "At the risk of
looking even more pessimistic, have you ever seen a corporate takeover where no one lost their job?"

He was quiet for several moments before answering, "No."

"I'm taking online business courses to get my degree. That will open up employment opportunities."

"That can't be easy to do while raising a child and working full-time."

"It's a challenge. But the full-time job is the most important. If I lose mine, I'm not sure I could get another one where I could make enough to support the two of us. And it will take me another year and a half before I can get my degree. I really need my job."

"I understand your concern."

"Even with it, I'm not sure how I'm going to handle our medical bills. I'm not even sure yet how I'm going to be able to go to work until she's feeling better."

"I can help."

The last thing she needed was to be further in his debt. "I have a support system. I just need to figure out what to do."

"You just said you've been under a strain the last few days. I can make this one easy."

"That's very generous of you, but—"

"Don't say it."

"What?"

"Anything negative."

"It never crossed my mind." She sighed. "The thing is, I already owe you more than I can repay."

"I'm not asking for anything." He looked at her. "You'd be doing me a favor."

"Oh, please."

"Seriously. I find myself with time on my hands."

"Because you volunteered—"

"Because I'm on vacation."

"Mommy?" Janie stood in the doorway, rubbing her eyes.

"Hi, baby. Did we wake you up?" Courtney held out her arms and the little girl walked over and crawled into her lap. "How do you feel?"

"Sleepy. I like my bed better than the hospital one."

"I know." She kissed her daughter's forehead.

"Let's let Janie decide," David suggested.

"'Cide what?" the little girl asked.

"Your mother has to go to work, and you're not ready to go back to school yet. And I don't have anything to do. What do you think about spending some time with me?"

"I can see if Mrs. Arnold downstairs can stay with you," Courtney suggested.

Janie made a face then met his gaze. "Can we play cards?"

"Sure," he said.

"What about milkshakes?" the little conniver asked, perking up.

"You drive a hard bargain, but I think it could be arranged."

"Okay. You can stay with me." Janie slid out of her mother's arms and scooted into David's lap. When she rested her cheek on his chest as if she'd been doing it for years, his strong arms folded around her as though she belonged there.

"I guess it's settled," David said, a smug tone to his voice.

"I guess."

How she'd love to relax and just let it be settled, but that couldn't happen. Her obligation to this man was mounting steadily and that was hard enough for her to take. But why was he being so generous to her when he'd ignored his father and family for so long? What kind of man was he? Charming playboy or knight in shining armor?

Either man could break her heart if she let him.

Chapter Six

"Dr. David, my ears are tired."

"Okay." He closed the book of fairy tales, pink cover of course, and looked down at Janie.

"I'm bored."

It was just a few days ago that Courtney had reacted so emotionally to those words. A hint of normal he understood better after spending a day with this munchkin.

"Do you want to play Monopoly? Or Scrabble?"

She shook her head, then crawled into his lap and rested her left cheek on his chest. The innate trust in the act squeezed his heart. At that moment if she'd asked for the moon, he'd have moved heaven and earth out of the way to get it for her.

"I guess I'm not much fun," he said, wishing he knew better how to entertain her.

"Yes, you are fun. I'm glad you stayed with me."

"I'm glad you're glad."

She sighed. "I don't think Mommy was very glad."

That was the understatement of the century. Yesterday when he'd brought them home from the hospital, Courtney had tried to talk him out of his offer because she didn't trust him. The truth was she probably shouldn't trust him because his motives *were* selfish. He had time on his hands and didn't look forward to doing nothing, even if he could afford to do it in the most expensive room at the Walnut River Inn. So Janie was actually doing him a favor.

"Thanks for going to bat for me with your mom," he told her.

"What's that mean?" Janie asked, looking up. There was something about a little girl in pink sweats and fuzzy slippers that made him want to stand between her and all the bad stuff in the world.

The lamp on the table beside them had little crystals dangling from the fluted beige shade. He liked it. In fact, he liked everything about this place, including—especially—its occupants. He'd paid more for a desk lamp than everything in this apartment had probably cost, yet there was something intangible here that made him feel good—something that money couldn't buy.

He smiled at the little girl. "*Going to bat* means you stuck up for me, pal. I appreciate it."

"It's okay." She caught her top lip between her teeth as a pensive expression filled the face so like her mother's.

"What's wrong, kiddo?"

She met his gaze with her one good eye. "I didn't tell Mommy, but I lifted up the bandage and looked."

With an effort, he kept his own expression neutral and tried to read hers. "Okay."

"My face looks gross." Her lips trembled.

"You have a serious injury, sweetie, but I'm going to make you just like before the accident."

A tear slid down her uninjured cheek. "What if you can't?"

He rubbed her arm then linked his fingers to snuggle her closer. "Have I ever lied to you?"

She thought for a moment. "No. In the hospital you said it would be a little pinch and then it wouldn't hurt. And it didn't."

"I'll always tell you the truth." He rested his chin on top of her head. "I can fix your face, but it will be a little different from before."

"How?" she said, turning a worried look up at him.

"I can't give you back your dimple."

"What if the kids at school make fun of me?"

She needed reassurance but this was way out of his league. He worked on kids, but he got in and out without emotional involvement. Not this time. Janie had stolen a piece of his heart. This required tact and diplomacy beyond his limited scope. Searching for the right words, he remembered having stitches as a kid.

At a neighbor's, he'd fallen on a sprinkler and took a chunk out of his knee down to the fat layer. The woman had turned white and he'd thought she'd pass out. Then his dad was there, telling him that there would be a scar, but that was cool for guys. Janie was a little girl. What would his father have told her?

"The kids at school are all going to be jealous of you," David finally said.

"Really?"

He nodded. "The girls will envy you because all the boys are going to think you look very mysterious with one dimple. You can tell them the other one was stolen by an evil sorcerer until your true love's first kiss."

"And I'll live happily ever after, like the story you read me?"

"Just like that." He met her gaze. "I promise you this, pal. It will take some time to heal, but eventually no one will ever know from looking at you that you were in a car accident." When she said nothing, he wished he could hug her tight enough to make her believe.

Finally he asked, "Do you trust me?"

She nodded and with her good hand she plucked the cotton of his white shirt. "Dr. David, how come you can't stay here in Walnut River forever?"

"Because my work isn't here," he explained.

"You could work here," she suggested. "You're going to make me better. You could make other people better, too."

"It's not that easy, squirt."

"Why not?" She rested her elbow on his midsection.

It was pointy and poked a rib, but he sucked it up because she was comfortable. "I have a practice in Beverly Hills. People there are depending on me."

"Aren't there other doctors there? Can't people go to someone else?"

"There are lots of doctors, but there are people who want to come to me. I've spent a lot of years working hard to be the best."

She thought about that for a few moments. "Mommy and me would have had to go somewhere to get my face fixed if you didn't stay. If you're the best, wouldn't people come here?"

"It's possible, but—"

"Then you could stay," she said, as if the problem were solved.

"Not forever, pal."

"I guess I knew that." She sighed. "Nobody stays."

"What do you mean?"

"My daddy had to go. Mommy said he wanted to stay with us but he had to be a soldier. Then he had to go to the war. When I was four, he didn't come back."

David had promised not to lie to her, but there were times the whole truth wasn't necessary. "Your father was a brave man."

"I guess." She shrugged. "I don't 'member him."

"You have that picture by your bed. I saw it when I tucked

you in." David remembered the good-looking guy in his army uniform. "I'm sure your mom talks about him."

Janie shook her head. "She won't. It makes her sad."

"She must love him very much," he commented. There were issues, but after all this time Courtney was still alone. Because she was still in love with her husband?

David knew that shouldn't make a difference to him one way or the other. He wouldn't lie to Janie and it probably wasn't smart to lie to himself. The fact that Courtney might still have deep feelings for her husband touched a nerve.

It was time to change the subject. "So, you like me better than Mrs. Arnold?"

Janie wrinkled her nose. "She snores when her soap operas come on TV."

"Since you kept me too busy to fall asleep, that wasn't an issue." David looked outside and noticed it was almost dark. Time flies when you're having fun. He realized it *had* been a good time. He stood with Janie in his arms. "Okay. Your mom will be home soon. Since I'm the only one around here with two good arms, I'll cook dinner."

"I can help," Janie offered.

"Can you set the table?"

"Yes." Her silky blond hair fell forward when she nodded vigorously. "Can you really cook?"

"I can dial the phone."

He didn't think his heart could melt more, but her sunny smile finished it off.

It was six-thirty when Courtney got to the door of her apartment and she was tired clear to the bone. Walking up three flights had almost done her in. That's what she got for teasing David about his masculinity. She let herself inside and was instantly besieged by delicious smells. Her stomach rumbled and she hadn't even realized she was hungry.

When Janie spotted her, she said, "Mommy's home."

David was in the kitchen bending over, peering into the oven. "Hi, there," he said, glancing over his shoulder.

When he straightened, she felt a twinge of disappointment because the man had a fine backside and she'd had a spectacular view. The thought proved that she was on thin ice here. Noticing something like that hadn't happened to her in a very long time.

"Hi." She stopped beside the sofa and pressed a kiss to her daughter's forehead. "How do you feel?"

"Okay. Me and Dr. David played games and watched *Nemo* and he read my fairy-tale book. And he taught me a card game and we bet with my pretend money."

She stood up straight and met his gaze. "Tell me it's not poker."

"Am I allowed to lie this time?"

She groaned. "If I try really hard, I can find a way to believe that poker is educational."

"Of course it is. Colors, shapes and patterns."

"Right." She sniffed. "I smell something good."

"There's an Italian restaurant on Lexington that delivers. Janie already had her pizza. I hope you like ravioli in tomato cream sauce, salad with oil and balsamic vinegar and garlic bread."

"It's my favorite. How did—"

"Janie told me." He joined her beside the couch and handed her a glass of wine. "How was your day?"

He didn't say "dear." Not even close, but for some reason her mind added it. "I was busy."

Work was a snap compared to coming home to David. It was too nice. And it would be too easy to get used to having him around, too easy to look forward to seeing his incredibly handsome face at the end of a day. Too easy to start relying on him. If not for his help, she wasn't sure how she'd have gotten through this. How could she ever pay him back? You could never go wrong being gracious.

She took a sip of wine. "I hope Janie wasn't too much for you."

"Yeah, she was pretty tough to take." He lifted his chin in her direction. "I think I wore her out. But it seems she wouldn't give in to rest until you got home."

The little girl was curled into the corner of the sofa, eyes closed, breathing evenly.

"This is early even for her," Courtney said. "I'll put her to bed."

"Let me." He rounded the sofa and lifted Janie, then carried her down the hall.

That was the second time and Courtney felt she was falling into habit territory. The man lived a life of luxury on the west coast, yet he chose to stay here and help her out. She would try to believe he was doing it because he really did need a vacation.

He returned and said, "She's in for the night. Mission accomplished."

When Courtney looked at the kitchen table, she noticed it was set for one. "You're not staying?"

"I didn't want to presume."

"Oh, please. Of course you're welcome. Stay." The last word came out as a plea to her ears but she hoped he hadn't heard it that way. Later she would worry about how much she didn't want him to go.

She put another setting on the table and they sat at right angles to each other after he served up portions on the plates. For several minutes they ate in silence.

David chewed thoughtfully. "Janie said she doesn't remember her father."

"She didn't see him much. Joe moved us to Walnut River to be closer to his parents."

"Morris and Elizabeth Albright, right?"

She nodded. "You know them?"

"They were friends of my folks. Nice people."

Not to her, but that was another story. And not pretty. "We were barely settled when he enlisted in the army and went to boot camp. I was six months pregnant."

He looked surprised. "He left before Janie was born?"

"Yes. After training, he didn't want to uproot us. We stayed here and he came home when he could."

"I see."

His tone said he didn't see at all. That made two of them. Joe had insisted on getting married when she found out she was pregnant and she'd thought he was incredibly honorable and decent. He'd brought her home to his family and she'd believed for a short time that all her dreams were coming true. But when things didn't go the way he wanted, Joe left her and Janie alone.

"He was killed shortly after his second tour of duty started in Iraq."

"I'm sorry."

"Me, too." She put her fork down and took a sip of wine.

"You've made it clear that life with Joe wasn't moonlight and roses, but it still must have been hard for you. Janie told me that talking about him makes you sad."

Instantly her gaze lifted to his. "I didn't know she'd noticed."

"She's a sharp cookie," he said.

"It *was* hard. For so many reasons. Making ends meet was always difficult."

"I thought servicemen have an insurance policy."

"They do. And each soldier receives counseling before deploying to a war zone." For some reason she found herself telling him more than she intended. "Joe neglected to name me as a beneficiary on his Serviceman's Group Life Insurance. The death benefit was paid to his estate but all the money went to legal fees to straighten out the mess he left behind. There's a small amount of money monthly, but it doesn't stretch far."

David's mouth thinned. "At the risk of speaking ill of the dead, that seems a bit irresponsible."

"That was Joe." Courtney shrugged. "I was blindsided when he joined the army. She was his child. I thought he'd want a relationship with her even though he and I had…"

"What?"

She shook her head. "Doesn't matter any more."

"So between your father and your husband, you had to be independent." He took her hand. "That explains a lot about why you have such a hard time accepting help."

He didn't know the half of it. And what she'd revealed wasn't the worst, but there was no reason to say more. Her husband hadn't provided the security she'd expected, but he had taught her that she really could only count on herself. It was a lesson she'd never forget. Although she hated the reminder because it felt really good when David gently squeezed her fingers.

"Court, do you ever think maybe you're *too* strong?"

"I don't think that's possible."

"Don't you ever get tired of doing it by yourself? Don't you ever want to let someone else in?"

She shook her head. "No."

For several moments, he looked at her as he brushed his thumb back and forth over her knuckles. "I see something else in your eyes."

"I'm not sure what that is, but I can tell you for a fact that I'm glad I'm strong enough to take care of Janie and me without help."

"It must get lonely."

"I have friends. This town is my family."

He stood and drew her to her feet, too. "But is that enough?"

"Yes, I—"

"Really?"

But the intensity in his eyes stole her breath and she couldn't answer. Then he cupped her face in his hands and kissed her. The way she leaned into him was answer enough. Her arm in the sling was between them, but he still managed to fold her against the solid length of his body. He threaded his fingers in her hair and gently urged her lips more firmly to his while her heart pounded and her breathing grew ragged.

She should have put a stop to it, but couldn't seem to find the will. Disappointment coursed through her when he pulled away, then pressed his forehead to hers and sucked in air.

"I've been wanting to do that from the first time I saw you."

"Y-you have?"

He nodded. "And you can tell yourself that you're content to be alone. But when you do, remember this—I'm not the only one who's breathing hard. And that makes me pretty damn happy."

He was right. It was so good. It had been so long since she'd felt like this and she didn't want it to end. But in the next instant, he kissed her forehead and stepped back.

"What—?"

"I'd better go."

"You're leaving?" Even she heard the whispered yearning in her voice.

"You need rest and recuperation as much as Janie. Although it's a waste of breath trying to convince you." There was regret in his eyes. "If I'm here you won't relax. So I'm going." He walked to the door and opened it, then looked at her. "But make no mistake. I'll be back."

She'd heard that before, but she'd never wanted to believe it as much as she did at this moment. Which was why he was so dangerous. That and the fact that if he'd wanted to take her to bed, she'd have willingly gone. She was pretty sure he knew it, too. She could understand if that's what he wanted from her. But he'd revved up her motor then left her idling. What was up with that?

No man was this noble and she simply couldn't afford to believe that David was.

Courtney put down the phone in her office, hardly more than a closet behind the hospital gift shop with barely enough space for her desk and shelves filled with inventory. The call had been from the insurance company. It had been a week since the accident and the adjuster informed her that the car was a total loss, so transportation was one more thing to worry about. Self-pity was a waste of energy, but just this once the thought sneaked in that she just couldn't seem to catch a break.

Karen Marshall picked that moment to peek in. "Sorry to bother you, Court." She looked closer. "Something wrong?"

"The insurance company just called. My car's a goner."

"Ouch. That sucks." Karen was a twenty-year-old redhead, a college student working part-time to help with expenses.

"I'll figure something out. Did you need me? Everything okay in the shop?" Courtney asked.

"Fine. Janie's here. With Dr. Wilder's brother."

"David." True to his word, he had come back to stay with her daughter that morning.

"Yeah." Karen's blue eyes narrowed in mock censure. "You never said a word about him being a hottie."

"Sorry." She shrugged. "What's wrong?"

"Nothing as far as I know. Dr. Hot Stuff just asked me to let you know they were here."

"Thanks." Courtney glanced at the clock on her wall. "It's time for you to go to lunch. I'll cover for you."

"Thanks, Boss."

Courtney followed her employee into the shop, as always glancing at the racks of greeting cards and stuffed animals. There was a small cold case for fresh flowers and shelves of porcelain and crystal figurines. A display of miscellaneous toiletries, candy bars and snacks lined up on the shelves in front of the cash register. Everything looked tidy and stocked.

Janie ran up to her. "Hi, Mommy."

"Hi, baby," she said, snuggling the little girl against her good side. "What are you doing here?"

"She wanted to come and see you," David explained.

"Is that all?" Courtney asked the little girl.

"Mostly." After a moment she said, "While I'm here, I thought maybe I could have some cafeteria ice cream."

"She loves the soft-serve here. Go figure," she said to David. Then she looked at Janie. "I can't take you, sweetie. I have to stay here while Karen goes to lunch."

"I'll take her," Karen offered. "I haven't seen her for a long time. We can catch up."

"Can I, Mommy?"

"Sure."

"Thanks, Mommy."

"Sorry about your car, Court," Karen said, then the two of them walked out into the hospital lobby.

They moved out of sight toward the elevator to the basement. And just like that she was alone with David. The last time she'd been alone with him he'd kissed her. When she met his gaze, something in his told her he was remembering, too.

Her cheeks burned, but she ignored the feeling. That was a whole lot easier than ignoring how good he looked in his worn jeans, white shirt and battered leather jacket. His hair was mussed in that sexy, trendy way. But in his case she had a feeling it wasn't deliberate as much as how he stepped out of the shower. Thoughts of David, showers, bare skin and muscles brought more heat to her face.

"So," she said, blowing out a long breath. "It was nice of you to bring her down here."

"There's another reason. It's been a week. Her stitches are ready to come out. I talked to Peter and he says there's a suite of offices in the new tower used for visiting doctors. When Karen comes back, can you slip away for a few minutes? I figured you'd want to be there."

"Of course. She'll be nervous."

"It's the easy part. I've already talked to her about what I'm going to do and promised that it won't hurt. She'll just feel a little pull. After that there are ointments I can recommend that will expedite healing and minimize scarring."

"Okay. Thank you, David. You're wonderful with her," Courtney said. "She trusts you."

"At least one of the Albright women does."

It was too much to hope he hadn't noticed. "Yeah. Well—"

"So what's the deal with your car?" At her blank look, he said, "Karen mentioned it before she left with Janie."

"Oh. Right." She let out a long breath. "The insurance company called and my little compact flat-lined. No possibility of resuscitation."

"They'll reimburse you for the loss, right?"

"Yeah. But it wasn't worth much. The thing is, it was paid for. I have to buy a new one and a payment is not in my budget."

He rested a lean hip against the glass case where knick-knacks were displayed. "Courtney, I could loan—"

"No." She held up a hand. "You've already done enough. I'll think of something. Part-time job, maybe—"

"You're already working full-time and taking classes. And raising a child. There are only so many hours in a day."

"You think I don't know that?" Her life was a house of

cards and it was collapsing around her. "It's my problem, David. And I'll deal with it."

"How?" He ran his fingers through his hair. "What about your in-laws? The Albrights?"

"No."

"Asking them for help is not weakness. My father knew them. They're good people."

"Your father liked everyone."

"I'm sure they'd help—"

"No, they won't."

"You said the people in this town are like family. But Janie is their actual granddaughter."

"That didn't seem to make a difference to them when Joe and I got married and moved here."

He frowned. "What are you saying?"

Courtney would never forget the coldness in their eyes when they said that Joe's unfortunate choices were his to deal with and they wanted nothing to do with his mistakes.

She started to shake and was angry that even after six years the humiliation of that moment hadn't gone away. She'd told herself over and over that success was the best revenge, but it was elusive. She kept working toward it, but every time she got close something happened and she slid right back to square one and started over.

And she would do it again now. For her daughter.

She met David's puzzled gaze. "I'm saying that the Albrights made it quite clear that they didn't approve of me. I won't ask for their help or give them the satisfaction of turning me down again."

"There must be some misunderstanding."

"Not likely," she defended, rubbing her arm. Her wrist ached but it was nothing compared to the pain in her heart.

"That just doesn't sound like the people I know."

"Maybe you don't know them as well as you think."

"Maybe not." He looked angry.

She didn't know how to deal with that. Fighting her own battles had been a way of life for so long, she didn't know anything different. And she was tired. More than that, she was afraid. Afraid this was the financial hit that would sink her. Afraid to drop her guard and lean on anyone. When David's support was gone, as she knew it would be, she was terrified that she'd fall and never be able to get back up.

Kissing him was dangerous. It opened a window to her heart, showed her how much he could hurt her. All that in spite of the fact that he had a questionable sense of loyalty. He was leaving. She was counting on it, because she didn't want to care about him.

That would be the death blow to her soul.

Chapter Seven

Late the next afternoon when Courtney arrived home from work to be with her daughter, David declined another dinner invitation from Janie. It bothered him to disappoint her and disturbed him even more how much he wanted to stay and talk to her mother. Maybe kiss her again. But he had something important to do.

He drove the BMW into the long driveway lined with sycamore trees and pulled up in front of the large brick house. Morris and Elizabeth Albright had lived here for as long as he could remember, but he didn't recall ever meeting their son. Joe was about nine years younger than he was; their paths had never crossed in school, then David had left for college.

He walked up several steps to the etched-glass front door and rang the bell. Lights inside went on just before the door was answered by Elizabeth Albright, who looked to be in her late fifties.

"Hello, David," she said.

He'd called ahead. "Mrs. Albright—"

"You're grown up now. Call me Elizabeth." She stood back and pulled the door open wider. "Come in, please."

"Thank you." He looked around.

The shined-to-perfection marble floor reflected the light from an overhead chandelier. On either side of the entryway twin staircases with intricate wrought-iron spindles topped by an oak handrail curved upward to the second floor. A mahogany table held a huge vase filled with fresh star lilies, daffodils, roses and baby's breath.

She closed the door then studied him. "You look a great deal like your father."

"So I've been told."

Elizabeth Albright was a tall, elegant woman with blue eyes and blond hair—probably not naturally blond. Her skin was still good, with minimal wrinkling and age damage even though, as far as he could tell without an examination, she'd not had work done. In her black silk lounging outfit and matching low-heeled shoes, she oozed an aura of wealth and privilege that could have intimidated Courtney when she was young and pregnant. He'd believed the Albrights were a kind and generous couple who would embrace a woman like Courtney and their only grandchild. But that's not what had happened—and he was here to find out why.

"Morris is in the library. We were just about to open a bottle of wine. Will you join us?"

"Thank you."

As he followed her into a room off the entryway, the floral scent surrounded him. In winter, fresh flowers were costly and again he wondered at the apparently callous attitude toward their son's widow and his child.

"Morris, David Wilder is here."

An older man looked up from a newspaper—the *Walnut River Courier*. He looked to be in his early sixties, silver-haired and fit. He stood when David walked into the bookshelf-lined room. A fire snapped and crackled in the fireplace on one wall. Two leather loveseats faced each other perpendicular to it with a cherrywood table between them.

David walked over to the man and held out his hand. "It's nice to see you, sir."

"And you." The man had an iron grip. He indicated the seat across from himself. "Have a seat, my boy."

"Thank you." David sat and Elizabeth handed them each a glass of red wine.

Morris took a sip and nodded. "An excellent pinot. Your father would have approved."

"I wouldn't know about that." The years when he could have shared an adult relationship with James Wilder were spent not speaking at all. The waste of it twisted and echoed inside him.

"You're a doctor, too?" he asked.

"Yes, sir. I specialize in reconstructive and plastic surgery. Designer medicine." Janie had heard it from her mother, who'd probably heard it from his father. "My father *didn't* approve of my specialty."

Morris merely nodded, then said, "I was sorry to hear about your father's death. He was a good friend and I miss him."

"Thank you, sir."

Elizabeth sat beside her husband. "Your father always spoke highly of you."

David didn't know how to respond. She was simply being polite because the words couldn't possibly be true. He'd been a lousy son and a severe disappointment to his father. Now, the man who had influenced him more than any other, who he'd respected more than any other and wanted so very much to please, was gone. Death was forever. David knew there was no way to reverse the damage he'd done.

"My father tried to see only the best in people," he finally said. James Wilder had tried his damnedest and failed to make his rebel son a better person. A better person would have swallowed his pride and contacted his father before it was too late. "How did you meet my father?"

Elizabeth's sigh was so deep it seemed to come from the depths of her soul. "It was when our daughter became ill."

"I didn't know you had a daughter."

"She died of leukemia many years ago," Morris explained.

"I'm sorry." He hadn't known, but then he'd been just a kid.

"Your father was her doctor and she spent a lot of time in Walnut River General. The people there took such good care of her, made the worst time in our lives tolerable. When she died we were inconsolable. Didn't know what to do with our grief. James suggested we endow the hospital pediatric department as a memorial. We did and have been involved ever since in fundraising and charitable endeavors."

David realized his father had a way of planting the seed of compassion and generosity. It was why his own medical intervention trips to impoverished countries had seemed natural when he'd finally had the skill and training to do some good.

Elizabeth half turned toward him. "Over the years we've donated money for equipment, toys, redecoration for a child-friendly environment and scholarships. The money is administered through a trust in our daughter's name. There's a plaque at the hospital, just outside pediatrics, a dedication to the Jane Elizabeth Albright Memorial Trust."

The name got his attention. "Your daughter's name was Jane?"

"That's right," Morris said. "We had a son, too. Joe. He was killed in Iraq."

"I'm sorry for your loss," he said automatically. But David was surprised when the older man's eyes turned hard. "Actually that's the reason I've come."

"Because of Joe?" Elizabeth asked.

"In a way, yes."

"Did he do something?" Morris leaned forward, wariness in his expression. "That boy—"

"Morris, don't start. We have to take some responsibility for Joe," Elizabeth said, patting her husband's knee. "After Jane died, we indulged him, protected him too much. *Enabled him,* I think, is the politically correct term today."

"That seems a natural reaction," David commented.

"Maybe. But he became manipulative and self-centered. Because he joined the army, everyone in Walnut River thinks he's something special."

Not everyone, David thought, remembering what Courtney had said. "He gave his life for his country. I'd say that makes him pretty special."

"You're James's son, all right. Seeing only the best," Morris said. "But it was hard to see any good in Joe." He met David's gaze, man to man. "What I'm telling you stays in this room. Joining the army had something in it for Joe. I'll guarantee you that."

"How can you be so sure?"

The older man's blue eyes turned hard, angry. "He never gave up trying to get money out of us and when we went soft and gave it to him, it ran through his fingers like water. He tried everything he could to rip us off and we did everything we could think of to help him be a better man. The only thing he has left is a reputation as a hero."

"He has a daughter," David pointed out. "Janie."

Elizabeth's mouth thinned. "I still can't believe that woman had the nerve to name her child after our little girl."

"She's not 'that woman,'" David said, keeping his voice even with an effort. "Her name is Courtney Albright. She's your son's widow and Janie is your grandchild."

Morris rested his clenched fist on his knee. "Maybe I

wasn't clear enough. Our son would have done anything to extort money from us. Including bringing home a woman who claimed to be pregnant with his child. It took us a long time, but we learned not to trust him or anyone who would marry him."

"I've gotten to know Courtney pretty well," David said. "She's not the type to use people."

Elizabeth's gaze narrowed. "Don't make the mistake of falling for her, David."

Not a chance, he thought. But if Courtney was an opportunist, she was putting on a darn good act. And even if it was an act, he was painfully aware of his own weakness for a woman who needed his help. Maybe it was some whacked-out need of his to fix his own life by fixing hers. Either way, he was on guard.

"Thanks for the warning, but I can take care of myself."

"I hope so. Losing Jane broke our hearts," Elizabeth said. "Joe's machinations and schemes broke our spirit. Trusting him and anyone who was with him wasn't an option." She sighed. "At least he died with a hero's reputation. And that's the end of it. We have no wish to dredge up all the pain again."

"The last thing I want is to open old wounds. But Courtney is struggling because your son didn't follow through on his responsibilities to her or his child. He joined the army, then his carelessness left her nothing but red tape and legal fees. In spite of that, she's made a warm and loving home. She's raising a bright and happy little girl while working full-time and taking classes online to complete her degree. She's doing it by herself, but she needs help."

"She's not our problem." Morris's lips pressed together until his mouth was a tight line.

"She's the mother of your grandchild. That kind of makes it your problem."

"We have no proof that child is Joe's," Elizabeth said, her voice shaking.

"What about a DNA test?"

"I have no wish to be made a fool of again. Or disappointed again," Elizabeth said softly.

David stood. "You wouldn't be let down."

"And how can you be so sure of that?" Morris asked.

"I reconstruct faces for a living, and without bragging too much, I'm pretty good at what I do. People from across the country come to me to have work done. It's my job to study faces, bone structure, to know every curve and angle."

"Your point is?" Elizabeth stood and met his gaze.

"Janie Albright has your chin, Elizabeth, and I've seen her lift it as stubbornly as you're doing right now." He looked down at Morris. "She has your blue eyes, sir. I would stake my considerable reputation on the fact that she *is* your granddaughter. And you're missing out on a lot if you turn your backs. Take it from someone who knows all about regrets."

Without another word, David walked to the front door and let himself out. He'd made his point and the Albrights had a lot to think about. Courtney had hinted at issues with her husband and his own parents had painted a pretty unflattering portrait of their son. That made him wonder what Courtney had gone through—and he intended to find out.

Courtney waited in the exam room for Dr. Ella Wilder. This was the moment of truth—surgery or no surgery. Obviously she was hoping for the latter. It would be the single bright spot in an otherwise sucky week. Actually, David was a bright spot, although she didn't like admitting that even to herself. After this appointment it was time to go home and the thought made her shiver. That happened every time she thought about seeing the handsome doctor, which was pretty much every day, since he was looking after Janie.

The door opened and Ella was there in her lab coat. Courtney often saw her in the gift shop, buying mints, a candy bar or bottled water. She was in her late twenties, pretty, medium height, with straight dark-brown hair worn in a bob, and warm brown eyes. In fact, her eyes seemed to sparkle more than usual.

"Courtney, hi. How are you?"

"Good, thanks."

"Let's take a look at that wrist." She removed the sling Courtney had begun to think of as an accessory to every outfit. Then she took off the temporary cast that now had room to spare and carefully examined the arm. "The swelling has gone down a lot more than I expected. We'll get another X-ray, but I'm pretty sure this is not going to need surgery. I'll put a cast on, probably for about four weeks, then we'll reevaluate."

"Thank God." Courtney let out her breath.

"I'm glad I could make you happy."

"Speaking of happy…" Courtney grinned at her.

The hospital rumor mill had been churning with tidbits about Ella and the good-looking businessman who had ended up in the hospital after losing his balance on the slippery sidewalk outside. Ella had been his doctor.

"What?" Ella looked clueless.

"You're looking especially glowing."

"Am I?" she said mysteriously.

"Duh," Courtney shot back. "The buzz is that there's a man involved. What's his name?"

"The rumor's name is J. D. Sumner." Her dark eyes radiated happiness even as a becoming blush pinkened her cheeks. "If I'm glowing, it's because love is good for the complexion."

"If love is what it takes, there's no hope for my skin."

"Don't be so pessimistic. You look great. The bruises are fading and the arm is healing nicely. How's Janie?"

"Doing great. Thanks to David. He's certainly gone above

and beyond the call of duty." And she didn't just mean his medical expertise. That kiss was way above and beyond. Courtney shook her head even as she felt the warmth in her own cheeks.

"I hear David is sticking around."

"For Janie's surgery, to repair her cheek."

Ella sighed. "I was hoping he'd change his mind about that."

"Doing the procedure?" Courtney asked, surprised.

"No. God, no. He's the best and that's what we want for Janie." She shook her head. "I was hoping he'd move back to Walnut River."

"His life isn't here any more." Courtney reminded herself of that every time that special shiver danced over her skin when she thought about him.

"For a man whose life is somewhere else, my brother is certainly—how did you put it? Going above and beyond the call of duty." Ella's eyebrow lifted knowingly.

"Me?" She tapped her chest. "I have no idea what you mean."

"I think my brother is smitten. Just today I was up in peds looking in on a patient and ran into one of the hospital's most generous patrons. She said David came to see her and it was all about you."

"Who was she?"

"Elizabeth Albright." Ella tapped her chin. "She's your mother-in-law, right?"

"Right," Courtney answered.

She was surprised her mouth worked at all after the cold that crept through her. Then anger set in and she welcomed the warmth of it to push out everything else.

Courtney walked up the three flights of stairs to her apartment and opened the door. David was sitting on the couch reading what looked like a medical publication. When she walked in, he smiled. God help her, she felt it deep down inside, where she carried the memory of his shattering kiss. It was a place she'd protected all her life. Joe had breached her defenses and that had been a disaster. But even he hadn't touched her as deeply as David, in spite of the fact that she'd seen with her own eyes that he was a flirt. She didn't want to care that he had smiled at another woman the way he was smiling at her now. But she did. It was time to put a stop to this.

She looked around the living room. "Where's Janie?"

"Taking a nap. You're home early."

"I had an appointment with Ella."

"I know, but I figured you'd go back to work. What did my sister say about your arm?"

She held up her neon-green cast. "It's healing nicely and surgery won't be necessary."

"Excellent news." He stood up, took three steps forward and pulled her into his arms for a hug.

She wanted to stay there so badly, which was why she forced herself to step away. Courtney went to the hallway and pulled the door shut. She didn't want her little girl to hear this.

"What's wrong, Court?"

She turned on him as outrage and memories of past humiliation made her shake. "How *dare* you go to see the Albrights!"

"Ah." He nodded grimly. "News still travels at the speed of light in this town."

"Ella saw Elizabeth Albright at the hospital. More likely the old bat was trolling for information. She wanted to know why in the world you'd champion someone like me."

His gaze narrowed. "What does that mean?"

"It means the Albrights didn't think much of me six years ago and there's no reason to change their minds now. Why didn't you stay out of it? You had no right to talk to them about me."

"Calm down, Court—"

"Don't patronize me, David."

Damn, she thought, as tears burned her eyes. All the painful memories rushed through her mind like a kaleidoscope of humiliation. Joe's parents had all but said she was trash—untrustworthy trash not good enough for their son. She'd been pregnant, newly married because of her condition, starry-eyed about starting life over in Walnut River with a man she believed would be there for her. One disdainful look from Elizabeth Albright had crushed those dreams. She hated sharing a name with them, but it was Janie's too and she wouldn't deprive her of that.

David stared at her for several moments. "Who picked out Janie's name? You?"

Where did that come from? "Yes. Why?"

"You never said that Joe had had a sister. And from what I learned, he wasn't the type to name his child after her."

It felt as if he'd knocked the air from her lungs. Joe had told her about Jane when they'd first met. The pain of loss in his eyes was what she'd fallen in love with because he'd seemed so caring about his sister who'd died. Courtney had bonded with him over the hardships of their pasts and he'd made a fool of her. The bitterness of that burned through her.

She lifted her chin and looked at David. "There was no reason for me to tell you that. Obviously the Albrights felt the need to share."

"Actually, they took the blame for his behavior."

What was he trying to tell her? "The dots are there, but you've got to connect them for me."

"They told me about losing their daughter in the context of explaining how their son became a selfish, self-centered, manipulative hustler."

Suddenly Courtney felt as if her legs wouldn't hold her up.

She rested against the arm of the sofa. "I'm surprised they acknowledged Joe's problems."

The Albrights had admitted as much to him, but not to her. Then the truth hit her. David was their equal, but she was nothing more than a hustler by association, an opportunist who would never rise above her shabby background. What they hadn't counted on was her determination to overcome the past and be gum on their shoes, an annoyance—someone they couldn't get rid of easily.

"They're not bad people, Court. Life kicked them around and they handled it the best way they knew how. After losing their child, they tried to pick up the pieces, but tragedies affect the whole family—including the healthy, surviving child. They cared enough about Joe to let him stand on his own because Jane's traumatic illness caused him to get lost in the shuffle—"

"Don't you dare defend him to me," she said hotly.

"I'm not. It's just that I have an idea why he turned out like he did."

"He voluntarily walked away from the opportunity to have a relationship with his child. Are you telling me you can understand that?"

"That's indefensible. I'd never turn my back on the people I care about."

"But you did, David."

"What?" His blue eyes went cold as ice.

"Your father talked about you all the time. He'd come in the gift shop and chat, ask about Janie. I'd tell him stories and he'd remember you at the same age. He loved you and needed you. Where were you all those years? Tell me how that's different from Joe."

A muscle jerked in his jaw. "My father had a life and could take care of himself. Unlike you and Janie counting on Joe."

He had her there, but she'd hit a nerve. Part of her was glad. She could only blame her harshness on the ever-present fight-or-flight mentality she'd known for as long as she could remember. Flight wasn't an option. She had roots here and wouldn't give them up. The men she'd let into her life had let her down, but Walnut River never had. Her only choice was to fight. But David didn't deserve to be her target.

She stood and started to put her hand on his arm, then curled her fingers into her palm. "I'm sorry, David. That was uncalled for."

"No harm, no foul." He shrugged.

"The thing is, I *can* take care of myself and my daughter. I don't need help from anyone and certainly not the Al-brights."

"Understood."

"I appreciate everything you've done."

She was walking a fine line and the edge was starting to cut her and Janie. The little girl talked nonstop about Dr. David this and Dr. David that. She was falling for him and didn't have the reserves of worldly wisdom to keep out the hurt when he walked away. Her little girl believed in fairy tales and happy endings and it was up to Courtney to protect her.

"It's no big deal." David walked to the door and grabbed his jacket from the hook beside it. "I'll see you, Court."

When he was gone she felt lower than a snake's belly in the deepest place on the planet. He'd only been trying to help, but old habits died hard. And because they did, she had to wonder what he got out of helping her.

On a whim, she booted up her computer tucked away on a small desk in the corner of the living room. When she'd logged onto the Internet, she typed in *David Wilder, M.D.*,

Plastic Surgeon, and a ton of stuff popped up. *Stunned* didn't begin to describe how she felt when she read about him.

The information should have been reassuring. Instead it made her afraid because all her defensive shields lowered in a heartbeat.

Chapter Eight

Courtney always manned—or was it womaned—the cash register at the hospital's gift shop when her staff was on a break. That was the case the next day when Dr. Peter Wilder walked in. She'd always thought him a good-looking man and still did. But she couldn't help making comparisons between the brothers and every time it was thoughts of David that made her pulse race. That condition had worsened after what she'd learned on the Internet.

"Hi, Courtney. How are you?"

She held up her injured arm. "On the mend, thanks."

"And Janie? How's she doing?"

"David—Dr. Wilder—"

Peter grinned. "I know who he is."

"Right." She brushed a strand of hair behind her ear. "He took out the stitches in her chin and that's healing nicely. To fix her cheek will require another surgery in about three weeks. Or less."

He nodded. "Check with Human Resources. You may be eligible for programs through the hospital to help with the expenses."

"Thanks for the tip. I'll do that." Apparently being a hero was a family trait. Their father had passed it down to both of his sons. "In fact, I'm glad you stopped in so I could thank you personally."

"For?"

"Bringing David in to look at Janie."

"Ella made the call."

"Then it was a joint effort. He's going to do the repair right here at Walnut River General. He assures me that except for her dimple, he can make her look just like she did before the accident."

She wished someone had warned her that David was one of the good guys before she'd revealed her snarky streak. According to what she'd read about him, he elevated benevolence and compassion to an art form.

"So he's coming back for the surgery?" Peter asked.

"Actually, he's taking time off and staying until the procedure," Courtney confirmed.

"That's news to me." Peter leaned against the counter. "I wonder what he's been doing with himself."

"Spending time with my daughter, for one thing," she said. "Janie couldn't go to school and I had to work. David offered to help out and keep her company."

"What a guy." Peter's dark eyebrows pulled together in a puzzled expression.

"Is that different from when you knew him? I—I mean growing up together?"

He thought for a moment, then said, "That's tough to answer. We haven't spent a lot of time together as grown men. I just remember that Dad always said David was the one who turned his hair white." He picked up a roll of mints and set them on the glass counter. "Is there any reason in particular you're wondering about David?"

So many reasons, so little time. Mostly she wanted to know because any piece of information that would help her keep David Wilder at arm's length would be greatly appreciated. She was hoping Peter would tell her that what she'd seen on the Internet about David fixing poor kids' faces was all about PR that would bring rich women to his office in droves. Somehow she wanted his brother to spin the good deeds into something that would crush the crush that got a little bigger every time she saw David.

"I looked David up on the Internet," she said.

"Checking out his credentials before he does Janie's procedure?" Peter teased.

"Something like that," she hedged. "The thing is, I found a lot of information on his work in third-world countries."

"I never heard Beverly Hills described that way before."

Courtney blinked. He had to be teasing. "No, I meant his trips to other countries. When he does surgery on impoverished kids with little or no access to medical care. The before and after pictures on the Net were pretty remarkable. Some of the children had incredible traumas or deformities and David performed miracles."

Peter straightened and stared down at her. "What are you talking about?"

"He's like the Indiana Jones of the medical community." She stared at him. "You don't know about this?"

"Not a clue."

"He never told you about these trips?" She needed to clarify, make sure they were on the same page.

"Not a word."

"Why?"

"I couldn't tell you." Peter ran his fingers through his hair. "Since he left home David hasn't been in touch regularly.

Something happened. A falling out with Dad. He wouldn't talk about it and as far as I know they never spoke before my father passed away."

Courtney felt a deep sadness for David and his father. James Wilder was probably the finest man she'd ever known and she'd have given anything if he'd been her father instead of the one fate had burdened her with. What had caused David and his dad to part ways? Why did he give of his time and skill to strangers yet drift away from his own family?

As a mother she could imagine the incredible pain and anguish if Janie turned away from her. She couldn't stand it if her daughter wasn't in her life. And she hoped she would always be that important to her child.

She met Peter's gaze. "It's not like he was trying to hide anything. It was all there on the Internet."

"Yeah. But he's my brother. Who knew I'd need the Internet to find out what he's been up to?"

"I'm sorry. I don't know what to say."

"That makes two of us. But David has some explaining to do." He took a bill out of his pocket, indicating he wanted to pay for his purchase.

Courtney ran the roll of mints across the scanner and gave him change for a twenty. "I'm glad I got a chance to say thanks for your help after the accident."

"Don't mention it. I appreciate the 411 on my brother. You can bet I want to know more about it."

That made two of them. While she watched Peter walk out of the gift shop a surreal feeling washed over her. Usually if something seemed too good to be true, it was. Not David. He turned out to be better than he looked. And he looked pretty darn good.

So, where did that leave her? With more questions than answers. She wanted answers because this was the man who was going to fix her little girl. Mostly that's why she wanted to know him. At least that's what she tried to believe. Because if he was really as good as he looked on paper, she didn't have a prayer of getting her heart through this unscathed.

Time off was a good opportunity to catch up on his professional reading. With a stack of medical journals beside him on the table, David sat in one of the wing chairs in his room at the Walnut River Inn. Dinner had consisted of an excellent Cornish game hen with all the trimmings served in the inn's huge, but homey, yellow-and-red gingham kitchen. He'd sat by himself at one of the tables for four.

This wasn't how he normally spent a Saturday night. At home it usually started with a movie or play followed by dinner at a trendy, expensive restaurant with a hot blonde, brunette or redhead across the table from him and hotter sex back at his place. For reasons he couldn't explain, he didn't miss it. The hot ladies, not the sex. That he missed quite a bit.

A vision of Courtney flashed into his mind, her lips wet and swollen from his kiss, her smoky eyes locked on his. Need slammed him like a sledgehammer to the chest. And how freaking stupid was that? The last time he'd seen her, she'd basically taken him to task for messing with her life. Where did he get this weakness for damsels in distress? She needed his skill as a doctor, but nothing else. And damned if that didn't make him *want* something else. Is that what had happened to him in college? Had he really learned nothing from that nightmare?

His thoughts went straight back to that time and the intensity of his desire to help the woman he'd thought he loved. When she'd got what she wanted and the manure had hit the fan, she'd dropped him like a hot rock. Once Janie's surgery was over, Courtney wouldn't need him. So, thinking about her like this was an exercise in futility. Or insanity. Or both.

A knock on the door saved him the trouble of deciding which. After setting his reading material on the table beside him, he crossed the room and opened the door.

"Courtney?"

"Hi, David. I hope I'm not disturbing you."

That was up for debate. Which was more disturbing? Thoughts of her driving him crazy or Courtney in person doing the same thing? He couldn't decide which form of self-torture was worse.

"Nope. Just reading." He opened the door wider. "Do you want to come in? We could go in the inn's living room—"

As voices of the other guests drifted to them, she shook her head. "No. Here is fine. I'd like to talk to you if that's okay."

More than okay, based on this feeling of being too happy to see her. "Sure," he said casually, standing back, then shutting the door behind her. "Where's Janie?"

"Spending the night at her friend's house. Melanie," she added, nervously twisting her fingers together. "Mel's mom is a nurse at the hospital and said she'd make sure the girls took it easy. No rough stuff. DVDs and dolls. Nothing more strenuous than that."

She was babbling, David noticed. And Courtney wasn't a babbler. So what was she nervous about?

"Have a seat," he said, indicating the matching wing chairs in the cozy alcove across from the four-poster bed.

"Thanks." She put her purse on the floor beside her.

"May I take your coat?" Subtext of the question was whether or not she'd be staying a while, and he hoped the answer was yes.

"Thanks again," she said, shrugging out of the fleece-lined windbreaker.

He settled it on the doorknob, then sat in the open chair beside her. "So, what brings you here? Now that I think about it, how'd you get in?"

"I know Greta Sanford and her husband. I took a history class from Mr. Sanford. He teaches college part time in Pittsfield and helps with the inn. So he can vouch that I'm not a serial killer."

"Good to know. So— What's up?" He rested his elbows on his knees.

"I looked you up on the Internet."

"I'm flattered."

"I didn't do it because I have a crush on you." And yet a blush crept into her cheeks.

"Okay."

"It was because I didn't trust you."

"So you do think *I'm* a serial killer," he teased.

"God, no." Her gaze jumped to his. "But you're too good to be true. That's not normal."

Maybe in her world, from what little she'd told him. The thought made him want to pull her into his arms and shelter her from everything bad. But he didn't and the self-torture ratcheted up.

"How do you mean *not normal?*" he asked.

"You know—if it walks like a duck, quacks like a duck—"

"It must be a duck. Yeah, I get that, but—" He shook his head. "I'm lying. I don't get that."

"You're a plastic surgeon. You look like a movie star. But—"

"Have I ever told you how much I hate the word *plastic?*"

Her mouth turned up at the corners. "But you're a really nice guy. I just wanted to know more about you."

"And did you find anything to change your mind? Prove I'm not a duck?"

"No. That is, you're not a duck. I found out about your trips to Africa and Central America to help kids with facial deformities. I saw the photographs of what you do and under what conditions. The thing is—"

"Yes?" he prodded when she hesitated.

"I mentioned this to your brother and he didn't know about it. Why would you not say anything to your family about the wonderful work you do?"

The subtext of her question was—what do you get out of it? He wanted to say "nothing" because thinking about his motives brought back all the bad stuff. But he wanted to be honest with her. Maybe because men had let her down on a regular basis and he didn't want to be one more on the infamous list. To answer her question, he needed to explain what had happened between him and his father. It seemed right finally to tell someone. It felt right to tell her.

"I don't broadcast it because somehow publicity and praise cancel out the lesson."

She inched forward on her chair in order to see his face without the lamp in the way. "What lesson?"

He stood and ran his fingers through his hair. "In college— There was a girl—"

"Your father didn't approve of her?"

Interesting she would go there. "No. Actually, they never met. His disapproval came after he was notified by the college when I was caught with answers for an exam."

"David—" She stood and looked up at him, questions swirling in her big, brown eyes.

"Not for me. They were for *her*." He held up his hand. "Stupid, I know. Don't ask."

She studied him intently, then nodded. "Okay. What happened?"

"I got thrown out of school."

"So— What? You're not really a doctor? You're the great imposter?"

"If there was any upside, it was that I only lost a year. I couldn't transfer my credits so I started from scratch at another school on the west coast. As far from my father and

Walnut River as I could get." He shrugged, not wanting to share the stupid, painful details. "What doesn't kill you makes you stronger. Starving student. Pick your cliché, although the starving part wasn't too far off the mark in my case."

"So you made it on your own."

He nodded. "In my residency I was mentored by a prestigious group of plastic—reconstructive—surgeons in Beverly Hills. Then they invited me to join the practice. They were approached by an international children's health care organization to have a doctor in the group volunteer a week in Central America doing surgeries on kids with cleft palates, facial trauma, burns, minimizing scars. I drew the short straw."

"Why the short straw? I found articles about your regular trips to other countries. It doesn't sound like you hated it."

"Yeah." He saw the look in her eyes, the doubt and skepticism. "Before you ask what I get out of it, let me just say the gratitude of those parents was payment enough. Some of them didn't speak English. There were translators, but the words didn't matter. God, they so didn't matter." He drew in a shuddering breath as he struggled to find the words to explain the power of the experience.

"Nothing mattered except the concern in their eyes for their children. And the soul-deep appreciation in their expressions. Word spread and people brought their kids to me to be fixed. I could see in their faces that they'd lost hope of a decent, normal life for their child. But if there was a single chance—" He held up his hands. "With these, I gave them back their hope. I changed lives for the better. I found out what my father meant."

"About what? What did he say?"

"He told me I would never appreciate the blessings I'd been born with until I learned to give back and not just take. He was right, Courtney." He rubbed the back of his neck.

"No, David. Obviously he was angry."

"Yeah. But it was more than that. Even then I was a good study of faces. I saw how much I'd let him down." He shook his head, remembering the desolate expression in James Wilder's eyes, the same eyes that stared back at him from the mirror every day. "In so many ways I disappointed him—" Emotion clogged his throat, he stopped and turned away.

"He loved you, David—" She put her hand on his back.

"I don't know any more."

The warmth of Courtney's fingers on his back burned straight into him, to a place he'd closed off so long ago. Something about her drew him in, lit a candle inside him, made him want to be close to her.

Needing to see her, he turned back. Courtney's eyes swam with sympathy just before she put her arms around him. He pulled her closer and buried his face in her sweet-smelling hair.

"David—"

He heard the need in her voice, recognized it as an echo of his own. Every thought went out of his head but one. If he didn't kiss her right now, his soul would dry up and blow away.

Courtney stared at him and braced for impact when his eyes darkened and his body tensed, urging her subtly closer to him. But nothing could prepare her for the heat, and, just like that, she was swept away, clinging to him as her safe harbor in the eye of the storm.

He tunneled his fingers into her hair and pressed the back of her head gently, making the contact of their mouths firmer, deeper, stronger. His breathing was fast and uneven. They were pressed together from chest to thigh, nearly as close as two people could get, making it impossible for her to ignore his erection pressing against her belly.

David eased his mouth from hers and stared into her eyes for several moments. The naked need in his gaze took her breath away and underscored his self-control when he gently kissed the tip of her nose.

He smiled. "I guess there's no point in lying about it. I want you. And the ball, as they say, is in your court."

Exhilaration speared through the sultry blast of heat holding her in its grip. He was turned on. She'd got his motor running. There'd been no one for her since Joe, and he hadn't wanted her after she'd told him she was pregnant, not even when he was home on leave. Courtney had forgotten what it felt like for a man to want her and to want him right back.

Could she turn off her head and simply let nature take its course? Worry about everything else later? For now she longed to just give in to the needs pouring through her body.

"Court?" His gaze moved over her face, studying her. "You're thinking. I don't like it when you think too much."

"Sorry. That's just me being me."

"What's going through your mind?"

"Not much, because I'm pretty sure all the circuits are shorted out. What I know is more instinct."

"Okay," he said warily. "What do you know?"

"I need you to touch me. Somewhere. Anywhere. I need to feel your hands on my skin."

He grinned and turned up the heat. "I can do that."

He put his hands at her waist and slid his palms beneath her sweater, up her sides, stopping when he brushed his thumbs over her nipples. The light touch produced a surge of electricity so strong it fried any brain circuits that might have survived his initial assault on her mouth. A shudder coursed through her body and the heavenly sensation made her mouth open and her eyes drift shut.

"Lady," he said, his voice husky with need, "when you look like that, it's all I can do not to throw you on the bed and ravish you."

She looked at him and smiled. "What's stopping you?"

He hesitated a heartbeat before saying, "Not a damn thing."

He yanked back the comforter and sheets and backed her up against the mattress, kissed her hard, then said, "Hold that thought."

He disappeared and a light in the bathroom flashed on for a moment. Then he returned holding a square packet and set it on the nightstand. Courtney was so far gone she hadn't even thought about protection. She didn't care why he had it; she was just grateful that he did.

Without words he slid his arms around her. His mouth captured hers, tasting of humor and hunger and heat. As his teeth grazed her bottom lip, she felt his hands at her waist, unbuttoning her jeans before sliding down the zipper and skimming the denim to her hips. She toed off her sneakers and let him draw the cloth over her knees and to the floor. When she had stepped out of the pants, he took the bottom of her sweater in his fingers and gently pulled it up and over her head.

Her left sleeve caught on her cast and he tenderly freed it before gently kissing each of her fingertips. As he unhooked her bra, she undid the buttons on his shirt and pressed her palm to his bare flesh. It was warm and appealingly masculine and soft, except for the sprinkling of hair across his chest.

While she was spinning in the headiness of the moment, he was busy removing shoes, pants and shirt. Just like that it was a level playing field, with both of them naked as the day they were born. Instead of embarrassment, Courtney reveled in his awed expression as he openly looked her over from head to toe.

He touched the colorful healing bruise on her shoulder, where the seatbelt had pulled tight in the accident. "Does it hurt?"

She shook her head. "Not unless you're talking vanity. Yellow does nothing for my skin tone."

Lowering his head, he kissed the mark. "You have incredibly beautiful skin," he murmured.

"Ah, flattery from the renowned reconstructive surgeon, Dr. David Wilder."

"I'm not trying to sweet-talk you, Court. That was a sincere compliment."

His vulnerable side was showing and it effectively lowered her defenses.

"I know. I'm nervous, David." She fixed her gaze on the center of his chest. "Gossip has you being with some of the most beautiful women in the world. And I'm just me. Battered and broken. On top of that I haven't done this for a really long time. I'm probably going to mess this up. It's a talent of mine—"

He touched a finger to her lips. "Stop thinking. More important, stop talking. Trust me."

Of the three, trust was the most difficult.

He lifted her into his arms, snuggling her to his chest. Her heart hammered against his, matching him beat for beat. Settling her in the center of the big, soft mattress, he slid beside her and touched his lips to hers again, effectively shutting down brain function.

When she opened her mouth, he didn't hesitate to accept the invitation and slid his tongue inside. As he stroked and sucked, liquid heat and pounding need pooled in her belly. He nipped her lower lip with his teeth as he kissed his way down her neck, over her chest and took her breast in his mouth. The soft, erotic touch coursed through her and she felt as if she were on fire.

That was nothing compared to the feeling of his hand inching down her belly before his fingers parted the curls between her thighs to slide inside her. She was wet and ready and nearly mindless with wanting.

"David, please," she whispered.

"In a minute."

Sixty seconds too long, she thought, writhing beneath his oh-so-focused attention. With his thumb, he rubbed the nub where all her nerve endings joined at the center of her femininity. Her breathing was shallow and uneven and she couldn't seem to get enough air into her lungs. The touch was simply too exquisite and she shattered into a million pieces, dissolving into all the colors of the rainbow.

"Oh, David," she said when she could speak. Her still-labored breathing was not conducive to conversation. "That was amazing— But you didn't—"

"I will."

He reached for the condom, opened the packet and slid the sheath on. Then he settled over her, bracing himself on his forearms as he stared, as if he couldn't look at her hard enough.

"That put some color into your cheeks," he said, sliding inside her.

She hooked her legs around his waist. "Let me return the favor."

His eyes darkened to navy blue, then his mouth claimed hers for an exquisitely sweet kiss. He started to move in and out, slowly. But in less time than it took a heart to beat he increased the rhythm. She gave herself over to it, losing herself in the texture and taste of his lips, the sensations of her body humming and her pulse pounding. And the sheer bliss of being with this man. Then he tensed and groaned, his face all angles, shadows, concentration. And intense pleasure.

Several moments later, he kissed her softly, then rested his forehead against hers. "For the record, the way you messed that up?" He blew out a long breath, then grinned the grin that rocked her world. "It really worked for me."

She laughed. "Me, too."

He rolled to the side and off the bed. "Don't move. I'll be right back."

She didn't have to move to start thinking again. Passion was satisfied. Doubts filled the void when need receded. She hated the doubts. But she'd learned life would bite her in the backside if she ignored them.

Chapter Nine

When David walked out of the bathroom, Courtney was putting her shoes on. "So much for doctor's orders not to move."

She looked up and straightened in the chair. Her gaze was locked on his face, which reminded him he was the only one in the room still naked. Her tense expression was a dead giveaway that the post-coital glow had dimmed.

He walked past her and, reaching into the drawer beneath the entertainment center, pulled out a pair of sweats, then stepped into them. "What's wrong, Court?"

"Nothing. I have to go."

"What's your hurry?"

"I need to get home. Janie—"

"Is spending the night with a friend," he reminded her.

"I guess I mentioned that." She twisted her fingers nervously.

"Yeah, you did. Which makes me wonder if there's something wrong."

"I just feel like I need to be home."

He folded his arms over his bare chest and had the satisfaction of watching her eyes darken as her gaze was drawn there. "So this isn't about running away."

"Of course not. I'm a responsible mother. Unlike my own," she added. "Scratch that. Ancient history."

"Right. A shrink could have a field day with that slip of the tongue."

David wasn't sure why he didn't just say adios, but something wouldn't let him back off. One minute Courtney was smiling, the next she was skidding straight into escape mode. What the hell had happened?

"What do you want me to say?" Courtney asked.

"We just had sex, and it was mind-blowingly good if I do say so myself. Now you're setting a land speed record for home and talking about your mother. What's up with that, Court?"

Her chin edged up, proud and independent. "I'm not like my mother."

"I never said you were."

"No, this is me saying I'm not like her. Trying to believe I'm not like her. This—" She swung out an arm, indicating the room, "This isn't like me at all. I don't sleep with men I've only known a short time."

He couldn't help thinking it had something to do with thanking him. She was strapped for cash and would be grateful to anyone who could do for her daughter what he could. It was an ugly thought and one he kept to himself.

Instead he asked, "Was that your mother's pattern?"

"She didn't stick around long enough for me to make inquiries." There was an edge of bitterness to her voice. "But in his drunken babbling, my father mentioned it a time or two."

"So why did you come here?" he asked.

"I wanted to ask you about the information on the Internet," she defended. "Because it didn't make sense that no one knew about your good deeds. I didn't come here to sleep with you."

"Do you mind if I ask why you did? Sleep with me, I mean."

"Bruised ego, doctor?" One corner of her full mouth curved up.

"Maybe. Mostly just curious. Why did you go to bed with me?"

Tension highlighted a haunted sort of pain in her eyes. "I thought I was going to die in that accident. When you go through something like that it changes you. Makes you painfully aware of regrets, the path not taken. You always believe there's time."

There was a lot of that going around. It had always been his intention to get in touch with his father and reconnect, put the past behind them. Now he never could. "Yeah. I know what you mean."

"I'm attracted to you." She laughed but it wasn't a carefree sound. "I guess I wanted to take the path. Just to see."

"And?"

"At the risk of resuscitating your ego—it was great." A blush put roses in her cheeks. "You already knew that."

"I sense a 'but' coming."

"It can't happen again," she said firmly.

"Because you're trying to live down your mother's reputation?"

"I'd like to avoid any comparison."

David wanted to wrap her in his arms, but for once listened to the warning that women in need were trouble. Besides, she looked brittle, as if she might shatter at the slightest touch. "Anyone can see you're an amazing mother. You don't have to prove anything to anyone."

"Except myself. I love my child more than anything in the world. And I'd do anything to protect her, keep her safe and not let her get hurt."

As she caught her top lip between her teeth, David saw the lingering effects of his kisses in her swollen lips. Her eyes were shadowed and her hair tousled from his running his fingers through it. His gut tightened in need and the intense reaction was as swift as it was unexpected. Moments ago he'd been so sure she was out of his system. Clearly he'd been wrong because he wanted her again. Which was exactly why he should let her go.

But he couldn't. She was carrying around a lot of baggage thanks to the men who should have taken care of her and lumping him in with the lowlifes. That bothered him.

"No one is disputing your devotion to Janie," he said.

"Good. Because she's my heart and that means she's at the heart of everything I do."

"So, even though she's not home and you have a cell phone in case she needs you, you feel required to be there?"

"I'm handling this badly." She shook her head. "I had a conversation with Janie just before she went to her friend's. She wanted to know if you have any kids."

"No."

"You're talking biological. The truth is you've got children all over the world. Every one you saved carries a part of you forever."

David was quiet for a moment. "I never thought about it like that."

"You should. Along with other things."

"Like what?" he asked.

"Like the fact that my daughter doesn't remember her father, so as far as she's concerned she's never had one. Until you."

"Me?" Like his wanting Courtney, that came out of nowhere. He'd gone from doctor to daddy?

She rubbed her temples and blew out a breath. "That didn't come out right. Since I'm not getting this accurate by beating around the bush in an attempt to be diplomatic, let me say it straight out. Janie wants a father. You're her hero for fixing her face and you pay attention to her. Everything she wants."

He ran his fingers through his hair. "Her standards aren't so high, are they?"

"What do you expect? She's six."

"I see what you mean. Do you want me to talk to her?" he suggested.

She shook her head. "Don't for one second think that I don't appreciate your kindness to my daughter. But I want you to stop spending time with her. David, we both know your life isn't here in Walnut River. We're adults. We understand the ramifications. But Janie doesn't. In her mind she's writing her own happily-ever-after where you chuck a lucrative medical practice and lavish lifestyle to stay here. If she gets too attached to you, it will break her heart when you go. I know what that feels like." She held up her hand. "I'm not an idiot with my head buried in the sand. I stopped doing that because it leaves other parts exposed, if you get my drift. I know sooner or later she'll be hurt—a crush that doesn't work out, misplaced trust in a friend. But this is one of the times I can do something to protect her. If I didn't, what kind of mother would I be?"

David didn't know what to say. He *was* leaving. There'd never been any question about that and he'd never deceived her. So why did he feel the urge to defend himself? Maybe because of all the men who came before him and crushed her dreams. He wanted her to know he wasn't like them. He wanted her in his bed with no promises, no strings attached, no regrets and no looking back. And if he said as much to her, she'd figure it was payback for his help. What he got out of it. His agenda. It was what he'd been after all along. So he said nothing.

As the silence stretched out, he watched Courtney's face and the expectant expression that faded to one of resignation followed swiftly by disappointment. It was as though the light went out of her. Her full mouth pulled into a straight line and she brushed past him to retrieve her coat from the doorknob.

"I'll just be going," she said.

"So this is all about protecting Janie?"

"Yes." She slid her arms into the sleeves.

He moved closer and lifted her hair free and over the collar, then pulled the sides together at her throat. "Are you sure?"

"What are you asking?"

"You're not running away to protect yourself?"

"I'm not saying you're right about that, but it makes good sense, given the fact that you didn't really try very hard to talk me out of it. Goodbye, David." She opened the door, then softly closed it behind her.

David blew out a long breath as he stared at where she'd been standing. For a small woman, she'd sure managed to fill up this room, and it felt pretty empty now.

He was going to try like hell not to see the biggest and most expensive room at the Walnut River Inn as a metaphor for his life.

At work bright and early Monday morning, Courtney breathed a sigh of relief that Janie had gone back to school. Soon the surgery on her face would be behind them and so would David. Something just this side of pain tightened in her chest. It had been her idea to put distance between them, but she found herself wishing that he'd tried harder to convince her she was wrong.

Probably she'd headed off trouble and that was a good thing. Slowly but surely things were getting back to normal. A vision of being in his arms flashed through her mind and she realized nothing would ever be normal again.

As soon as the thought was there, she shut it down. She'd lived in the moment. She'd wanted to be with him and couldn't make herself say no. Part of surviving an accident such as she'd had was a clearer, deeper appreciation of life. It was permission to live fully. No regrets. Probably. Maybe.

After counting out change for the cash register and making sure the shelves were neatly and fully stocked, promptly at 9:00 A.M. she unlocked and opened the gift-shop doors.

Behind the glass counter, she checked over her list of inventory and made notes for her monthly order. At ten she had an appointment with a woman who hand-crocheted baby blankets, afghans, hats and gloves, and who wanted to display her items in the shop. Courtney thought the idea had potential. She had the nurses on the floors let her know when a patient didn't get visitors and made it a point to send up a balloon bouquet or something cheery, and a cozy, handmade lap blanket could bring a bit of comfort and a sense of home. There was nothing happier than a baby being born and visitors were always looking for a special gift.

When she heard footsteps, she looked up. "Hi, Ella."

"Hi, yourself." The doctor was wearing blue scrubs under a white lab coat which meant a rotation in the E.R. today.

"How are you?"

"Never better."

Courtney figured as much. The woman still glowed so brightly she needed a lead shield for radioactive containment. "That's good to hear. What can I do for you?"

"I need a card," she said.

"All along that wall." Courtney pointed with her left hand. The green cast caught Ella's attention. "How's the wrist?"

"I'd say never better," she commented wryly, "but it was better before I broke it. Now I can tell you it doesn't hurt, but it itches like crazy."

Ella nodded with satisfaction. "As it should."

"We can put a man on the moon, float a space station and

send ships there to supply it. Wouldn't you think someone could invent a cast that doesn't itch?"

"Sometimes there's no substitute for the tried and true."

"If it ain't broke, don't fix it?" Courtney said smiling.

"Yeah." Ella stuck her hands in the pockets of her lab coat. "How's Janie doing?"

"Back to school."

"That's good news."

"Yeah." It meant she didn't have to see David when she got home from work. Janie had said she wanted to call his cell and invite him to dinner. Courtney had managed to talk her out of that with a lot of verbal tap dancing and a heart-felt plea to wait and see how she tolerated getting back into her regular routine. "I left instructions with the school staff that if she got too tired or complained of anything more than a hangnail, they should call me."

Ella nodded. "Kids are so resilient. They bounce back pretty quickly."

"Thank God."

"I'm sure you know this, Courtney, but the accident wasn't your fault."

David had told her the same thing. Thinking of him made her heart stutter and her stomach flutter. "I appreciate you saying that."

"I'm not patronizing you. The road was icy. You didn't do it on purpose, that's why they're called accidents. Otherwise they'd be known as deliberates."

Courtney smiled. What was it about the Wilder clan that could make her smile when it was the last thing she wanted to do? David did that to her all the time. He'd been a light in the darkness during this horrible time. Now she knew he was a light in the darkness for a lot of people all over the world. Now she knew he had no agenda for helping her except maybe personal demons of his own. Somehow that got to her more than his looks and personality. He wasn't perfect. It made him human. Like her.

"Thanks for saying that," she said.

Ella nodded. "It's the truth. Give yourself a break. Get off the guiltmobile."

"I'll try."

"Okay. I'm stopping the Ella Wilder lecture tour. At least long enough to pick out my card."

"Let me know if I can help you with anything."

"Will do."

Courtney looked down at her paperwork, but concentration was elusive. David's siblings both worked at Walnut River General, which meant that as long as she had a job here she was going to see them. Every time she did, she'd think of him. How could she help it? There was a resemblance in looks and personality. She'd have been better off not meeting David Wilder, but Janie wouldn't have. And so she bought a ticket for another ride on the guiltmobile.

Ella came to the counter and handed her several cards. "Thanks to the Internet, the fine art of note- and letter-writing is dying out. Because I'm busy like everyone else, this is my way of putting it on life support."

Courtney rang up the purchases, took Ella's twenty-dollar bill and handed her her change, then put the cards in a small plastic bag. "There you go."

"Thanks." She stuck the bag in her lab coat and started to turn away, then stopped. "I heard about David's trips to developing countries to help the children. You were the one who ratted him out to Peter."

"Yeah." Courtney's cheeks felt hot, as if she'd been caught doing a drive-by. In this technological age, the Internet was a way to cruise past the cute guy's house without getting caught peeking. Usually.

"I often think about David and wonder what he's up to,

but it never occurred to me to look him up on the Web." She frowned. "We were so close growing up, but everything changed after David went to college."

Courtney knew why, but it wasn't her place to say. She'd done enough meddling. If she'd minded her own business, she'd never have learned about his unselfish side. Ignorance of it would have kept her from going to see him, which would have kept her from…sleeping with him. Every time her mind turned a corner there was another memory to make her blush.

"Your brother is a very nice man," Courtney said.

"He is." One eyebrow rose in what looked very much like an aha expression. "So, the rumors are true."

"Rumors?" Courtney went still. "What would those be?"

"It's come to my attention that you and David are spending a lot of time together."

"A lot of time is probably an exaggeration. Because he's Janie's doctor we've seen him. And he offered to stay with her when I came back to work."

"I see."

"One good deed and all that. He stayed for dinner a few times." She shrugged. "But it's nothing personal."

Although sex was about as personal as you could get. But that was nothing more than a weak moment and wouldn't happen again. It was on the tip of her tongue to say so. Then she stopped herself. There was no reason to assure Ella that her intentions toward David were strictly honorable. She had no intentions toward the man.

Still, she tensed. Growing up she'd carried the label of the town drunk's daughter. She'd get glances that held everything from pity to distaste, as if she was not good enough, as if the disgrace of her family background was contagious or would rub off. It was a good thing she'd had school and work to keep her busy or she'd have had a lot of time to feel sorry for herself because no one would let their kids be her friend.

Going to college had been like wiping her slate clean. No one knew about her past until she'd trusted Joe enough to share it. He'd lulled her into a false sense of security, then pulled the rug out from under her when he'd brought her home to meet his folks. That had been a disaster and she'd kicked herself for letting her guard down. It wouldn't happen again.

"Nothing personal?" Ella studied her. "Then you have to tell me how you keep your skin so flawless."

Courtney blinked. "Excuse me?"

"Love is good for the complexion. Right? Yours is glowing—at least it is when you talk about David."

Ella had always been friendly, but Courtney still tensed, waiting for the warning to stay away from her brother. "There's really nothing between me and David."

"Well, darn." Ella sighed. "I was hoping there was something to talk about."

"You were?"

"Big-time. Tell me I'm a selfish witch, but if you and my brother hit it off, we might see more of him."

"His practice is in California."

"There is that. Still, he's drifting, I think. Something's missing in his life and when he decided to stay in Walnut River for a while, I'd hoped he'd find what he was looking for."

"Even if that was me?" Courtney blurted out. She wanted to call the words back but it was too late.

Ella smiled. "You're smart and beautiful. And yet I still like you."

"You do?"

"Why do you sound so surprised? Courtney, you're an inspiration. Single mom raising a terrific kid. I admire you tremendously."

"I—"

"Just say thank you," Ella advised.

"Thank you," Courtney answered automatically.

"I have to go back to work now. See you."

Courtney was too stunned by the words to answer. Dr. Ella Wilder admired her? That was amazing. She'd expected a different reaction. Because David's recent contact with the Albrights had triggered her defensiveness? Everyone else she'd met in Walnut River had accepted and supported her from day one.

That's when she realized that she owned this problem. It was all about attitude. She was so accustomed to being the girl from the wrong side of the tracks, she'd never let herself live on the right side.

She was a decent person trying to be the best person she could be, just like everyone else. The Albrights had rejected her, but that didn't mean she was lacking. It was their problem. And if David hadn't done what he'd done, she might never have seen the difference, had this aha moment.

It was another in a growing list of things to thank him for. Another in a long list of things that could keep him in her heart forever. Janie wasn't the only Albright woman who was falling under his spell.

And she couldn't let it happen.

Chapter Ten

With fifteen minutes to spare, David pulled into the parking lot at the Walnut River Elementary School. The facility was at least fifty years old but had been meticulously maintained. In the front, a flagpole stalwartly flew the Stars and Stripes. Bushes were neatly trimmed and mature maples and sycamores separated the school from Concord Avenue.

He chirped the Beamer's locks, then walked up the familiar path past the administration offices and buildings that housed the upper grades. The primary classes were the farthest from the outside world—whether to protect the most vulnerable or give them fewer distractions, he didn't know.

What he did know was that his chest tightened because it all looked just the same. Janie's first-grade classroom was the exact one he'd gone to.

He stood in the doorway and glanced around. People were just starting to arrive. Instead of the individual desk he'd used there were tables neatly marching the length of the room with two tiny chairs at each. Crayoned and painted artwork was tacked up on boards and strung around the room. The smell of paint and chalk unleashed a flood of memories. Most of them bad. Disappointment was right there at the top of the list. And, although he was pretty sure Courtney would have an issue, he was here because he wouldn't be responsible for a little girl's bad memory.

A woman he assumed was the teacher stood in the front of the room by an adult-sized desk, although she looked small enough to use the kids'. She was giving him a thorough scrutiny and didn't look reassured.

He navigated his way through pint-sized furniture and headed straight for her. "Hi. I should probably introduce myself since I'm crashing this awards ceremony. I'm David Wilder."

"Dr. Wilder." She smiled and the warmth made her look less like the Wicked Witch of the East and more like a kindly fairy godmother. "I'm Carol Hart, Janie's teacher. She's told me all about you."

"Should I be afraid?"

She laughed. "No. It was all good. There's a little hero-worship going on, I think."

"She's a terrific kid."

"Indeed she is. Welcome. It's very nice of you to come."

"She's getting an award. I wouldn't miss it."

She looked past him, then met his gaze. "If you'll excuse me—"

"Of course."

Looking around he noticed the desks had names printed on poster board folded over so it would stand. He found Janie's in the last row. Her seat buddy was Melanie Kier. Probably the friend she'd been visiting the night Courtney had come to see him. He hadn't deliberately kept his humanitarian endeavors a secret, but didn't see any reason to make a big deal out of it. Except, if he'd known Courtney would look at him as though he'd hung the moon, he'd have said something sooner.

Because that was maybe the best and worst night he could remember in a long time. Having her in his arms had been twice as sweet as he'd thought it would be, and he'd imagined it would be pretty sweet. Then she'd gone Jekyll and Hyde on him. One minute warm and soft, the next cool and tough. Warning him against spending too much time with her child because Janie saw him as a substitute father and would be hurt when he went back to his life.

Was it only three days ago? Seemed longer, much longer. He'd liked seeing Courtney every day and spending time with Janie. Maybe coming here was an excuse to see Court. Maybe he was selfish. It wouldn't be the first time and he was paying for that. But this was about a promise and he intended to keep it.

As the hands on the clock closed in on seven, the room filled up with adults and children and the noise level rose accordingly. That didn't drown out Janie's voice when she spotted him.

"Dr. David!"

"Hi, kiddo." He squatted down and she threw her arms around him, her cast scraping his neck.

"You came." The bandage still covered half her face, but the other half was all smiles. "I wasn't sure you would."

"I'm happy to be invited," he said. "It's not every day you get a student-of-the month award."

Courtney put a hand on her daughter's shoulder. "David, I didn't know you'd be here."

"I forgot to tell you. I asked him to come, Mommy." Janie left one arm on his shoulder. "Mrs. Hart said I could."

David stood. "I met your teacher. She's very nice."

"Yes, she is." Courtney's tone was cool, but the pulse at the base of her throat was jumping like crazy.

Janie tugged on his hand. "I have to go, Mommy. I have to sit by Mrs. Hart to get my award."

"Okay, sweetie. I'll be right here. I've got the camera," Courtney said, holding it up.

A few minutes later Mrs. Hart asked for everyone's attention and began the ceremony. There were scholastic achievement medals, citizenship awards and then the all-around student of the month. When Courtney tried to manage the digital camera with one good hand, he took it from her.

"I can do it," she protested.

"I can do it better." He looked down at her. "Height and dexterity."

"Thanks. I appreciate that."

Maybe. But she wasn't happy about him being here. He did his best to ignore the chill as he took pictures and did his level best to get most of them from Janie's good side. When the awards were over, everyone was invited to stay for cookies and juice. Janie was busy visiting with her friends.

Courtney took her camera back and stashed it in her purse. "May I speak to you outside?"

"Sure."

He followed her and they stopped several feet from the door, by an overhang support. An outside light on the wall beside the classroom emphasized the tension in her face. "What's up?"

"I think you know."

"Okay. Yeah. In my defense I have to say that Janie invited me."

"And I explained that spending time with her could generate expectations that you're not prepared or in a position to meet."

"I understand. But I promised her before you made your little speech. Promises trump ultimatums."

"David, I'm not ungrateful for your time. And Janie is beyond excited that you're here. But what about the next time there's an event in her life and you're on the other side of the country? This is just the sort of thing I meant about not getting attached."

"I'll explain—"

"She doesn't really understand anything except that she's getting used to having you around. After her surgery you'll be gone. How is she going to feel then? I'm trying to protect her."

"Me too. Because I showed up she'll remember that I didn't lie to her."

"David, I just don't want her to be let down."

"Neither do I. If anyone knows disappointment, it's me," he said, surprised at the welling of anger and resentment in his voice.

Courtney's eyes widened. "What happened? Who lied to you?" she asked gently.

He let out a long breath as he looked around. "I went to school here. Feels like a million years ago."

"With the dinosaurs. Must have been exciting. You're lucky they didn't have you for lunch," she teased.

"I was pretty fast. They couldn't catch me." Then he turned serious again. "But for everything else, I couldn't catch a break."

"What do you mean?" She folded her arms over her chest. "You've got it all."

"Now. Not then. This was where I learned that bad behavior got my father's attention."

"I don't understand. James Wilder was incredibly generous with his time and interest. He was caring to Janie and me when I was a stranger and didn't know anyone. Why would you, his own son, have to act out for him to notice you?"

"I sound like a spoiled brat, don't I?" He met her gaze. "Now that I'm an adult, and a doctor, I get that he was a busy man. My inner child is okay with that part."

"Then what part is still bugging your inner spoiled brat?"

"The part where he promised to show up for a school function or a soccer or football game and didn't. The part where he put everything and everyone else in the family on hold for Anna."

"Your sister?"

"*Adopted* sister."

"That shouldn't matter."

"It wouldn't," he protested. "If the sacrifice had made a difference. But she's deliberately put distance between herself and the rest of the family. It sounds stupid to say *repay*, no one expects payback for giving her a home. But to turn her back is a slap in the face when Dad bent over backwards at the expense of the rest of his family to make her feel like a Wilder. There are obligations."

"You're not walking in her shoes, David."

He frowned. "What does that mean?"

"Maybe she has a good reason for her behavior. When you had a falling-out with your father, I'm guessing you felt justified in turning your back." When he opened his mouth, she said, "Don't try to tell me you didn't do that. You had a choice. You could have blinked first and contacted him."

She was right. He knew that. Finding a way to live with that regret wouldn't be easy. "What's your point?"

She put her hand on his sleeve. "I'm not trying to hurt you, David. Truly I'm not. Just playing devil's advocate. I'm just pointing out that we all do what we think is best at the time. My father was drinking himself to death and I stayed because he was family and I was obligated. Was it best for me?" She sighed. "Probably not. You struck out on your own and made something remarkable out of your life and career."

"Is that a compliment, Mrs. Albright?"

"Not for you. It's for your inner child. He's got issues." The corners of her mouth turned up. "My point is that we shouldn't judge someone without hearing their side of the story. Maybe Anna is choosing to exercise her free choice and is waiting until she feels sure of herself before committing to the Wilder clan."

"Maybe." He wasn't so sure, but he didn't want her to take her hand off his arm and challenging her would do that. "I didn't mean to go Psych 101 on you."

"It's okay. Nice to know Dr. Perfect has flaws."

"More than you know. But breaking promises isn't one of them." He put his hand over hers. "I never meant to upset you, Court. That's the last thing I'd do."

"I know."

"And my only intention tonight was to give Janie a good memory."

"Thanks for that. It means a lot to her." Courtney's voice thickened with emotion. "We should go back inside. She'll be wondering where we are."

David didn't really know where he was. It was absolutely true that he'd come tonight because of his promise. But if he was being honest with himself, it was all about Courtney. She was constantly on his mind, no matter how hard he fought against it. And now… Looking at her…

In his bed she was pretty memorable. By moonlight she took his breath away. That was bad on more levels than he could count and he could count really high.

"Mommy, I can't sleep."

Courtney glanced up from the computer where she'd just started working on an assignment for her online class. Janie stood in the doorway to the hall.

"Janie, you only went to bed five minutes ago."

"That's a long time."

"Maybe for you, but not for me." Courtney got up and squatted in front of her. "Is anything bothering you?"

The little girl's small fingers plucked at her pink flannel nightgown. "I was thinking about my daddy."

Courtney held in a groan. "Do you want to talk about it?"

She wanted to groan again when Janie nodded. As much as she would have preferred to blow it off and pretend the man had never existed, that wasn't a good idea. It had all the makings of a bad session with Dr. Phil. Janie needed to express her feelings, so that's what they'd do.

"Okay."

"Hot chocolate might help me talk. And sleep," she added.

Courtney suppressed a smile. "Coming right up."

After putting cocoa and milk in two mugs, followed by just the right amount of nuking, the two of them sat side by side on the sofa.

"So what's keeping you awake, baby?"

Janie took a sip. "I was just thinkin'. About my daddy."

"I see." Damn. Damn. Damn. "What about him?"

"Just that I don't 'member much. Can you tell me stuff? About what he was like?"

"He was handsome." Many women had thought so. They'd flirted openly with him and he'd returned the favor. More often than not it didn't stop there.

"What else?"

"He was smart." Smart enough to not get caught when he didn't stop there. Until that last time.

"What did he do in the army?"

Courtney wasn't sure. Their communication had been almost nonexistent after he'd suddenly gone into the army. Because he hadn't discussed the decision, it should have been a clue that they had no relationship. But she was too dense to get the message. She couldn't tell Janie any of that.

"Your father worked hard to make America a safe place for you to grow up."

"Because he loved me?"

"Very much." She hoped that wasn't a lie, but Joe hadn't done much to show whether or not he cared.

"And he loved you."

Fortunately that was stated as a fact and not a question because Courtney's only truthful answer could be that Joe never really loved anyone but himself. Wasn't it supposed to be the good stuff you remembered when someone you'd shared so much with was gone? When she looked back, all she recalled was self-indulgence and manipulation. Even now the hurt lengthened and stretched until it filled every crack in her soul.

She'd shared more with David than she ever had with the man she'd married. The man who had fathered her child. She'd been angry earlier tonight when she'd seen David in Janie's class-room. Angry that he'd ignored her request to keep his distance, but mostly she'd been irritated with herself. Her reaction to seeing him there had been an instantaneous, involuntary spurt of sheer joy that scared the living daylights out of her.

If only she could think of him as the shallow-as-a-cookie-sheet plastic surgeon she'd first believed him to be. But her own snooping had backfired on her. David Wilder was not just a pretty face, there was depth and substance there, too. He'd taken care of her child. He cared about people and actually did something positive because of it. He used his powers for good all over the world.

And the man had a killer sense of humor. If he'd been a toad who had to wear a bag over his head the wit and charm would still have attracted her. She'd known David only a short time, yet a substantial collection of warm memories would remain when he was gone.

How could she sustain a level of anger enough to keep her feelings for him in line? How could she possibly stay mad at a man whose only thought tonight had been to give her baby girl a good memory?

"Melanie thinks Dr. David is a hottie," Janie said.

"Where did Mel hear that kind of language?"

"From her older sister."

"God, help us," Courtney mumbled.

"What?"

"Nothing. Go on."

"Do you think Dr. David is a hottie?"

An honest, straightforward answer to that question could be an entrance exam for admittance to the diplomatic corps. "I think David is very nice-looking."

"Is he your boyfriend?"

"I consider him a friend." A friend with benefits. At least that one time. "And he's a boy." A man, actually, with magic hands that could heal as well as take her to heights she'd never reached before. *Hottie* was definitely the word to describe David.

"Mo-om."

"What?"

Janie finished her hot chocolate, then scooted forward and set the empty cup on the coffee table.

As she looked at her own cast, it crossed Courtney's mind that the two of them were adapting to life with limitations. Probably because they'd had a lot of practice adapting to everything life could throw at them.

"Are you and Dr. David going out?"

Courtney knew what this meant. Some of the nurses with children a little older than Janie joked that their kids were "going out" but never actually went anywhere. They were talking crushes and attraction. She was attracted and would probably get crushed. So how did she answer truthfully?

"David and I have spent a little time together."

"It was a yes-or-no question, Mommy."

Courtney looked down at her child. "Who are you? Perry Mason?"

"Who's that?"

"A famous TV lawyer." She shook her head. "Maybe you should think about law as a career choice when you grow up."

"You're changing the subject," Janie pointed out.

"Yes, I am. Go with it."

"I think Dr. David loves me."

"I'm sure he does, sweetheart." She kissed the top of her daughter's head and snuggled her close. "When you're not grilling me like raw hamburger you're a pretty easy kid to love."

"Mom, I think Dr. David loves you, too."

That was a stunner and made her heart skip a beat or two. "You do? Why?"

"I don't know," she said, shrugging. "I just think he does."

"We've talked about this, sweetie."

Janie sighed. "I know he doesn't live here in Walnut River."

"That's right," Courtney agreed. "He works all the way across the country in California."

"That doesn't mean he can't love us."

"You're right about that."

Though it *would* rule out the traditional family that her little girl was hinting at. Right then and there Courtney's heart shuddered and cracked. She tried so hard to be both mother and father to her child, to give her everything. She still struggled with guilt about the accident and didn't think she'd ever be able to forget the horrific sound of Janie's screams followed by the sound of grinding metal and shattering glass.

There would be financial fallout from the crash that worried her. But this conversation worried her *and* broke her heart. She'd always thought her biggest problem was a tight budget. That was nothing compared to not being able to give her daughter what she wanted most and money couldn't buy: a father, a family.

Courtney couldn't fault her daughter's taste in men. David

would be a fabulous father. And husband? As her one and
only attempt had gone horribly wrong, Courtney felt her
taste, not to mention her judgment, was questionable at best.
Clearly Janie's instincts were better, even though her match-
making efforts were doomed to failure. Courtney had no illusions that she and David would work out.

Janie frowned. "You got quiet, Mommy. What's wrong?"

"Nothing, sweetie."

"Do you think Dr. David loves you?"

"No."

Make that no way he'd be attracted to someone like her.
He'd been linked to some of the world's most beautiful and
sophisticated women. Courtney couldn't compete with that
even if she wanted to. Which she didn't. The only way to win
was not to play.

"I think you're wrong," Janie said on a big yawn.

There was nothing she could say to that because a part of
her couldn't help hoping she was wrong, too.

"Come on, little bit, you can't fall asleep here because I
don't think I can carry you into bed."

David could. If he was here. The traitorous thought made
her just as hopelessly romantic as her daughter. Apparently
it was true that the fruit didn't fall far from the tree.

She walked Janie down the hall and tucked her into her
impossibly pink bed. Courtney was so tired she wanted to
crawl in with her and curl up. It would be a couple of more
weeks before Janie's surgery. A couple of more weeks with
the potential for a David sighting. More possibilities for her
to slide farther down that slippery slope.

Janie was already crushing on him big-time and Courtney
wasn't far behind. But one of them had to stay strong enough
to get them through when he was gone.

Since Courtney was the grown-up, it was up to her not to
fall in love with him.

Chapter Eleven

Courtney was just about to enjoy a cup of tea and fifteen minutes of quiet before Janie came home from her friend's house when there was a knock on the door. She set her steaming mug on the coffee table and went to check. It wasn't often unexpected visitors dropped by and she couldn't help hoping it was David. That night at the school he'd revealed another layer of vulnerability that somehow hiked up the attraction factor for her. As soon as the thought was there she pushed it away. That was dangerous thinking. That was a recipe for disaster.

She peeked through the peephole. That recipe for disaster would be a thousand times better than this; even with the eyepiece distortion she recognized the Albrights. In her opinion, the peephole view was an improvement.

Letting out a long breath, she leaned back against the door and wondered if the fates had it in for her. Between the accident, her and Janie recovering and trying not to make a fool of herself over Dr. Hottie, wasn't life giving her enough challenges? Did karma really feel it necessary to make her face the in-laws who believed she was the spawn of Satan?

It was easier to believe they were the ones with the problem when she didn't have to talk to them. This was all David's fault. Why couldn't he leave well enough alone?

There was another knock and she figured it would be better to get this over with so they'd be gone by the time Janie got home.

She twisted the lock and opened the door and looked from one to the other while her hands shook. "Mrs. Albright. Mr. Albright. This is a surprise."

"Hello, Courtney." Mrs. Albright held herself stiffly and not because of the chilly weather. "We heard about the accident. You're looking well."

"I'm feeling fine. Thanks for asking."

"And...Janie?" Morris asked.

Was there censure in his voice or was her own guilt putting it there? "She's doing remarkably well."

Her mother-in-law unbuttoned her camel-colored cashmere coat. "May we see her?"

"She's at a friend's house."

"I'm sorry to hear that."

The older woman was dressed in a black sweater and co-ordinating slacks. Courtney had a pretty good idea that the cost of the outfit would supply them with groceries for a month. Or more. This was really awkward and she figured the visit meant only bad stuff. It was on the tip of her tongue to suggest they leave.

Mr. Albright mopped his forehead with a pristine white handkerchief. "May we come in for a moment?"

She'd rather poke herself in the eye with a stick, but what was she supposed to say? "I'm sorry. Of course. Please come in." When the door was closed behind them, she asked politely, "May I take your coats?"

"Thank you." The older man slipped off his overcoat and took his wife's before handing them over.

Courtney hung them on the coat tree beside the door. "Won't you sit down?" She turned back and noticed her mug. "I was just going to have some tea. Would you care for some?"

"No. Thank you," Mrs. Albright answered.

They sat side by side on her home-covered sofa. Reading between the lines of their rigid body language she figured they were thinking this place was tacky times ten. She might not have a lot of money but she had buckets of pride. The rent was paid, there was food on the table and her little girl would never go without while Courtney had breath in her body.

"Charming place." Mrs. Albright's voice was clipped.

"Thanks. We like it."

Mr. Albright drew in a deep breath. "Lots of stairs."

"We like those, too." No matter how hard she tried, she couldn't seem to lose the defensive tone. Why didn't they just go?

The two looked at each other and the starch seemed to go out of them. Mrs. Albright met her gaze. "We came to apologize to you, Courtney."

"What?" The defensiveness wavered. It was hard to maintain defenses when the breath was knocked out of you.

"We misjudged you," Mr. Albright said.

"Our son did not grow into the man we'd have preferred him to be," his wife interjected diplomatically. "He tried numerous times and various schemes to extract money from us. Sadly, it worked most of the time. Not that we were stupid. We simply held out hope that he would change."

"He never did," the older man said. "The time came when we were forced to cut him off."

Not unlike what David's father had done, she thought. But in his case, the strategy was an unqualified success. Not for Joe.

"What do they call that these days? Tough love," the older man answered his own question.

"Tough on whom?" his wife said wryly. "I think it hurt us more than him. Especially in the long run."

"I don't understand." Courtney sat in the secondhand chair across from them.

Joe's mother twisted her fingers together in her lap. "We assumed that when our son came to us with the story of you being pregnant that it was another ploy for money. We had doubts that there was a baby. Even after she was born, we weren't convinced that—"

"She was Joe's?"

"Yes. And then we heard you'd named her Jane." Her eyes closed for a moment as she sighed. "We hardened ourselves to the probability that any young woman who would associate with our son was unsavory and disreputable."

"Ten-dollar words for *sleazy tramp*," Courtney commented.

Mrs. Albright winced. "We're not trying to hurt you, Courtney. Quite the contrary. We were wrong about you."

"James tried to make us see," her husband added.

"David's father?"

"Yes." The older man leaned back. "He'd gotten to know you, taken a liking to you, got you a job in the gift shop. Watched Janie grow up," he said wistfully.

"He was a good man." Courtney's chest felt tight. "I think about him a lot."

"As do we." Mrs. Albright said the words and her husband nodded sadly. "David is very much like his father," she added.

"Yes." A good man. The knot in Courtney's chest pulled a little tighter.

"He forced us to face the truth." Mrs. Albright met her gaze. "That Janie *is* our granddaughter. If you can forgive us, we would very much like the opportunity to get to know her."

"I—"

Just then the phone rang and Courtney was grateful for the distraction. She walked to the kitchen counter and answered it, hearing the crackle of a cell phone. "Hello?"

"Hi, Court. It's Susan Kier. I'm parked out front and I'm watching Janie walk to the door. She's on her way up."

"Thanks, Susan. I appreciate it."

"I'll see you tomorrow at the hospital."

"Sounds good. Next time it's my turn to keep the girls."

"You're on. Bye."

"Bye."

She looked back at the older couple. Minutes ago she'd wanted them gone before Janie got home. Now…

"Janie's on her way up. Excuse me a moment. I'm going to watch for her in the hall."

She walked out, leaving the door open, and listened to the sound of her daughter's steps on the stairs. When she appeared at the bottom of the last flight, Courtney smiled. "Hi, sweetie."

"Hi, Mommy. Mel and I baked cookies."

"All by yourself?"

"Her mom wouldn't let us. But we got to stir in chocolate chips and mix up the dough. And put it on the baking sheet."

"Did you eat any?"

"Yes. They were really good." Janie climbed the last stair and opened her arms for a hug.

"I'm glad you had a good time." Courtney gathered her closer than usual. She took a deep breath and said, "There's someone here to see you."

"There is?" Janie looked first excited, then confused. "Who?"

They walked inside and Janie stepped a little closer to Courtney's side when she spotted the older couple. "Janie, this is Mr. and Mrs. Albright."

"They have the same last name as me." She glanced up questioningly.

"They're your daddy's mother and father."

"They are?" Janie looked back at the sofa, her one visible eye wide.

"I see what David meant." Elizabeth Albright studied the little girl before she stood and moved in front of them.

"Do you know Dr. David?"

"I do indeed." She crouched down to little-girl level and at her age that couldn't be easy. That got her some positive points. "That's quite a boo-boo on your face."

"Dr. David's going to make me like I was before. Except for the dimple. But he said that will make me look mys— mystery— What's that word, Mommy?"

"Mysterious?" Courtney suggested.

"Yeah."

"Then I'm sure you'll be good as new," Mrs. Albright said. "But you're quite beautiful just as you are."

"That's what Dr. David told me, too."

The older woman stared in awe for several moments, then said, "This is your grandfather, and I'm your grandmother, Jane."

Janie looked up uncertainly, then back at the older woman. "It's nice to meet you."

"I'm very happy to meet you."

Janie glanced up doubtfully, then said, "Do you want to see my room?"

"I'd love to. But first I'd like to speak with your mother for a moment. Why don't you show your grandfather?"

"Okay." She walked over to the couch and said, "Want to see my room?"

"It would be my pleasure. But first I have to get up. I'm old," he said with a wink.

Courtney couldn't believe it. Crusty Morris Albright had winked at his granddaughter. Points to him for that. Next thing you knew lightning would strike.

Janie held out her small hand to him. "I could help you."

He took it and pretended to let her assist him to his feet. There was a suspicious thickness in his voice when he said, "Thank you. I needed that."

When they were alone, Courtney said, "I meant no disrespect in naming my little girl after—"

"—*my* little girl?"

"Yes. When I first met Joe, he talked about his sister. He seemed so caring and I fell hard and fast."

"Seemed caring?" The other woman nodded knowingly. "I suspect my son inflicted numerous emotional wounds and I appreciate the fact that you didn't rush to articulate them all."

"There's no reason to pile on," she said, remembering her complete humiliation and distress at learning Joe had really joined the military to run away from the responsibility of being a husband and father. There was no point in adding to his mother's grief. "And it serves no purpose to speak ill of the dead. Janie will only ever know that her father was a hero who died in the service of his country."

"That's very generous of you, Courtney."

"No. I'd do anything to protect my little girl."

"Then we have something in common," Mrs. Albright said. "Because I'd do anything to protect your little girl, too."

Emotion squeezed Courtney's throat as moisture filled her eyes. The surprise wasn't that Elizabeth Albright had made her cry, but the fact that she'd acknowledged Janie was family. "I appreciate that," she finally said.

Janie came running from the other room with Mr. Albright behind her. "Mommy, he—" She stopped and looked up. "What should I call you?"

"*Grandpa* has a nice ring to it," he said, looking at Courtney. She nodded and blinked rapidly.

"Then, by default, I'd be *Grandma*," Mrs. Albright said.

Janie frowned. "Whose fault?"

Everyone laughed.

"Never mind, sweetie."

"Can Grandma and Grandpa stay for dinner?" she asked.

"Of course. But are you hungry after all those cookies?"

Janie nodded enthusiastically. "Grandpa is going to play dolls with me."

"Are you sure?" she asked him.

"I've got a few years to make up for," he said, before being willingly dragged back down the hall.

"And I'd be pleased if you'd call me Elizabeth."

"It would be my pleasure," Courtney said sincerely.

The older woman drew in a shuddering breath before saying, "I'm glad you named her after Jane. It's fitting. That little girl is like a ray of sunshine from heaven. Thank you, Courtney for not throwing us out when you had every right to."

"How could I? You've given my child a gift. She has grandparents. How cool is that?"

"Very cool, indeed."

When Elizabeth leaned over and pulled her into a hug, Courtney felt every last trace of resentment slip away. David was right. The Albrights *were* good and decent people. And though Joe hadn't left Janie any money, he'd left her something money couldn't buy. A family.

Thanks to David, she was able to cash in on that. Courtney realized her debt to Dr. Hottie was mounting daily. And the days until he was gone were flying by.

As David climbed the three flights of stairs to Courtney's apartment, his respect and admiration for her soared while he pictured her lugging in groceries on a regular basis. If she and Janie weren't home, this cardiovascular workout would be for nothing. The target date for the little girl's surgery was fast approaching and he needed to check her out and see if there were any setbacks or contraindications to the procedure now.

He was here because of Janie, he told himself. And if he actually swallowed that line, there was probably beach-front property in Arizona someone would be more than happy to sell him.

On the landing in front of apartment 3, he blew out a long breath and let his heart rate return to normal. When he knocked and Courtney answered, the sight of her convinced him there was no such thing as a normal heart rate when he was near her.

"Hi," he said.

"Hi." There was surprise on her face. Also shadows in her eyes—and they were swollen and red.

Didn't take a rocket scientist to know she'd been crying. "What's wrong?"

"Would you believe nothing?"

"No." But he respected the fact she'd tried.

She blew out a long breath. "I got the insurance check today."

"That's good."

"Yeah. I can put a down payment on a skateboard."

"Court, can I—"

"I'm just feeling sorry for myself. The first of the month is looming and it seems like everything's due. I just worry." She shrugged. "And Janie's surgery is coming up. And I have to buy a car to replace the broken one. Don't mind me." She brushed the back of her hand over her cheek. "But you didn't stop by to hear me moan." She stared at him. "Why did you stop by?"

"House call. Take a look at Janie's face to see how the swelling looks."

Courtney leaned against the doorjamb. "That's very nice of you. But I'm sorry you came all this way, because she's not here at the moment."

He looked at his watch. It was after supper and time to be settling in for the evening, even if it was Friday night. "It's Friday night. Does she have a hot date?"

"Kind of."

"Oh?"

"Her grandparents stopped by yesterday."

"The Albrights?"

"Since there aren't any on my side of the family, those would be the ones." A small smile tugged at the corners of her lips. "You were right."

"Words to warm a man's heart. About what?"

"About them. They're very nice people. She's spending the night with them."

"Care to tell me how all this came about?"

It would sound as pathetic as it felt, but he wanted very much for her to invite him in. Another night alone at the Walnut River Inn was about as appealing as walking naked in a hail storm.

Courtney hesitated, and he held his breath. She was good at talking tough, but not so much at hiding her feelings. Conflict swirled in the depths of her huge brown eyes, churning up flecks of gold and green. Sensuality radiated from her like sound waves and need rolled through him as relentlessly as a line of thunderstorms pushing through tornado alley. Tucking a strand of hair behind her ear and chewing on her lip made her probably the sexiest thing he'd ever seen.

He'd dated models, actresses and TV personalities—all beautiful women. But there was so much more to Courtney than her looks. She had substance and a spine of steel. She was creative and loving and fiercely protective. And he'd never wanted anything more than an invitation to spend some time with her.

Finally, she stepped back and opened the door wider. "Come in. Would you like some coffee?"

"I don't want you to go to any trouble."

Her look was wry as she filled the coffeemaker with grounds and water, then flipped the on switch. "It would be easier to list the things I don't need to thank you for. Janie is over the moon about having a grandma and grandpa. They stopped by because of you. Because of whatever you said to them."

A few minutes later the coffee was made, and she poured two mugs that he carried into the living room. She sat on the sofa and David sat down beside her. When she angled her body sideways and tucked a foot beneath her, her knee grazed his thigh and set off sparks like a falling log on a campfire. He'd really wanted to see Janie, but he was far happier than he should be that he was alone with her mom.

"Thanks for the coffee."

She took the mug he held out. "It's the least I can do to show my appreciation."

"For what?"

He blew on his own. "I didn't do anything but give the Albrights something to think about."

"They apologized for misjudging me and admitted that in their eyes I was guilty by association with Joe. They're painfully aware that he had flaws and believed any woman who was with him had the same flaws."

"I see. What did you say?"

"That Janie would only know that her father was a hero." Her eyes were bleak when they locked with his. "I hate lying to her. Isn't a lie to protect her better than the awful truth?"

"For sure when she's little. I guess that's something you'll have to decide on a case-by-case basis as she gets older."

She took a sip of her coffee, then set it beside his on the table in front of them. "You mean if she's in danger of making the same mistake I did, I can hold myself up as a horrible warning."

"That's not exactly what I said."

"It's true, though." She wrapped her arms around her waist. "He definitely wasn't the poster boy for self-sacrifice. When I got pregnant, I thought he loved me because he insisted we get married. The truth is that he wanted to use me and his child to get money out of his parents."

Anger hummed through David and he struggled to remain expressionless. This was Courtney's story to tell and get off her chest. She didn't need his emotions getting in the way.

"At that point they were on to him," he pointed out.

"Yeah." She smiled without humor. "As hard as that was on me, I'm glad they didn't let him use them. Instead he used Uncle Sam."

"How so?"

"He didn't finish college and without skills he couldn't make a living. So he decided to join the army and see the world."

"The armed forces expect something out of their recruits."

"True. And he performed as needed. Putting on an act was as easy for him as breathing. Basic training and various assignments gave him an excuse to be away from me. The old ball and chain."

"Courtney, I'm sure—"

She held up a hand. "Don't say it. He never cared for me or his daughter. I'm not really sure why he didn't file for divorce, except that maybe he held out hope that his parents would come to their senses and cough up something for their granddaughter. He joined the army because he didn't want marriage or responsibility. He wanted to do what he wanted to do. He wanted freedom and women, and being stationed all over the country gave him exactly that—being away from me."

Joe Albright was a cold-hearted son of a bitch, David thought. He got lucky and found Courtney, had a beautiful little girl and walked away from it for the illusion of freedom. What really burned him up was that everyone believed the man a hero when he was nothing but selfish and self-centered.

"For what it's worth," he said, "I think this is one time when perpetuating the lie is the right thing."

"I'm not taking the easy way out for me," she protested. "I don't care for myself. It's hard on Janie. She doesn't understand why she never knew her father—" A sob choked off her words.

Courtney's tear-filled gaze met his own as moisture gathered in her eyes, then spilled over and trickled down her cheeks. "Oh, God. I'm sorry."

She scooted forward and started to stand. He put his hand on her arm. "Don't be sorry. There's no reason to apologize."

"The last thing you need is a weepy female. It's just—" The tears kept coming. "I didn't mean to say anything. It's just that I—I've been holding it in for so long."

She angled her body away and put her hands over her face. Instinct to comfort made David slide a forearm beneath her knees and one behind her back, then lift her into his lap and fold her in his arms. Curling against him, she shook with the weeping, deep wrenching sobs tore up from inside her. All he could do was hold her and be angry that she'd been used so badly. He tightened his arms around her because it was either that or put his fist through the wall. He wanted to hurt the man who'd hurt her, but doing damage to a ghost wasn't possible.

Finally, the emotional storm weakened and she sniffled. "I messed up your sweater."

"It'll dry," he said.

"I'll have it cleaned." She pulled back and the barest trace of humor sparkled in her red, swollen eyes. "Snot doesn't dry without leaving marks."

He laughed. "If it will make you feel better."

"It will. That and—" She ran a finger over his chest. "Thanks for—listening."

"My pleasure."

Her gaze locked with his and something electric arced between them. Something that said she wasn't vulnerable now.

David's body tightened with need, but he had a feeling this was more than just the physical release they could find in each other. He'd lived with a faint, hollow feeling in his gut for a very long time. It only went away when he was with Courtney. He wasn't about to make any promises based on this, but he knew for sure he'd regret it forever if he didn't kiss the living daylights out of her in the next second.

David touched his mouth to hers and sighed with satisfaction. Then she slid her hands over his chest and locked them around his neck, pressing herself fully against him as she nibbled small kisses over his lips. The banked fire inside him burst into flame and his heart went from zero to off the charts in three seconds flat. At this moment he couldn't care about right or wrong, and especially not the future.

There was only him, her and now.

Chapter Twelve

The second Courtney knew David intended to kiss her, every vow, every lecture, every warning she'd given herself about resisting him melted away. The why was a mystery to her, but this man—this sexy, handsome, successful, caring man—wanted her. Loneliness fell away and that felt so darn good. How was she supposed to stand firm against that?

Easy. She couldn't.

David took charge and settled his lips on hers, sending a delicious ache straight down the center of her body. He gently rubbed his hands down her back, over her arms even as he kept kissing her, demanding, making her want to give more. When he slid his warm palm beneath her sweatshirt and settled it on her bare skin, her breath caught.

He stopped and said against her mouth, "Is my hand cold?"

"Hardly. It's perfect. The healing touch."

"It's not healing that's on my mind."

"Or mine," she agreed.

He tucked her hair behind her ear, then rubbed a strand between two fingers. "Your hair is like silk."

The compliment produced a fast and furious jolt of pure lust. "Glad you like it."

"And your eyes." He stared directly into them. "Big, brown eyes. Warm. Soft."

She blinked at him. "Thank you, kind sir."

He grinned, then kissed the tip of her nose. "Cute. Saucy." He nipped her chin. "Stubborn."

"Flattery like that will turn my head," she said breathlessly.

After taking her earlobe gently in his teeth and nipping, he trailed his tongue down her neck, then blew softly on the wet skin in that oh-so-sensitive place. Her pulse instantly spiked and blood pounded in her ears.

And she desperately wanted to return the favor. She settled herself in his lap, straddling him, her legs on either side of his thighs. Resting her cast on his shoulder for balance, she traced a finger down one side of his neck while she nibbled kisses on the other side. His sharp intake of breath, along with little involuntary jumps of his muscles whenever she touched him, made her smile. It was incredibly arousing and she needed to feel her hands on his skin.

Leaning back, she took the bottom of his sweater and tugged up. He lifted his arms, eager to cooperate, and she pulled it off, tossed it aside. Then she went to work on the buttons of his long-sleeved white shirt. One by one she undid them, feeling her anticipation build as she watched the smoky look in his eyes simmer into a slow burn. She finished and pulled the shirt from the waistband of his jeans, then spread it wide and flattened her palm against his chest. His breathing grew more unsteady.

"You're playing with fire," he said, his voice husky with banked passion.

"It's been a long winter. I'm tired of being cold."

"I know just how to warm you up."

Without further warning, he pulled her sweatshirt up and over her head. After gently easing it off her left arm, he tossed it on top of his sweater. Then he traced a finger over her nipple, through her bra, and put a hitch in her breathing. She was definitely not cold any more. He reached behind her and expertly unfastened the hooks, then swept aside the flimsy material.

He cupped her breasts in his hands and brushed his thumbs over her nipples until they grew taut.

Dragging his gaze up to hers, he said in a ragged voice, "You are so beautiful."

Coming from him, the man who fixed the flaws nature dished out, that was high praise and it went straight to her head, nicking her heart on the way.

She kissed him slowly, softly, and sucked on his bottom lip before drawing back. "How odd that the less clothes I'm wearing, the hotter I get."

He braced his forearms under her butt and stood with her in his arms. "Then I think I know how to really warm you up."

Courtney knew where he was taking her, and she was all for it. But when he got to the doorway of her bedroom, she stopped him.

"What?" he asked.

"I just thought you should know that my bedroom is a virgin."

His eyes darkened. "Are you saying what I think you are?"

"I haven't been with anyone else in this room."

As the significance of her words sank in, he smiled. "But no pressure."

"Of course not."

"So the last time, when we were together in my room was—"

"My first time in a very long time."

"Duly noted," he said. "And appreciated. Are you trying to tell me you've changed your mind?"

"No. I just— I guess I just wanted you to know I don't make this a habit." She'd told him same thing last time, but it mattered very much that he believed her.

"It never occurred to me you did." He smiled. "So, are you ready to deflower the room?"

Wrapping her arms around his neck, she said, "Oh, yeah."

Chest to chest, skin to skin, he carried her to the bed then let her legs slide along his thighs until her feet touched the floor. He reached down and turned on the bedside lamp, the fringe of crystals around the shade catching the light.

Looking around he said, "*Deflower* is definitely the right word."

Seeing it through his eyes, she realized it was all girl. Floral comforter, curtains and throw pillows. Shades of pink, burgundy and olive green were everywhere.

"It works for me."

When the loneliness pressed relentlessly in on her, she comforted herself with the fact that there was no man she had to compromise for. No one to please but herself. Now with David, she wanted to compromise. Wanted to please.

She pulled down the quilt and blankets beneath, baring the sheets. When he reached out and flicked the button on her jeans, her stomach quivered. Then he lowered the zipper, his knuckles grazing her bare flesh and leaving sparks in their wake. Resting his big, gentle hands on her hips, he brushed her jeans and panties down her legs until she stepped out of them.

"Turnabout is fair play," she said.

She locked her gaze on his as she started to unbuckle his belt. Because she was clumsy with the cast on her left arm, he took over and finished, standing before her all muscle and flesh and masculinity. She ran her palm over the dusting of hair on his chest and savored the tingle of her skin. Being horizontal with David beside her seemed suddenly urgent. She sat on the bed and took his hand, sliding to the middle to make room for him. A heartbeat later the mattress dipped beneath his weight.

The chill of the cold sheets was chased away when he took her in his arms and pulled her to the hard, hot length of his body. He captured her mouth with his own and drew her top lip gently between his teeth. Then she felt his hand slide over her belly and lower, until he slipped a finger into her moist warmth. Sudden demand cut to her core and her breathing grew shallow and rapid. Something frantic built inside her and scratched to be liberated.

Reaching between them she took him in her hand, reveling in the hard and smooth contradictions of his texture. He sucked in a breath at her touch and tensed, his hands becoming eager as he stroked and molded. She felt the wild beat of his heart against her own and gloried in the feeling of power that she could wield.

He rolled her onto her back, then straddled her, pressing himself between her legs. Then, with one powerful thrust, he was inside her. He lifted her hips to go deeper and plunged. Her senses were filled with his taste and scent even as her body was filled with his essence. She felt the tension inside her build to breaking, just before her mindless cry of release ravished the virgin room.

David was only seconds behind her. He tensed just before shudders wracked his body. When it was over, he pressed his forehead to hers while their breathing returned to normal. Then he rolled onto his back and folded her into the shelter of his warm body.

"The room is happy and so is its occupant," she said, resting her hand on his chest and the hammering heartbeat that was still slowing.

"I'm glad."

"How did you know I needed you tonight?"

There was an almost imperceptible jump in his skin and he covered it well. She probably only noticed because she was so relaxed and suddenly he wasn't.

"Like you said—I'm the babe whisperer." His voice was casual but had a slight edge.

"Does that mean you think I'm a babe?"

"Unquestionably." But the fingers cupping her shoulder curled into a fist.

The body language was classic distance and she'd experienced it often enough with her husband to recognize the signs now. And just like that he booted her contentment out the door.

Surprisingly, David spent the night with her. When he'd grown detached last night, she'd thought he would stay in her bed long enough so it wouldn't look bad, then make some excuse and go. Instead, they'd fallen asleep in each other's arms and awakened in the same bed, as comfortable as if it happened every day.

She'd made breakfast, nothing fancy, just eggs and toast. He'd said it was the best he'd eaten in a long time, which was a bald-faced lie because she knew for a fact that Greta Stanford's breakfasts at the Walnut River Inn were to die for. Still, his compliment made her feel good. Happy. She hated happy because it didn't last and you somehow felt worse when it was gone.

So Courtney tried to get rid of him by mentioning that with Janie occupied at her grandparents, she was going to take the opportunity to look at cars. After he'd caught her in a cry the day before, she thought that would scare him off, but not so much. He'd insisted on coming along.

So here they were, walking around the lot at Reliable Used Cars on a beautiful March morning. It was on Lexington, just down the street from Buns 'n' Burgers. The temperature was a little chilly, but overhead the sky was a cloudless blue. With David beside her, happiness threatened to bubble to the surface and that made her nervous.

"It's awfully nice of you to go car-shopping with me."

"No problem. I'm at loose ends today. I—"

"Hi, folks." The salesman was short, portly and bald. The black leather jacket, although stylish, made him look like a hit man for the Sopranos.

"Hi," Courtney said.

"My name is Chad. And you are?" He looked at David.

"I'm Courtney and this is David," she said.

"Nice to meet you," he answered shaking hands. "Something for the missus?" he asked, looking at David again.

"He's not my mister. I'm buying the car." A breeze kicked up and blew her hair across her face. She tucked it behind her ear. "I need something that's in good shape. Fuel economy is important," she added. "And the crash-test safety is a concern."

"And you want to spend a dollar and a half," Chad teased.

"Exactly."

"I'll show you some of my best deals. You pick something out and take it for a spin. Then we'll talk deal."

"Okay."

When she'd decided on a small compact, Chad led them into his office/cubicle, complete with cluttered metal desk, computer and two chairs. She and David sat. She told him what she intended to put down and he left to crunch numbers with the dealership's financial guy.

Courtney looked at David. "This is the part that makes me nervous."

"Did you like the car?"

"Yeah. It's in decent shape as far as I can tell. The gas mileage is good. Peppy for a compact. And it's red."

"Color is important?" His grin was teasing.

"Of course. I need wheels, but preferably without a body that's neon-green or puce."

He frowned. "What shade would that be?"

"Not a clue. I'd have to look it up in the dictionary," she admitted. "What do you think of it?"

"Pretty much the same. Although I'd prefer a zippy silver model. And it couldn't hurt to have it checked out by an independent mechanic." He thought for a second. "Also an extended warranty, if it's available, wouldn't be a bad idea."

"Both good thoughts, but not especially economical," she said. "My budget is screaming for mercy now, and that's without a car payment." She twisted her fingers together. "How long does it take to run a few numbers?"

"Maybe it won't be as bad as you think." David reached over and took her hand in his own.

"Maybe." But she'd learned in her life that not only was it always as bad as she thought, usually it was worse.

When Chad walked in and sat behind the desk looking supremely confident, Courtney knew it was the latter.

"I think you're going to like this payment," he started. He put a piece of paper in front of her with monetary amounts scattered over it. Then he circled one. "That's a steal."

Her stomach dropped, then knotted up. Tears that smacked of desperation were very close to the surface. "Thank you, Chad. I'll—" She was trying to think of a polite way to say "not in this lifetime."

David slid forward and glanced at the numbers. "It's not a bad price. I'd like to talk about throwing in that extended warranty."

"Are we talking about a done deal here?" Chad asked.

"Yes," David said.

"What?" Courtney stared at him. "David, I'm not sure I can handle the payment."

"You won't have to," he said.

Why wouldn't she have to? What was he saying? She looked at Chad. "Can you give us a minute?"

"Sure thing." He stood. "I'll check with my manager on that extended warranty."

"You do that." David met her gaze.

When they were alone, she slid forward on the chair and angled her knees toward him. "What do you mean I won't have to handle the payments?"

"Because the loan will be paid off."

"By who? My fairy godmother?"

"Be reasonable, Court."

"When did I start being unreasonable?"

"Look." David sat up straighter. "I want to help."

"Just so I get it right before I become unreasonable, I'd like to clarify something. By *help* you mean buy this car for me outright?"

"I can afford it."

"That's not what I asked. Do you or do you not intend to pay for this car?" When he started to answer, she said, "A simple yes or no will suffice."

"All right then. Yes."

"Why, David?"

"Because you need it."

"And I'll figure something out," she protested.

"What's to figure? I'll write a check." He shrugged. "The money isn't going to make a difference to me one way or the other. But you're raising a child and could use the help. It's as simple as that."

If something looked too good to be true, Courtney had learned that it usually was. No one in her world had ever done something without expecting a return on the investment. More than likely there was something in this for David.

"*Simple* is hardly the word I would use," she said.

"What does that mean?"

"I have to ask this. What do you get out of buying me a car?"

"The satisfaction of giving assistance to a hard-working single mom." His gaze narrowed.

"That's it?"

"What else could there be?" The irritation in his voice said there'd been a direct hit on a nerve.

"Oh, I don't know," she said. "Maybe it's about putting a muzzle on your conscience when you go back to L.A. with your hometown hero hat firmly in place."

"What the hell does that mean?" he said.

"It means we've had a good time. I'm not denying that. I like you, David. I appreciate what you've done, what you're going to do for Janie. Believe me, I know I sound like an ungrateful hag, but it's got to be about more than giving me a helping hand."

"Do you know how paranoid that sounds?"

"It's not paranoia if someone's out to get you," she shot back.

Chad walked back in and glanced warily between the two of them. "If you're paying cash, my manager authorized me to give you—"

"Hold that thought," Courtney said. She stood. "I'll have to get back to you on this."

"David?" Chad looked to him.

He stood and blew out a long breath. "We have to talk this over."

"I can't guarantee—"

"Good-bye, Chad." Courtney walked out and kept walking.

She would have walked all the way home if David hadn't taken her arm and steered her wordlessly to his BMW parked in the lot. Neither of them said a word on the way back to her apartment. In her case it was because she didn't trust herself not to cry and she'd done enough of that in front of David. When he pulled up in front and turned off the car, she opened the passenger door and started to get out.

"Court?"

She made the mistake of looking at him and when she did something in the region of her chest grew tight and achy. "What?"

"Can we talk about this?"

"What is there to say?"

"Aren't you being overly suspicious?" he asked, resting his wrist on the steering wheel.

It was such a blatantly masculine thing to do and oddly sexy. And the fact that she noticed at all when she was so angry and upset really ticked her off.

"If I'm exceptionally suspicious, it's not without good reason." Still in the seat, she pulled the door closed against the wind and stared out the front window. She didn't trust herself to look at him. "My father lost himself in a bottle of whiskey and left me to raise myself and take care of him. He was never there for me. I thought Joe was different, but I was wrong. He just left me in a different way, because he was never there to begin with. He ran out on me and looked like a hero when he did. I learned the hard way that I can only ever count on myself." She looked at him. "I can't accept the kind of help you're offering and I don't understand why you're doing it."

"I truly do want to help. Not because of some imagined payoff, a way to not feel guilty for going back to my practice." He blew out a long breath. "Although there's probably some truth to the guilt part, but it's not what you think."

"Then what is it?" she asked.

"When I told you about the falling out with my father, I left out the details."

She closed her eyes and stifled a groan. This was where she felt like the world's biggest jerk. If only she hadn't looked at him, she'd be safely inside. She was going to hate herself for asking, but that couldn't be helped. "What details?"

"I fell in love. At least I thought I did, and all I could think about was being together forever. But she was flunking a class and I was prepared to do whatever I could to make sure she didn't get kicked out of school."

"If the story had a happy ending there would have been no disagreement with your father."

"You're right about that." Grimly, he shook his head. "On the final exam I was going to slip her the answers, but I got caught."

"Oh, David—"

"I finally got my father's attention." He laughed, but the sound was bitter and dark. "To make a long story short, he said he didn't raise me to be a cheat. Stupidly I said he didn't raise me at all because he was never there, so who was really the family disgrace? He couldn't condone or support cheating or anyone who engaged in such reprehensible behavior. I was on my own in every way, including financial."

She didn't know what to say so she asked, "What happened with the girl?"

His expression was wry but his eyes darkened with anger and bitterness. "She let me take the fall, then dumped me."

She sucked in a breath at the callousness. She knew what young love felt like. She knew what being used felt like. It made you not want to put your heart on the line again. And David lost his father, too. And his support. Yet he'd found a way to go on. How had he managed it? "You've told me that you still became a doctor. I guess what I'd like to know is…how?"

"With the black mark on my record, I couldn't transfer any credits, so I had to start over. Fortunately the lesson came early in my academic career. I got student loans, grants, scholarships and worked my ass off because school was all I had."

Because he'd lost the father he'd spent his whole life trying to impress. It all made sense now. The charity work. Helping Janie and her. David's core belief was that if he did enough good it would cancel out that one bad decision and make things right. The problem was that all the good deeds in the world wouldn't give him the absolution he craved from the father who was gone forever and couldn't give it to him.

"I'm so sorry, David."

"Not your fault." He shrugged. "The story is as old as Adam, Eve and the apple. Boy meets girl. Boy falls head over heels and when girl bats her eyelashes and says she needs him, boy wants to fix problem."

Needs. That word was like a punch to the gut.

Courtney remembered how he'd reacted after making love, when she'd said she'd needed him. He'd grown distant and his behavior today was all about pushing her buttons in the worst possible way—because he knew she wanted to be independent. Correction, because she had told him more than once that she could take care of herself.

"So—" She swallowed. "When I said I needed you last night— It was a red flag for you."

He glanced sharply at her. "What are you talking about?"

"You…withdrew, I guess is the best way to say it."

"No—"

"I know what it feels like when a man pulls away from me, David. The thing is, I'm not asking for anything."

"I never said you were." His voice was deep, dangerous.

"That defensive tone says you're not being honest with yourself. We shared something pretty wonderful. And, for that moment, I needed you. I'm healing physically and emotionally. It wasn't about forever."

He smiled, but it was his bedside manner face. The one he hid behind because he'd been used and thrown away and lost everything. "Okay."

But she knew it wasn't okay and never would be. He had no reason to trust that she wouldn't take his heart and throw it away. And she didn't trust him to be there for her.

"I guess we have something in common."

"What's that?" he asked.

"Neither of us wants to be used."

He frowned. "I'm not using you."

"Yes, you are. I'm the latest in a long list of charity cases. If you help enough people, you'll get back what you lost with your father."

His gaze narrowed as his eyes darkened. "You should give up the business major and take up Psych 101."

"It doesn't require an advanced degree to understand you. The dots were all there and you just connected them." She took a deep breath and opened the car door, then stepped out. She leaned down and looked at him. "Like I said before, you've got demons, David. And so do I. But the bottom line for me is that Janie and I will not be your current pity project."

"That's not—"

"Good-bye, David." She closed the door and it took all her self-control not to look back as she went to the door of her building and let herself inside. When she was out of sight, she rested her forehead against the cool wall.

What ticked her off the most was that she couldn't even blame him for how much she hurt. She knew what it was like to have nothing and David did too. She understood why he was protecting himself. Why should he believe that she wasn't after him for what he could give her? He had no reason to believe that her refusing his generosity wasn't simply a ploy to manipulate him before reeling him in.

He would never let down his guard to care about her. He had no reservations about making her his pity project, but the real pity was that she'd fallen in love with him.

Chapter Thirteen

It was the pity-project crack that finally pushed David to make the call.

During the last two days, the whole conversation with Courtney had gotten him to thinking about his father. If he was being honest with himself, he'd been remembering James Wilder since learning he'd died and there wouldn't ever be a chance to make things right between them.

David had never told anyone about what happened. There was no way to put into words the depth of disgust, disappointment and disgrace he'd seen in his dad's eyes. That look had carved out an empty feeling inside him and nothing he'd done since had come close to filling it up.

Then he got to thinking about why he'd done what he'd done, pushed the envelope the way he had. He'd had a lot of time to think, what with not being able to sleep. A lot of motivation for his behavior went back to his childhood, when his father had brought Anna home. Then his parents had adopted her and said, *She's your sister now.* Translation: *You have to love her.* From an adult perspective, it was like a man bringing home his secretary and telling his wife to love and accept the interloper.

David realized that a lot of the resentment he felt toward his father was entrenched in memories of the attention lavished on Anna. His parents took her in as an infant when she'd been abandoned. His feelings were childish and stupid, and he was an idiot times ten, but that didn't alter the fact that it was past time to deal with it.

He realized he knew very little about Anna's life since he'd left home. Opening his laptop on the desk in his room he accessed the wireless Internet connection and signed on. Courtney had used it to find out about him. He typed in *Anna Wilder.* What he found only amplified his negative feelings.

She was working for the company trying to take over the hospital.

He called and after being transferred several times, was put through to her secretary.

"Anna Wilder's office. How may I help you?"

"I'd like to speak with Ms. Wilder."

"May I tell her who's calling?"

"Tell her it's Dr. David Wilder."

"Hold, please."

He held just long enough to consider the possibility that she was going to blow him off. Then he heard a click and a woman's voice.

"Hello, David." The voice was coolly polite. "How did you get this number?"

"I looked you up on the Internet."

"Ah."

"It's a sad commentary on our family that we have to use the Web to find out what's going on with each other." Hypocritical, he knew. But he was in kind of a black mood and figured the pot calling the kettle black sort of went with the territory.

Anna ignored the dig. "How are you?"

"Fine. And you?" He stood and paced the room.

"Couldn't be better." There was an awkward silence before she said, "To what do I owe the pleasure of a phone call from the famous physician to the stars?"

"I've been doing a lot of thinking since Dad's funeral."

"Me, too." There was a deep sigh. "Something like that— Losing him—"

He couldn't be sure, what with the cell phone connection, but it almost sounded like she choked up. "Yeah. I know. It makes you take stock of your life."

"Yeah," she agreed. "It does. And in that spirit, how is your life?"

"Busy." But empty. And the feeling had gotten worse, lonelier somehow, after the way Courtney had called him on his behavior yesterday. "And like Ella and Peter I'm guessing by that physician-to-the-stars crack you're under the impression that all I do is implants and nose jobs."

"No?"

The teasing note in her voice brought back memories of her when they were growing up. Her light blond hair and blue eyes. All the intensity in her waiflike, Precious-Moments-doll expression. She would argue her opinion first, then ask questions later. Always on the defensive.

"No," he said. "As a matter of fact, I've taken trips to developing countries and done facial reconstruction on kids with some pretty severe injuries."

"Doctors without Borders?"

"No. But a similar organization." Why did he feel the need to tell her and not Peter or Ella? Didn't take a shrink to point out that neither of his siblings made him feel the need to be special enough to earn his father's affection.

"That's great, David. It must be very rewarding. So is there anyone special in your life? Are you dating someone?"

Courtney's face flashed into his mind along with the reminder that she believed he was using her to cancel out his youthful indiscretion. It was impossible for her to let herself believe that some good deeds don't have an ulterior motive. Whether or not she trusted his reasons, he was going to fix Janie's face. Then he'd return to his practice. Move forward.

Alone.

The thought was like being swallowed by a big, black hole. It was as if all the light and color were suddenly sucked out of his world. His chest felt like someone had whacked him a good one to shock his heart into normal sinus rhythm. When he left Courtney would his heart stop for good?

"Earth to David?"

"Hmm?"

"Thought I lost you for a second. The question wasn't that hard. Are you dating anyone special?"

Courtney was special, but they weren't exactly dating. And after yesterday he was pretty sure she didn't like him very much. "No. How about you?"

"How about me—what?"

"Is there a man in your life?"

"No. My job is pretty demanding—" She stopped. Probably because of the can of worms she'd opened.

He took the ball and ran with it. "What the hell are you doing working for Northeastern HealthCare? The last I heard you were in Mergers and Acquisitions at a large Manhattan investment bank. Peter and Ella have no idea you're working to undermine them."

"I saw a lot of potential for growth with this company. And I'm not hiding anything. You found me."

"Growth? You call growth swallowing up everything in your path?"

"Size matters, David. If it didn't, all those Hollywood starlets wouldn't flock to your office so you could give them bigger breasts."

"It's all part of the service. They're going to do it anyway. At least I can do the job right and make sure there are no medical complications that will compromise their health down the road."

"And you put a silencer on your conscience by fixing kids?"

It they'd been face to face, she'd have seen him flinch at that zinger. "It's not about me—"

"And my job isn't about me. It's for the greater good. Bigger means revenue that can be channeled into research, equipment, programs to actually help people."

"Walnut River General Hospital *is* helping people. If it ain't broke, don't fix it."

"What's wrong with making it better?" she argued.

"You should stop buying the company policy hook, line and sinker, Anna. Northeastern HealthCare isn't known for improving the facilities they acquire. They have more of a scorched-earth policy. Suck the life out of it and move on."

"Some things never change," she said, her voice cool again.

"What does that mean?"

"I mean putting down my job."

"This isn't about you, Anna." Staring out the window, he thought about that and shook his head. "Maybe partly. How can you live with yourself? Is career advancement worth betraying your father?"

"I'm good at what I do. Dad would have been proud of me," she said defensively.

"Proud that you're helping destroy his work?" He gentled his voice. If anyone understood the yearning for a father's pride and respect, it was him. But he couldn't let this go unchallenged. "Dad and Mom took you in, gave you a home, made you part of the family. They loved you. Now you're repaying that by undermining the institution he gave his life for."

"David," she said with exaggerated patience. "We're coming at this from two different directions—business and medicine."

"That's because they're diametrically opposed."

"It doesn't have to be that way. You have the skill to heal people, but you're also a businessman. You have office space, staff, supplies and it doesn't come cheap. There's a common ground where business and health care can co-exist—"

"Don't patronize me, Anna. If this was good for the hospital, Peter would be on board. He's a pretty smart guy and he's opposed to this takeover. It's not in the hospital's best interest and I'm guessing deep down inside you know it, too."

"Oh, please—"

"Why is it that no one in the family knows you work for Northeastern HealthCare?"

"How do you know they don't?" she asked.

"Because I'm pretty sure Peter would have mentioned it when he told me what's going on. If you were a doctor, you'd understand what this is going to do to the people in town."

There was a long silence before she said in icy tones, "It's clear that we have to agree to disagree."

"Look, Anna, I didn't call to argue with you. I really wanted to—"

"I'm sorry, David. I've got another call I have to take."

"Wait, Anna—"

"Good-bye, David."

There was a click on the other end and he sighed as he flipped his cell closed. That went well, he thought. Not. Whatever he'd been looking for, he hadn't achieved the goal. But he got the feeling that he and Anna did have one thing in common—the need for their father's approval. It was a terrible thing to disappoint a parent. He wasn't sure why his sister felt that way, but his own sins stood out in stark relief against the blackness of his soul.

Despite what Courtney had said, he wasn't using her or Janie to ease his conscience. He genuinely cared about them. From the first moment he'd seen them, battered and bruised, but not bowed, the Albright women had taken hold of his heart and wouldn't let go.

As he looked out the window at the grass, trees and bushes just starting to show signs of spring, the thought of caring about a woman that way made his blood run cold. He'd learned that tender emotion was like an explosive device that could detonate without warning. The repercussions were painful and life-altering.

Trying not to let on that she was apprehensive, Courtney held Janie's hand as they walked into the medical exam room. It was a suite for visiting doctors to see patients, located in the tower behind the main building of Walnut River General Hospital. David had left a message on her cell asking them to meet him here so he could take a look at Janie's face and determine whether or not to schedule the reconstruction. The nurse was Susan Kier, the mother of Janie's best friend. A familiar face was comforting since the two of them were pretty jumpy.

Courtney looked around. It was a typical room with the exam table, sink and anatomy posters sharing space with various drug advertisements on the beige walls.

"Okay, J.J., if you'll just hop up there on the exam table." Susan Kier slid the foot stool over so Janie could climb up. She was the only one who shortened Jane Josephine to J.J. Janie liked it.

"Thanks, Mrs. Kier." The paper covering the table crackled when the little girl sat and settled.

When all was quiet, Courtney said, "I didn't know you worked here in the tower."

"I don't." Susan took the blood-pressure cuff from the wall and secured it around the small arm while Janie watched in fascination as she squeezed the black bulb and pumped it up. "At least not full-time. But when there's a guest doctor here, the nurses take turns assisting when he, or she, is seeing outpatients."

"That was tight on my arm," Janie said.

"Sorry, J.J. It has to be snug to get a good reading. But it's all done now." After making a notation in the chart, Susan looked up. "James Wilder believed patients' health issues resolved faster with a personal touch. He'd be pleased that the hospital is continuing in the spirit and standard of care he championed while he was with us. He'd be enormously proud of both of his sons."

"Yes, he would," Courtney said.

She knew the man who was the closest thing to a father she'd ever known would have fought the takeover by Northeastern HealthCare just as hard as his son Peter. And whether David wanted to admit it or not, he was his father's son, too.

It had been a week since their disastrous excursion to the used-car lot. A thousand times since she'd wished to call back the words. They were abrasive, ungrateful and he didn't deserve the abuse. A simple "no, thank you" would have been sufficient. But she had to go psycho-babble on him. The ugly, selfish truth was that she'd instinctively pushed him away to protect herself. The problem was, it was like closing the barn door after the cows got loose, because she'd already fallen in love with him.

Susan smiled at them. "Okay, you two, I'll be just outside if you need anything. Dr. Wilder should be here in a few minutes."

"Thanks, Susan."

"Bye, Mrs. Kier."

"When you're finished with the doctor, J.J., how about I take you to the cafeteria for ice cream?"

"Can I, Mom?" Even with only one eye showing—especially with one eye showing—Janie's face took on a pleading, puppy-dog expression that worked big-time.

Courtney sighed. "How can I say no?"

"Then we've got a date." Susan closed the door softly.

Courtney stared after her and realized it was easier not to be scared when she didn't have to be the strong one all by herself. Janie was relying on her for reassurance and when puppy-dog changed to worried, anxious and nervous, she forced herself to smile cheerfully even though breaking down in tears held a lot more appeal.

"That's nice of Mrs. Kier to take you for ice cream," she said, trying to distract her daughter.

"Is it going to hurt, Mommy?"

"What? When Dr. David looks at your face?" When Janie nodded uncertainly, she shook her head. "He's just going to see if the swelling has gone down enough so that he can fix it."

"Is it going to hurt when he fixes it?"

Courtney winced inwardly. It was an invasive procedure and there was no way to do it without discomfort. She didn't believe in lying, but it was important to choose her words carefully.

"Well, sweetie, it's unlikely that—"

The door opened suddenly and she was incredibly happy to see David. For so many reasons. But relief at not having to answer was at the top of the list. Also very high up was the fact that he made the white lab coat look sexy.

"Hi," she said brightly.

"Dr. David!" Janie held out her arms and he walked over to give her a hug.

"Hi, you two." He stepped back and stuck his hands in the pockets of the lab coat. "How are you?"

"Okay," Janie said.

"Me, too," Courtney added. She noticed circles under his eyes and lines on either side of his nose and mouth. For a man taking a rest from work, he looked not very rested. She stood on one side of Janie and he was on the other. "Have you been sleeping? You look tired."

"I'm fine." He turned his attention to his patient. "Let's see how this looks, princess."

"I'm not a princess."

"Says who?" With the long fingers of one hand, he held her small chin still while he carefully removed the tape and gauze bandages.

"Says Mommy." Holding very still, Janie slid her a look from the corner of her good eye. "She says I'm not a princess. Just a regular girl."

Courtney wasn't looking straight on but could still see the damage. Where Janie's cheekbone should have been, there was what she could only think of as a hollow, a depression. The dimple that matched the good side of her face was missing in action.

David glanced at her and somehow the expression in his eyes told her not to worry. Everything would be fine if she trusted him.

"I hate to be the one to tell your mommy she's wrong," he said, "but you're not a regular girl. You're special."

He tilted Janie's face up and gently touched the area around the trauma. "Does that hurt?"

"No."

"How about this?" he asked.

Janie shook her head.

"Good." He brushed her hair off her forehead and play-fully tweaked her nose. "The swelling has receded nicely. I'd like to schedule the repair as soon as possible."

Courtney didn't know whether to laugh or cry. She wanted

this over and done with. Put behind them. A distant memory. At the same time she knew that when all of the above happened, she and David would be done with. A distant memory. But it would be best to take it one trauma at a time. She'd think about her own heart damage later because she'd reached the worry threshold and just couldn't hold any more.

"How do we arrange it?" she asked him.

"Susan will set it up with the hospital." Instead of calling the nurse, he replaced the bandage on the injured half of Janie's face.

When he finished, she said, "Dr. David?"

"What, princess?" He gave her his undivided attention.

She twisted her fingers in her lap. "Is it gonna hurt when you make it better?"

He met her gaze directly, without hesitation. "You know I won't lie to you."

Janie thought for a moment, then nodded. "Yes. Because you said you'd come to my school for awards night and you did."

"Okay. This is what's going to happen. Your mom is going to bring you to the hospital. We're going to give you some medicine so you'll go to sleep when I fix your face. You won't feel any pain. When you wake up, there will be some discomfort. But we can give you something to make it not so bad until it's gone for good. Do you believe that I'm going to make you better?"

Without hesitation, she said, "Yes."

He called Susan back in and asked her to set up a surgical date, then said, "When it's arranged, Susan will let you know and you'll be given pre-surgery instructions."

"Mommy? Can I go have ice cream now?"

"Of course. I'll meet you there after I talk with David."

David started to lift Janie from the exam table and she put her arms around his neck and hugged tightly. "I'm only a little scared now, Dr. David."

He pressed her close. "I'm going to take extra special care of you, princess."

When he set her down, she slipped her hand into Susan's and the two left. David turned back and frowned. "What's wrong, Court?"

Tears filled her eyes when she said, "I'm a lot scared."

Without hesitation, he pulled her into his arms. "I can't tell you not to be. It wouldn't do any good."

What did her good was being right where she was. She pressed her cheek against his solid chest and listened to the strong, steady beat of his heart and tried not to hate herself for relying on him. It wasn't as though she was going to make it a habit, but he was here now and she needed him.

"You're her mom and I think worrying about facial reconstruction is part of the job description," he said.

Moments ago it seemed impossible that she could laugh, but she did. "I can't argue with that."

"Wow." He rubbed his chin on the top of her head. "You not arguing. Let me mark the date on my calendar so I can remember it always."

"Smart aleck."

He tightened his hold. "I promise you that I will do my best. I'll take extraordinary care of your child."

"I know you will. You're extraordinarily wonderful with her."

"It's easy. She's a wonderful kid."

"Your father would be very proud of the man you are," she said, sliding her arms beneath the lab coat and around his waist. "In fact, of all of his children. Susan and I were just commenting on the fact that his memory and spirit are still alive in this hospital and the personal care offered."

He tensed, just before he dropped his hands and stepped back. His expression was grim. "That may not be enough to keep it going."

"What do you mean?" She touched his arm and ignored

the shiver of awareness that jolted her system like defibrilla-tor paddles. "What's wrong, David?"

"I had a long talk with my sister, Anna."

"That's good, right? Communication and all that."

He shook his head. "Not when she's communicating that she works for the company trying to take over this hospital."

"You didn't know?"

"No. And I don't think Peter and Ella do either. I've got to break the news."

"Did you try to talk to her?" Courtney asked, shocked that a member of the Wilder family was in the enemy camp, so to speak.

"Of course I did. She grew up in the same house as the rest of us. She knows how much time and energy our father put into building the hospital. All the blood, sweat and tears that went into giving it a heart and soul. Molding the mission statement to put the care in patient care. My sister is a company person all the way and to her it's just a business."

"And?"

He shoved his hand through his hair. "She's essentially on the team that's destroying my father's dream. She's tearing down the life's work of the man who gave her a home and family."

"I'm sorry the conversation didn't go well." She took his hand and linked her fingers with his. "Maybe if you and Peter talk to her together—"

"I don't think so." He slid his hand from hers. "You don't understand. My father doted on her because she was an orphan. But adding Anna to the mix changed the family dynamic. My mother withdrew emotionally. I can't speak for Ella and Peter, but I resented being pushed aside. She took all the affection and attention and instead of thanking her lucky stars, she's siding with the enemy. Just goes to show what happens when you give up everything for a woman."

Courtney went cold inside as her heart interpreted the message. He would never get over the trauma of being used and abused by a woman. And there was no surgical procedure to repair the invasive trauma he'd experienced. She didn't know the rug was there until he'd pulled it out from under her.

"David," she said gently, struggling to keep her voice even. "Maybe I don't understand. My upbringing was about as dysfunctional as it gets. Your father was the first to show me what a caring, considerate man looks like. So I have no frame of reference for growing up in a family that gives a damn about you. But I'm pretty sure that your father would be deeply troubled if he knew that the message you took away from giving an abandoned child a home is not to love at all."

There was nothing left to say so she walked out, down the hall and around the corner. When he didn't come after her, she ducked into the ladies' room and struggled to breathe against the crushing pain inside her.

She'd finally met a man who was as selfless and noble as he appeared to be. A man who didn't have an ulterior motive. A man who made her want to give her love, which was all she had to give. But he was also a man who would never accept her love because that meant he had to risk caring again.

She felt as though she'd been fighting her whole life. To get ahead. To make something of herself. For survival. But there was no way to fight this. And the sadness of it went clear to her soul.

Chapter Fourteen

After checking the O.R. scheduling for Janie's surgery the following day, David brushed by someone as he headed toward the E.R. exit on his way out of the hospital.

"If it isn't the hotshot, golf-playing face-lifter from La La Land."

The mocking female voice was painfully familiar and David turned to see his sister Ella. She grinned and waggled her fingers at him. "I thought that might get your attention."

His little sister was paraphrasing what Courtney had said about him after their first meeting. After her earlier remark about disappointing his father, he figured Court would stand by her first impression.

"Hi, El." He smiled back, but his heart wasn't in it. "For the record, I don't play golf."

"Beach volleyball?" she teased.

"Hardly. To maintain this godlike physique, I have a treadmill, elliptical and weights from the sporting goods store. All tucked away in a spare bedroom."

"It's working," she said, giving him a once-over. "What are you doing here?"

"Making sure everything's set for Janie's surgery to-morrow."

"Excellent." She smiled. "I'm so glad I called you. And that you came, of course. Janie couldn't be in better hands. You're good, but you're also family. Courtney's worked here for so long, she's like family and families look out for each other."

"Yeah." That's the way it should be. Although you couldn't prove it by him.

"What's wrong, handsome?"

"Nothing. Don't be dramatic, El—"

She frowned at the bustling E.R., then tugged him into the quietest corner of the waiting room, beside a silk plant. "Don't play that game. I'm your sister, and I'm not blind. I know when something's on your mind, so spill it, David."

Her soft, pretty features tensed into determination and he knew there'd be no escape until he—shudder—talked. "You're not going to drop this, are you?"

"Not even for money. What's putting lines in that pretty face of yours?"

He snorted at her compliment, then turned serious. "It's something Courtney said."

Instantly his sister looked troubled. "I was teasing a minute ago. I'm sure she no longer thinks you're a shallow surgeon from L.A."

He shook his head. "That's ancient history, sis. She had some razor-sharp comments about my relationship—or lack thereof—with Dad."

"What did she say?"

"I'd rather not get into it."

"Bet you'd talk to Dad—if he was here." Sadness crept into her dark eyes.

"When I need to talk to him the most, he went and died on me. Damned inconvenient."

"Yeah, I'm sure he's not real tickled about it either," Ella said dryly.

"This isn't being shallow, El," he protested. "It's more about feeling sorry for myself."

"And you clarified that because self-pity is so much more attractive?"

"I didn't say that. It's the simple truth."

And it wasn't just because he'd lost his father, who could have been his best friend, and would never get back the wasted years. Somehow Courtney was all mixed up in these feelings, too. He didn't know how to fix it and that was damned frustrating for a man whose whole life was about fixing what was broken.

"Okay, then," Ella said. "As long as you're being honest about your pity party, I suggest you take it somewhere it will do some good."

He stared at her for a moment. "That bracing little piece of advice made absolutely no sense to me, El."

"Then let me put it bluntly. Go talk to Dad."

"You might want to have your head examined, and you've come to the right place, I might add." He touched two fingers to her forehead, teasingly checking to see if she was feverish. "Can you say CT scan?"

"I'm serious, David. I've had the same feeling about wanting to talk to him. So I go to the graveyard, to his head-stone, and—" She shrugged sheepishly. "Talk."

"You're kidding, right?"

She shook her head and looked a little hurt. "It always makes me feel better. But go ahead and laugh. I heal broken bones for a living, what do I know about feelings?"

He knew he'd hurt hers. "I'm sorry. It's just a little far out."

"Dad's a little far out now, which is why it works. Besides, confession is good for the soul. The upside of baring that soul in the graveyard is that it's full of souls who don't talk back. At least we hope they don't." She nodded for emphasis. "Look, I've got to get back to work. Good luck with the surgery tomorrow."

"Thanks."

It wasn't the procedure that bothered him, but what would happen after. That was the part where he left town and the thought was about as appealing as—well, talking to a ghost.

If anyone saw him talking to himself in the cemetery there'd be no doubt he was crazy. But it was certainly a beautiful day for crazy, David thought. The sky was clear and blue, as it could only be in Walnut River. April was approaching and dragging spring along for the ride as the grass turned green and trees were beginning to bud. Bouquets of flowers and plants dotted the cemetery's rolling hills.

He parked the BMW in the sector where his father had been buried, then turned off the engine. Was this really insane? Or did it just feel that way?

After locking the car, he laughed. Who was going to steal the thing in a cemetery? Then he started walking and headed for his father's eternal resting place and the maple that shaded it. The tree was easy to find, the tallest one around. And how fitting was that? He'd always had the impression that James Wilder was the tallest, strongest, wisest person on the face of the earth. Now his father was under it and the emotion brought on by the thought made his throat and chest tight.

He coughed, then tentatively said, "Hi, Dad. Long time no see."

And he would never see him again. Looking around at the tree branches swaying and rustling in the breeze, he remembered the saying—if a tree falls in the forest and no one is there to hear, does it still make a sound? "Here's a philosophical question. If a man talks to his dead father and no one is there to hear, is he still crazy?"

No one answered. Good thing.

The simple headstone was in place, with the dates of his father's birth and death and the words, "Do no harm."

"The Hippocratic Oath," David whispered.

Every doctor swore first to do no harm in the treatment of patients. But sometimes an invasive procedure was required for the greater good. Like Janie, he thought. He had to go in to repair her shattered cheekbone. No pain, no gain.

"Dad, I know you never understood why I wanted to go into plastics. Ella is in orthopedics. Peter is following in your footsteps. And I'm the black sheep—Botox and boob jobs. Superficial stuff. It's not practicing medicine in your opinion. Once a screw-up, always a screw-up."

He let out a long breath as he ran his fingers through his hair. "You always said that a doctor uses every skill, all the science and a black bag full of tricks to cheat death. And no one questions that. But what about after that, Dad? What happens to the scars? What if they're so bad a person wants to hide? Or wishes you'd let them die?" He went down on one knee. "That's where I come in. After doctors like you cheat death, I give patients back their life."

The wind blew suddenly and he pulled up the collar of his leather jacket. "I help kids, Dad. The ones with facial trauma so acute that they have no prospects for a decent quality of life. Kids like Janie."

He smiled. "You know her. Cute little thing. Blond hair, blue eyes. Princess attitude. And her mom. Blond hair, brown eyes. Sexy, sassy and sweet in equal parts. Spine of steel and a heart of gold. A soft heart that's been stomped on one too many times, and that's sort of shut down her ability to trust. She's been abused by men who handed her hope, then snatched it away.

"You were there for her at a difficult time, Dad. Courtney appreciates it, by the way. But you're gone now and I'm going to—" Fill your shoes? Never in a million years, he thought. "I'm going to fix the damage to Janie's face. Then I'll go back to California. No excuse to stay after that."

The breeze stirred the tree branches above him and the rustling almost sounded like whispering. He heard the word *coward*. Or maybe he just felt like one.

He wasn't running away. He had a practice in California and people were counting on him. But who could he count on?

There was no little girl so happy to see him she raced into his arms to give him a hug, or chatter like a magpie about whatever was on her mind. No Courtney to tell about his day, make him laugh to take the edge off. Make love to. The familiar blackness opened up inside him. Except it wasn't familiar any more.

Since he'd come back to Walnut River, the empty feeling had disappeared. Janie and Courtney had moved into his heart and taken down the vacancy sign. But it would be up again soon when he went back to his glass-and-chrome life in Los Angeles. Compared to the warm, girly world he'd be leaving behind, it seemed cold and hollow and—not pink.

The breeze swirled through the trees and this time he swore there was a whisper. *Don't leave the woman you love.*

David wasn't sure if a soul had spoken or if the thought was simply there in his mind. He looked around, confirmed that he was still alone, kneeling by his father's grave. Maybe he should have been creeped out. Oddly enough, he wasn't.

"The thing is, Dad, I don't want to be another man who comes along and hurts Courtney. I care too much about her. Do no harm."

Don't leave the woman you love. He swore he heard the words again, and God, he was tempted. However the thought had come to him didn't make the reality of it any less true. Or any less complicated.

He'd fallen in love with Courtney.

The next morning before Janie's procedure, David went to see his brother. He knew Peter would be there early and it was the best time to talk, before patients demanded his attention.

He knocked, then entered the office where his big brother was doing paperwork. "Hi. Got a minute?"

Peter looked up and smiled with genuine pleasure. "Hey. Sure. Come in."

"Thanks." He took a chair in front of the desk.

"You're out and about early."

"I'm doing the reconstruction on Janie's face this morning."

Peter nodded. "How's Courtney holding up?"

"She's putting on a brave face for Janie, but she's scared."

"You look concerned. Is there reason to be?"

"Not about the surgery." David blew out a breath. "I care a lot about that little girl."

"And her mother?" Peter set his pen down and focused his full attention on the conversation.

"Yeah. Her mother, too."

"Is that going to affect your concentration in the O.R.?"

"You mean is my objectivity compromised?" David asked.

"Yeah. Something like that."

"I gave Janie my word that I'd make her look as good as new and I won't let her down. I'm very good at what I do. The truth is that I wouldn't trust her to anyone else."

"For you? Or for her mom?"

"For both of us."

"Wonders never cease," Peter said. "You're in love with Courtney Albright."

"What is this? Junior high?" They weren't kids any more, David thought. Dodging the truth was stupid. "Yeah. I am."

"When did this happen? How?"

"There's no procedure manual. No single moment when the clouds parted and the hand of God smacked me upside the head." He decided not to share his experience in the cemetery. Or his very real feeling that their father was somehow responsible for his epiphany. "It just happened."

"Congratulations. I couldn't be happier for you."

"Not so fast, bro. There's this small matter of the continental United States between us."

"A minor detail to be worked out."

"You think my work is minor?"

"Hardly. But people on the west coast aren't the only ones who can use your expertise." There was a gleam in his brother's eyes.

"Are you saying there'd be a place for me on staff here at Walnut River General?"

"That's exactly what I'm saying. Ella and I would both be giddy with joy if you came back."

"Giddy?" David's eyebrow rose as he fought the threatening grin. "I can see Ella giddy, maybe. But you?"

Peter shrugged. "Dad would be happy to know the prodigal son returned."

"I let him down, Peter. There's nothing I can do to change that. You'll never know how much I wish I could talk to him now—face to face—and make things okay between us. I wish I could hear him say he's proud of me."

Peter snapped his fingers. "That reminds me. I've got something for you."

"What?"

His brother reached into a drawer and pulled out a thick publication. "I was going through some of Dad's things and found this."

David reached across the desk and took the periodical—a medical journal. There was a sticky note marking a page. He opened the journal to the article he'd written about his positive results with scar-camouflage techniques and examples of successes in children from one of his trips to Nicaragua. The publication had come out in January, the month his dad had died. There was a note on the page in his father's handwriting.

He cleared his throat. "It says, 'Proud of David. Excellent work. Note to self—children make a liar out of you every time. Good excuse to call. About damn time.'"

After reading the words, David drew in a deep breath.

"What did he mean? About making a liar out of him?" Peter asked.

"I did something in college that I'm not very proud of." He met his brother's gaze. "No point in going into detail. But Dad found out. He said I was a disgrace to the Wilder name and wouldn't amount to anything."

"Ah."

"I never had the chance to tell him I was sorry, Peter."

"And he never got a chance to tell you he was wrong. Sounds like an even playing field to me." His brother glanced upward, then met his gaze again. "He knows, David. He's looking down on us right now and smiling and thinking his children are doing him proud. They're all together—"

David snapped his fingers. "You're not the only one who forgot something. I talked to Anna." Thoughts of Courtney had pushed everything else out of his mind.

"Our prodigal sister?"

"More than you know." David brushed his hand over his father's note. "She's working for Northeastern HealthCare, Peter."

"What?"

"The company trying to take over the hospital our father built. You remember."

"Of course I remember." Now he looked worried.

"What's wrong?" David asked.

"I just found out that the state attorney general's office is sending an investigator. There have been allegations and stories leaked to the press about the hospital. This investigator is supposed to dig through everything and separate fact, fiction and rumor."

"Is that a problem?"

"Any time a government agency does an inspection it's a problem. What makes it worse is that NHC wants this hospital. The question is how far they'll go to make the deal happen."

"You think they have someone on the inside here at the hospital?"

"Who knows?" Peter shrugged. "And I'm not sure that matters now. It's ugly and likely to get a lot worse. And it doesn't help that one of the Wilders works for them."

"Sorry to be the bearer of bad news." Especially when his brother had given him something so special. He closed the medical journal and felt a weight he hadn't been aware of lift from his heart.

"It's one of many reasons that I'm glad you'll be here to watch my back. I'll need all the help I can get to save the hospital."

"Count me in." David stood, magazine in hand. "Thanks for this. I have to get down to the O.R. I want Janie to know I'm there before they put her to sleep."

Peter nodded, then stood and held out his hand. "She's in excellent hands."

"Thanks." It meant a lot to have his brother's respect.

"Good luck."

"I thought you said she was in excellent hands."

"She is. And that's not what I meant. Good luck with Courtney."

From his mouth to God's ear. Maybe his dad could pull some strings up there because David needed all the help he could get. He had his doubts that Courtney would be willing to take one more chance on hope.

Especially when he was the man handing it to her.

Chapter Fifteen

In Walnut River General's second-floor lounge, reserved for family and friends of surgery patients, Courtney stared out the window, not really seeing much of anything. The room behind her was hospital-standard-issue—tweed chairs and a leather-padded bench along one wall. Magazines were scattered on tables and a TV was mounted in the corner, turned off at the moment. None of it took her mind off the fact that her baby was down the hall having an operation on her little face and the waiting was hell.

She remembered when David had told her the repair couldn't be done until the swelling subsided. She'd wondered how she was going to get through the wait because she so desperately wanted Janie well and back to normal, right then, right there. Somehow time *had* passed, relatively quickly and painlessly. If she admitted the truth to herself, the reason was David. He'd even made sure to be with them before Janie went to sleep. This was the day she'd been both anticipating and dreading and she trusted him absolutely with her child's welfare.

She'd been able to move forward and get through each day by leaning on him, looking forward to seeing him. Loving him.

In spite of her highly developed emotional defenses, the man had gone over, under, around and through them until she'd waved the white flag and fallen for him. Part of his reason for hanging around was to confront the demons she'd once accused him of having. She sincerely hoped that he'd found a measure of peace because he deserved it. Since their first meeting she'd wondered about the price of his generosity and knew now that it was going to cost her her heart and soul.

"Courtney, any news yet?"

She turned at the deep, familiar voice and saw Peter Wilder in the doorway. "Not yet. It's only been a little while. David said the procedure would take at least several hours."

"Janie's going to be fine." Peter walked over to her and put a comforting arm around her shoulders. So like his father. "My brother was a dweeb growing up, but he's matured since then and is a competent surgeon."

"Dweeb? Is that the official medical term?" she asked, looking up and smiling in spite of the situation.

He looked thoughtful. "Yes. But rest assured. There's every indication that he's left his dweeb days behind him."

It would never have occurred to her to call him a dweeb. Maybe hunk and hottie—even Janie knew that one. Sweetie. Steadfast. Compassionate. Caring. Complicated.

"So he probably wouldn't respond if I called him Dr. Dweeb?" she asked.

Peter's mouth curved upward in a smile. "Paging Dr. Dweeb. I like that."

He reminded her of David in a teasing mood and she could almost see the wheels turning.

"Don't you dare call him that," she warned. "And if you blame the nickname on me, I'll deny it."

"I could be bought off," he suggested, dark eyes twinkling. "Baked goods of any kind. Peanut butter cookies are especially effective in helping me keep mum."

"Because they stick to the roof of your mouth?" she suggested.

"Good one." He laughed.

"What?" Ella Wilder stood just inside the door.

"Did you know your brother is a sugar slut?" Courtney asked.

"His dirty little secret," Ella agreed. "He can be had for as little as a candy bar or scoop of ice cream. Absolutely shameful. And why are we going to give him a sugar rush?"

"Courtney doesn't want David to know she called him Dr. Dweeb."

"I did not!" she denied. "You're the one who said he wasn't so cool when he was a kid."

"That implies I think he's cool now," Peter commented thoughtfully. "I would never say such a thing."

"Merciful heavens, no," Ella said in mock seriousness. "The planet wouldn't be large enough to contain his ego."

Courtney smiled as the two of them good-naturedly bashed their brother, all in the pursuit of taking her mind off worrying about Janie. What a special family the Wilders were. When she missed their father, which was often, it brought her a measure of comfort to know that he'd raised his children to be considerate and caring human beings. That meant his kindness would live on.

"Any word on Janie?" Ella finally asked.

Courtney shook her head. "Not yet. But it hasn't been that long."

"You know," Ella said, "sometimes a procedure can take a little longer than estimated. We make educated guesses based on test results, but until we're there, we don't really know for sure what's going on."

"It doesn't mean there's anything wrong," Peter interjected. "Just that he has to see for himself what the situation is."

"That's what I just said." Ella glared, but there was a gleam in her eyes. "Just because I'm the youngest doesn't mean I'm incompetent."

"I never said you were, but if the stethoscope fits…" Peter looked at her and shrugged.

"I'll have you know—" She stopped, and wagged a finger. "I refuse to get sucked into an argument. Let me simply say that David's not the only one with ego issues. What is it with the Wilder men?"

"They're good and kind," Courtney said. "Caring enough to distract me. If you guys weren't here, I'd be a basket case."

Peter slid his hands into the pockets of his lab coat. "We aim to please. Patients aren't just the sum of their medical problem. They're flesh and blood and have families who worry. We look at healing through mind, body and spirit. Janie's going to need you most when she comes out of surgery. If your spirit is ailing, how can you take care of her?"

"How is she?" Elizabeth Albright walked in the room with her husband right behind her. "Is there any word on my granddaughter?"

"Not yet," Courtney said.

In her hands, the older woman carried a cardboard holder with a hot beverage cup and a bag. She held it out. "I brought you tea and a muffin."

"I couldn't eat anything—"

"You must keep up your strength," Elizabeth interrupted. "How can you take care of Janie if you're weak and undernourished?" She took Courtney's arm and steered her to a chair with a table beside it. "Come. Sit. Eat."

Morris Albright sat beside her. "She's not a puppy, Elizabeth."

"I know that. I'm just trying to help."

"I know." Courtney met her gaze. "Thank you."

"You're welcome." A small smile curved her mouth and softened the tension on her gently lined face. "We'd have been here sooner, but we stopped in the gift shop to order a balloon bouquet for Janie's room. While we were there, we took the liberty of making sure all was running smoothly in your absence. Everything seems under control."

"Karen assured me she'd take care of everything."

"That impossibly young girl we met?" Elizabeth asked.

"Yes. She works part-time. A college student." Courtney thought for a moment. "She's about the same age I was when I came to Walnut River."

Morris squeezed her hand. "We weren't there for you then, Courtney."

"I didn't mean— I was just commenting—"

"It's all right." He smiled. "We're here now. Better late than never."

"I appreciate it so much—" A multitude of emotions pressed on her chest and choked off her words.

She looked at them all. Peter. Ella. The Albrights. Tears gathered in her eyes.

Elizabeth pushed the muffin and tea out of the way and sat on the table since there was no chair available beside Courtney. She took Courtney's good hand between her own. "It's okay to cry, sweetheart. We're here to pick up the slack. You're not alone any more."

"The truth is I haven't really been alone since I came to Walnut River," she said, smiling through her tears. She glanced at Peter and Ella and thought again of James Wilder. "People who work here in the hospital are a tight-knit group and made me one of them right from the start." She looked at her in-laws, Janie's family. Her family, too. "And having you here means the world to me."

David was responsible for that. If he hadn't reached out, she'd have gone on assuming that they would reject her. She'd have deprived her child of the special relationship between granddaughter and grandparents.

Ella pulled a chair closer and sat in front of her. "Don't cry, Court. She's going to be the way she was before the accident."

"But will I?" The words slipped out before she could stop them. "And I don't mean that in a selfish way. But you can't go through a trauma like this and…meet the people you meet…and not be changed forever."

Peter walked closer, joining the little protective circle around her. "For what it's worth, David feels the same way."

"He's a nice man," she said, brushing more tears away when Elizabeth put an arm around her. "I'm grateful he put his west-coast life on hold to help Janie. He's probably anxious to get back."

"How do you feel about my brother, Courtney?" Peter slid his hands in his pockets.

Ella glared up at him. "That's an inappropriate question. I speak for the rest of the country when I say I'm glad you practice medicine and not diplomacy." She looked back at Courtney. "Don't answer that."

"She's right," Peter said. "It's none of my business. But I want you to think about something. When you see Janie's face after the surgery you're going to wonder if the reconstruction is a success, because it will look worse before it gets better."

"David warned me," Courtney said.

But she had a feeling Peter was talking about more than the surgery, trying to let her down easy and prepare her to be alone. She knew how to handle it because she'd been alone all her life. But it had been so much easier before she knew David.

He'd been there for her and she couldn't help being sad that he was going away. He was the kind of man who would take a lifetime to get to know, the kind of man who would never be boring. Part of her wanted to feel sorry for herself that he'd walked into her life and would walk out again taking her heart with him.

She would always remember him. He was one of the good guys and she was grateful to him for showing her they did exist.

When David walked into the lounge, everyone stood up as one. He looked tired, Courtney thought. And darn sexy in his blue scrubs.

"How's Janie?" she asked.

He stood in front of her and ran his fingers through his hair. "Still out from the anesthesia, but she'll be awake soon. The procedure went better than I could have hoped. We have to watch for infection. As with all invasive techniques, there will be a scar, but too small and inconspicuous to cause her any anxiety. Bottom line, I expect her to make a full recovery." Finally he grinned down at her.

After three beats of dead silence, everyone cheered, hugged and high-fived. Courtney buried her face in her hands and cried. Instantly she felt strong arms around her as she was folded against a wide chest that felt familiar and safe.

"Please don't cry, Courtney," David said.

"I cried when Peter and Ella came to sit with me. I blubbered when the Albrights showed up. I've cried so much there's a real danger of dehydration. Trust me, these are happy tears." Mostly. But some were because now he would be going home and she would miss him desperately. But there was no way she'd tell him that. "I feel like I've been crying for a month. Why stop now?"

"Because Janie needs you now."

So holding her wasn't personal; it was all about him being a doctor. She sniffled and lifted her head. Everyone else had quietly and tactfully left and now she was alone with David. His handsome image wavered through her tears.

"Just stop?" She struggled to put a teasing note in her voice. "Is that part of your bedside manner for dealing with a hysterical mother? If so, I have to tell you it needs work, doctor."

"I see no hysteria. And the scared, unhappy mother is you. Seeing you cry rips me up. I can't stand it."

"What?" Who knew shock, not dehydration, could dry up tears? When she tried to back up a step, he curved his fingers around her upper arms.

"I'm in love with you, Courtney."

She couldn't believe she'd heard right. Maybe all the crying had caused flooding that short-circuited her brain *and* her hearing. Surely he hadn't said he loved her. Maybe it was part of the Wilder family conspiracy to let her down easy. He could say it because he was leaving town and no follow-up would be required. He'd look like a hero, and there'd be no guilt to infect his conscience.

This time she pulled away. "That's just— You don't have to say that."

"Yeah, I do."

"And why's that?"

"Because you were right. My father would be deeply disappointed if I took away the wrong message from him loving a child." He blew out a long breath. "But it's not just about that. I've felt empty for a very long time. And now—"

"What?"

He shrugged. "I don't any more."

"Since when?" she asked.

"Since meeting you. And Janie." He glanced toward the window for a moment, then looked back. "I didn't hang around because I needed a vacation from work. It's because I was emotionally spent. I had nothing, no one to fill up the void. You and Janie got to me in a way no one ever has."

She stared at him. "It was the bump on my head, wasn't it? You're a sucker for a woman with a broken wrist and a concussion."

"Joke if you want—"

"I don't need your permission. Humor has gotten me around every lousy pothole on this road we call life. I'm not about to stop now."

"Good. I think it's that sassy, in-your-face attitude that first made me fall in love with you."

"Not the contusion?" she asked in a small voice.

"No." His mouth curved up, then he got serious. Cupping her face in his hands, he kissed her softly. "It was the combination of sarcasm and the unconditional and bottomless love for your child that I fell for."

"I'm not sure I know how to respond to that."

He brushed his thumb across her mouth, then dropped his hands. "You could start by saying you love me, too."

"How do you know I do?"

"I know."

"Dr. Hottie strikes again?"

"Courtney—"

She sighed. "I'm not sure what good it will do for me to say it."

"Why?"

"Okay, if I have to give you a geography lesson, I will. I live here in Walnut River. East coast. And you live—" With her finger, she made an arc in the air to the left, indicating the entire continental United States. "All the way on the other side of the country. West coast."

"So?"

"Okay. Now we'll have a lesson in relationships doomed

to failure. You have an enormously profitable medical practice in California that you've been neglecting."

"I love you. That's more important than an address."

She ignored that although her heart started pounding. The man had gifted hands and a silver tongue. And she wasn't sure why she was resisting, except that self-preservation instincts were a hard habit to break.

"When you go back, you'll have every intention of making it work with me. We'll promise to take long weekends, get together every chance we get. But you'll get involved with your patients. I'm busy with work, getting my degree and raising Janie. She's got school, which narrows our window of opportunity to be around her holidays. Eventually we'll move on." She shrugged. "I think it would be easier if I just move on now."

"Easier for who?" His eyes narrowed. "I know you've taken some hits in life, but it never crossed my mind that the gutsy woman I met in the E.R. was a coward."

"I'm not." But the accusation hit a nerve.

"Then why are you giving up without a fight?"

"Because the only way we'll work is if I give up my life." The tears threatened again. "Only an idiot would expect you to sacrifice a lucrative medical practice and I can't give up what I've built here."

"I love you. I want you to be happy. I—"

She put her fingers to his lips to silence him. "You have to understand, David. I raised myself. I didn't grow up with anything resembling a family. When I came to Walnut River, I was pregnant and scared. Janie was born in this hospital. It's the heart and soul of this town thanks to your father. He gave me a job and I was determined not to let him down. So I worked hard. The silver lining was that I made friends. Put down roots. This is more than a town to me. It's the first and only family I've ever had. It's part of my heart."

"I understand."

"Do you?"

"Yeah. It's part of my heart, too, and the reason I came back." He searched her eyes. "But I'd still like an answer. If we'd met in the elevator of our mutual condo complex in Los Angeles, would you be afraid to tell me how you feel?"

"Yes." She shook her head. "No. It's just so hard to be this close to everything you've ever wanted, you know? What if I reach out and it all falls apart? If the worst-case scenario happens—"

Then she remembered what Peter had said about things getting worse before they got better. When David went back to his life would she hurt any less if she never told him how she felt?

With her knuckle, she brushed away a single tear that slid down her cheek. Then she looked into his blue eyes and her mouth trembled. "I love you. Are you happy now?"

"I will be if you'll agree to marry me."

"But—"

This time he put his fingers to her lips. "The thing is, it's fortunate that you're happy living in Walnut River because I'm going to be living here too. I accepted a position on staff at the hospital and plan to move my practice here. I've missed the town and my family."

"Let me get this straight. You're giving up your life for me?"

"I'm not giving up anything," he countered. "And I'm getting everything. For the record, my reasons are completely selfish because living without you and Janie isn't living at all. I love you, Court. I love your strength and stubbornness, although not at the moment because I'm not fond of suspense when everything I've ever wanted hangs in the balance. Just say you'll marry me."

In the end it was easy. A no-brainer.

"Okay." Her heart was so full, she'd never imagined it was possible to be this happy. "I would love to marry you."

He kissed her then snuggled her against him. "We'll have to go tell Janie." There was a hint of nervousness in his voice, an indication of how deeply he cared for her little girl.

"You know she wants you to be her dad, Dr. David." Courtney managed to skip words past the lump of emotion in her throat.

"I'd like nothing better."

"Life is funny," she whispered, blinking back tears. "When your sister paged you to come and examine my daughter, I knew I'd be getting a famous physician, but I had no idea that doctor would turn out to be a daddy, too."

And the man who would make all her dreams come true.

* * * * *

A sneaky peek at next month...

By Request

RELIVE THE ROMANCE WITH THE BEST OF THE BEST

My wish list for next month's titles...

In stores from 15th March 2013:

☐ To Tame the Playboy – Susanne James, Ally Blake & Kate Hardy

☐ The Brides of Bella Rosa – Raye Morgan, Barbara Hannay & Rebecca Winters

3 stories in each book - only £5.99!

In stores from 5th April 2013:

☐ Wilder Hearts – Judy Duarte, Karen Rose Smith & RaeAnne Thayne

Available at WHSmith, Tesco, Asda, Eason, Amazon and Apple

Just can't wait?

Visit us Online

You can buy our books online a month before they hit the shops! **www.millsandboon.co.uk**

0313/05

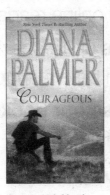